# SHE WRITES IN RED

## DEAR CELESTE

### J.R. ERICKSON

*For the Cronies.*

# 1

————

Dear Celeste,

I stumbled on your column tonight as I was scouring the Internet for an exorcist.

How's that for an opening line?

I'm almost embarrassed to write it. And by the way, I didn't find one. Maybe I don't even need one. My sister, Torrie, says I need a therapist. Perhaps she's right. It *has* been a year—a breakup, loss of my job, the death of my beloved sheepdog Bo, who I'd had for fourteen years. The list goes on.

So yeah, could those things be at the heart of my troubling experiences? Could be. But I don't think so.

Let me start with some backstory. Sorry to turn this into a mini-novel, but this bit matters.

Fourteen years ago, I was eleven years old and living here in Frankfort. My two best friends, Marco and Gwen, lived on the same street as me, in a little subdivision on the outskirts of town. On Devil's Night, we decided to get into some mischief. That's the whole idea of Devil's Night, right?

We swiped a few rolls of toilet paper and a carton of eggs from Marco's garage, pulled our hoods up, and slipped into the dark. Hitting houses on our own street was out of the question —our parents would've smelled the guilt on us before breakfast. So, we crept a few blocks over to Fulton Road.

Fulton was quieter. The houses there sat back from the road on wide, lonely lots, half swallowed by trees and tall grass. Our target was an old farmhouse, the kind of place that looked so old people had probably died inside. The house wasn't particularly large or fancy—white paint peeling like old scabs, shutters barely hanging on—but it radiated something. A presence.

Call it energy, if you want. I know that word's been overused into nonsense. But I trust you know what I mean.

So that night, just after ten o'clock, we snuck out and headed for Fulton Road. We hit two other houses first—strung some toilet paper in trees, egged a dark porch.

Then we got to *the* house.

Marco decided this was the place he wanted to do the dog poop dash. You've probably heard of it—fill a paper bag with dog poop, set it on the porch, light it on fire, and ring the doorbell. Marco had gathered a bag of poop at his place, thanks to his black Lab, Meatball. Gwen and I stayed back, hunkering down behind some chokecherry bushes.

I saw a light on near the back of the house and told Gwen I wanted to creep around and try to get a look inside. I made it to the back of the house, and through a gap in the curtains, I could see into this big room with sofas and lamps. The woman who lived there—I'd seen her a few times over the years—was big and pregnant and standing on a little step stool, writing on the walls. She had one of those old-fashioned quill pens, and the writing was red. She dipped the quill again and again into this dark bowl, and I had this terrifying thought she was writing in blood. Probably not, right?

Anyway, she suddenly looked up, face all sweaty and feverish, and I realized Marco had rung the doorbell. I shot back to the bushes at the front just as Marco came skidding in beside me.

The woman opened the door and, even though I couldn't see her face clearly, I swear she stared *right* at us. I don't think she even looked down at the burning bag.

It scared the daylights out of us. The second she closed the door, we tore out of there. We hadn't even made it back to our street when the cramps started for Marco. They got so bad, he had to duck into the woods, drop his pants, and relieve himself. Any other time, we would've made fun of him and thought it was hilarious. But he'd gone as white as a ghost, and all three of us had this terrible feeling we'd made a mistake going to that house.

I told them what I'd seen in the room, and we went from scared to downright terrified. We wanted to run home, but we couldn't—Marco could barely walk. We ended up knocking on the door to Sid Patt's house for help. Marco was slurring his words and falling every couple of feet. Sid got right on the phone and called Marco's parents, then an ambulance, then my parents and Gwen's.

Marco's mom took one look at him and started praying to Saint Anthony.

Marco died that night.

The doctors said his appendix burst, but in the hours after his death, I dreamt of the woman from the house. In my dream, she'd written Marco's name on her wall and I woke up knowing somehow, she had killed him.

Fast-forward fourteen years.

A month ago, I moved into that old farmhouse on Fulton Road.

You're probably thinking, *Well, there it is, proof positive this woman is insane.* And who knows, maybe it's true.

I was living in Ann Arbor when my life took a nosedive. One morning I'm sitting there, and what pops up in my email but a list of new rentals in Frankfort. I'd been searching for rentals in the town I lived in, but shoot, I no longer had a job or a boyfriend, so what difference did it make if I moved back up north?

The truth was I missed Northern Michigan. Missed my hometown. And a part of me even missed that horrible house. Maybe *missed* isn't the right word. I *yearned* for it. I felt like I'd left something behind there, and someday I'd need to come back and retrieve it.

I talked myself out of the decision a dozen times. The rent would be unaffordable. By the time I reached out, the house would be rented. I wouldn't find a job up here. On and on.

Then I called the guy who was renting it. It was still available, and furnished—no need to move any stuff, which was perfect because I didn't *have* any stuff. My ex, Luke, had bought all our furniture and made it pretty clear he'd be keeping it after the breakup.

I agreed to the rental, still not sure if I'd find a job. I'm an elementary school teacher, so I logged into the substitute system in Frankfort and—boom—a long-term subbing job for kindergarten.

The first week or two passed without incident. I told myself the silence was a blessing. I had only days to settle in before school started, and maybe that rush kept me blind. Or maybe the house was just waiting.

The sounds started small—barely there footsteps, something shifting just out of view, a feeling of not being alone.

I'm not going to unravel the whole story here.

But I'll tell you this much: There's something in this house.

And it knows I'm here.

Can you help?

–Andi

**2**

---

Celeste read the Dear Celeste email a final time, allowing her eyes to get soft, her shoulders to relax. She tried to open to any awareness about the house or Andi, a spirit reaching out, a bit of guidance.

Nothing but the tick of the still-cooling engine in her truck, the birdsong outside the windows, a van rumbling by on the street.

She'd already responded to Andi days before and they'd set a meeting for that afternoon in Frankfort to meet at the allegedly haunted house. Still, Celeste had tried in the previous days to get a line on what she was walking into with no luck.

She'd moved into the mother-in-law suite at Eliza's house, in Traverse City, a month earlier—oddly during the same time frame Andi had moved to Frankfort. Jonathan was still missing. And the ever-present knowledge that a new life was growing inside of her felt a bit like lying on the wooden frame from Poe's "The Pit and the Pendulum," watching the razor-sharp pendulum inch ever closer.

She closed her email and dropped her cell phone into her purse, hoisting her tired body out of her truck.

Eliza lived in a ranch-style home on a quiet cul-de-sac near Traverse City's East Bay. The mother-in-law suite Celeste had moved into was quaint, with a small covered porch facing the road. It contained a single bedroom, a small kitchenette, bathroom and living room.

Celeste gathered her groceries from the back seat and followed the flagstone path to her door. Cash and Romeo crowded forward, both streaking onto the porch and then racing back inside.

"You guys trying to kill me?" Celeste grumbled as the cats tripped her up. She clutched her paper sack of groceries with one arm and reached a steadying hand for the doorframe.

The cats had mostly acclimated to their new environment, though Cash had sulked for the first few days after their arrival. His demeanor improved once she allowed the cats to start going outside to explore for a couple of hours every day.

Eliza also owned a cat, a large orange fluff ball named Pumpkin, and a small dog named Sassy, who'd most definitely earned her name.

Celeste plopped her groceries on the little Murphy table and sat in the accompanying chair. A vague queasiness settled in her belly and she took a few slow, deep breaths, waiting for it to pass. Morning sickness with actual vomiting had been rare, but nausea crept up anytime she exerted herself for more than a few minutes. Throw in the tiredness, frequent urination and sore breasts, and she'd begun to forget what it felt like to have a normal, healthy body. Perhaps strangest of all was an overwhelming desire to eat spinach, a food she'd loathed her entire life. Now she often stood in front of her little fridge eating spinach by the handful right out of the bag. She cooked it down and added it to eggs, soups, and slapped it on her sandwiches. She couldn't get enough of it.

Celeste hadn't told anyone about the pregnancy. After researching online for weeks following the initial positive test, a part of her suspected she'd lose the baby. It was far more common than she'd realized. Eighty percent of miscarriages happened during the first trimester and every day, she anticipated blood spots in her underwear, dampness on her sheets. It hadn't happened.

She rested a hand on her belly and tried to imagine what lay inside. Who? She hated to admit it even to herself, but she'd begun to think the baby was a girl and girl names had started to drift through her thoughts when she nodded off to sleep at night.

"Nettie," she murmured. "Nettie Clementine Cleary." After her mother and aunt, but Cleary was Jonathan's name. Did she intend to keep it?

Detective Bowman called once every week or two with updates. A possible sighting in Detroit, another in Ohio. A stakeout at his parents' house turned up nothing, likewise at his sister's. In the first weeks after he'd vanished, Celeste's nights had been plagued with dark dreams of waking to find Jonathan at her bed, pillow in hand to smother her or a bottle of pills he'd force her to take so it looked like suicide. Would he try to kill her even if he knew she was carrying his baby?

"Stop it," she told herself, breaking her mind out of the rabbit hole of Jonathan's disappearance.

She couldn't go there. The Memento Mori group was meeting at Eliza's that night and Celeste had offered to bake a cake. She'd bought a boxed yellow cake mix at the grocery store and a can of chocolate frosting. Celeste hadn't baked a cake since college when she'd made one for her roommate Lacy's birthday. The cake, intended to look like a champagne bottle for Lacy's twenty-first birthday, had instead looked disturbingly like a penis. The white piping at the edges added the final, unintentionally vulgar touch.

Celeste smiled at the memory, dumping the box of cake mix into a bowl she'd borrowed from Eliza. Celeste knew Lacy had died. She'd sensed it during her ferry ride to meet River the previous spring, but she'd meant to reach out, make contact with her old college friends, and discover what happened. Instead, she'd been sucked into the black hole of her own unraveling. Survival mode, Harris called it. Someday soon, she'd discover what had become of her old friend.

Celeste carried her slightly sunken cake outside, along the stone pathway to Eliza's side door and into her house.

Eliza stood at the stove in her kitchen, a green apron cinched at her waist.

"I tried," Celeste said, sliding the cake on the counter.

Eliza smiled. "I love it. Nothing worse than those picture-perfect cakes no one can stand to cut into."

"No threat of that here." Celeste eyed her deflated cake. "I have the meeting with Andi in a couple of hours. I'm going to take a quick shower and get going, but I'll be back in time for dinner with the Memento Mori group."

"Perfect," Eliza said. "This is the haunted house girl?"

"Yeah."

On the wall above the kitchen table hung a display of sepia-toned photographs, all depicting one little boy.

Eliza saw her looking. "That's Simon."

"Your brother who was abducted?" Celeste remembered Eliza's story of Simon from their first meeting. Eliza had originally believed her near-death experience occurred so she could discover what happened to her little brother who'd vanished during their childhood. Despite her mediumship gifts, she'd never found him.

Eliza nodded and moved closer to the framed images. She pointed to a photo of the dark-haired little boy delicately cradling a mouse in his cupped hands. "He caught that in the house. My mom jumped up on a kitchen chair and screamed like a madwoman, but Simon just cornered him, scooped him up, and carried him outside. I ran out and took the picture. Mostly to later show my dad the little beast that finally shattered my mom's steely facade. I'm so happy I did now. Back then, we didn't have smartphones. Cameras were expensive. At least the kind we owned and money had always been tight. My dad saved up for two years to buy that camera and he taught me to use it. He said since he was gone at work so much, he needed me to capture the highlights."

Celeste's gaze moved through the many iterations of Simon. A toddler in a diaper and a T-shirt. Simon tucked neatly into a little suit, gripping a pretty woman's hand, their mom, Celeste thought, who wore a yellow dress with a tulle skirt. Another showed Simon posed before a glowing birthday cake, proudly clutching a wooden ball painted with a grinning clown's face.

"My uncle made him that ball for his fifth birthday, his last birthday. Hand-painted it. He had it that day ... when he disappeared."

"Is there an open investigation?"

"It's not closed, so they say."

"Is Harris involved at all?"

"We grew up in Honor, not far from Frankfort actually. The Benzie County Sheriff's Office had the case, so technically no, but as a personal favor, he's spent some time on it."

"And what about the Memento Mori group? Have they tried to ... find out what happened to him?"

Eliza nodded. "Oh yeah. We've tried a lot of stuff over the years. Group meditations with that question in our minds, Ouija boards, multiple séances. Nothing clear has ever come through. A year or two ago, Taylor got an image of a woman in a car with him. He was in the back seat and the woman had lured him into the car by offering him candy."

"Do you think it was real?"

"Taylor's visions are pretty powerful. That being said, she couldn't get anything else, so whether it was real or not, it didn't help much."

Celeste thought of her own experience with Taylor's sight. Taylor had described in vivid detail the bedroom where Dee Simmons was later murdered by River's tormentor. She'd seen the vision weeks before the attack occurred.

Celeste studied the pictures and something inside her shifted. Her skin prickled and for a moment, Simon's image blurred—not physically, not really, but emotionally, like a memory forming just out of reach.

Nothing came through.

Eliza shifted her attention back to the stovetop, then turned back, forehead creased. "Are you getting something, Celeste?"

Celeste shook her head. "No. I'm sorry." It wasn't entirely true, but what was coming through might have nothing to do with Simon, and she didn't want to get Eliza's hopes up.

---

Though Celeste had showered that morning, she stripped off her clothes and stepped beneath the spray. She seemed to be constantly hot, regardless of the weather; sweat clung to her skin, encased her.

After toweling off, she stood in front of the full-length mirror in underwear and a bra. If the baby had begun to show, she couldn't see it. But she felt it, felt the tiny, almost indiscernible presence of another. Her skin appeared stark and pale against the 'evolve' tattoo on her leg, the raven.

"Evolve," she said.

One way or another, the universe seemed intent on forcing that to happen.

**3**

---

Andi forced a smile and did the grown-up thing of inviting the woman, Celeste, into the house because Andi was after all a grown-up. Even if she didn't always feel like it, a feeling compounded by returning to her hometown of Frankfort, the streets and businesses awash in her girlhood memories.

"It's much nicer inside," Andi assured Celeste as she led her in.

Andi didn't know why she felt the need to make excuses for the house's worn-down, and frankly ugly, exterior. It wasn't her house. She was renting it for the sole purpose of making sense of what happened to Marco all those years ago.

"Even when we were young the outside had started to get ... run down. I guess that was part of the appeal for us kids. Most people in this area were really house proud. God forbid someone let a few dandelions pop up in the yard, but this house would be so overgrown even our school bus driver would complain about it."

Andi watched Celeste scan the hall, eyes drifting up the stairs and then into the living room.

"Where should we start?" Andi murmured, fidgeting. "In the room where I saw the woman writing on the wall or ... umm ... do you want a tour of the whole house?"

"We can start in that room," Celeste murmured. "Talk for a bit."

"Great. OK, sure." Andi pushed open the double glass parlor doors. "This is it." Andi chewed her lip and gestured at the wood-paneled walls. The memory of that night had faded after she'd moved away from Frankfort, but since returning to the house it had all rushed back.

Celeste walked into the room, rested a hand against the wood-paneled wall.

Andi, unsure what to say, sat on the edge of one stiff sofa and watched her. She looked to be in her thirties, but something about her felt older, like she'd figured out stuff Andi hadn't even started thinking about.

After a moment, Celeste sat opposite her.

"In your letter you said you moved into this house about a month ago?" Celeste asked.

Andi nodded. "Bizarre, right? My whole family thinks so."

"And you did it in part because you'd gone through a breakup?"

"Yeah. I couldn't commit. I have this story that he, Luke, broke up with me, but the truth is ..." She shook her head. "He started talking about getting married over a year ago and I kept saying I wasn't ready until finally, he said, either we're getting married or we're breaking up. Weird, right? It's usually the other way around. My sister badgered her husband for like two years to get an engagement ring.

"Anyway, Luke asked me to move out and it was only fair because he owned the condo. I'd been an elementary teacher, but we were on summer break. In the middle of apartment hunting, I got a call from the principal that enrollment had dropped and they were combining the first-grade classes into one and the other teacher had seniority." She swiped a hand through her chin-length cinnamon-colored hair.

"Then Bo, my sheepdog, got sick. And it shouldn't have been such a shock; he was fourteen. That's at the far end of their typical lifespan, but still ... I just ..." The damn tears tried to creep up, but she fought them down. "We got him the year after Marco died. I'd been in such a dark place and my parents were trying to lift me up. I came home from school one day and there he was, this little wiggly ball of black-and-white fur. Then recently, as my life fell apart, Bo suddenly stopped eating. He struggled to walk, kept getting disoriented and running into stuff. Luke and I took him to the vet. He was heartbroken too, Luke. We'd been together three years by then. Bo was like our baby. After they put him to sleep, I had this sudden urge to leave Ann Arbor forever. I needed to get out."

"So, you packed up your life and moved here?"

"Crazy, huh?"

Celeste shook her head. "I don't think so. We have this idea that life will fall on some linear continuum with a clear beginning, middle and end, but it's more like a scatter plot, chaotic and unpredictable."

"Chaotic and unpredictable," Andi repeated. "Check, check."

Celeste smiled and Andi felt slightly more at ease. She wasn't sure what she'd expected. Some of Celeste's columns— she'd read back through years of questions and answers—had come across as heavily researched and scientific. She'd feared the woman might arrive in a lab coat with a team of researchers ready to pick apart the house.

"I am curious why you'd choose to move into this particular house after what happened in your childhood."

"You and me both." Andi released a dry laugh. "I guess it's because ... I thought it might dispel the myth, you know? It's like that idea to never meet your heroes or never peek behind the curtain. I thought if I moved into this house, I'd realize it was just a house and the woman who lived here was just a woman and this whole idea of something evil or magic or whatever wasn't real."

"Except you said in your letter stuff is happening in this house."

Andi chewed her lip. "Yeah."

"Tell me about it."

Andi pulled her legs into her chest and rested her chin on her knees. The thought of some of the things made her want to curl into the fetal position and get one of her mom's famous back rubs. But her mom was more than seven hundred miles away and they hadn't talked in weeks. Her mom didn't approve of Andi's choice to uproot her life. Andi, rather than talking through their disagreement like an adult, had opted for ignoring her calls.

"Weird little stuff at first. Umm ... sounds. Creaking. I figured it's an old house and I didn't exactly move in without preconceived notions. My memory of what happened to Marco is alive and well. It's why I came here in the first place. So, I thought my mind was playing tricks on me. I saw shadows from the corners of my eyes a couple times, woke up hearing things, crying one time, a child crying."

"You said you started searching for an exorcist. Clearly the sounds and other things started to feel more real?"

"Yeah." Andi picked at a scab on her wrist, thought about where it had come from, a nightmare so vivid days before that she'd leaped from bed and scratched her arm on a nail poking from the wall. "I woke up one night to get a drink and heard scratching in the parlor."

"Like an animal scratching?"

Andi shook her head, recalling the low groan of the parlor doors as she'd pushed them open that night. Moonlight spilled into the room, pooling at her feet, and there—against the far wall—stood the woman. Her pale arm moving in frantic strokes, scrawling red, glossy letters, wet, that bled toward the floor.

"No. It was the woman from that night when Marco died. I saw her at the wall there and then ..." Andi wiggled her fingers. "She was gone, just gone. The room was empty and I tried to tell myself it was a dream, I'd sleepwalked, which I've never done, but the next day I started searching for exorcists online. I didn't actually call one. I found your column."

"Have you seen her again?"

Andi nodded. "Glimpses mostly, the tail end of a dress going around a corner in the house. I came home from school one day last week and saw someone, her, watching me from an upstairs window. Another time, I umm ... had just gotten out of the shower. I wiped the fog off the mirror and for a second, just so quick, it was her reflection, not mine, in the mirror."

That last experience had about sent Andi packing. She'd forced on her clothes, her body still wet from the shower. Her T-shirt and shorts had clung to her as she ran to her car without a backward glance. She'd driven south for two hours before some part of her finally came to her senses. Andi had pulled off at a truck stop and sat at a picnic table, drinking a milkshake and pondering her next move. She had school the next day. Not to mention she'd sunk all her money into the deposit and first and last month's rent on the house. Ultimately, she'd returned to the house, avoiding the upstairs bathroom for the next several days.

"And you're sure it's the woman you saw in childhood? The one who lived here when your friend died?"

Andi squinted, tried to make details of the woman click into place. "I think so, but honestly ... no. It was so brief each time I saw her, there and then gone. A part of me still thinks that I ..."

"Imagined it."

Andi nodded.

"The night Marco died and you saw the woman writing on the wall, could you read the words she'd written?"

"No. The adrenaline of the night and the words were small, chicken scratch, you know. My handwriting's not great, but this writing looked"—she frowned—"illegible."

"Maybe that was by design."

"You think so?" Andi asked. "So, if anyone peeked in a window, they couldn't read it."

"Possibly, yes." Celeste gazed again at the paneled wall, a small crease between her eyebrows.

Andi wondered if she were trying to imagine the words that had been written there.

"I'd like to hear more about Marco," Celeste said. "Was there ever any question at all about the cause of death?"

"Ruptured appendix," Andi said. "Case closed. His funeral happened a few days later and so many people went. Hundreds, maybe a thousand. He came from an Italian family. Here in Frankfort, it was just him and his brother and his parents, but the extended family was huge. They came from downstate, New York, even California. And then like half the kids from school attended and teachers and ..." Andi shuddered at the memory, the wave of bodies, cloying perfume and pungent, too ripe roses and the sounds of voices and clacking heels and murmurs and sobs.

Andi had nearly run out of the church, managed to stay in place only because when she looked down the row of people she sat squeezed in the center of, the heads went on and on. She'd imagined tripping on their feet, their hands grasping, their eyes boring into her.

"That must have been really hard," Celeste said.

"It was. And harder still because no one knew the truth. No one except me and Gwen and you know what? Gwen didn't go to the funeral. Her parents were there and said she had the flu, but I knew she just couldn't handle it and I wished so bad I hadn't gone too, at the time anyway. Now I'm happy I did even if the memory is … not a good one."

"Andi, is it possible that Marco's death really was just a terrible coincidence? That he'd had appendicitis and the stress of that night triggered something already dormant in his body?"

Andi frowned and looked away. It was the same story she'd heard before. She'd tried to tell Marco's parents and her own and they'd all insisted the two were not related. They shouldn't have pranked the house on Fulton Road, but Marco didn't die as a result of their actions.

"Sure, it's possible," Andi grumbled, unable to hide the annoyance from her voice. "It's possible I'm crazy. It's possible this is just an old creaky house and the woman who lived here was just some nutter who used gross-looking maroon paint to keep a diary on her walls."

"But you don't think so?"

"Obviously not."

Celeste tilted her head. "OK. Then we'll drop that line of inquiry for now. I can see the theory bothers you, but I think it's worth examining for yourself, the possibility that the shock of his death caused the night to become something more extraordinary, supernatural even and that survivor's guilt is playing a part in your belief that you guys targeting this house led to his death."

Andi fiddled with a button on the sofa and nodded. She didn't bother telling Celeste she had thought about those things a million times. It was more than that. She'd known it that night and knew it still.

"What can you tell me about the woman who lived here?" Celeste asked.

"Her name was Vivian Walters. I asked around and found someone who remembered her, but they really didn't know anything at all about her."

"Vivian Walters," Celeste repeated, as she added the name to her notes app on her phone.

"It took some digging to find her name and then I couldn't find anything else," Andi admitted. "No clue when she moved out. Maybe she even died. She might have died in this house."

# 4

I n the short time they'd been in the once-parlor, a terrible feeling had fallen over Celeste as if someone had tossed a black sheath over the windows though sun still streamed in. Her body had grown cold, her brain on edge. She realized she'd clenched her teeth and forced her jaw to relax, attempted the detached eye of a scientist merely taking in the space. She couldn't do it.

A gilt-framed painting of a barn with two children in front hung above the dark fireplace. Something flickered in the glass, a shift of light perhaps, but as Celeste stared at it, long-ago sounds, muffled, played in her mind.

The scratchy sound of a phonograph, notes, hollow and faint. Then came voices—low, indistinct, speaking over one another in a muted hum. She couldn't make out words, only the cadence of conversation, the rise and fall of human presence long gone.

Suddenly, an agonized scream cut through it all.

Celeste jumped, startling Andi, who dropped a ceramic cherub she'd picked up from a side table. It hit the wood floor with a crack.

Andi knelt and held the figure up. Its painted smile and too wide eyes made Celeste's skin crawl.

"It's not broken.," Andi confirmed. "Are you OK?"

Celeste's heart continued pounding, but she nodded and forced a smile. "I thought I heard something."

Andi cocked her head as if listening for the sound.

"Why don't you show me the rest of the house," Celeste suggested, ready to get out of the parlor.

In the hall, Celeste shuddered and cast a final glance at the, now-closed, parlor doors.

"Do you get a bad feeling in there?" Celeste asked Andi.

"Just the opposite," Andi said, appearing surprised. "It's the room I spend most of my time in. I have had half a thought to put my bed in there if dragging the mattress down the stairs wouldn't be such a pain in the ass. Which I know sounds so weird since it's the room where I saw her ... writing with ... well, I don't know if it was blood. It couldn't have been, right?" Andi chuckled, as if the idea were absurd.

"Don't sleep in there," Celeste said, quickly glancing back over her shoulder, expecting to see someone watching them through the glass parlor doors, could feel their eyes. No one was there.

"Did *you* get a bad feeling in there?" Andi asked, rubbing her hands along her arms.

"Yes."

"Really?" Andi paused and looked back at the room. "What kind of feeling?"

"I'm not sure how to explain it, but ..." She shook her head. "I would limit your time in there."

Andi appeared disappointed, but didn't push for more. Celeste didn't want to scare Andi. She was, after all, living alone in the house and in the previous months had undergone enough upheaval without the addition of Celeste making her afraid to go home after work.

Celeste followed Andi to the kitchen, which was warm with aged pine and painted cabinetry. A cast-iron stove occupied one corner. A small square table sat in an opposite corner scattered with markers, paints, and poster board.

"I usually organize my stuff for school in here," Andi said.

Celeste followed Andi back down the hall. The wallpaper was a delicate print of faded violets. A time-worn floral runner lay on the wood floor.

"Half bathroom." Andi pointed through an open door. "Main living room."

Celeste cast a glance into the next room. It felt calmer than the parlor, lighter somehow. Sunlight streamed through a large picture window overlooking the front yard, warming the space. The furniture was modern: a well-worn recliner and a brown sectional arranged for comfort, not style. Against one wall, a mostly empty bookshelf stood like an afterthought.

"There are three bedrooms up here." Andi led the way up the staircase. "And a full bathroom." Andi paused at the first bedroom, spacious with a four-poster bed. The walls were painted red. "I sleep in this room."

In the corner, Celeste eyed several totes, their lids askew, still piled with stuff.

"I'm still kind of unpacking," Andi admitted.

They walked through the other bedrooms. Andi pointed out the bathroom, but appeared reluctant to go inside. Celeste glanced through the doorway to see a shower, a heavy dark curtain obscuring the interior, a toilet and an older mirror with a small spiderweb crack at the bottom of the frame.

Back downstairs, Celeste checked her phone. "I have dinner with friends, so I need to get going, but I'm going to see what I can find out about this house and the woman who used to live here."

"That'd be so great. Thank you. And umm ..." Andi tucked

her hair behind her ear. "I meant to ask you what you charge? I probably should have asked before you came."

"Nothing."

"Nothing? But you're driving here and ..."

"No charge. I have friends who work with ... spirits, haunted places. Do you mind if I talk to them about what's happening here?"

"Not at all." Andi's body visibly relaxed, as if the money question had been weighing on her mind. "I guess that means you believe me about this house?"

Celeste nodded. Despite her initial misgivings, the potential that Andi's experiences in the house were born from the trauma of her childhood, she too sensed something, someone, other than Andi inhabited the house.

"I do. I feel something here."

Andi leaned forward, eyes shining slightly. "I've wondered if ... well, if maybe Marco is here too. If the woman's ghost is here, doesn't that mean Marco could be as well?"

Celeste scanned the room and then went back to the open doorway. She thought she heard the faintest creak from one of the parlor doors inching open. Gooseflesh rippled up her arms. "It's possible. Andi, can I ask what you're hoping to get from all this? Moving back here?"

Andi looped her thumbs through the straps on her overalls, face thoughtful. She suddenly looked very young, more like a teenager than a grown woman.

"The truth. I need to know the truth about what happened to Marco. I feel like if I can get that I can ... move on, have a life that isn't so ..." She bit her lip. "Stuck."

## 5

-------

Celeste walked into Eliza's kitchen to find the Memento Mori group seated around the kitchen table. Plates of half-eaten Mexican food scattered before them.

"There she is," Eliza announced. "I'm afraid we started without you. Jack said he was so hungry, Sassy was starting to look like a rotisserie chicken."

Hearing her name, Sassy trotted into the room and gazed expectantly at Eliza.

"No more table food, Sassy-pants, or you'll have to go on a diet."

"She does vaguely resemble a chicken," Jack said with a grin as he stood to hug Celeste.

One by one, Taylor, Lena, and Harris followed suit, each rising to embrace her. As Lena settled back into her seat, she covertly slipped Sassy a tortilla chip under the table.

Celeste's face was flushed, her body still buzzing with the strangeness from Andi's house. She'd felt weirdly guilty driving away and leaving Andi behind there.

Eliza handed Celeste a plate. "We have chicken or beef

tacos and Harris made guacamole that is delicious but so full of garlic we may have to open the windows soon."

"Between the guacamole and the black beans there's going to be more gas in this room than a truck stop," Lena said.

Celeste's stomach gurgled and a flutter of queasiness squirmed through her belly. "No, umm ... beans for me. Thank you," she told Eliza, who stood at crock-pots scooping food onto Celeste's plate.

"How'd the visit to the Frankfort house go today?" Harris asked when Celeste sat down.

They'd spoken at least every week, usually more, since she'd moved to northern Michigan. He called it his weekly check-in, which honestly, she appreciated.

"It was pretty good. There's definitely something going on in the house."

"Ooh. Haunted?" Lena asked.

"Considering you've lived and breathed this stuff for years, how is it you still sound like an excited teenager right now?" Jack asked.

"Because a lot of the places I check out aren't haunted," Lena quipped. "Not legit haunted anyway. It's usually some emotional chaos because the teenage daughter just hit puberty or the parents are going through a divorce. I really should be getting a commission for all the therapists I've sent clients to."

"I'm going back tomorrow," Celeste explained. "Today we went over what she's experienced. Tomorrow I want to see if I can get a read on who's there, take some pictures and stuff."

"Want some ghost hunting equipment?" Lena asked, taking a messy bite of taco and spilling half the meat and cheese onto her plate.

"What is it?"

"The usual stuff: EMF detectors, spirit box, digital recorders."

"I wouldn't bother," Taylor said. "If anything, that stuff

muddles the signal. Remember"—she tapped her temple—"you just have to tune into the right station."

"Rubbish," Lena argued. "The ghost stuff helps you narrow down the likeliest place to spend some time, that's all. You're not going to get much from heat signals and electromagnetic fields, but they'll give you a room, a corner in the house where something is off."

For the next little while, the group debated the effectiveness of modern ghost hunting equipment. Eliza cut the cake and everyone assured Celeste that despite its ugliness it still tasted delicious.

She'd never really belonged to a group before, not like this. Aside from a fleeting couple of years in college, the idea of a close-knit circle had always felt like something other people had. She hadn't grown up around a noisy dinner table full of stories and teasing and second helpings. Her childhood kitchen had been quiet, restrained. Just like the one she'd shared with Jonathan.

Now, with her stomach full and the soft murmur of voices all around, her eyelids grew heavy.

"Celeste?"

She blinked at Harris, who stared at her.

He smiled. "I think you nodded off for a minute there."

She yawned. "Did I?"

"If that isn't a sign that this conversation is boring, then I don't know what is," Jack said, standing and twisting from side to side. "I, for one, need to stretch my legs."

Taylor winked at Celeste. "Typical guy behavior. If we talk for more than an hour, Jack starts clipping his nails and checking his watch."

"It's been over two hours!" he said, pumping his legs. "My feet, like Celeste, have fallen asleep."

"I'll stick the cake pan in my apartment quick and meet you guys back here," Celeste said, starting toward the door.

"I'll help," Taylor offered, plucking the pan from Celeste's hand.

"Is it a secret?" Taylor asked, closing Celeste's apartment door.

"Is what a secret?"

Taylor furrowed her brow and rested a hand on her belly. "The baby."

Celeste closed her eyes, swallowed. A part of her had suspected one of the Memento Mori group would sense her pregnancy.

"Does anyone else know?" Celeste asked.

"Not that they hinted to me."

"How did you know?"

Taylor smiled. "I dreamt it last night. You with a belly out to here." Taylor held her hand in front of her. "I thought it could mean something else, a new creative project, but then I saw you and ... I can't quite explain it. The energy of a pregnant woman is different."

Celeste sat in one of the kitchen chairs and sighed. "I haven't told anyone. I just ... I'm struggling to even come to terms with it. Jonathan is gone, on the run for trying to kill me, and now I'm going to have his baby."

"Your baby," Taylor corrected. "Did you want children?"

Celeste rubbed the hollows of her eyes. Had she? They'd never really talked about it. Work had been their child, their shared love, their purpose. "I never gave it much thought. Most of my time and energy, and Jonathan's too, went to the lab ..." Which suddenly struck her as absurd. Whose life purpose was developing pharmaceutical drugs in a lab?

Taylor sat opposite her and took one of her hands, squeezed. "I think this is wonderful. I do. Scary, yes. I completely understand why you're scared, but ... this is your baby, Celeste. Your life. Jonathan is shit. It's time to let him go and just live for you."

Celeste considered what that life looked like. The frightened part of her conjured the dismal story—single mother, jobless, homeless, parentless, alone. But there was another part of her, the part that still clung to the idea of happily-ever-after, to the belief that all things could work out. Celeste had begun to envision a little cottage on a lake. A rocking chair like the ones at River's house, her baby tucked in her arms, watching the sun set over the water. She wasn't sure where that image had come from, but she retreated to it now as she tried to fit Taylor's words into her uncertain future.

"I've never been great at imagining a happily-ever-after," Celeste murmured. "I feel like I need to do that, be constantly focused on how I want our lives to unfold, mine and this baby's, and yet I get hung up on the darker possibilities. The brain literally has a negativity bias, an adaptive mechanism that heightens our sensitivity to threats, demands we pay attention to the worst possible outcome. I'm not sure how to get past all that hard wiring."

"After the year you've had, you sure don't want to turn it off. I can tell you that much," Taylor said. "But, and this is a big but, you don't have to live in survival mode 24-7. The best way I've found to shift the focus is meditation. Remember when we laid out in my yard?"

Celeste nodded.

"It's time for you to start carving out twenty minutes a day and make it a focused meditation. Imagine one future moment with your baby where everything is exactly as you want it to be. One vision, that's it."

"I think I've got one." Celeste pictured again the cottage on the lake at sunset, added a wind chime hanging from the eave of the house's porch, a bird feeder surrounded by ravens.

"Good. And when you're meditating on it, don't just see it in your mind. You've got to feel it. What are you feeling in that future place? It makes all the difference, Celeste. Before I found my house in Fruitport, I started visualizing exactly what I wanted down to the trees in the backyard. I even made a vision board, and poof, three weeks later I see my dream house in an ad online."

Celeste groaned. "A vision board?"

Taylor laughed. "Fine, no vision board. Just the vision, one moment. Don't overcomplicate it. It's a daydream. It's meant to be fun and easy."

---

They walked as a group down to the lake. Sassy trotted on her leash with the confidence of a parade leader, her tail high and ears perked. Every few steps, she glanced over her shoulder with an impatient flick of her head, as if urging the humans to pick up the pace.

Harris fell into step beside Celeste.

"You're taking it on then? This situation with the house in Frankfort?"

"Yeah. Andi needs help. She's in her twenties, but something about her seems younger, in over her head. It's tied to what happened when she was young. I know that much. And honestly, since I moved up here, I've felt a little"—she gestured at a leaf falling from a tree—"adrift."

"I can understand that. Gotta give yourself some grace, though. You're in a big transition. Things will settle again."

"I hope so."

"How's the apartment at Eliza's?"

Celeste gazed ahead to where Eliza had been pulled slightly into the grass by Sassy, who desperately stretched her nose toward a large birch tree. She pictured the wall of Simon's photographs and remembered the niggling sense she'd had earlier that day.

"It's been amazing, really. Eliza is welcoming and the apartment's perfect."

"But ..."

"No but."

Harris looked at her sideways. "I can feel you holding back. What is it?"

Celeste returned to the daydream of cradling her baby on the porch of the cottage, the glassy lake stretching out before them. "Ever since I spent time at River's last spring, I've been envisioning a little cottage with rocking chairs." She laughed. "Which is preposterous. I don't know how to fix anything. I have no business buying some old cottage in the woods, but ..." She shrugged. "Maybe the desire will pass."

"It doesn't have to pass. This is the twenty-first century. You hire people to fix stuff. Or you can call me. I was only electrocuted once a few months back when I replaced an outlet in my kitchen."

Celeste laughed.

"Joking aside," Harris said, "The cottage should wait until Jonathan is arrested. Right now, you're safer at Eliza's."

Celeste sighed. "I know. I'm learning to live in limbo."

## 6

Andi drove through the tall iron gates that enclosed the Woodland Cemetery. The road forked, and she turned right, following the narrow, winding path to the base of a small hill that rose toward the woods.

She grabbed the bouquet of flowers, stripped the cellophane and rubber band free, and walked up the hill to Marco's grave.

Two potted plants flanked the dark granite headstone. Fresh flowers bloomed in each, yellow and blue marigolds. Marco had always been a Michigan fan. Andi wondered who'd planted them. Marco's mom? His brother, Dante, hardly seemed the type, but then again, his brother wasn't an unruly teenager anymore. Like her, he must have grown up.

"Grown up," she murmured, kneeling on the soft grass and laying the flowers in front of the headstone.

*Marco D. Lombardi. Beloved son.*

Marco had never grown up, would never grow up.

"I'm back," Andi told him. "Crazy, right? I used to talk so much about getting out of Frankfort, anywhere but here. I only made it to Ann Arbor. I hate to say it never felt like home. You wanted to go there, be a U of M grad. It's not all it's cracked up to be. Game days are so wild, you might as well not leave home because you just get stuck in a gridlock of traffic. Good grief, listen to me. I sound like our parents."

Andi stretched out in the grass, crossed her arms behind her head and stared up at the scattering of wispy pale clouds.

She blinked away the tears.

"There were a few good restaurants, though. An Italian place I ate at every Friday for bottomless spaghetti. Not as good as your mom's spaghetti. Gosh, she could cook, huh? Remember that time you came to my place and my mom broke all the noodles in half before she boiled the pasta for spaghetti? You looked like she'd sprouted horns."

Marco would watch Andi's mom prepare dinner like he'd been beamed onto earth from an alien planet and had never seen anything like it.

"Is this meat?" he'd asked once when Andi's mom plopped microwave Salisbury steaks in front of them.

"Andi?"

She opened her eyes and gasped. It was Marco, but older. Glossy dark curls, hazel eyes. And then she made the connection: Dante, Marco's brother.

She struggled to sit up, cheeks warm.

"Dante. Hey."

"What are you doing?" His expression was puzzled.

"Yeah ..." She pushed up to standing and tugged a leaf from her hair. "Bizarre to find me napping on your brother's grave." She offered an awkward smile. "I just moved back to town last month. Thought I'd come... catch up."

He raised an eyebrow. "With Marco?"

She chuckled. "Yeah. Sorry. I know. It's strange." Her eyes drifted to the paper bag from his parents' Italian deli and bakery. "Or maybe it's not. Have you brought him lunch?"

"I brought myself lunch. Sometimes I sit here and"—he shrugged—"eat. It's peaceful."

"You're still in Frankfort? Never moved away?" she asked.

"I did for a couple of years. I went to Kalamazoo for college and then my dad had a heart attack. They needed help with the store and honestly, I was wasting time in school, racking up debt, drinking way too much. It was a blessing in disguise. Why did you move back? Your parents aren't here anymore, right?"

She brushed off the back of her shorts and then down to her legs, where bits of grass clung to her calves.

"No, they moved to Tennessee. That's where Torrie is, so ..."

"How is Torrie?"

Dante and Andi's older sister, Torrie, had dated in high school. It had been a difficult relationship for Andi, because Dante and Marco had always looked so alike. More than once, she'd caught glimpses of Dante in the house and, for a moment, believed she was seeing Marco.

"Torrie's good. Married, two kids. Seems to have gotten the hang of this adulting thing at record speed."

He raised an eyebrow. "I'm not surprised. She had that 'nothing gets in my way' attitude. She wanted to go to college for physical therapy. That happen?"

"Oh yeah. Somehow managed to graduate with honors while taking care of a one-year-old and being pregnant out to here." Andi held her hand in front of her stomach, a memory of Torrie waddling across the stage, carrying an extra thirty pounds on her petite frame to accept her diploma.

"What does her husband do?"

"Engineer. Don't ask me what kind. He's told me, but my eyes glaze over when Calvin talks about his job."

"How about you? Do college and the whole bit?"

"Yeah. U of M. Got a degree in elementary education. I'm teaching kindergarten at our old elementary school. Technically it's a long-term subbing position while their kindergarten teacher is on leave."

He smiled. "That fits. I can see you spending your days wiping runny noses and gluing popsicle sticks together."

"Wow. Thanks."

He laughed. "It wasn't an insult. You were nice to little kids. I remember."

Andi didn't tell him that was because she was hardly more than a kid herself, a kid trapped in an adult body. Marco had insisted if Andi were a teacher, she should opt for PE. "What could be better than playing dodgeball all day?" he'd ask.

"Are you renting an apartment or a house in Frankfort?"

"A house." She knew he'd ask the questions, which one, where at, and she couldn't tell him it was the Fulton Road house. "So, how are your parents? I didn't realize your dad had a heart attack."

"Yeah." He swiped a hand through his bouncy curls. When he and Torrie had broken up, she'd said one of her issues was that Dante was prettier than her. She couldn't handle being with a man better-looking than she was. "It happened about four years ago. Nothing major. He didn't almost die or anything, but it was a wake-up call for him and my mom both. They'd always wanted to travel, visit family in Italy, do some of that bucket list stuff. I offered to come back and manage the store so they could have some freedom. They're in Ireland right now."

"Oh wow. That's great."

"It was good to see you, Andi. Stop into the store sometime. My parents would love to see you too."

"I'll do that. I've been craving your mom's amaretti cookies."

"They're one of a kind."

"That they are."

Andi yawned and moved from room to room in the farmhouse, flipping off lights. She hadn't realized what a chore it would be to turn off the lights every night. At times, it made her miss the condo with Luke. Two bedrooms, one bathroom, efficient. Not to mention he usually turned off the lights, locked the doors and checked the windows. He didn't sleep well on nights he forgot.

In the kitchen, Andi poured a glass of water and forced it down. She rarely drank enough water. Preferred juice or pop, but had noticed more headaches lately and again, thanks to Luke, associated headaches with not enough water. A fact he'd drilled into her head so many times she'd sometimes avoided drinking water just to spite him.

The water in the Fulton Road house came from a well and tasted slightly metallic, sulfurous even. She grimaced as she swallowed the last bit and put her glass in the sink.

She flicked off the light and started toward the doorway. Before she made it into the hall, a bark sounded behind her.

Andi spun around and stared through the darkness.

The bark came again, undeniably familiar—Bo. The hair on her neck prickled.

Andi shuffled across the dark kitchen. She stopped at the door to the basement.

A third bark, followed by a whine and a scratching sound.

"Bo?" she whispered. Then repeated louder, "Bo?"

Hand trembling, she reached toward the door, silence now on the other side. When she touched the knob, it was ice-cold. As she started to twist it open, the memory of sitting next to Bo on the big metal table as the vet—Jodie was her name—slid the needle into his backside. Bo's eyes had blinked at her once, twice, and then they'd closed and his body had stilled. Andi had lain on his big fluffy body and cried so hard she nearly vomited. Luke had stood in the corner, hands shoved in the pockets of his jeans, tears streaming down his face. The room had been too bright, reeked of something antiseptic and bleach.

The memory washed through her with such clarity, Andi jerked her hand from the knob and stepped back. She hit a chair positioned behind her. It hadn't been there moments before, had it? And she nearly fell over it. She wobbled, managed to plant her feet and regain her balance.

The bark came again, the whine, but it sounded different this time, not like Bo so much as something trying to impersonate Bo.

*It's not real. It's in your head.*

Was that true?

Andi shuddered and hurried from the kitchen. She slipped on her sandals, grabbed her keys from the bureau near the door and walked to the car. Before she'd slid behind the wheel, the absurdity of fleeing sunk in. Where did she intend to go? Drive south again until she lost her nerve and returned. Burn up valuable gas money she didn't have to spare?

"It's not Bo," she said out loud. "It's not anything that can hurt me."

She didn't know that, was relying on her woefully limited experience with horror movies that included hauntings. *The Sixth Sense, Stir of Echoes, The Others.* None of those ghosts hurt people. They just wanted help, answers.

"I'm not leaving," she whispered and then said it louder, made sure the house could hear her. "I am not leaving!"

As Celeste turned onto Fulton Road, her cell phone rang. Her brother, Adam's, name appeared on the screen.

"Hi," she answered.

"Hey. How are you?"

"Decent. What's up?"

"Well, I'm at the prison in West Virginia. I'm getting ready to see Dad."

"Oh." Celeste tightened her grip on the wheel. "I had no idea you were planning to visit him."

"I wasn't. Not really. I put my name on the visitors' list, but didn't decide until last night to actually drive down. It's probably a terrible idea, but ..."

"No. I get it. Call me after. OK?"

"Will do."

Celeste sat for a moment in the car and stared up at the Fulton Road house. She imagined Adam at the prison in West Virginia preparing to get buzzed through steel doors, patted down, maybe even searched. What would their dad tell him?

The truth or some watered-down version of justifications and excuses.

Their dad had seemed remorseful after the night on the lake when Hannah died. He'd apologized for what he'd done to Nettie, for the affair, for hiding the death of Elliot Thacker. But how much of that remorse had drained away in the hours after? When he realized he'd be spending the rest of his life in prison for what he'd done.

Celeste grabbed her cell phone and stepped from the truck, aware that as her belly grew, getting into and out of the truck might become a problem. She couldn't think of that now.

She held up her cell phone and snapped a photo of the house.

At the front door, she knocked.

A door slammed inside the house and then another. Celeste waited, the gooseflesh tittering down her spine. The minutes ticked by.

She knocked again and called out. "Andi?"

No answer.

Down the street, she heard the squeal of tires and turned to see a small car careen onto Fulton Road. It moved fast and whipped into the driveway. A squeal of brakes as the nose of the Civic stopped inches from the bumper of Celeste's truck.

Andi jumped out, paper bag in hand, freckled face flushed. "Sorry. I meant to get back earlier, make some tea or something."

Celeste stared into the car. A child sat in the back seat. His face pale, his eyes huge as he looked back at Celeste.

By the time Celeste reached the car, the child was gone.

Celeste leaned closer, peered into the back seat.

"What is it?" Andi asked, following Celeste's gaze.

Celeste shook her head. "Weird. I thought I saw ... I don't even know."

Andi leaned closer to the window. "Nothing but junk. I've been meaning to clean it out, but ..." She shrugged. "Life."

"Is there someone else home?" Celeste asked, turning back toward the house.

Andi smiled, seemed confused, then shook her head. "No, just me, well not even me." She laughed nervously.

"I thought I heard doors slamming."

Andi picked at a button on her polka-dot blouse. It pulled loose, and she stuffed the button in her pocket. "That's what I mentioned before ... the sounds in the house."

Celeste followed her up the steps and through the front door.

"Did anything happen since I was here yesterday?" Celeste asked.

Andi turned back, her expression pinched and Celeste suspected she might lie to her. "I'm here to help you, Andi. For me to do that, you've got to tell me what you're experiencing."

"I heard something." She broke eye contact and gazed at the floor, cheeks flushed.

"What?"

She tucked a strand of hair behind her ear. "Bo. My dog."

"Your dog who died?"

Andi nodded.

"OK. Well, we'll talk about it. First, I thought I'd just walk around and try to get a sense of things if that's all right with you," Celeste explained.

"Of course, yeah." Andi held up the paper bag. "I'm getting supplies ready for a craft project in kindergarten, so I'll be in the kitchen. Can I get you a cup of coffee or ... well, I don't actually have coffee." She chuckled. "I've not yet managed to acquire the taste for such a grown-up drink. I do have orange juice though, or Dr. Pepper."

"I'm good. Thanks."

Celeste returned to the front of the house, stepped outside, and closed the door behind her. She took a few deep breaths and emptied her mind.

When she felt clear, lighter, she returned to the house, twisted the knob and stepped into the front hall. She formed a question in her mind, whispered it.

"What do you want to show me?"

She did her best to gaze at the house with a scientist's eyes. Gleaming mahogany floors stretched through the living room to her right by a faded maroon rug. Also, in the room a tall grandfather clock, the metronome ticking down the seconds. Dark floral wallpaper, several paintings of cherubic children running in fields, picking wildflowers. The reclining chair was covered in cracked, worn leather. The brown sectional sofa held a mishmash of faded throw pillows. A chipped marble coffee table sat in front of it.

The furnishings were an odd array of old and new.

She stepped again through the double glass doors into the parlor, felt an instant hardening in her stomach, a pit of repulsion. Celeste scanned the space, forcing a detachment her body refused to participate in.

Faded dusty rose print rug, a velvet fainting couch, a wood fireplace mantel arranged with porcelain cherubs and figures of children. Wood-paneled walls. More pictures of children. All the pictures in the house, Celeste realized, were of children. The frames were big and gaudy and ornate.

Celeste stilled her mind and tried to be open to the spirit in the house. Outside, a car rumbled past on the road. Goose bumps prickled along Celeste's arms.

There was something in the house, but it wasn't like anything Celeste had previously experienced.

No sounds, no visions. Nothing.

*It doesn't want me to know it's here.*

The thought bothered her and yet ... she sensed it was true.

She stared at the wood-paneled wall where Andi said she'd

seen the woman writing. It was plain, indistinct and unlike many of the other walls, free of paintings.

Celeste moved to the painting above the fireplace. A red barn beneath an overcast sky. Celeste studied the image. Tall weeds sprang up in front of the barn, wildflowers among them. Two children, one holding a chicken, stood in front of the barn.

A sort of trance fell over her as she stared at the painting. Somewhere deep in the dark maw of the open barn door a child was crying, the sound growing from a whimper to a wail of terror so sharp that Celeste jerked away, took a startled step back and nearly toppled over a footstool she'd not noticed situated just behind her.

Celeste steadied a hand on her chest and waited for her heart to slow. When it had, she made her way upstairs. She paused in the doorway of each bedroom and snapped a picture. She stepped fully into the bathroom where Andi had described seeing the woman in the mirror and took a selfie of her own face reflected back to her. She stared at her phone, half expected to see another figure behind her, but the image revealed only Celeste.

Celeste found Andi in the kitchen, her craft project spread across the kitchen table that had, the day before, been in the corner. It now stood pressed against a white door.

"Where does that lead?" Celeste asked her.

Andi's face darkened. "The basement."

"Is there a reason you put the table in front of it?"

Andi sighed and plopped a handful of mismatched socks back into the paper bag. "That's where I heard Bo. He was whining and scratching at the door. Well ..." She looked flustered. "Obviously it wasn't him."

"But it sounded like him?"

"Yeah."

"Have you been down there?"

Andi cast a wary glance at the door. "Steve, the property

manager, warned me away from it when I signed the lease. Lead paint and asbestos and God only knows what—his words, not mine—but frankly I'm good at avoiding it."

Celeste felt a tug to go down there, to explore it as she had the rest of the house. At the same time, the door repulsed her. The thoughts of what lay beyond it took her instantly back to the cellar in the schoolhouse in Graves and Katie Ellis's walled-up corpse. River's mother too had been buried in a basement in Wild Rose, Wisconsin. And in West Virginia, her own father had buried the child, Elliot, in his crawl space at Moon Lake. Celeste had begun to think of basements as the graveyard of the house.

She shuddered. "I'll skip it for now."

"Steve told me it's just an old Michigan basement, not much down there anyway."

Celeste nodded. "I'm going to head out, but I'd like to come back again with some"— Lena's words popped into her mind, *ghost hunting equipment*—"gadgets to see if anything is off here in the house. Temperature drops, electromagnetic frequencies, that kind of thing."

"Like paranormal ghost hunter type stuff?"

Celeste smiled. "Basically. Yes. Those friends I mentioned yesterday have some. I figured it wouldn't hurt to try."

"Absolutely. I'd be curious to know if you find anything. I teach tomorrow," Andi explained, "but I don't mind leaving a key for you."

The thought of spending time in the house alone made her skin crawl, but she intended to do it. If Andi's trauma was somehow causing the strange happenings in the house, using the ghost equipment in her absence might be the best option.

"Great. Maybe I'll see you tomorrow if I'm still here."

As Celeste climbed into her truck, she cast a final glance at the dark windows. No faces peered back at her and yet she sensed someone, something, watching.

**8**

───────────

As Celeste drove back to Traverse City, her cell phone rang. Adam.

"How did the visit with Dad go?" she asked him.

"He cried," Adam said.

"Really?" Celeste tried to imagine it, but couldn't. Her father's grief, if it existed, had always worn a mask.

"Yeah, and apologized a lot. The visit was ... good. That's the wrong word, but he's never been so open, ever. And he admitted bottling up what happened all these years. Trying to bury it had made him retreat further and further from us and now finally confessing has ... opened the floodgates. He said the jailers keep having to get him fresh toilet paper because he's blowing his nose all night."

The story sounded so little like their father she struggled to reconcile it with the man she knew. Had it really been that simple? Confess your sins and you're saved?

"Do you believe him? That he's sorry."

"Yeah. Without a doubt. You should call him, Celeste. Just hear him out. I know you're mad. I'm mad too. I went into the jail ready to rip him a new one and let him know not to expect to ever hear from me again. By the end I was bawling my eyes out and promising to come back tomorrow."

Celeste pictured their father in a cramped county jail cell in West Virginia, clad in a stiff orange jumpsuit, choking down watery eggs each morning, his gaze fixed on the bleak stretch of the years ahead.

"Is he safe there? No one has tried to hurt him?"

"Right now, he is. He said there's a young guy, Gino, who keeps telling him how he looks like his grandpa who died. He's keeping an eye on him, but Gino's getting released in two weeks, so ..."

"And eventually he'll go to prison. That's going to be different from jail. Is he afraid?"

"No. At least he didn't seem to be. He kept saying he's exactly where he deserves to be."

"Did he hire an attorney?"

"Nope. Has a state-designated lawyer, and he's sticking with him. But I think he should hire one, right? Not that I want him to get away with what he did. Not at all, but ... maybe a better attorney could make sure he doesn't die in prison. Especially now that he's changed, that he's remorseful."

Celeste chewed the edge of her fingernail, but said nothing. Adam had always been more forgiving of their dad, more willing to believe in his potential to be a good father. Celeste had given up hope for that long ago.

"Maybe I'll call him," she murmured, unsure if she was ready. "How long are you staying in West Virginia?"

"Until the day after tomorrow. I hate being gone like this at the start of the school year, but I couldn't put it off any longer. Last night was my first full night of sleep since you told me what happened here."

"Did you visit our old house?"

"Yeah. It was eerie. Crime scene tape everywhere. It brought back some memories, that's for sure."

"It makes me sick to think about it now," Celeste murmured. "What happened in that house ... Even if Hannah dealt the final blow, Dad killed our mom, Adam. She caught him having an affair, and he strangled her."

Adam sighed. "I know. I'm not excusing what he did, but he's still our dad. Any news on Jonathan?" Adam asked, clearly desperate to change the subject.

"No. He's still running. Hopefully he's made it to Mexico by now and he never comes back."

"But then he gets away with it. Screw that. I want him caught. Don't you?"

Celeste imagined the last time she'd seen Jonathan, how out of sorts he seemed, desperate to mend what had been broken beyond repair. Had it all been an act? She suspected that yes, it had been, and yet she now carried his child. Someday she would have to tell that little girl about her father.

"I don't want to talk about Jonathan."

"OK. I get it. Really. But how are *you* doing, Celeste?"

"I'm"—Celeste searched inward, felt the chasm of grief and worry she'd been hovering on the precipice of for months and slowly backed away from it. She hadn't told Adam she was pregnant, that he was going to be an uncle—"fine. It's different living up here. But ... it's nice."

"And you're living with a woman you met at a near death conference."

"Yes, Eliza. In her mother-in-law suite."

"Hmm ... you could have moved in with me, you know? I have a spare bedroom."

"I know. And I'm thankful you offered, really. It's just ... When I was up here in Graves helping Joanna Ellis last winter, I felt ... weirdly at home. Right now, this feels like the place I belong."

Adam sighed. "Are you sure you're OK? I lie in bed at night

thinking about everything that's happened to you and have to get up and drink baking soda, my indigestion gets so bad."

"Stop thinking about it, then. You know what my friend up here says? Worry is a meditation on what you don't want. Tell your brain to go to sleep."

"Ha. When has that ever worked?"

"Are you still taking your antianxiety meds?"

"Yeah, but all this stuff with you and now with Dad." He burped. "Oh boy, here we go again."

"No. We're not. We're stepping off the runaway train of the mind. Tell me the best thing that happened to you this week."

He didn't answer for a moment and then said, "Truthfully?"

"Yeah."

"Seeing Dad cry. Sad, right?" Adam asked. "But it's true. In that moment, I felt ... like he was real, finally. Like he was a real dad with real feelings and that maybe he did always love us in his own twisted way."

"I'm sure he did," she agreed.

But that didn't make him any less of a murderer.

**9**

―――――――

Andi stopped at The Shoreline market and grabbed a basket. Seymour Finnegan, the owner since Andi was a kid, stood at the cash register eyeing her suspiciously like she might shove a handful of bubble gum in her pocket when no one was looking. She fought the urge to stick her tongue out at him.

She grabbed a box of powdered donut holes, crackers, a package of American cheese slices, and four prewrapped chicken salad sandwiches for lunch at school.

Luke had been the cook in their relationship. The one who insisted they buy lettuce and watch it rot in the refrigerator. Still, she'd eaten better with him. Managed vegetables most days of the week—usually carrot sticks dipped in ranch, which he often clucked his tongue at despite Andi's expectation that he'd be proud of her for picking a snack that didn't come wrapped in plastic.

At the counter, Seymour raised his eyebrows with the same judgmental expressions she'd previously seen on Luke.

Next to the register stood a tall, clear container of rainbow pinwheel lollipops. She grabbed four and added them to her purchase.

Seymour scanned the lollipops and put them in her paper bag. Perfectly ordinary movements that seemed loaded with criticism, and Andi's face grew warmer by the second.

A sudden urge to snap at him lit through her.

"I can eat whatever I want," she told him, jerking the bag away harder than necessary. "And I suggest you keep your judgments to yourself or I'll drive a few more miles down the road and go to that new Quick Mart."

He blinked at her, eyes wide with surprise as if the comments had come out of nowhere, as if instead of sitting in judgment about her junk food dinner, he'd been in his own thoughts, some other place far from the store and she'd suddenly snapped him back with a baseless accusation he couldn't even find words to respond to.

"Umm… okay. Thanks," she mumbled, looking down as she hurried from the store.

Andi's cell rang as she carried in her meager groceries, the shame of her attack on old Seymour Finnegan still burning like a wildfire in her face. Her sister's name appeared on the screen.

"Found your calling yet?" Torrie asked.

Andi pulled the lollipops from the bag and set them on the table, wondering what had compelled her to buy them. She didn't even like suckers. "That's not why I moved up here, but also no. Unless my calling is lying in bed at night contemplating the purpose of life."

Andi popped open the donut holes, removed two and walked out to the porch. The aged gray wood groaned beneath her feet. She sank onto one of the two plastic chairs she'd bought at a yard sale the week before.

"That's not a purpose. It's a diversion from the purpose. Less thinky, more do-ey. How's the house?"

"Other than the occasional creaking floorboard or slamming door, it's pretty good." Andi popped a donut hole in her mouth and watched the woman across the street blowing bubbles in the front yard for her two young children.

"Maybe it's the ghost of that old hag who lived there trying to tell you to take a hike."

Andi felt the presence of the house behind her, thought of the woman scrawling red on the walls. "Very funny."

"Well Mom and Dad won't tell you, but they're freaking out. They came over for dinner last night and Mom practically started hyperventilating listing all the ways you're ruining your life. Dad chimed in with his own list of potential hazards in that old house. Let's just say it was not the most cheerful dinner."

"Is it ever? Denver is what? Two years old? Doesn't dinner consist of him flinging peas on the floor?"

"Green beans. He likes the peas."

"Tell them I'm fine."

"Maybe you could tell them. Mom says you're not answering her calls."

"I saw Dante today," Andi cut in.

A brief pause. "Really? Huh. How is he? How'd he look?"

"You remember you're married, right?"

"Oh, shut up."

"Dante and Torrie sitting in a tree ..." She sang the song she and Marco had often sung to their older siblings in their younger years when Torrie and Dante seemed to have a shared crush long before they dated in high school.

"If I could reach through this phone and yank your hair, I would."

"Oh, believe me, I know. He looked good. Like himself, but older."

"Whoa. Insightful."

"What do you want me to say? He's got a chiseled jaw and shoulders that would make a linebacker envious?"

"Does he?"

Andi imagined him. "Pretty well-defined jaw, but as for the shoulders, nah. He's got the runner's body. Same as he always did. Long and lean."

"And what'd you guys talk about?"

"Not you."

"Ugh. You're so annoying."

Andi laughed. "Just doin' my job. We did talk about you, actually. He asked how you were. I said, pumping out kids like a factory."

"Jesus."

"I said you were good. Two babies, a husband, physical therapy career, living the dream."

"Hmm ... And what about him? What's he doing?"

"What else? Running the family store."

"Is that where you saw him?"

"At the cemetery, actually. I was visiting Marco's grave, catching him up on the times."

"Tell me you're joking."

"Nope."

"Good grief, Andi. You know he's dead, right? Has been dead for ... I don't know what, thirteen years?"

"Fourteen."

"OK. So ... maybe it's time to ... let go."

"I didn't dig him up. I just sat and had a chat with him."

"Let me reiterate what I said in our last conversation. You need a therapist."

When Andi climbed into bed, her eyes lingered on Bo's urn sitting on the bedside table. Navy blue porcelain covered in paw prints. His name was printed in elegant white calligraphy on the side.

"Goodnight, Bo."

She thought of the bark she'd heard in the basement and shuddered, rolling to face away from the urn.

For a while she lay and stared at the wall, thought of her conversation with Torrie. "You need a therapist." And then of her parents, her mother's calls unanswered, her desire to shut everyone out.

Andi woke to the sound of scratching—not like an animal worrying at the door as Bo sometimes used to do when he had to pee in the middle of the night, but something more deliberate.

She blinked into the dark room where a shape, inky black, stood at the opposite wall, one arm raised as it dragged the quill slow and then quick, paused to dip the end and the scratching resumed. A dense, pungent odor of metal filled the air.

Frozen with fear, Andi observed the woman. Cold sweat formed under her shirt as she strained to decipher the dark letters illuminated by a sliver of moonlight. The woman turned slowly, unnaturally, moving as if guided by something other than herself. She approached Andi, who tried to retreat but found herself paralyzed.

The woman thrust the quill pen, blood dripping, across Andi's pale sheets, and into Andi's hand.

Andi jolted up in bed, flinging open her right hand and expecting the quill pen to clatter across the floor.

It didn't.

Her hand lay empty. No woman stood before her, no red writing on the wall. It was still dark outside, but dawn had begun to lighten the sky.

## 10

Celeste had just poured her coffee when someone knocked on her door. She opened it to find Lena, dressed in a flowing silver skirt with a black lace tank top.

"These are for you." Lena thrust a box into her hands.

Celeste studied the image on top. "The Gossamer Veil Tarot," she read aloud.

"They're not your thing, right? That was my reaction when Jazzy told me in the middle of the night that I woke her up and insisted I needed to give these to you."

"You dreamt it?"

"Something like that. I have a sleepwalking thing. It's interesting, sometimes a pain. Twice my neighbor has woken up to find me rooting around in his refrigerator." She laughed. "But good stuff comes through too, important stuff."

"What do I do with them?"

"Ask questions. See what comes up. Sometimes the cards just reveal what's buried in our subconscious; other times ... they can be weirdly accurate. Before I met Jazzy, literally the day before, I pulled the Hierophant card from my tarot deck.

It's a card associated with doctors, healers. Jazzy's a doctor in Traverse City. I'd stay and give you a quick rundown on reading them, but one of my employees, Mallori, just got a job offer downstate and quit out of the blue. I'm short-staffed and have back-to-back readings." Lena swiped a lock of hair out of her face. As she did, a butterfly landed briefly on her fingers. "I know, I know. Trust the universe to do her thing. I get it. Bye, Celeste."

As Lena started to climb into her car, Celeste followed her out.

"Lena, if you want, I'll come work at the store." Celeste hadn't worked a retail job since college and never in anything like a new age store, but for weeks she'd been feeling the pressure to find a job.

"Really?" Lena paused with her door open. Her expression shifted from surprise to delight. "Heck yeah. That'd be awesome. Can you come by tonight after we close at six? I'll show you the ropes."

"I'll be there." Celeste considered Lena's outfit. "Dress code?" Celeste asked.

Lena looked down at herself and grinned. "No dress code, Celeste. This is just me. You can wear a potato bag if you want."

"I think I can manage something more presentable than that."

"I have no doubt."

Celeste sat crisscrossed on the bed and took the stack of tarot cards from the box. Each card held a dreamy, colorful illustration. They were labeled with words like Four of Cups and the High Priestess. She'd never used tarot cards, felt strange doing it now, but she thought of Lena's advice and shuffled through the cards, allowing her eyes to drift shut. She thought of Andi's house and allowed a loose question to form.

*What do I need to know to help Andi?*

She pulled a card from the deck and turned it over. The Moon. A bulbous blue moon dangled in a starry sky. A half-wolf, half-woman being howled beneath it.

A little booklet accompanied the deck and Celeste flipped to the section on the moon and read the brief description: illusion, deception, and hidden truths.

"Is there something in Andi's house?" she whispered, again shuffling the cards and drawing one out.

She turned the tarot card over. A hunched, ghoulish figure reached toward a young girl, its eyes burning with malice. At the bottom, in ornate lettering, was the title: *The Devil.*

Celeste shook her head, stuffed the card back into the deck, and tucked them into her bureau drawer. Deciphering tarot cards was difficult, but Celeste knew how to do research and she wanted to find out more about the woman who'd lived in the Fulton Road house when Andi was a child.

Celeste opened her laptop and searched for Vivian Walters in Frankfort, Michigan, but found nothing.

She logged into her newspaper archive subscription and searched again for Vivian's name. This time she found an old wedding announcement in a Chicago newspaper.

If it were the same Vivian Walters, she'd married a man named Conrad Walters in Chicago. Celeste searched for Conrad's name and began the painstaking process of sifting through articles and websites.

Eventually she found a phone number and address for a Conrad Walters in Rockford, Illinois. On a social media site for professionals, he was listed as a mortgage broker with a business contact number.

"Walters and Associates," a man answered after Celeste punched in the man's number.

"Hi. Is this Conrad Walters?" she asked.

"Speaking."

"Were you once married to a woman named Vivian Walters?"

The man said nothing. Celeste wondered if he'd hung up on her.

"Hello?" she asked.

"Who is this?" he demanded, his cheery customer service voice gone.

"My name is Celeste Cleary. I'm trying to find Vivian. It's about something that happened a long time ago, but ..."

"Vivian is gone. I doubt you'll ever find her."

"What does that mean?"

"It means she lost her mind and took off years ago."

"Was she reported missing or—"

He scoffed. "By who? She had no one left. I didn't even know she'd disappeared until a neighbor called to tell me the mail was piling up."

"This was your wife? And you just ... didn't care."

"Ex-wife," he said sharply. "Ex-wife who tried to kill me in my sleep and our little son, too. She was insane. I tried to get her help. She wanted nothing to do with it."

"She has a son?"

"I have a son. You're not a parent just because you birth them. I don't care what anyone says."

Celeste thought of Andi's description of the woman as heavily pregnant.

"Were you living in the house on Fulton Road in Frankfort when she had the baby?"

"What is this about? I swear to God if this is some deranged scheme to get money—"

"It's not. I'm helping someone who once knew Vivian. I'm trying to get some information on her."

"Who? Who are you helping?"

Celeste wondered if it was appropriate to share Andi's name and decided against it. "It's a person who met Vivian as a child and she's now ... living in the house on Fulton Road."

"Our son was born in Frankfort. Yes."

"Can you tell me what happened with Vivian? You said she lost her mind."

"No. I can't tell you what happened. Only she could answer that, but honestly, I doubt even she could. I worked in Chicago then and came home most weekends. If something happened to cause her ... mental issues, she never told me about it."

In the background, Celeste heard a voice, but couldn't make out what they said.

"I have to go," Conrad told her. "My eleven o'clock just walked in."

"You said she tried to kill you and your child? Was she arrested?"

"I'm ending the call now, but," Conrad said, his voice lower, little more than a whisper, "if you find her ... I'd like to know."

"And yet you've never bothered looking for her yourself."

"It's for Jeremy, my son. Sometimes he asks and, well, he deserves to know what became of his mother."

---

## 11

Andi high-fived and hugged the students as they trailed into her kindergarten room. The crying for most of them had subsided in the previous weeks, though she saw Ellie sniffling as she hugged her mother goodbye in the hallway.

Andi looked away, remembered her own difficulty starting school, her mother prying Andi from her leg in the same hallway. She'd cried for days every morning at drop-off, begging her mother not to leave. It had been Marco who'd popped out of their kindergarten class clutching a clear plastic cage.

"Andi, look!" he'd said.

She'd been surprised he remembered her name, even more surprised he singled her out to be friends.

She'd stepped away from her mom to get a closer look at the little plastic cage containing the class pet, a hamster named Waffle.

From that point on they'd been borderline inseparable, their pack growing by one when they realized another little girl in their class, Gwen, lived on the same street as them.

Since returning to the school at the start of the month, Andi had been overwhelmed daily by memories of Marco. Every room contained the long-faded echoes of his laughter, his presence.

Andi stepped into class and walked to each student, asking if they'd selected the lunch on the whiteboard and told them to get out that morning's coloring page. She broke up two arguments and had to ask Hunter Williams to stop drawing on his arm with a marker. By the time the bell rang, she'd managed to wrangle all eighteen of her students into their chairs.

"Ms. Cooper?"

Andi looked up. Paisley Kincaid stood holding up her hand painting.

"Isn't that pretty?" Andi said, taking the messy painting and lying it flat on her desk so the colors wouldn't run.

Andi had passed out the paint only a few minutes before and was surprised Paisley had finished so quickly.

"You're a fast painter, huh?" Andi said.

"Almost everyone's done." Paisley looked back at the other kids, many of whom were talking, or had begun to move around the room, made their way to the toy corner or worse, had started to paint their desks.

Andi blinked at her watch, then up at the room clock. Twenty minutes had passed though it had felt more like two. She'd just sat down at her desk, opened her planner to check the school calendar. Andi blinked and rubbed her eyes. For a moment, the room seemed wrong—slightly off-kilter.

After she guided Paisley back to her seat, Andi felt oddly floaty, as if she'd stepped onto unstable ground. Twice more, she stared at the clock and tried to understand the lapse in time.

"All right, guys. Great job." She forced brightness into her voice. "I see most of you have finished up. I'm going to excuse you by table to carry your pictures to the back counter to dry. And if any of you turned your table into a canvas too"—she gave them a mock stern look and raised her eyebrows—"you will be on Team Cleanup. Grab some paper towel from the back. Then everyone line up to wash hands."

One boy held up a green-smeared palm. "Miss Andi, I made a monster!"

"Ooh scary, Max," Andi murmured, offering an expression of exaggerated horror at his green and black hand with a red gaping mouth in the center.

As they moved to the drying table, Andi returned to her own desk.

Near the energy drink she concealed in an insulated U of M cup, lay a sheet of construction paper with a large handprint, bigger than a child's, bigger than her own hand even. It appeared as if someone had dipped their hand in dark red paint and dragged it down the page.

Andi had no recollection of creating the painting.

"Miss Andi?" Paisley tugged on Andi's hand. "Hunter is squirting soap on everyone's hands when they're asking him not to."

Andi shifted her attention to the sink in the back where the kids squabbled.

"All right, Hunter. Shake your tail feathers back to your seat. Everyone who's done washing, return to your chairs."

When Andi looked back at her desk, the red handprint was gone. She gazed at her hands. Her palms and fingertips were clean.

Andi pushed open the door to the Italian bakery that belonged to Marco's family. A rush of nostalgic scents enveloped her.

Yeasty bread and almond cookies and a heartier smell with fennel seeds. Mrs. Lombardi's soup likely in one of the hot pots at the soup and salad bar.

The black-and-white checked floor squeaked beneath her feet and she stopped and stared at the wall of family photos, hundreds of photos of Marco's big Italian family. Most of the images were old. They were black and white and sepia-toned. Images of weddings and vineyards and enormous family gatherings.

A dozen memories of skidding into the store with Marco and Gwen, each getting an amaretti cookie and running through the kitchen much to the dismay of Marco's dad, bursting through the back door and racing down the road to Frankfort Beach streamed through her mind.

"Andi?"

She looked up to see Dante, sleeves rolled to his elbows, standing behind the clear glass counter that displayed racks of colorful baked goods.

"Hi," she told him, her voice slightly croaky. It took her a minute to get her legs moving, but when they did, she made her way back to him, eyes drifting over the rainbow cookies, biscotti, and cannoli. She'd often salivated at the sight of the pastries and wished Marco's mom would let them try something other than amaretti cookies, but the glass display was off limits to Marco and his friends.

"Looking for something?"

Andi shook her head, tried to force the tears filling her eyes to stay put. "I just wanted to stop by." She pushed her hands into her pockets and clenched her teeth together. The wave of emotion had begun to subside, but she blinked hard at the glass case until her eyes cleared completely. "Actually"—she pulled out a hand and pointed at the case of baked goods—"I'll take a cannoli."

He reached in the case and, with a piece of parchment paper, grabbed one.

"And a fruit flan and an amaretti cookie. Three amaretti cookies."

Dante grinned. "You always did have a sweet tooth. Marco too."

He handed her the little paper bag of pastries.

Andi took out her wallet, but Dante shook his head. "On the house."

"No way. I don't want your mother banging on my door in the middle of the night because you gave away pastries. What did she use to call your dad when he did that?"

Dante laughed and slapped the counter. "The patron saint of freebies. I can't believe you remembered that."

"I spent as much time here at the bakery as I did my own house. How could I forget?"

Dante took the cash she handed him and gave her change.

"Want an espresso?" He tapped the machine.

"It's almost six o'clock!"

He grinned. "So. Don't you want to be able to outrun the monsters in your dreams?"

Andi's thoughts slipped to the nightmare of the woman thrusting the bloody quill into her hand. She shuddered.

"Fine. Make me one, heavy on the cream and sugar."

He made a face. "I said espresso, not latte."

"What's the difference?"

"Sophistication."

Andi laughed. "Dante, I get my caffeine from Dr. Pepper and energy drinks. If it's sophistication you're after, you won't find it here."

He scowled as he added milk and sugar to the little white cup.

"If I end up reorganizing all my school holiday craft bins at two in the morning, I'm blaming you," Andi told him. "I'll text you pictures so you can be awake with me."

"Good. It'll be nice to get a middle-of-the-night text that's not my dad asking if I remembered to turn the bakery lights off."

Andi perched on a barstool, letting the warmth of the bakery sink into her.

"So what's this I hear about you moving into that old house on Fulton Road?" he asked.

"Where'd you hear that?"

He raised an eyebrow. "This is Frankfort, remember? There are no secrets."

"It's not a secret," she murmured. "It was available, so"—she shrugged—"I rented it."

"Oh, come on. You think I don't remember what you said about that house after ..." He paused as if he didn't want to say it out loud. "After Marco died."

She cupped the espresso, letting the heat anchor her. Dante wanted a reason, some logical explanation. Dante, Torrie, her parents. She didn't have one, at least not one that could be communicated through words.

"My life fell apart in Ann Arbor. My dog died, my boyfriend and I broke up and he owned the condo we lived in. I decided I wanted to come back to Frankfort."

"You moved back to Frankfort into the creepy old house you insisted was cursed because a few things went awry?" He stared at her, disbelieving. "Why stay in Michigan? Why not move to Tennessee, where your sister and parents are, after the breakup?"

"Unfinished business."

"And what business is that?"

She couldn't tell him it was Marco and the old house and the woman who'd once lived inside of it. Andi had to come back. It hardly felt like a choice at all. Since that long-ago night she'd lived in purgatory, a half-life, and would never be able to fully exist in her own life until she dealt with the past. Everyone felt a little trapped in their childhood, a sliver of their kid-self remaining, but for Andi it was so much more than that; half of her, 75 percent maybe, still looked in the mirror and saw Andi at eleven years old—forever frozen by that fateful night.

"I don't know exactly. I just felt like ... I needed to come back here. Maybe when it's all over I will move to Tennessee."

"When what's all over?"

Andi waved a dismissive hand. "Tell me about your parents. Where else have they traveled to?"

He stared at her for a long moment, clearly aware she was changing the subject. She thought he might push, but then he leaned back, took a sip of his espresso and started talking about Egypt.

**12**

---

Celeste knocked, unsure if Andi was home. Her car wasn't in the driveway, but might have been parked in the little garage behind the house. It was four in the afternoon, after school.

Celeste had texted her on her drive from Traverse City, but had not gotten a response.

From somewhere inside the house, she heard Andi's muffled shout, "Come in."

Celeste twisted the knob, and the door, without a push, swung open.

"Andi?" she called.

No answer.

Celeste paused in the foyer, scanning the shadowy hall. She'd heard Andi invite her in but now the house sat eerily quiet. No creaking floorboard as Andi moved, no doors opening.

The silence seemed weirdly alive. Celeste sensed something trying to remain undetected, crouched, waiting.

"Andi?" she yelled, louder this time.

Again, no response.

Her cell phone pinged.

Celeste took it out.

Andi: *Running a few errands after school. I might miss you. Please let yourself in. The door's unlocked.*

Celeste thought of the voice she'd heard. "Come in."

She caught sight of her reflection in the hall mirror and paused. Her brown hair appeared static, lightly floating. She touched it and felt the undercurrent, an electricity in the air.

Deep in her womb, the baby, not even the size of a raspberry according to the baby books, seemed to tug, draw her attention down. Celeste moved her hand there.

So quickly that her sudden movements startled even her, Celeste backed out of the house. She closed the door firmly behind her and practically leaped off the porch into the yard. Only when she stood on the sidewalk in front of the house did her chest loosen enough to allow a full breath.

The house loomed before her. Silent and still. It appeared to be an ordinary, empty house and yet Celeste knew something inside of it watched her.

She slid into her driver's seat and stared at the house. Celeste checked the time on her phone. She needed to be back in Traverse City by six to meet Lena and didn't want to have driven all the way to Frankfort for nothing. She glanced at the houses on either side of Andi's. Her own search for her mother in West Virginia had been aided by talking to neighbors. It was possible people in the surrounding houses had known Vivian.

When her heart rate had returned to normal, Celeste stepped from the truck. She didn't love the thought of knocking on the neighbor's doors. Anyone could be tucked behind the cheery facades, waiting. As she approached the house next to Andi's, she slowed. A for sale sign was staked in the yard and the windows were dark.

The next house appeared to be occupied with a green Land Rover in the driveway. Celeste rang the doorbell and a middle-aged woman in jeans and a Lake Michigan T-shirt pulled it open. She held an oven mitt in her free hand.

"Yes?"

"Hi. I'm sorry to bother you. I'm trying to track down someone who used to live in that big house two doors down, the old farmhouse. I wondered if you've lived here for more than fifteen years?"

"Sorry. No. We moved here three years ago, after my husband retired. Try Maureen Sinclair. She lives three houses down. The big greenish-colored house. My husband calls it the avocado. You can't miss it."

"Thanks."

Celeste followed the walkway to the large green-tinged house. The roof was mossy, and the gutters stuffed to overflowing with leaves. The windows appeared slightly murky, as if they hadn't been cleaned in many years.

An elderly woman sat on the front porch in a rocking chair, a crochet project in her lap.

"Who is it?" the woman called as Celeste drew closer.

The woman's eyes were both cloudy, the faint blue irises barely present beneath her heavy lids.

"Hi," Celeste said, pausing before taking the steps to the porch. "My name is Celeste Cleary. I'm looking for anyone in the neighborhood who knew a woman who used to live on this road. Vivian Walters."

The woman fumbled with her crochet project. It looked vaguely like a cat, but it had far too many legs. Seven, Celeste counted.

"I knew Vivian," the woman said. She reached, flailing one age-spotted hand for a small side table to set her crochet cat on.

"Would you mind telling me a bit about her?" Celeste asked.

"Do I mind?" The woman chuckled. "Child, get up here and

sit down. You know how many visitors I have in a month? Zero."

Celeste walked onto the creaking porch. An unpleasant odor emanated from the woman. Something sour. Celeste sat on a little wicker chair that groaned. Celeste gripped the arms, waiting to see if it would hold her. It did.

"I'm Maureen, Celeste. It's a pleasure. Could you hand me my sippy cup?" She gestured at a purple cup with a straw on the table. "Lost my sight about ten years ago. Cataracts. I get around all right, but if someone stops by, I get to be lazy."

Celeste grabbed the purple cup and placed it in Maureen's gnarled hands.

She took a long slurp and then deftly returned the cup to the table. "Vivian was a beautiful woman and when she first moved into that house, she was very friendly. She brought me a plant." Maureen chuckled. "She didn't realize I can't keep a cactus alive, let alone an orchid. Poor thing wilted and browned in a matter of weeks."

"How long have you lived here, Maureen?"

"Hmm ... that's a good question. Moved here with my third husband, Hugo. The kids were all grown by then. Twenty-two years, maybe twenty-three."

"Were you close with Vivian?"

Maureen shifted in her chair, released a little groan. "Not close. No. I didn't get the sense she was the kind of woman who got close to many people. She had her husband, Conrad." Maureen said his name like it tasted rancid. "Maybe back in the city they had friends, but I never saw 'em around here. Even when she was pregnant with the babies, there wasn't any kind of baby shower. I secretly hoped for an invite. I make the most precious little booties. But nope. No party at all."

"Babies? As in more than one?"

Maureen held up two fingers. "Two. Lost the first, and she was pretty far along. Lots of women lose their babies early on. I lost three myself, but one day Vivian had a belly and the next she didn't and rumor got around."

Celeste shifted in her chair, the tiny life inside of her suddenly more present. She'd expected to have a miscarriage, considering all the trauma at Moon Lake, but it hadn't happened and with each day that passed, she discovered she was more and more attached to the little person living in her body. Vivian Walters had lost one of her babies. Had it been the baby inside of her the night Andi, Gwen and Marco visited her house?

"That must have been terrible for her."

"Oh I'm sure it was," Maureen agreed. "But some babies aren't meant for this world. And it's an ugly world, isn't it? For some of them."

"Yes. It is."

Maureen sighed. "But that was a long time ago, wasn't it? And you're here now. So, what is it about Vivian you'd like to know?"

"Do you have any idea what happened to her? Where she is now?"

"Oh no. I guess she moved out. Couldn't tell you where."

"And was Vivian into ... anything weird?"

"Weird like getting the mail in her nightie or weird like howling at the full moon?"

"Anything at all?"

"Truth is, after the first few months, Vivian kept to herself. That husband of hers, Conrad, was indifferent, down-right negligent. He let the grass grow wild. He'd leave for work and sometimes not bother to come home on the week-ends. I know a struggling marriage when I see one. She started off real put together, pretty dresses, face all made up, hair curled. By the end, she was skin and bones draped in a grimy T-shirt and sweatpants. He left and took that baby. The police had been around there a few times by then, the ambulance once. I heard she spent a few weeks in a mental-type place."

"Conrad said she tried to kill him and the baby."

"That so?" Maureen picked up her crocheted cat and fingered each of the legs, frowning. "I'm not saying it ain't true, but if it is, if she'd gone as mad as he claims, he half drove her to it. Gone all the time. A young woman alone in a big ole house in a place like this. Winters here, they're ..." She shook her head. "Difficult. Enough to cause a person to lose their wits."

"Did you ever hear of bad things happening to people after they interacted with Vivian?" Celeste thought of Andi's story the night Marco died, how she'd spent her life convinced that Vivian cast some kind of spell, cursed the boy.

Maureen rubbed at the crusted yellow goop that gathered in the corner of one of her eyes. "What sorts of bad things?"

"People getting sick, dying even." Celeste knew the line of questioning sounded like crazy talk and yet she suspected Maureen was a believer, the type who threw salt over her left shoulder and walked around rather than beneath ladders.

"No ..." Maureen shook her head slowly. "Nothing comes to mind."

"Any idea who might know more about Vivian? Or how I might track her down. Conrad said she took off, just disappeared."

"She did do that," Maureen agreed. "I remember the house sittin' and sittin', empty, forlorn. That house was sad after Vivian left."

"Did someone eventually move in?"

"Just last month."

"No one else? In all the years after Vivian left?"

"Nope. Some houses are particular if you catch my drift. They wait for the right one to come along."

Celeste did not catch her drift and the implication made

her uncomfortable. "You're saying the house chooses who moves in?"

Maureen raised an eyebrow. "I'm saying no one lived there after Vivian until this latest girl."

"Who lived in the house before Vivian?"

Maureen rocked back in her chair. "Let's see. It was vacant for a few years and before that it was ... a woman, but her name plum slips my mind."

"Do you remember if the police were involved in the alleged attack by Vivian on her husband and child? Did Vivian get arrested?"

Maureen rocked forward, head cocked slightly as if she could hear something Celeste could not. Celeste scanned the front yard and the street beyond. Empty and other than the chatter of a few birds and the far-off bark of a dog, she heard nothing unusual.

"Mighta got shipped off to the looney bin again. Not the kind we used to have, mind you. All the big asylums closed down decades ago. A shame too. Now they send 'em to the hospital and they're lucky to get a few days' respite before they're turned loose. If she did mean to kill him, I almost don't blame her. I told you, grass up to here." She held her hand flat in front of her chest. "A disgrace to the neighborhood, really. Course, now ..."

She turned her head toward the house as if she could see it. In her memories, she likely could. "It's been neglected. That's what Sue Miller says. She lives down the road a bit. The big white house with green shutters. Takes a lot of pride in curb appeal. At our neighborhood potluck last year, she called that house an abomination." Maureen laughed. "I'll tell you what's an abomination. Her daughter running off with Ronnie Monroe, the postman. He delivered our mail for years, then one day I hear he and Sue's daughter took off and got married in Las Vegas. When she was engaged to a boy right here in town.

An absolute scandal, but you don't hear Sue talking about that at the potluck."

---

When Celeste returned, Andi's car still wasn't in the driveway. She hesitated, tempted to slip back inside and poke around for traces of Vivian Walters—old boxes, forgotten papers, anything she might have left behind. But halfway up the walkway, her steps stalled.

She couldn't make herself cross the threshold.

A sleek black raven dropped onto the porch rail, its beady eyes fixed on her. It let out a sharp, rasping cry.

A warning.

She turned and hurried to her truck.

## 13

———

Celeste called Conrad on her drive back to Traverse City. When he didn't answer, she left him a voicemail message.

As she wound along the bay, Lake Michigan sparkled beside her. The sun had begun its descent and cast a halo of orange across the smooth surface. Celeste parked downtown and walked to Lena's store, The Spirit Lantern.

A brass bell jingled as she pushed through the frosted glass door. The scent of lavender and some earthy incense greeted her. Amber lamps offered the primary lighting, with additional fairy lights strung across tall shelves brimming with crystals and various stones. Velvet-draped tables displayed decks of tarot cards, guided journals and candles. A beaded curtain shimmered at the back, parting just slightly with the draft from the door.

"Celeste!" Lena exclaimed, popping up from behind the counter, two handfuls of colorful beaded strands that looked like rosaries clutched in her hands. "Welcome to The Spirit Lantern, my home away from home."

"More like your primary residence these days," a woman

grumbled as she carried a box through the beaded curtain and set it on the counter.

"Not for much longer," Lena exclaimed. "Celeste, this is my partner in life, not business, Jazzy."

Jazzy rolled her eyes. "As much as I work in here, you might as well call us partners in business too." Jazzy walked to Celeste and offered her hand. "Good to meet you, Celeste."

"Likewise."

"Jazzy, you spend more time at the hospital than you've ever spent with me or in here, so don't start."

Jazzy frowned and squinted at her watch. "Which reminds me, I've gotta go home soon and catch some sleep. My next thirty-six-hour marathon starts at the crack of dawn."

"Lena mentioned you're a doctor," Celeste said.

"Not any doctor either," Lena added. "She's an ob-gyn."

"No lesbian jokes, please," Jazzy said.

"Before you go," Lena cut in. "You need to look through the astrology cards. You wanted to pick one out for Norm's birthday, remember?"

"Right, yeah."

The bell over the door rang.

"We're closed—," Lena started then stopped. "Oh, it's Harris."

"Coffee delivery!" Harris held up a cardboard tray of to-go coffee cups.

Jazzy cocked an eyebrow. "You realize it's after six?"

He shrugged. "I'm a detective. Coffee's for the night." He winked at Celeste. "But don't worry, I got a decaf for you, Jazzy."

Celeste took a coffee and had a tiny sip. She'd been trying to limit her caffeine intake to a single small cup in the morning, but tiredness tugged at the corners of her eyes.

"I'm working, but figured I'd pop in and see how the employee onboarding is going. I hope Lena's not working you to the bone," Harris said.

Celeste twiddled her fingers. "No exposed bones just yet, but we'll see once I have to learn to use the cash register. I haven't worked one of those since dial-up Internet."

"Ha!" Lena grabbed a large coffee and took a gulp, scowling and squeezing her eyes shut. "Hot. Ouch damn, hot."

"Gotta prepare for winter," Harris said.

"Don't even say that word." Jazzy glared at him. "It's blasphemous to speak of until December."

"*Farmer's Almanac* is predicting the first snow in October."

Jazzy groaned. Lena put an arm around her and squeezed. "Have no fear, honey. Now you get to try out that faux fur coat we got at the estate sale last summer."

"The one you said smelled like mothballs and dead old lady?"

Lena nodded, wide-eyed. "That's the one. Now, come on, let's go dig through the astrology cards."

Jazzy followed Lena through the beaded curtain.

"How's the Frankfort house going?" Harris asked.

"Strange. I went over there today and got a really bad feeling in the house like ..." Celeste tried to put into words the sensation. "Like it didn't want me there."

He peeled the lid off his coffee and blew on it. "Maybe you shouldn't be there. I get that you want to help, but the last what, year and a half, two years have been pretty rough. You could give yourself a break."

"And do what? Sit at Eliza's and stare out the window? Reminisce about the tragic turn of my life?"

He sipped his coffee. "Read, work here at the store, heal."

"Is that what you did?" Celeste felt instantly guilty for asking the question, plunging him back into the tragedy of his wife's and daughter's deaths. Still, she didn't apologize.

He sighed. "No. I didn't. But I should have. The years after might have been easier if I'd given myself permission to recover instead of diving into the next distraction."

"I'm not trying to distract myself. I'm helping a young woman who's in over her head. There's something going on in that house."

"Any leads on the history of the place?"

"Andi gave me the name of the woman who lived there when she was a girl. Vivian Walters. I called her husband. He told me Vivian took off after trying to kill him and their son."

Harris whistled through his teeth. "That's dark. And you said the girl who lives there now…"

"Andi."

"Yeah, Andi. She had a friend who died after they pranked the house as kids?"

"Yes."

"But now she's living in the house."

"Yep."

"The same house where this lady tried to kill her husband and son."

"Apparently. The only source of the attempted murder is the husband, Conrad, and he says Vivian disappeared, abandoned the house after he fled with their son."

"And you think what? Vivian is haunting the house? If she died there, who killed her?"

"Maybe she killed herself."

"And concealed her own body?" Harris looked skeptical.

"I know. It doesn't add up, but I'm just getting started."

"Be careful. If your gut is telling you something is wrong in that house, trust it."

---

After two hours learning the basic store operations, Celeste bid goodnight to Lena and walked to her car.

As she slid behind the wheel, her cell rang: Conrad Walters.

"Hi, Conrad," she answered.

"I'm returning your call," he said stiffly. "Did you find Vivian?"

She avoided his question, knowing if she told him no, he might end the call. "I spoke with a neighbor on Fulton Road today who said your relationship with Vivian was quite troubled, that you basically neglected and abandoned your wife. Worked instead of going home on weekends."

"Who told you that?"

"Maureen."

"Oh Jesus. That's your source? Good grief. I'm amazed that the woman is still alive. She didn't like men. If you spent ten minutes with her, nine of them would be devoted to how her departed husband never so much as lifted a finger to fix a shutter or paint a door. The husband before him never changed a diaper. The one before him went off to the war and contracted syphilis from a prostitute. I never heard her say a kind word about any of the men in her life and there were quite a few. So am I surprised that she insists I was the source of all Vivian's problems? No, I'm not.

"And I didn't leave Vivian in that house. I begged her to move to Chicago. We both loved the house when we saw it, had a dream of raising our kids in Northern Michigan. But a month in, I knew something was wrong. I'm not into all that woo-woo business people talk about, but ..." He didn't speak for a long time. When he did, he'd dropped his voice, though Celeste suspected he was alone. Still, the mere thought of anyone overhearing him, thinking he believed in ghosts and goblins, was apparently more than he could handle. "The house wasn't right. Weird stuff went on there and Vivian got attached to it. She wouldn't leave."

"What weird stuff?"

"I don't know ... it's all ... I haven't thought about that place in a long time." He let out a long sigh. "Sometimes we heard crying at night and ... umm ..." Something in his tone told

Celeste he was holding back, reluctant to disclose the more troubling things that had happened.

"It's OK, Conrad. Please just tell me."

"Blood. A couple of times there was blood on the wall and on the floors. I don't know where it came from. Vivian said she didn't either and, in the beginning, before she ... changed, I believed her. Now looking back, I wonder if it was her all along. The crying and the blood. I don't know how she did it."

"Where was the blood at?"

"In the sitting room with the double glass doors. The parlor, Vivian called it."

**14**

---

Andi had a late start at school and spent the morning organizing a craft bin so the kids could make popsicle stick picture frames. She loaded her supplies into a plastic tote and sealed it.

Handling the popsicle sticks sent her thoughts skittering to the fudge pops in her freezer. She dug one out, peeled off the wrapper and walked into the backyard, flopping onto a distressed vinyl lawn chair, its center sagging beneath her.

The backyard was quiet, save for a few birds squabbling in the trees.

Despite getting to sleep in that morning, Andi's eyes had felt gritty since she crawled out of bed around nine. She wanted to blame Dante and the espresso for keeping her awake, but in truth, the instant her head hit the pillow the night before she'd been gone.

"Andi!"

The voice startled her and as Andi bolted upright, the last of the vinyl gave out and ripped beneath her. She fell through the lawn chair onto the mossy stone patio. Her fudge pop landed in her lap.

Andi blinked at the woman who'd spoken, trying to make sense of this familiar, and yet wildly different, person standing in her heels in the backyard.

"Gwen?" Andi barely recognized her. She'd last seen her friend the summer after high school graduation, more than seven years before, but by then they'd grown apart, the tight bonds of their adolescence frayed by the shared trauma of losing Marco.

Back in elementary school, the other kids labeled Gwen "Giraffe"—a cruel nod to her tall, awkward frame. It was one of the things that had bonded Andi, Marco, and Gwen. Cody Braud, the burly kid whose dad rumbled up to the school on a Harley most mornings, had singled each of them out for his own brand of mockery. Marco had been "Meatball," Gwen "Giraffe," and Andi "Chicken Pox"—a dig at her freckled face.

Together they'd shrugged off the insults, but when Marco died, Andi and Gwen had drifted apart. Gwen seemed to sink into depression. Through middle school and into high school, Gwen haunted the hallways like a shadow, long dark hair veiling her face, her body hidden beneath oversized sweatshirts and baggy jeans. She had perfected the art of invisibility. Andi had done her own version of vanishing. Sports, volunteer projects, and running a kids' club.

This Gwen was not the one Andi remembered.

Tall, as she'd always been, but elegant and self-assured. She wore black silk pants and a pearl-colored sleeveless blouse. Everything about her reminded Andi of the women she and Gwen had obsessed over in magazines like *Cosmo* and *Seventeen*.

"You look amazing!" Andi said, stunned as she struggled to her feet. When she finally got her legs beneath her, the partially melted fudge pop dropped to the ground and splattered her bare feet.

"I'm so sorry! I didn't mean to spook you."

Andi waved a dismissive hand and tried to wipe off the fudge pop that smeared her jean overalls. She thought of what Torrie liked to say anytime she wore the overalls: "You look like a giant toddler in those things."

"Seriously, Gwen. Wow. I barely recognize you."

Gwen laughed and flipped her shiny, dark hair. "Oh stop it." She put her hands on Andi's shoulders. "Look at you! All grown up. We both are, apparently."

Andi pulled back slightly, afraid to soil Gwen's pretty blouse and vaguely wishing the stone patio would crack open and swallow her whole.

"I cannot believe you are living in this house," Gwen said, smoky-tinged eyes scanning to the roofline. "After ... What happened?"

Andi chewed her lip, nodded. "Nuts, right? It was for rent and ... I needed a place, so ..."

"Huh." Gwen gazed past her toward the back door. "Mind giving me a tour? I've always wondered ..."

"Sure, yeah. Of course." Andi waved her in, grimaced at her bitten-down nails and curled her hands into fists. The back door opened into a hall to the right of the kitchen. Andi made a beeline for the paper towel, her sticky feet suctioning with each step.

"The kitchen obviously," Andi explained, wiping off her bib and feet.

Gwen nodded and gazed around. "Old-fashioned."

"This whole place is. I don't know if it's been updated since ... well, ever." Andi moved into the hall, Gwen trailing behind her, peering into each room, making little sounds of curiosity.

"I heard you're teaching at the school?" Gwen asked, pausing in the hall to gaze at a framed painting of a little boy sitting on a dock, feet dangling over the side.

"Yeah. Kindergarten. That's what I was doing before I

moved back up here; got lucky they had a long-term sub position open up, so …"

"You were living somewhere downstate?"

"Ann Arbor." Andi tried not to stare at Gwen, at the easy way she moved in her skin. Envy tugged at Andi's heart.

How had Gwen shrugged it all off? How had she not only emerged from it, but seemingly transformed into an entirely different person? Andi had waited for that change, that shift. It had never come.

"You stayed here in Frankfort?" Andi asked.

Gwen pushed open the glass doors into the parlor with a flourish. For a moment, Andi froze. The walls were covered in words, dripping crimson, incomprehensible words. The room reeked of blood, coppery and dank. It pooled on the floor beneath the walls.

"Andi?"

Andi's eyes snapped to her old friend, Gwen's voice breaking the momentary trance. She opened her mouth, but as she looked beyond Gwen, she saw the walls were as they had been. Brown paneling in parts, floral wallpaper, paintings in ornate frames. No writing, no blood.

"Andi," Gwen repeated, stepping closer, putting a warm hand on her forearm. "Are you OK?"

Andi blinked, rubbed her still grainy eyes and swallowed the bile that had risen up at the stench of blood. "Yeah." She brushed hair off her forehead, felt the dampness of perspiration, wondered if she was coming down with the flu. "Working with kids," she murmured.

Gwen nodded knowingly. "I completely get it. Petri dishes. Better start taking zinc and vitamin C. That works for me every time."

"Yeah. I'll grab some after school." Another thing Luke had been in charge of: supplements. He'd kept their cupboard stocked with echinacea, elderberry, and multivitamins. Andi rarely took them unless they were the gummy kind. Then she had a tendency to eat more than the suggested dose.

"Where are you working, Gwen? And living?"

"At the art gallery by the lake. Living in the new condos and working at the gallery. It's in the old Coast Guard Station. Such a beautiful spot. Remember how we used to jump off the pier?"

"Oh yeah. Marco was always the first one in."

"A daredevil, that's for sure," Gwen agreed. "I spend a lot of time there now. Walking the pier, looking at the lake."

"I've gone a couple of times since moving back, but I need to do that more. Some of my best memories happened there."

Gwen smiled, a shadow of sadness flitting across her face. "I better get going. It's good to see you, Andi."

"You too, Gwen. Maybe we can grab a drink or dinner sometime," Andi suggested as she walked her down the hall to the front door.

Gwen paused in the doorway, turned back. "Andi, before I go. Why did you come *here*?" Her tone was light enough, the easy breezy stance she'd held for the last twenty minutes still in place but her eyes had narrowed and the creases in her mouth revealed she was unsettled by Andi's choice to return, not so much to Frankfort, but to *the house*.

There was that question again. Andi fidgeted, brushed her fingers over the stain on her overalls that had hardened into a brown crust.

"I ... I needed to understand what happened to Marco. I need to understand."

Gwen stared past her into the house, lips thinned. "He died, Andi."

"I'm aware of that." Andi couldn't hide her irritation at the comment.

Gwen moved closer to her, her perfume, something strong and floral that reminded Andi of funeral flowers, wafted off of her. She touched Andi's arm.

"Don't let your obsession with this house take your life, too."

---

By the time the final bell rang at school, Andi's head throbbed. She'd downed a couple of aspirin at lunch, eating her sandwich at the cracked window as the screams and laughter of kids drifted in from the playground. Throughout the day, her thoughts had circled constantly to Gwen. Gwen who'd clearly healed, moved on, thrived.

Andi had often wondered if she'd gone into elementary education as a way to avoid growing up. She'd never told anyone of her secret fear, that maybe she was less interested in the shaping of young minds and more drawn to a desire to forever live in the safe world of dancing alphabets, crayons and story time.

She sat now in a too-small chair at the back of her brightly colored room sifting through the children's hand paintings. There wasn't anything to grade or judge. That was the beauty of art, at least in kindergarten. Art for the sake of art.

Andi ripped a blank sheet of paper from a notepad and opened up several of the small plastic jars of finger paint. She dipped her index finger in black and drew an outline for a butterfly.

"Girl! What are you still doing here?"

Andi looked up, startled. Kim, who worked in the front office, stared at her. One penciled-in eyebrow raised.

Andi looked down at the mess of papers. She'd ruined them, covered most of the children's paintings from the previous day with her own finger-painted words.

*Keep one. Kill one.*

"Need help packing up?" Kim started into the room.

Andi scrambled to gather all the pictures, crumpling them

together, practically falling across the table to catch one that whooshed across the room, landing at Kim's feet.

Kim bent down and picked it up, head cocked to the side as she studied the image. She walked it to Andi. "A handprint flower. How cute."

Andi held the other papers clutched to her chest, realized how unhinged she must look, and tried to steady her trembling hand as she took the sheet. It was one of the few she hadn't painted over.

"Well ..." Kim took a step back and then another, a slight crease of worry marring her otherwise smooth forehead. "Have a good night."

---

The scratching woke Andi, but she didn't sit up. She lay perfectly still, eyes clenched shut, trying to steady her suddenly shaky breath.

The sound of the quill dripping, the metallic smell. A breath low and ragged and phlegmy.

A squelching sound suddenly, as if someone (*she!*) were walking across the room in wet slippers.

Andi swallowed the lump in her throat, cringed at the loudness of it.

The breath was closer now, hot and rancid. A hand, slick and warm, touched her.

"Mine ...," the whisper rasped into her ear.

Andi's body trembled, but still she didn't look, didn't move.

Time passed and the heat of the room seeped out and with it the smells.

When she finally blinked her eyes open, pale morning light trickled through the curtains.

## 15

Celeste pulled into the parking lot at the Frankfort Library. The well-maintained light brick building was flanked by flowering bushes. Only one other car, a small yellow coupe, occupied the lot.

Celeste walked to the circulation desk where a girl who looked little more than sixteen stood scanning books. The girl's messy white-blond bun bobbed to whatever song played from the single earbud she wore, the other dangling from its wire against her shoulder.

"Hi," Celeste said. "I just had a quick question about Frankfort newspapers. I have a subscription to an online newspaper archive but couldn't find any Frankfort publications listed."

"That's because the library board voted against adding the digitized records to the public databases. It's an ongoing saga that you're more than welcome to weigh in on at the township meeting next month."

Celeste stared at the girl, surprised by her apparent knowledge of library politics.

"Anyway, the newspaper database is on an ancient IBM computer at the end of the aisle along those big windows." She pointed toward the back of the room. "It looks like something out of Moriarty's Antique Store and freezes if you breathe too hard near it. But it works. Mostly."

"This'll be interesting. I haven't used an IBM since … I don't know, grad school."

"They don't let the old ways die in these parts. Not without a good long death rattle, anyway." She returned to her books and Celeste started away. "If you need help to operate it, I've got a cheat sheet taped to the wall. With that and a few prayers you should be good," the girl added.

Celeste laughed. "Thanks." She searched the girl's shirt for a name tag.

The girl, quick as usual, pointed at herself. "Bjork."

Celeste nodded. "That's an unusual name."

The girl rolled her eyes. "Tell me about it. My mom was obsessed with Bjork, this Icelandic singer-songwriter in the nineties. Thus"—Bjork curtsied—"I was blessed with a name no one, myself included if I just woke up, can pronounce."

Celeste grinned. "Thanks, Bjork."

"Bravo." The girl clapped. "Got it right on the first try."

Celeste found the beast of a computer on a rickety-looking desk tucked against a back wall. It looked well ready for retirement. Above the computer hung a poster that depicted a stack of colorful books beneath the quote "Life's short, read fast." The cheat sheet hung lopsided from a tack beside it. Login information posted in bold at the bottom read: User: guest / Password: 123.

"A pretty secure system clearly," she murmured, tapping a key and logging in.

She typed in Vivian Walters first. Five newspaper archives populated. Three from the 1940s. She disregarded those and clicked on the more recent ones, which likely focused on the Vivian Walters who'd lived in the Fulton Road house when Andi was young.

*Woman Arrested After Assaulting Husband and Minor Child*

Police in Frankfort responded to a 911 call late Friday evening after neighbors reported screams coming from a house on Fulton Road. Officers arrived to find a chaotic scene and arrested thirty-nine-year-old Vivian Walters, who allegedly attacked her husband and infant son during a domestic dispute. Authorities say the husband sustained minor injuries while the boy was treated at a nearby hospital. Walters was taken into custody without incident and is being held on charges of assault and child endangerment. The motive behind the outburst remains unclear, but officials say mental health issues may have been a factor.

Celeste printed the article. The next article had occurred nearly a year after the attack on her husband.

*Woman Apprehended Attempting to Remove Infant from Hospital Ward*

Traverse City, MI — In a disturbing incident late Thursday afternoon, a woman identified as forty-year-old Vivian Walters was apprehended while attempting to carry an infant out of the neonatal ward at Munson Medical Center. Hospital staff became suspicious when Walters, who was not wearing an identification bracelet, was seen cradling a newborn and heading toward a service exit. Security intercepted her just outside the maternity wing, where she claimed the baby was hers. Authorities quickly determined she had no relation to the child or its family. The infant was safely returned to its mother, and Vivian was placed in police custody pending psychiatric evaluation and formal charges.

Celeste frowned, disturbed at the vision of the woman spiriting a newborn from the neonatal ward. What would have happened if she'd made it out? Celeste printed the second article.

It was clear Vivian Walters had suffered some type of mental health crisis. Celeste considered what Maureen had said about Conrad, *"indifferent, downright negligent."* She'd also mentioned two babies, the first a miscarriage. Had that caused some sort of traumatic break for Vivian?

Celeste thought of the house on Fulton Road, the sense of something lurking inside it. Had Vivian died there and haunted it now? And if she did, what had become of her body? Unless Conrad or someone else had murdered her and hidden her somewhere in the house or on the property. Or did the energy have more to do with her psychosis? Could a person's trauma haunt a house?

Celeste returned to the newspaper database and typed in the address of the house: 506 Fulton Road. A series of articles populated.

She started with the earliest result.

*Tax Delinquency Notice*: Taxes unpaid on property at 506 Fulton Road for year 1913; payment due to avoid public sale. – Benzie Co. Treasurer, Mar. 4, 1914.

The next two from 1953 listed the house in conjunction with other properties on the road that had been affected by a utility easement.

She opened the fourth article.

*Local Authorities Remove Deceased Infants From Fulton Road Residence*

June 14, 1941 — Early yesterday morning, officials from the county coroner's office, accompanied by local law enforcement, quietly removed three deceased infants from a private residence located at 506 Fulton Road. The circumstances surrounding the deaths remain under investigation. Neighbors expressed shock and sadness, but no further details have been released at this time. Authorities have asked the public to refrain from speculation as the inquiry continues.

*Letter to the Editor: What Really Happened on Fulton Road*
June 16, 1941
By Dirk Craven, First Aid Worker

I was one of the first on the scene at 506 Fulton Road. What I saw there will stay with me for the rest of my life. The paper said three babies were "quietly removed." That's not even close to the truth.

Those babies weren't just dead. They looked drained, gray and shriveled, lips blue, eyes open but empty. Like something had taken everything out of them. Blood. Life. Soul. I've seen a lot in this job, but never anything like that.

And you want to know what's worse? No one in that house seemed shocked. No tears. Just silence. Cold silence. We all felt it. Something was wrong in that place.

This wasn't natural. Someone in that house did something terrible. Call it what it is. Those babies were murdered.

And now we're supposed to look the other way?

A terrible stillness had fallen over Celeste as she read the article. Somewhere in the deep recesses of her mind or perhaps not in her mind at all, but in some doorway that opened into the past, she heard the sounds of crying, long, drawn-out sobs and then gurgles and then silence.

Celeste stood and paced away from the computer, was halfway to the door when she realized she was on her feet and trying to flee the library as if by walking from the building she could shake off the horror story that happened in that house, the cries of those babies.

Three, the article said, all dead and gray and shriveled as if all their blood and their souls too had been siphoned out. And though Celeste's scientist mind could usually take such data and file it away, this new Celeste—the one who now shared her body with another living being—felt a terrible urge to scream as a vision of her own baby, a daughter emerging from her womb not wriggling but shriveled and gray, little more than an apple left to dry and rot on the forest floor, pummeled her.

And that vision of the apple cast her in an instant back to Wild Rose in Wisconsin, the rotted scent of the old apple orchard and the rain-soaked night as she fled from the old farmhouse and attempted to rescue River who Curtis had begun to drown in a puddle of water.

Black pinpricks swam behind her eyes, and her chest constricted, her lungs narrowing, vanishing. She couldn't suck in a breath. As she stood in the row of books, mouth agape, her body feeling almost separate as if she'd begun to float away, Bjork stepped into view. She looked at Celeste, and her eyes shot wide.

Celeste could barely see her. She groped for the wall. One hand on her throat, still no breath, the other knocking books from the shelf as she clawed her way toward what? She couldn't think of where to go, which direction to turn.

Bjork spoke rapidly into a cell phone.

Celeste heard the words: "*Emergency, hurry,*" as she sank onto the floor, prickly carpet beneath her hands.

Still no breath.

Darkness swallowed her.

## 16

"A panic attack?" Celeste repeated.

She sat on a hospital bed in the emergency room, sterile paper crinkly beneath her, unable to hide her embarrassment.

"It's more common than you'd think," the ER doctor, who looked about twenty years old, told her. "I can't say it's that for certain, but it fits. We'll draw some blood and run a panel and see if anything else comes up."

"I'm pregnant," she blurted. "Could that ... cause it?"

He nodded. "Absolutely. A lot of changes happening in your body, not to mention pregnancy itself, can be a stressor. Have you told your OB about how you're feeling?"

"I don't have one." Celeste's face flushed. She was a grown woman, a scientist and yet hadn't done the basic thing of finding a doctor.

"Do that. Sooner rather than later. We have some great OBs here in Frankfort."

"I live in Traverse City, but I'm sure I'll have no problem finding one."

"You won't."

Celeste's drive back to Traverse City seemed endless, her eyes constantly flickering to the little cotton ball beneath the clear plastic tape on her arm where they'd drawn her blood.

A panic attack.

It shouldn't have felt shameful and yet it did. Not only shameful, but scary. Nothing truly dangerous had even happened. But what if she'd had a panic attack when Randy Mills walled her into the cellar at the schoolhouse in Graves or when she'd needed to help save River in Wisconsin? Or most recently when Hannah intended to kill Celeste and her dad at Moon Lake? She'd have been dead three times over by now.

Celeste pulled into the parking garage at the hospital in Traverse City. At the reception desk in the front lobby, she requested directions to the labor and delivery floor.

At the nurse's station, she asked for Jazzy. Several minutes later Jazzy, dressed in blue scrubs and a white lab coat, a stethoscope around her neck, emerged from a room at the end of the hall.

"Celeste!" Jazzy exclaimed, smiling. "Is everything OK? Did something happen at the store?"

"No. Everything's fine." Celeste fidgeted, picking at the tape on her forearm. "I actually stopped by because I need ... well, you. I need an OB. I'm pregnant."

Jazzy's mouth fell open. "You are? Lena didn't tell me. I had no idea."

"She doesn't know."

Jazzy closed her mouth and lowered her voice. "Sure. I totally understand. Technically, you'll need to schedule with our receptionist, but let's pop into a room for a few minutes and talk."

Jazzy walked into an empty room and pulled a blue curtain closed behind her.

"How far along are you?" she asked.

"Almost two months."

"And any issues so far? Cramps? Bleeding?"

"Nothing like that."

"Anything at all that feels wrong or off?"

Celeste nodded. "I had a panic attack today in Frankfort. At least that's what they called it. My vision got blurry, I couldn't breathe. I passed out and they transported me to the ER by ambulance."

Jazzy's eyebrows knitted together. "Today?"

Celeste nodded. "I drove straight here from that hospital."

"That was a good idea. Let's do a quick check on the fetal heartbeat, hmmm?" Jazzy pulled a Doppler from a cabinet and gestured. "Lie back. Shirt up."

Celeste reclined on the bed, her heart thudding.

Jazzy worked in silence for a moment, then angled the device. A moment later, a rapid *whump-whump-whump* filled the room.

Celeste stared at Jazzy. "Is that her heartbeat?"

"Her?" Jazzy raised an eyebrow.

"I think it's a girl."

Jazzy smiled and set the Doppler on the counter. "She's as healthy as a horse, or more like a tadpole. You can sit up."

Celeste pulled her shirt down and pushed back to sitting.

"Panic attacks aren't totally unusual, but passing out, that's extreme and obviously dangerous as you get further along. I don't know your whole story, but Lena has told me a bit. Your near-death experience resulted from a hit-and-run?"

Celeste nodded.

"And you found out your husband was involved?"

"Yeah."

"And he's the father of the baby?"

The surge of emotion pushed up; unwanted tears streaked down her cheeks.

Jazzy grabbed a piece of paper towel and handed it to her.

"Yes," Celeste admitted.

"Well, that seriously sucks, and it's no wonder you're experiencing panic. You're going to need to talk to someone, a therapist. Lena would tell you meditation and some Reiki would do the trick, but you're a scientist, right?"

Celeste nodded.

"Us left-brained folks need a bit of logic with our magic. I can give you some names."

"That'd be great."

"And you need to tell everyone. I mean it, everyone. Don't hide your pregnancy. No shame. Shame is its own kind of poison. Pregnancy is awesome, OK? And for the parts that aren't awesome, you're going to need your tribe, a support system. You've got them in the Memento Mori group, but you need to tell them what's happening."

Celeste had long been someone who carried her pain, her troubles inside of her. There'd been no tribe in her childhood and she'd been careful to protect her little brother from the daily struggles of life with an emotionally distant father and an absentee (*murdered*) mother. A lot of good it had done for either of them.

"OK," she agreed.

---

Eliza was gone when Celeste returned to the house, likely at her office in downtown Traverse City, seeing clients. Celeste breathed a sigh of relief. She would tell the Memento Mori group, but was grateful that evening to simply slink away to her apartment and be alone.

Celeste opened her door and squatted to pet Romeo and Cash, who both rushed to greet her. After a quick dinner of half a bag of spinach and a turkey and cheese sandwich, she showered and climbed into bed.

She rolled to her side, readjusted her pillow, and wished for sleep. Her body was exhausted, but her brain buzzed with a constant stream of thoughts.

Celeste would soon tell her friends about her pregnancy. A pregnancy the father of her child wasn't even aware of because he was on the run from the police. Seven weeks and counting. Where had he gone? Where was he at that moment?

Celeste stared at the ceiling and tried to imagine why he'd followed her to West Virginia. He'd acted as if he wanted to put it all behind them, as if he wasn't aware of the noose tightening around his neck. Or had he gone to kill her? To finish her off and paint it as a suicide in the hopes that her death would cause the case against him and Darlene to fizzle and die.

It defied logic that he had fled. Nothing in their life together had revealed that side of him. But then nothing had revealed he'd be the kind of man to have an affair and plot her murder. Why had he done it? Why didn't he just ask for a divorce? Ride off into the sunset with their coworker?

The loneliness, the fear, came on suddenly. A rush of absolute clarity about the reversal of her life from a driven, successful scientist, a wife, a woman who had it all figured out, to this wrecked person, unmoored in a turbulent sea, the sky sick above, the depths below filled with the lurking unknown.

She missed her life with Jonathan. She missed the Celeste who had trusted in the course of the road before them. A memory of him swam up. Their second date, him showing up at her apartment with an injured sparrow. It was nestled in the folds of his sweatshirt.

"I didn't want to be late for our date," he'd explained sheepishly, "so I scooped it up and..." He'd smiled. A smile in those days that lit up his face, his brown eyes and peeled open his sweatshirt to reveal a little brown and white sparrow, its dark shimmery eyes blinking at Celeste.

That evening, rather than dinner and a movie, their original date plan, they spent hours scouring campus and the surrounding city in search of a bird rescuer with no luck. So they'd stopped for fast food cheeseburgers and hit the road, drove an hour north to Whitehall. They'd delivered the bird to a funky little compound of trailers and brick buildings that housed Wildlife Is Cool. An older man, wearing a tie-dyed bandana had assured them the sparrow would be right at home in their aviary. The aviary, if it could be called that, was a converted greenhouse filled with plants and birdcages.

On their drive back, Jonathan had detoured to Lake Michigan and they'd walked to the top of the sand dunes and stared out at the lake. The water was placid, a mirror of the starry sky. They'd shared their first kiss, him leaning in, wrapping both arms around her waist and pulling her against him. The kiss had taken her breath away, largely because she wasn't expecting it, but there'd been something else in it, a comfort, a familiarity.

From that night on they'd been together. He stayed over at her place most nights, though sometimes she joined him and his two roommates in their off-campus house. They studied together, worked out at the rec, began working side by side at Dynamic Labs once they'd each completed graduate school. Jonathan had not been a stranger to her. She had known him better than anyone and he had known her too, known more about her than a single other person in her life.

Celeste curled into a ball on the bed and pulled the crocheted pillow closer, pressing it to her belly. She sank her fingers into the soft loops of yarn and cried. Her body shook with the effort. Tears soaked the pillow beneath her face, and she whimpered to keep from crying out loudly, though Eliza was not home to hear her.

What did it mean then that he'd done this to her, betrayed her, tried to kill her? It didn't matter if Darlene was the weapon he used. Jonathan had tried to kill her, had intended to kill her. Had he already rehearsed how he'd act when he discovered she'd died? What he'd say to her dad and Adam when he called to break the news? What type of funeral he'd have for her?

Celeste thought again of calling Jonathan's family.

She'd never been close to Jonathan's parents. It hadn't seemed unusual. She wasn't close to her own dad. Why should it be any different with her in-laws? She tried to imagine Jonathan's mother, Beverly, learning the news her son had conspired to kill her daughter-in-law and was now on the run from the police. Would they harbor him?

No. Celeste didn't think so. Like Jonathan, the Cleary family were rule followers. They didn't make a fuss, preferred to stay solidly in the good graces of their community.

Aware that sleep was likely hours away, Celeste sat up and, without giving herself a moment to change her mind, called Jonathan's parents' house.

"Hello?" Beverly's voice sounded strained, tired.

"Hi, Bev. It's Celeste."

Silence.

Celeste pictured her at home, probably in the kitchen, wiping down the counters or rearranging her spices.

"Celeste," she said finally. "How are you?"

*Alive. No thanks to your son.*

"I'm okay. How are you?"

"Oh ... well ... we're fine."

"I'm assuming you've been contacted by Detective Bowman?" Celeste asked.

Muffled sounds came through the phone as if Bev had wrapped it in something to obscure her voice. "It's Celeste," she whispered.

Albert must have walked into whatever room Bev was in.

"Umm ... yes. He called us ... well, he's been calling us practically every week. But I told him, we haven't seen Jonathan since ..."

Whispering in the background.

"Since July."

"You're aware they've charged him with my attempted murder?"

More muffled sounds.

Albert's voice came on the line. "Yes. We are. And we don't believe it. Not for one minute. I hope you agree, Celeste. Did you know Jonathan won an award in high school for perfect attendance? Perfect. He didn't miss a single day."

Celeste frowned. "I'm not sure what that has to do with him cheating on me and then plotting my death."

Albert made a frustrated sound. "They've brainwashed you. I spoke to Bowman, and I said, show me the evidence. One piece of irrefutable evidence that Jonathan was involved and you know what he said—it's an open investigation and he can't disclose details. In other words, they're flinging spaghetti at the wall to see what sticks."

In the background, she heard Beverly adding her own chorus of agreement. "And now this business with Lorna," Bev said. "Complete and utter nonsense."

"You of all people, Celeste, know Jonathan is not the type of man—," Albert continued.

Celeste pulled the phone from her ear and ended the call. She couldn't do it. Couldn't listen to Albert and Beverly continue to sell the pristine image of their perfect son. She'd believed the lie that was Jonathan, too. But she was done.

These were the grandparents of her future baby. Her own mother was dead, her dad headed for prison. In an instant, Celeste decided Albert and Beverly would never know the baby existed.

And neither would Jonathan.

As Celeste pulled the covers back up and allowed Romeo to make a nest in the crook of her arm, a name popped into her head.

"Lorna," she murmured.

Jonathan's mother had said, "Now this business with Lorna."

Who was Lorna?

## 17

Andi stood in the hall outside of class as students streamed into the room.

The remaining stragglers stood at their lockers, parents huddled close by, trying to help them shuffle off backpacks and pull out lunch boxes.

Andi yawned, covering her mouth too late.

"Not sleeping?" Carrie Davies, who taught first grade, asked as she stopped near Andi.

Andi blinked at her. Her eyes gritty, her brain dragging. "Not great. No."

"How come? Hard to turn off the brain? I have that problem some nights. Melatonin is your friend."

"I'll have to pick some up."

"A bunch of us are going to Lake Effect Brewing after school today. Wednesday night is Teacher's Night, so we get everything half off. Go with us. It's always super fun."

She needed to say yes. Andi had put zero effort into making friends since returning to Frankfort. She taught and went home. Ann Arbor Andi would have agreed in a heartbeat.

She'd had a vibrant social life, she and Luke spending at least two or three nights out with friends a week.

She thought of the house on Fulton Road, sitting on the floor in the parlor with her beloved coloring books, listening to music, and zoning out. Somehow that seemed better, so much less exhausting.

"Come on!" Carrie fixed her with the stern gaze Andi had most often seen her use on her unruly first graders. "Just this once. If you have a terrible time, I'll never ask again."

Andi rocked back on her heels. Paisley tugged on the hem of her shirt.

"Hunter is sticking pencils in his nose."

Carrie grinned. "Half off everything on tap. And their cinnamon apple hard cider is to die for," she said. "After today, you might need it."

"All right, fine." Andi sighed. "I'll meet you there after school."

Before the first bell, Andi slipped quickly into the bathroom. When she glanced in the mirror, Carrie's question about sleep suddenly made sense. Purple skin dragged beneath her eyes, which had a squinty, just-woken-up look. Andi turned the water cold and splashed her face several times. It did little to smooth her haggard appearance.

She hurried back to class, plastered on a smile and started the day.

---

"Damn, girl, look at you go. You're like the air hockey champion," Carrie enthused, grabbing her cider and taking a sip.

The other teachers, six in all, stood around a high-top table at Lake Effect Brewing, sharing stories from the day and complaining about the never-ending standardized tests.

Andi smiled, didn't mention that she'd learned in Marco's basement where he had an air hockey table, a television and a sectional sofa. They'd spend hours in tense air hockey games. Dante occasionally flopped on the couch watching *That '70s Show* and telling them to stop yelling so he could hear the TV.

After school, Andi nearly bailed on the brewery and just gone home. Instead, she forced herself to make the short drive and join her coworkers. She didn't regret it. As she laughed at Carrie's story of her student Zander proudly holding up a used band-aid at show-and-tell that day as proof that he'd fallen off his scooter the week before, it struck Andi that she hadn't been out a single time since she'd moved to Frankfort. Sure, she'd gone to the grocery store and the graveyard and once to Marco's family's bakery, but not a single time to a restaurant or bar with friends.

Ginnie Arnold, who taught fourth grade, strode to the table and handed Carrie and Andi each another hard cider.

"I'm done after this one," Carrie announced. "Those little beasts will eat me alive if I'm hungover tomorrow."

"Me too," Andi agreed, taking the cider and sipping it.

"Andi, I have an enormous favor to ask you," Ginnie said.

Andi set her glass on a table and pulled the hockey puck from the goal. She dropped it and immediately shot it into Carrie's goal.

"Ugh! You're slaughtering me, here."

"What do you need?" Andi asked hoping Ginnie didn't want her to cover recess again. She'd already done it once for Ginnie's fourth-grade class, thus missing her own lunch and had spent the rest of the day with her stomach rumbling, daydreaming about her uneaten sandwich.

"My husband's college roommate is spending the weekend with us, but Friday night we have a wedding to go to. My husband told him we'd set him up on a date."

"A blind date?" Andi asked.

"Ooh! How fun! I wish I wasn't already married. I could use a date," Carrie said.

"Please, please, please, Andi? He sells insurance, and is super cute, all the good stuff."

Andi, who'd already drunk three hard ciders, tried to apply critical thinking to the question, but her usual faculties were dulled by the booze.

"Sure," she said. "Why not?"

Ginnie squealed and clapped her hands. "You're saving us, seriously." She kissed Andi on the cheek and pranced back to the table of teachers.

***

After sobering up with two plates of french fries and two Dr. Peppers and watching most of a U of M basketball game on a TV suspended above the bar, Andi left the brewery and climbed into her car.

As she drove toward Fulton Road, she turned and took a detour down her old street passing first her childhood home, sold months after she'd graduated from high school. The new owners had added a garage. She slowed at Marco's house, a red brick split-level. The basketball hoop they'd played on dozens of times as kids still hung above the garage, the tattered hoop shifting with the breeze. The windows were dark. The house closed up as the Lombardis traveled.

The last time Andi had walked inside Marco's house had been the day of the funeral. Flanked by her parents and sister, her mother carrying a bowl of fruit. The house had been hushed and claustrophobic. Andi had felt as if she'd walked into an alien replica. Gone was the laughter and blare of the television and boisterous voices. Even the color of the photos on the wall appeared muted. Marco's mother had sat on the edge of the couch like she might slide off and vanish into the floor. Her eyes were puffy, and her hands twisted a damp tissue.

Dante had been nowhere to be seen, but Andi had found him in the basement, the television on too low to hear, an uneaten plate of funeral food on the table. The room had been filled with remnants of Marco. His marble collection, a half-finished game of Monopoly, his discarded basketball shoes. When Dante looked at her, his eyes had been red-rimmed, his mouth fixed in a hard line. Andi, whose tears had felt trapped until that moment, began to cry. She'd sat on the couch beside Dante, neither of them talking, and cried.

The memory of that day made her stomach feel sick, the hard cider and french fries churning. She shouldn't have taken the detour down memory lane. Everything happy had long ago been painted over by Marco's death.

She took a left onto the little cul-de-sac where Gwen grew up. Andi slowed in front of Gwen's childhood home. Another rush of memories skipped through her mind. Sitting on the twin bed in Gwen's room, the walls covered in posters of the Jonas Brothers, complaining about their older sisters and gossiping about boys at school.

A for sale sign poked from the front lawn and the driveway stood empty. The picture window that looked into the large living room, which in their youth held matching blue suede sofas, appeared forlorn. Gwen's mom had been obsessive about her flowers, but the once flower bed in front of the windows had, at some point, been replaced by a concrete patio and a set of plastic chairs.

Gwen had mentioned visiting her parents, but clearly, they'd moved to another house in Frankfort, a fact that surprised Andi. They'd built the house when she and Gwen were in elementary school and Gwen's parents both loved it.

She wondered if they'd downsized and opted for one of the beachside condos, perhaps on the same floor as Gwen. She imagined Gwen's mom walking down the hall, tipsy in high heels after a boozy dinner in Gwen's swanky apartment. Gwen's dad would likely be out walking the beach looking for Petoskey or pudding stones. He'd been a rockhound when they were young. The sound of his rock tumbler a constant backdrop whenever they passed his hobby room.

The memories made Andi sad; she'd allowed the friendship to fade. Why hadn't she tried harder to stay close with the one person who understood what it had been like that night. And why didn't Gwen seem haunted by what had transpired on Fulton Road so many years before?

**18**

Celeste had not slept well the previous night. The residual emotion of her conversation with Jonathan's parents led to uneasy dreams.

Morning brought no relief. Halfway through her desperately needed cup of coffee, Cash retched and dropped a glistening wad of hair onto the rug. The sight, the sound, the smell were too much. Nausea surged, dark and sudden. She stumbled to the bathroom, collapsing in front of the toilet as the coffee came up, bitter and burning. She didn't cry. She didn't have the energy.

When the episode passed, she remained seated on the tile floor, back against the wall.

Her cell phone rang and she dug it out of the pocket of her sweatshirt.

Detective Bowman's name on the screen.

"Hello."

"Hi. Celeste. How are you?"

She looked at the toilet.

*Just grand.*

"I'm fine. How are you?"

"Can't complain. The reason I'm calling is that Darlene Stiles has requested to talk to you."

Celeste wiped spit from her lower lip. "She did?"

"Yes. And if you're up for it, I think you should talk to her. The call would be recorded obviously."

"Why does she want to talk to me?"

"Honestly, I'm not sure. She hasn't spoken to me or any other law enforcement since she hired her lawyer. He's the one who contacted us requesting an opportunity to speak to you. Our hope is she knows where Jonathan is and might be willing to tell you."

"Why would she do that?"

"Because she's sitting in jail and he's on the run."

Celeste sighed. "All right. Yeah. I'll talk to her."

"Great. I'll set it up and be in touch."

"Detective, before you go. Can you tell me anything about a person named Lorna?"

Silence on the line.

"Are you still there?"

"Yes. Sorry. I guess I should have called about that. Things have been busy. Can I ask what you've heard?"

"I spoke with Jonathan's parents and his mother mentioned the name. To quote her, she said, 'Now there's this business with Lorna.'"

"Had you ever heard that name before associated with Jonathan?"

"No."

"OK. That's interesting."

"Why? Who is she?"

"She *was* a girl he dated in high school."

"Was. So she's ..."

"Dead. Yes. She died their senior year about three weeks after she ended her relationship with Jonathan."

Celeste leaned her head against the lip of the bathtub,

searched her memory for Jonathan ever mentioning a high school girlfriend who died. He hadn't. She would never have forgotten.

"How did she die?" Celeste's voice sounded far away, small. For a moment, the toilet, the tile, the door on the opposite wall shrank and blurred.

"Hit-and-run. The driver was never caught."

The air left the room. Celeste's chest grew tight; her lungs compressed.

"Celeste?"

She blinked against the narrowing of her vision. "I'm here," she rasped. She sucked in a shallow breath, managed a second deeper one.

"Are you OK?"

"Yeah. Just ... got short of breath for a minute."

"It's a lot to take in."

"Are you saying you think ... you think Jonathan was involved in Lorna's death?"

"It's an angle we're looking into."

"How did you find out about her?"

"Anonymous tip."

"No idea who called it in?"

"Unfortunately, no. And they sent it through our website, so we don't have a voice or anything, but I don't think it matters."

"All right."

"One last thing," he said. "We found two more life insurance policies on you."

"In addition to my personal policy and the one at Dynamic Labs?"

"Yes. Jonathan took out another two policies in the year before you were hit."

"Did he stop paying the premiums after I survived?"

"No. He's still paying them."

"Still ...?"

"Yes. Which is to say ... be vigilant. OK? I think it's highly unlikely he'll try to track you down up north, but you can never be too careful."

Celeste closed her eyes. "Sure. Thanks."

After Celeste ended the call, she considered Bowman's belief that Jonathan might have murdered his high school girlfriend. She searched her memory for a mention of Lorna, but found nothing. Why hadn't he talked about her? They'd shared at least a cursory background on their previous relationships. Celeste had dated a few guys during undergrad, never anything serious. Jonathan had claimed to share a similar dating history, a few girlfriends, but no one worth mentioning.

Her head ached from the effort of sifting through years in search of a clue as to the man Jonathan secretly was, a liar, a manipulator ... a murderer.

She thought of what Jazzy had told her the day before: You need your tribe on this, your support system. She'd meant Celeste's pregnancy, but as she sat on the cold tile of the bathroom floor, she realized she needed them for so much more than that. It was just after eight in the morning. She texted the Memento Mori group chat.

Celeste: *Any chance everyone can meet for coffee this morning? Excluding Taylor and Jack obviously since they live hours away.*

Jack: *Three and a half hours to be exact, but this Detroit traffic has me considering moving north.*

Eliza: *I'm up and drinking a cup of coffee as we speak. I'll start another pot. Are we meeting here?*

Celeste: *That'd be great, Eliza. Thank you.*

Lena: *I'm opening the store at nine, but I have a half hour and never say no to coffee.*

Harris: *On my way.*

Taylor: *Wish I could be there.*

Celeste waited until she saw Lena's and Harris's cars in the driveway to make her way to Eliza's house. They stood in the kitchen, Eliza handing out mugs of coffee.

"There she is," Eliza announced extending a cup of coffee to her. "Is everything OK?"

Celeste didn't drink the coffee. She sat the mug on the counter, noticed the slight tremor in her hands.

"I'm pregnant," she said.

Harris, who'd been mid-sip, dribbled coffee down his lip. "You're ..."

"Pregnant, yes. There. I said it." Celeste released a loud, heavy breath and leaned against the counter. She hadn't realized what a relief it would be to say the words out loud.

"My money's on a girl," Lena said. "Twenty bucks? Who's in?"

Eliza smiled and bumped her hip against Lena's. "Congratulations, Celeste. And also, I second Lena's girl."

Harris looked from Celeste to Lena and finally Eliza. "Did everyone know but me?"

"I didn't tell them," Celeste said. "Taylor asked me when she was here the other day, but—"

"I wasn't positive," Eliza cut in, "but I've wondered."

"Really?" Celeste stared at her. "How? I mean I have this"— she twiddled her fingers—"psychic stuff and I don't get any sense from women walking down the street they're pregnant."

"Not enough time," Lena said. "I need an hour with someone, minimum, and sometimes I get it wrong. Pregnant with a new idea can feel weirdly similar."

"Did Jazzy tell you?" Celeste asked Lena.

"My Jazzy? How would she know?"

"I went and saw her yesterday. I need a doctor so ..."

"Oh ..." Lena nodded slowly. "Now I get why she was acting so weird on the phone. Huh. No she didn't tell me. Jazzy's big on patient-doctor confidentiality. I have to use my"—she tapped her finger on the space above and between her eyebrows—"sixth sense. I've been getting the vibes though and after you left the store the other night, I pulled a tarot card just to see and sure enough, I got the Empress—motherhood, fertility—and the Moon—a secret—so voila, some basic deduction. Celeste is carrying a secret baby."

"Holy shit," Harris murmured turning red. "Sorry, that was the wrong thing to say. That's great news ... Yeah?"

Celeste fingered the handle on her coffee mug. "I don't know. It's hard to see it that way considering the current crash course of my life ... but ..."

"It's amazing news," Eliza said.

"Here, here," Lena added.

Eliza took Celeste's hands and squeezed. "It's scary, yes. Life has dealt you a lot of difficult cards lately, but this ... it's a miracle."

"Thank you. All of you." Celeste gazed at each of them. "I don't know where I'd be without you guys. Harris, you've been such a good friend; all of you have, and I really ..." Another surge of emotion. Celeste's throat grew thick and for a moment, she didn't talk, couldn't.

Harris put a hand on her shoulder and squeezed. "It's all right. We know, Celeste. And thank you. This last year has been a lot more exciting with you in it."

"And now a baby!" Lena exclaimed. "I can plan a blessingway."

"Better pump the brakes, Lena," Harris told her. "Celeste, you tell us what you need, and it's done."

Celeste smiled at Lena. "Thank you, Lena. I have no idea what a blessingway is, but maybe you can fill me in at the store. And right now"—she shifted her attention to Harris—"I don't need anything. Just ... for all of you to know."

Eliza rubbed her hands together, eyes sparkling. "A baby."

**19**

———

After sharing her news, Celeste walked with Harris down to the lake. They sat on a bench that faced the massive stretch of blue-gray water, calmly reflecting the strips of thin white clouds above.

Harris stretched his legs long and crossed his feet at the ankles, set his coffee mug on the bench between them. "Do you want to talk about it?"

Celeste sighed and pulled her feet onto the bench, hugging her knees, aware she would soon be unable to do so. "According to Jazzy, I need to talk about it. Except not with you."

He raised an eyebrow.

"She gave me the names of several therapists. I have an appointment with one tomorrow."

"Not a bad idea."

"Probably not. I'm sorry I didn't tell you sooner. My head's been spinning since I found out. For a few weeks, I let the move up here take my full attention and I sort of pushed it into the back of my mind. And then I had a panic attack at the library in Frankfort. I passed out and the girl working had to call an ambulance."

Harris frowned, uncrossing his legs and bending his knees. He gazed at her, forehead creased. "Is something wrong? With the pregnancy?"

"No. Apparently, it's not uncommon. I'm not sure if it's a result of the pregnancy or just ... everything, but obviously I need help."

"Any idea what triggered the panic attack?"

Celeste thought of the article in the Frankfort newspaper: *The babies looked drained, gray and shriveled.* She rubbed beneath her eyes, willed the images in her mind to recede.

"I found out some stuff about Andi's house. Years ago, three babies were found dead inside. I'll spare you the details, but it was ... disturbing. Former me could have read that and been fine, but apparently new me has a vivid imagination. I miss the world of spreadsheets and molecules."

"Did someone murder the babies?"

"The article didn't say that. It was weird, but I didn't do a deep dive into the story because I was too busy hyperventilating on the floor."

"Ugh. That must have been rough. I'm sorry it happened to you."

"Put some fire under my butt to get a doctor, so maybe it's a good thing."

"Three babies," he murmured, shaking his head. "Despicable."

"Yeah." The emotion crept up and her eyes welled with tears that spilled down her cheeks. Why couldn't she keep it in check? From zero to bawling in three seconds.

"Hey now." Harris took her hand, threaded his fingers through hers and squeezed. "It's okay. I know it's a lot. But I'm here all right. Whatever is weighing on you, tell me all about it."

"I talked to Bowman today," she said, wiping the wetness from her eyelashes. "He told me Jonathan took two additional life insurance policies out on me. Four total. He tried to kill me for money. That's it." She laced her fingers together and pressed them against her gritted teeth. She wanted to scream, to break something. Her anguish was giving way to rage.

"He's a sick person, a lost person."

"Does that make it forgivable?"

"No. Probably not for a long time, anyway. He's lost connection with his soul. I suspect he's living in a hell of his own making and his time for freedom is running out."

"What if it's not? What if he never gets caught?"

"He will."

"How can you say that? You're a detective. How many bad guys get away? Look at Randy in Graves? Kurtis in Wisconsin. My own dad and his girlfriend killed Elliot and my mother decades ago. Not everyone gets caught."

"You're right. But those guys got away with it because no one knew what they'd done. Jonathan's deception has been exposed. He's going to get caught. I can feel it. But that doesn't mean you shouldn't be furious and, most of all, careful. I can't say how long it's going to take or what he might do as the hammer starts to fall."

"I never knew him. I've spent my entire adult life with a stranger. I shared a bed with him, a life."

"It's infuriating. I can only imagine how you're feeling."

"Darlene wants to talk to me."

"I assumed she would at some point."

"Really?"

"Yeah. It's not uncommon. I've seen more than a few cases where the mistress and the wife team up to take down the cheating husband. Not to say you're teaming up," he added quickly.

Celeste watched the water crawl across the shore and flow back out. She conjured a memory of Darlene working beside her in the lab. They'd been testing the metabolic stability of an antipsychotic. Darlene had seemed small that day, out of sorts, and when Celeste had gotten a good look at her, Darlene's eyes were red-rimmed.

Celeste normally wouldn't have asked what was wrong, too focused on the task at hand, often oblivious to those around her in the lab, but that day she had. And Darlene, as if desperately waiting for a listening ear, had begun to cry and poured out the story of euthanizing her beloved seventeen-year-old cat, Daisy, the day before. Daisy had been the kitten of her grandmother's cat and since her grandmother had died years earlier, the cat had become the lasting remnant of that relationship. Celeste had felt sorry for Darlene, sensed the woman was lonely and other than her cat and dog, had few companions. Even now, after so much had been revealed, Celeste struggled to imagine Darlene having an affair with Jonathan and trying to kill her.

"No teaming up," Celeste murmured. "But I would like to hear her side of the story."

"As you should."

"Bowman told me something else," Celeste added slowly, hoping her next words didn't unleash another torrent of emotion.

"What?"

"Jonathan had a girlfriend who died in high school, an ex-girlfriend. She was killed in a hit-and-run a few weeks after she broke up with him."

Harris shook his head. "No way."

"Way."

"So this wasn't a one-off thing. He's been living in darkness for a long time."

"They never accused him of it, apparently. But Bowman is thinking now he might have been involved."

Harris nodded slowly. "He was."

"You think so?"

"Yes. I do."

## 20

Andi sat, cross-legged on the floor in the parlor coloring in the Mythical Beasts coloring book Torrie had sent her for her birthday. Radiohead played on her cell phone. Songs she, Marco and Gwen had listened to ad nauseam in Marco's basement, considering themselves so sophisticated to be into such serious music.

She stared at the wall where the woman, Vivian, had been writing all those years ago. It was covered by paneling. No evidence it ever existed at all.

*What if it hadn't?*

She glared at the thought in her mind's eye. Gwen had been the first to suggest it when they were young, that maybe Andi had imagined it. Later it had been echoed by her parents and sister. Eventually, she'd stopped sharing the story altogether. No one believed her.

What did they all think now? She'd uprooted her life, moved back to her hometown and back into the house that had so terrified her in childhood. Her sister and parents wanted to know why. She still had no clear answer.

"What am I doing here?" she asked.

No one answered, and yet ... she didn't feel alone in the house.

*Because you're not ...*

She'd explored most of the house when she first moved in and hadn't found anything groundbreaking. Old furniture, a mishmash of time period pieces abandoned throughout the years. In all the abandoned stuff, she'd found no evidence of Vivian Walters. No old photos or mail.

Despite the seemingly ordinary house, each time Andi had opened a drawer, she'd expected to see bones held together with twine, books on the occult, black candles. In the years since Marco's death her imaginings about the woman who lived there had grown and morphed. She was Ursula the Sea Witch, Baba Yaga crouched on chicken legs in the forest, or the sugary sweet witch in the woods waiting for Hansel and Gretel. She was a real-life monster.

But now Andi'd uncovered few traces she'd ever existed at all and her desperation to find her, to know more about her, seemed to be slipping away. Since moving into the house, Andi's singular focus on uncovering what truly happened to Marco felt more distant, like a dream that she'd finally woken up from.

It was almost as if her true life could not begin until she returned to 506 Fulton Road.

From the front of the house, she heard a knock on the door.

After stuffing the rattle in a bureau drawer, she hurried down the hall.

Dante stood on the front porch, a box from the store in his hands. "I had a surplus of almond cookies. Thought I'd bring some by."

"Oh, cool. Thanks. Come in." She glanced down and realized she'd never changed after school. They'd done watercolor paintings and Hunter had spilled an entire plastic cup of blue-tinged paint on Andi's gray slacks.

Dante stepped inside and followed her down the hall. "I always wondered what this place looked like inside. Pretty odd how they've let the exterior go, but kept the inside pretty tidy. And here I was picturing you over here living in a veritable shack."

Andi led Dante through the double parlor doors. Her mind momentarily slipped to Celeste's advice to limit her time in the parlor.

Dante sat on the velvet sofa.

"Want one?" Andi peeled open the lid on the box and plucked out a cookie. She took a bite, crumbs spilling down the front of her shirt.

He shook his head. "I ate about four fresh out of the oven. If I keep it up I'm going to have to go up a pants size."

She glanced at his body, the press of his arms against his T-shirt, narrow waist. She doubted he had an ounce of fat on him. "I don't understand how you're an Italian baker. Shouldn't you have started to grow round at some point?"

He laughed. "I get about twenty thousand steps a day." He held up his arm where a smartwatch encircled his wrist. "Between that and my nightly workout, I manage to keep the cookies from taking hold. How was school today?" His eyes landed on her stained trousers.

"Watercolor flower paintings," she explained, sitting in a chair and balancing the box on her knees, tempted to eat another one, but not wanting to look like a sugar junkie.

"So you like being a teacher?"

"Yeah. It's always felt like the right thing for me, the right fit. How about you and the store? Is that good? Are you happy?"

Dante's expression looked troubled, but he nodded. "Mostly, yeah. It's complicated." He shrugged. "Marco was always the one who really loved the store, you know? Perched on a stool next to my dad, learning to hand roll the pasta or with my mom kneading dough for cookies. He wanted nothing more than to run the store one day. Sometimes I feel conflicted about that, like I'm living his dream."

Something creaked in the hallway, and Dante's eyes flickered toward the door, the crease between his eyebrows deepening. "How do you live here with all the sounds? I'm not a paranoid person, but that sounded like a footstep."

Andi shrugged. "It grows on you."

"What grows on you, exactly?"

She opened her eyes wide. "The ghosts!"

Dante paled, and Andi grinned, shaking her head. "I'm kidding. The house itself. It's charming. The condo I lived in downstate was so sterile. White walls, white carpet, white tile in the kitchen and bathrooms, white cupboards. It felt like living in a padded room."

"So you opted for a century-old haunted house."

"Is that what this is?"

"Andi, I remember what you said all those years ago. You, Gwen and Marco came here the last night he was alive. You did the dog poop thing here and then he got sick. You said the woman who lived in this house cursed him."

"I did say those things."

"And what? Now you don't believe any of that?"

Andi fiddled with the friendship bracelet Paisley had made for her. She did believe it and yet ... she still wanted to be in the house. It made no sense. "Not really, no," she lied.

"That still doesn't explain why you'd move in here. I looked at the rental listings yesterday. I saw five rentals: houses, apartments. Why choose this house?"

"You looked at rentals? Why? Because you think I'm crazy?"

"Crazy? No. Honestly, I don't know you well enough to have those opinions about you. You were friends with Marco. Your and my relationship was ..."

"Nonexistent. Yeah. I know."

"So, enlighten me. Make it make sense. The other day, you said you had unfinished business here."

"Maybe it's realizing once and for all there was no curse, that Marco's death was really just ..."

"Burst appendix."

She nodded, wondered if her face gave away the lie.

"It was. The woman who lived here didn't touch him, didn't even talk to him. You and Gwen both said so. It was a crazy coincidence. That's it."

---

Andi woke to the sound of crying. She sat upright, hot and disoriented, sure at first it had followed her from a dream. The house was quiet, the air thick and muggy.

It came again, a wailing sound from downstairs.

She shoved off the comforter and groped through the darkness, not bothering with the bedroom light, but flipping on the hall light. Clumsily, she made her way down the stairs, gripping the banister, straining to catch the sound again.

She reached the first-floor landing, silence and then another shriek, high-pitched and long—a child's wailing.

"Hello?" Andi called. She moved first into the living room, scanned the furnishings, peered quickly behind the couch. Back in the hall, she opened the closet, rifled through old musty coats. As she opened the parlor doors, the wail again split the quiet, not from the parlor, but the kitchen.

She spun and ran the rest of the way through the house and into the kitchen, searched for the light switch. The yellow glow from the fixture illuminated the table, appliances...and the basement door.

It stood open. The table shoved aside.

Another cry from the dark doorway into the basement.

The sound catalyzed her. Andi surged forward then froze in

the open door staring into the darkness. She remembered Bo barking in the basement. Bo who was dead.

The cry, as if in response to her hesitation, rose once more, louder, as if the child were in pain.

Shivering, Andi plunged into the cellar, each floorboard protesting under her bare feet.

"Where are you?" she screamed, hands flailing against the stone walls and through the air in search of a light switch, a string light, something.

She caught the string, tugged it hard, and a single lightbulb sparked and fluttered to life.

The basement was a cramped, cluttered maze. Stacks of dusty cardboard boxes teetered on wobbly wooden crates. Against one wall, a moth-eaten armchair slumped beneath a sagging sheet, its faded fabric mottled with dark patches of mold.

Amidst the chaos, Andi saw her.

A little girl stood barefoot on the stone floor. She wore a pale green, stiff-looking dress, a uniform, streaked in dark stains, molded at the collar and cuffs. Her head was down, dark ringlets falling over her face. Her shoulders trembled as if she'd just finished sobbing.

Andi couldn't move, couldn't breathe.

Slowly, the girl lifted her head. Her eyes were vast and dark, empty. A single black tear slipped from one eye and left an inky trail down her pale cheek. Then she simply... thinned out, faded and was gone.

Falling over her own clumsy feet, Andi backed away, turned and sprinted up the stairs. She shoved through the basement door and slammed it shut behind her.

## 21

Bjork stood behind the Frankfort Library circulation desk, one headphone dangling from her ear, sketching in a notebook.

"Hello again," Celeste said.

Bjork looked up. "Survived the hot foot soup then?"

"The hot foot soup?"

Bjork shrugged. "Hospital food. I was in for three days last year for some gnarly infection I got after a skateboard crash. Thought if the infection didn't get me, the hot foot-flavored soup would for sure."

"Unfortunately, I wasn't there long enough to have the pleasure of the hot foot soup, but I might have to pop back in for lunch after that description."

Bjork smirked. "I hear it's a bestseller."

"I wanted to thank you for calling an ambulance. And to apologize if I scared you."

"It's cool. Ernie Johnson actually had a heart attack in here last summer. Pretty soon the 911 operator will know me by name."

Celeste smiled. "I really appreciate it."

"Panic attack?" Bjork asked.

Celeste nodded. "The doctor thinks so. How did you know?"

"My older sister gets them. The first few were a lot like what happened to you. Now she's adjusted to them, so she doesn't freak out."

"Does she have any idea why they started?"

"Yeah. She got into an accident a few years ago and rolled her car. She didn't get hurt, really, just scraped up. About six months after the accident, she suddenly started getting panic attacks when she drove. Not all the time, but I was with her the first time and it was pretty scary. All of a sudden, she was saying she couldn't see and couldn't breathe. She started to swerve. I grabbed the wheel, and we made it onto the side of the road. I drove her to the ER and they said panic attacks."

"Does she take something or—"

"Nah. She's a purist. Won't even take ibuprofen unless she has a rager of a headache. Anyway, the ER doc told her anxiety meds won't necessarily help. He recommended yoga, so she's all about that now."

"Has it helped?"

Bjork shrugged. "She hasn't passed out in her car yet."

Celeste had never done yoga. They'd offered it at the gym she attended in her previous life, but she'd always opted for spinning or some other intense cardio, any activity that pushed her until her brain went quiet. In those days, it had been one of the few times she wasn't thinking about whatever drug she was working on at the lab.

The lab had been her home away from home, her sanctuary in many ways. It had been the place where she discovered she could disappear into work, shrug off her troubled childhood, her distant father, the constant sense of inadequacy birthed by the belief (the lie!) that her mother had abandoned her.

For a moment she let herself really remember the lab, the

rhythmic hum of centrifuges, the silent language of pipettes and vials.

If she added $x$ to $y$, the result would be measurable. Predictable.

Not like people.

Not like Jonathan.

Or Darlene.

Bjork pulled a stack of several papers from behind the desk. "I can't say I'm surprised you crashed out with the horror stories you were reading."

"Thank you for saving those," Celeste said, taking them. "You read the articles?"

"Just the one about the babies." Bjork shuddered. "Crazy, you can live in a small town your whole life and have never heard of something so sick happening right down the road."

"Are you familiar with the house in the article? 506 Fulton?" Celeste asked.

Bjork shook her head. "I live out by Crystal Lake. I wouldn't mind doing a drive-by after reading that though. How come you're looking up stuff about the house? Thinking about buying it or something?"

"No. I'm just doing some historical research into the place. In fact, maybe you can help me. Is there a town historian? Anyone here in Frankfort that's been around for ages, hangs on to the old stories, knows the behind-the-scenes stuff."

"OK, sure. You want the Porch Prophet, Gus."

"The Porch Prophet?"

Bjork laughed. "I know, right? I aspire to someday have such a title. I'll probably be called something like Lady Grumpleton. Anyway, Gus lives in Golden Oaks, the assisted living house over on Hall Street. Cool-looking place, but smells god-awful inside. No offense to the oldies, but ..." Bjork wrinkled her nose. "Push me off a cliff before I start fermenting."

"Gus," Celeste repeated. "Last name?"

"Talbot. But you'll only need to ask for Gus. You probably won't need to ask for him at all. He'll be on the porch. White beard about to his knees. If I had to describe him in two words, I'd say emaciated Santa Claus."

A gurgle of laughter drifted from Celeste's belly.

"I'm for real," Bjork said, grinning. "Make sure you set aside an afternoon or a whole week. He's going to talk to you until your ears bleed."

---

Celeste considered turning her truck toward Traverse City, putting off her conversation with Gus—the so-called Porch Prophet—for another day. The queasiness she'd woken with clung to her, and exhaustion pressed heavier than usual. But then she pictured Andi in that house—a place where police had carried out the bodies of dead infants, where a woman had once scrawled words on the wall in blood, where something unnatural still seemed to linger.

She found the Golden Oaks Assisted Living Home easily. A large painted sign stood in the corner of the well-maintained yard near the road.

It was a pretty Victorian with gingerbread-style trim, painted a deep blue. A long wheelchair-accessible walkway angling from the front porch was the only feature that marred the otherwise dollhouse-like facade. Lace curtains fluttered in the front windows as Celeste walked toward the porch.

Three people sat in high-backed chairs. Two older women, one with her eyes closed, another reading a book. In the third chair sat a scrawny man with a long white beard. His bony, age-spotted legs were propped on a cushioned stool.

"Who are ya here to see?" he called as Celeste started up the steps. "It's market day and most of the girls have run off. Run might be giving 'em too much credit. They hobbled off. 'Cept

Jilly and Fran here." He gestured at the two women beside him. "All the boys are inside except Mike, who wouldn't miss market day even if he couldn't walk, which mostly he can't." He guffawed.

The woman next to him reading the book rolled her eyes. She dog-eared her page, stood and shuffled into the house. The other woman didn't so much as crack an eye open.

"I think I'm here to see you," Celeste told him. "Gus?"

"Little ole me?" His eyes widened. "If that ain't the best news I've had all month. Assuming you're not here to cancel my insurance or tell me one of my kids has been arrested? Or my grandkids. Stevie is always gettin' himself into trouble with the law. I told his daddy, my son Ray, that he needed to ship that boy off to military school when he was thirteen. You think he listened? Might as well have told a brick wall for all the good it did me."

"I'm not here about any of that," Celeste said. She made her way down the porch and started to sit in a chair on his opposite side.

He waved a hand at her. "Hold on now. Milly had an accident in that one yesterday. The banana pudding runs through her like a mudslide. Best flip the cushion."

Celeste's already fragile stomach clenched and sour bile crept into her throat. She turned away for a moment, waited to see if she'd have to plunge to the rail and puke into the flowers. She didn't.

"Whatcha doin' now?" he asked. "Admiring the sage? I like the smell myself, but some of the folks here say it makes their eyes and nose itch something awful."

Celeste turned back and forced a smile, wishing she'd opted to just go home. She sank into the chair. "Gus, I wanted to ask you about the house on Fulton Road. The big farmhouse, 506 Fulton."

He finger-brushed his beard, staring at her curiously. "Huh.

All right, now that's interesting. Coulda given me a thousand guesses about why you popped by and I wouldn't have picked that once."

"Do you know the house I'm referring to?"

"I surely do. That's the old Atwater place. It was a prize in its day. Course time don't play favorites. It'll peel your paint and wrinkle your siding, whether you're a house or a man."

"Did you know a woman who lived there named Vivian Walters?"

"I heard of her, yep. I did. My wife, Bertie, God rest her soul, saw her now and then down at the beach. She liked to walk out on the pier, Vivian, not my wife. I remember Bertie telling me she saw Vivian out there one day when the wind was blowin' and the water was crashin' against that pier like it meant to wash it away and Vivian was pregnant out to here." He held his hand in front of his stomach. "Bertie hollered at her to get back to the shore, but Vivian acted like she didn't hear a thing. Wasn't too long after that when the whole fiasco with her husband went on and then they were all gone."

"The fiasco with her husband?"

"Yep. Tried to kill him, according to my son. He was dating a girl whose daddy was a copper here in town, so he'd get the news of the goings-on and come over for Sunday breakfast and tell me and his ma all about it. Vivian went after her husband with a butcher knife. Might even have gotten him though I can't be sure. Police carted her off to jail and then to a mental ward somewhere. The husband and baby moved away. Bertie was heartbroken. She didn't know the woman, but figured she musta been afflicted by the postpartum business, you know? The kind that has mamas drowning their babies in the bathtub. Nasty business."

Celeste shrank away from his words and the terrible vision they conjured. She locked her gaze on the stained glass hummingbird feeder, willing herself into the numb distance she could reach less and less these days. "I read about some other things that had happened in that house. About babies killed there in the forties."

"Oh yeah, gosh, forgot all about that." His finger caught on a snag in his beard and he scowled as he tugged it loose. "I was still a pup back then. I'd just learned to ride a bike. I remember that because my dad was teaching me and my ma and the other neighborhood ladies were all standin' around talking in hushed tones about them babies. Let's see"—he tapped his fingers on the arm of his chair—"the Tuckers or Turners ... No! The Millers, that's right. I remember now. Anyhow, the Millers, not so unlike the Walters, were just an ordinary couple far as I remember. Course I was a kid so what did I know? Then one day their names are on everyone's lips and the house is crawling with po-lice and they've got that creepy yellow tape strewn from one end of the yard to the other. I remember, I drove by it with my parents, two, three times. That road was the busiest thoroughfare in Frankfort that summer, and not because it took you anywhere you needed to go. Clogged right up with lookie-loos."

"Do you know what happened?"

"Nope. It all got hushed right up. What came out after a few weeks of people rantin' and ravin', demanding answers, is the woman had given birth to dead babies—stillborns people call 'em. A pair of twins and one single and she kept 'em all, hid 'em in the basement. That's the story anyhow. Lot of people didn't believe it."

"What happened to her?"

He frowned. "Died in that very house. Not sure how, but I can tell you that for certain."

"Anything else you remember about that house?"

"Oh sure, yeah. I heard a guy once call that place cursed on account of its evil origin story." Gus laughed. "His words, not mine. You see the family who built that house, the Atwaters, had some troubles. Fred Atwater had that place built for his family in the early 1900s, give or take. He was a railroad guy, into politics too. He was a name around Frankfort in those days. His wife was Mary. The Atwater family would tell you they had a lovely daughter who lost a baby and went mad in her grief. The rumor mill would make sure you knew that young woman was a nun in training and the priest was that baby's daddy."

"Is it true?"

"Well, I ain't old enough to have seen it with my own two eyes, but I've heard a thing or two."

"So they had a daughter who got pregnant by a priest and lost the baby?"

"That's the watered-down version. You've heard the saying 'promised my firstborn baby to the devil.' Well, the story around town goes something like that. The girl fled her rectory and returned to her parents' home on Fulton Road. She was a Catholic nun who'd fallen pregnant with the priest's child. Obviously, this was a terrible sin, committed not only by the girl who was all of nineteen, but especially by the priest who led a thriving congregation in Northern Michigan. The nun became convinced they meant to kill her, not only to abort the baby and hide the sin, but because she'd fallen hopelessly in love with the priest and despite their repeated attempts to silence her, she refused to be quieted.

"Her father was furious and turned her away, but her mother slipped her into the basement and hid her there. Eventually she gave birth to the baby in secret and the baby died. The girl went insane with her grief and prayed to the devil to bring her baby back. The girl was sent off to the madhouse and that was that."

"Nonsense," the woman, who'd seemingly been asleep, suddenly snapped.

"Lord Jesus, Fran!" Gus exclaimed. "I nearly pulled a Milly and shat myself. I thought you was sleepin'!"

"You talk so loud, you probably woke up my Great-Aunt Shirley, who's buried at the cemetery up the road," she grumbled.

"Loud as you always got your TV blaring, I figured I could scream and you wouldn't hear me," Gus retorted.

"Unfortunately, not. Your voice is like nails on a chalkboard. Can't hear nothin' but you gabbing twenty-four hours a day."

"Gus." A woman in blue scrubs poked her head from the house. "It's time for your medicine."

Gus grinned. "That means I get a cookie." He winked at Celeste and dropped his voice. "I tell them I get an upset stomach with my pills and they give me an oatmeal cookie. Best part of the whole day." He stood, his long thin legs creaking and popping, and made his way into the house.

"Did you hear something different happened in the Fulton Road house?" Celeste asked.

Fran started to speak, then a raspy cough took over. She pulled a grimy-looking hanky from her pocket and hacked into it.

Again, Celeste felt the sudden queasiness rise up and she looked quickly away.

"I know it didn't go that way. My mother's best friend Rosa was one of the midwives at the house that night."

"And did she tell you what happened?"

"Oh yes, yes indeed. A story that has haunted me my whole life. I wouldn't so much as drive down Fulton Road for a very long time after I heard the tale. Now they didn't know I was listenin' mind you. My mother would have whipped me bloody if she'd caught me eavesdropping on the conversation.

"Rosa had come over for tea and she confided to my mother she was having the most terrible nightmares. After a bit of coaxing the whole story came pouring out. About fifteen years before, she'd been summoned by Mary Atwater to 506 Fulton to assist in the birth of Georgina Atwater's baby. Three midwives were called that night. It was storming out, wind raging, rain beating against the roof like God himself was furious about that baby. And who knows. Maybe he was.

"It's true Mary had hidden Georgina in the basement because Fred had turned her away. On this night, Fred was on a hunting trip, gone for two nights with the guys, and when Georgina went into labor, they moved her into the parlor.

"Well, Fred musta gotten wind of Georgina being at the house and having that baby. His hunting party returned. Those men came in with blood lust, furious, carrying their hunting knives. They fell upon Georgina and her baby in a frenzy. Fred leading the pack. One midwife, Edith, was never seen again and Rosa said Edith had just caught that little baby and when the men started slashing, they took Edith down as well.

"Rosa got hit in the head, woke up hours later locked in an upstairs bedroom. The men had closed her and Mary Atwater in the room. God knew what they were doing downstairs, hiding the bodies most likely and cleaning up the evidence of their crime."

**22**

———

Celeste drove into downtown Traverse City the following day plagued by thoughts of Fran's story from the day before. A hundred years ago, a teenage girl had died just after giving birth in 506 Fulton. No, not died. She'd been murdered, brutally murdered.

Celeste imagined the nun who'd become pregnant by her priest. She'd loved him, Gus said, and intended to keep her baby. The carnage at the house made her want to double over, curl tighter around the baby inside of her, shield her from the dark world she would be born into.

As she parked on the street and fed the meter, Celeste did her best to shake off the ruminations before walking to The Spirit Lantern for her first official shift.

"Please tell me you brought some good luck this morning because I'm seriously about to lose it," Lena said when Celeste walked into the store.

"Why, what's going on?"

Lena held her tablet, angrily swiping. "Apparently Mercury is retrograde because this hexed rectangle that I need to accept credit card payments has decided it hates me today." She turned it to face Celeste, who saw the words, Login Error.

"Here, let me try." Celeste took the tablet, closed the app, and powered it off.

"If that works, I'm giving you the keys to this place and retiring."

Celeste powered it back on and opened the app. "Ta-da." She handed the tablet back to Lena.

"Good goddess, that's embarrassing. Well, at least you know straight away the shitshow you've signed up for. Despite my Only Love and Light May Enter Here sign"—Lena gestured toward the front window—"I bring my little black bag of bullshit every day."

Celeste laughed. "You're juggling a lot here."

"Need a refresher on anything?" Lena asked. "I have readings most of the day, but I'll pop out and check on you."

"I think I remember everything."

"How's the haunted house going?"

"Weird. It has the kind of history that's so grotesque you'd think it's made up."

"Ooh do tell." Lena leaned on the counter and propped her chin in her folded hands.

"A young woman, the daughter of the original owners of the house, died there during childbirth, but it was a scandalous birth. She was training to be a nun. Rumor had it the priest was the father of the baby. The family claimed the baby had been stillborn and the girl, Georgina, went insane and was sent to a mental hospital. But a midwife who was there that night said the father and his friends murdered the daughter and the baby and a midwife too."

Lena whistled. "A tale as old as time. Priest impregnates nun, the powers that be silence her."

"Yeah, and then years later in the forties, three babies were found dead in the house. I haven't found out what happened.

Supposedly the babies had been stillborn, and the mother kept them. An op-ed I read in the newspaper called it foul play and the guy who wrote it had been one of the first at the scene."

Lena stood up, shuddered and brushed both hands down her arms, jangling her silver bracelets. "Now that is freaky."

"Yeah, and the woman Andi met in childhood, the one she saw writing on the wall in red, blood she thought, disappeared after attacking her husband and infant son. I spoke with her husband. Allegedly, she abandoned the house and just vanished."

"Huh. And this is the woman Andi believes killed her friend?"

"Not directly killed, more like cursed."

"And these are all different people who have lived in that same house?"

"Yeah."

Lena straightened up and plucked a pencil from the cup on the counter, rolling it between her palms. "Well you've definitely got something nasty on your hands then."

"But what? I've experienced ghosts now, quite a few, in fact, but nothing like this. Is it a spirit? What do you make of ... evil or demons? I keep thinking back to my near-death experience and the overwhelming sense that everything is love. That the energy of existence is this benign, beautiful currency. I can't reconcile those beliefs with what's happened in Andi's house."

Lena chewed on the eraser end of her pencil. "I think the hard part of how we view reality after our NDE is we don't necessarily get the whole picture during our near-death. We move from human to spirit, but most of us understand there's a lot going on. There are beings here on earth: angels, ghosts, guides. I met a woman at an NDE conference years ago who had a very terrifying experience when she first died. Dark beings were dragging her down. She thought she was being pulled into hell. For some period of time she was terrified and then she called out to her father who'd died years before, '*Help me, take me into the light,*' and suddenly the dark beings were gone. Are they psychological? Another dimension? Another life-form? Not human, but not spirit. I've seen some things. It's real, but that doesn't tell us what it is. You know?"

"How do I help her, then? If I don't even know what's causing it?" Celeste asked.

"Shine the light on it. Secrets, mysteries, all that stuff that lives in the dark, that people don't want to talk about, all the buried history. Start there."

---

Celeste carefully wrapped several crystals for a customer and handed her the little paper bag stamped with The Spirit Lantern. As the customer exited, several women, laughing and carrying shopping bags, entered the store.

It took Celeste a moment to register the woman at the front, Liz, from Dynamic Laboratories. Their eyes locked and Liz's mouth fell open.

"Celeste Cleary? Are you working here?"

Celeste's face grew warm. She didn't bother smiling. "Yes. Anything I can help you with?"

Liz exchanged a meaningful glance with her friends, an *I'll tell you later* expression, and shook her head. "Nothing in particular. We're here for Beth."

"Are you doing my reading?" another of the women, this one tall and thin with frizzy blond hair tucked beneath a white derby hat, asked. Apparently, this was Beth.

"No. I don't do readings." As Celeste said the words, something flickered near the woman, a small child, hand reaching toward hers and then disappearing.

The woman, noticing Celeste's gaze, looked down as if she might have spilled something on her khaki pants.

As her friends wandered the shop, Liz stopped in front of the counter and dropped her voice, though not so low her friends couldn't hear her.

"Everyone at Dynamic Laboratories was absolutely shocked to hear the news. Darlene and Jonathan having an affair, trying to kill you. I am still reeling from it. How are you?" Liz seemed incapable of feigning any real empathy, so her words came off as mildly accusatory.

"Never better," Celeste said.

Lena emerged from behind the beaded curtain, her arm draped around the shoulders of the young man she'd completed a reading for.

"Remember what I said, Ian," Lena told him. "Keep an eye out for the feathers."

Lena made her way to Celeste, eyes shifting for a moment to the group of women. "What's up?" Lena asked. "Feels like a cauldron about to boil over in here."

Celeste lowered her voice. "The woman in the striped dress is a former coworker."

"And not a nice one from that black aura."

Celeste tried to hide her smile. "Pretty much."

"Want me to shoo them out, say we need to close during Beth's reading for your lunch break?"

"No. I'm fine." Celeste held up a box of tarot cards. "No time like the present to get a hang of these."

"That's the spirit."

"And before you take her back, I saw a child near her a moment ago. A little boy, I think."

Lena studied the woman, squinted her eyes slightly. "OK. I think I'm picking him up. Her son." She rubbed her hands up and down her arms. "This is going to be a sad one."

"Beth?" Lena asked.

"That's me." The woman in the white hat stepped away from the group.

Beth and Lena disappeared through the beaded curtain.

Celeste watched Liz and her friends as they pawed through the aromatherapy candles. She shuffled the tarot cards and spread them on the counter, asking a silent question for guidance on what she most needed to know.

She flipped a card. The Seven of Swords. The booklet listed the card's meaning as manipulation, deceit and hidden enemies.

Celeste considered the image of a man carrying seven swords.

"What does this one do?"

Celeste looked up to see Liz standing in front of her, a shiny black stone pinched between her fingers.

Celeste shook her head. "I don't know, Liz. The little cards next to the bowls of stones describe their properties."

"Huh. And do you believe in all this nonsense, then?" Her eyes had narrowed on the tarot cards, a slight smirk on her lips.

Celeste shrugged. "I believe there's far more to reality than our brains can conceive."

"I have to tell you, Celeste, this is not how I pictured you."

"And how did you picture me?" Celeste asked, unable to keep the edge from her voice.

Liz drew back as if surprised. "Well ... in a lab, obviously."

"Liz, there's a Cherry Republic a block away," one of her friends called. "Let's walk down there."

"Shouldn't we wait for Beth?"

"We'll come back to get her after. I'll buy her a bag of chocolate-covered cherries."

Liz turned back to Celeste. "I wanted to ask you really quickly if you've spoken to either of them? Darlene or Jonathan?"

Celeste stared at her, but said nothing.

After a prolonged and terribly uncomfortable silence, Liz huffed and strode toward the door.

As the women trailed out, Celeste noticed her heart had begun to thud faster. She stared at the picture window revealing the street beyond, rested a hand on her chest.

"Please, not now," she murmured, but of course it was already too late.

Her breath wheezed in and out and no matter how she tried to deepen it, her lungs had gone slack, two deflated balloons. Black spots popped behind her eyes. She braced her hands on the counter, tried to focus on the smooth, cool surface beneath her fingertips.

As Celeste tried to make it to the back room, her vision blurred and went dark. She flailed a hand, hit a row of incense and sent them crashing to the floor.

Her knees buckled and she sank to the ground. She curled her arms around herself, forehead against her knees, trying to slow the tremor in her limbs. The walls closed in.

Then, suddenly—

A pair of small black Converse stepped into view.

Startled, Celeste lifted her head. A boy stood a few feet from her. Eleven, maybe twelve years old. Dark hair fell across his forehead, nearly into his eyes, and he wore a hoodie with a faded Michigan Wolverines logo on the chest. He looked out of place—not just because she hadn't heard the bell, but because everything about him appeared indistinct. She rubbed her eyes, tried to clear her blurred vision.

He knelt before her, placed something in her hand, smooth and cool. A blue and yellow marble.

Celeste drew in a shaky breath, then another deeper one. She needed to pull it together for this kid. Did not want a repeat of Bjork calling an ambulance.

Her heart continued thudding, her vision blinking in and out of focus.

She closed her eyes, pressed the marble to the skin above and between her eyebrows, the third eye space.

After a moment, she drew in a deeper, solid breath.

"I'm OK," she assured him.

She tilted her head to look at him, but the space before her was empty.

No Converse. No boy.

She stared at the marble in her hand.

**23**

———————

Celeste crossed and uncrossed her legs for what felt like the fiftieth time. She glanced at the clock above the closed door. A sign on the door read "In Session, Quiet, Please."

The therapist was running twenty minutes behind and occasionally Celeste heard a high-pitched sound through the door, a woman crying.

She would have minded the wait less if she weren't in a therapist's office. Something about it put her on edge, reminded her too much of her and Jonathan's sessions with Gail. Appointments he'd insisted on and then lied through.

That morning she'd also had her first official appointment with Jazzy and had waited in that office for nearly a half hour before Jazzy, flustered, had charged into the room full of apologies. The important thing was that after a series of checks, Jazzy felt confident everything was fine with the pregnancy. Celeste was scheduled for an ultrasound and had a prescription for prenatal vitamins.

The door across the room swung open and a middle-aged

woman clutching a box of Kleenex emerged. Head down, she hurried to the door and disappeared into the parking lot.

"Celeste?" The therapist, Doctor Stachulski, had silver-streaked hair in a loose bun. His face was weathered, his clothing casual, jeans paired with a plain black T-shirt. A beaded necklace swung gently against his chest.

"Hi," she said, standing and extending her hand. "Dr. Stachulski?"

"Most of my patients call me Doctor Dave, or just Dave is fine. I've long since passed the age where I feel the need to be addressed by my title. Despite the way I dress." He grinned.

"OK, well, good to meet you, Dave."

"And you, Celeste. Come on in."

She walked into the small but cozy office. A well-worn plaid couch stretched along one wall, a suede chair angled toward it. In the corner of the room sat a desk, the surface bare except for two framed photos Celeste couldn't see.

"The couch?" she asked.

"Unless you prefer the chair."

"No. This is fine." She sat down and laced her fingers together in her lap.

Dave picked up a notebook and sat. "Let's start with why you scheduled the appointment today."

Celeste thought back to the library, reeling down the aisle, knocking books to the floor, convinced she was dying. And since her near-death, Celeste didn't fear dying, not really. So why such terror when her lungs suddenly refused to inflate, when her vision went dark?

*The baby.*

The answer appeared before she'd even completed her thought. She no longer lived only for herself.

"I had a panic attack."

"Your first?"

"No. There have been others, but I didn't realize they were panic attacks."

"That's not unusual. And what do you think is causing them?"

Celeste's eyes drifted to the window, to trees beginning to change, the green draining away. Soon the forests would be red and gold. The morning her life had combusted, it had been spring, the green just returning, the natural world waking up again.

"A year and a half ago I was hit by a vehicle during my morning walk. I died on the operating table. Doctors brought me back, but ... I saw things, experienced things. I know now we don't really die. That this world"—she patted the cushion—"is an illusion. That we're here to experience physical reality and then we'll all be energy once more." She looked up, thought he might be scribbling furiously, a prescription, a recommendation to have her committed. Not really, that's what therapists did in movies and yet she expected at least some incredulity, doubt, even pity.

His eyes were bright, curious. He smiled. "I've heard stories similar to yours. That must have been a transformative experience."

"It was." She dropped her shoulders, surprised but grateful for his reaction. "You've heard near-death stories from patients?"

He nodded. "More than you'd think. I worked for fifteen years at a veterans' hospital. Honestly, I was shocked at how many of them shared stories of dying, visiting an alternate reality, returning with secret knowledge if you will. I have a colleague who wrote a book about near-death experiencers. It's truly fascinating."

"It is," she agreed. "Before I died, I worked in a pharmaceutical lab. I lived a very routine, left-brain sort of life. After I woke up, I was different. I am different. My marriage started to fall apart, which originally, I believed was because my husband couldn't accept the new me. Then I found out he'd been having an affair with a woman from the lab and she was the person who hit me. It appears they planned it together."

Dave sat back, put his pen to his lips.

"Exactly," she agreed, though he'd said nothing. "That woman, Darlene, is now in jail and my husband, Jonathan, is on the run. He hasn't been seen for more than six weeks."

"I'm beginning to understand the panic attacks," he murmured.

"No. You're not," she told him. For the next half hour, she laid out the events of the previous year and a half, beginning with the secret Dear Celeste advice column and the letter from Joanna Ellis. She finished with her near murder at the hands of her dad's ex-girlfriend, the one who'd usurped their mother and then ultimately murdered her, with her dad participating in the crime.

Dave had listened, rapt, interrupting only once, to ask Celeste to clarify some Hannah/Rose confusion.

"Oh, and I'm pregnant." She sighed back into the couch, relieved to be done with the story.

"I honestly don't even know where to begin with unpacking all that," he admitted. "But here's what I want to do. We only have twenty minutes left. Your situation deserves a much deeper examination, but I'm booked through the afternoon. I want to talk about the panic attacks and come up with some workable solutions.

"I've worked with many clients who've experienced major trauma. We see a lot of that in military veterans. They're living with their squads and platoons day in and day out for months and they are experiencing extremes, adrenaline and stress together. They become closer to these people than perhaps anyone else in their life and in some instances, they watch these people who they've grown to love die in very violent, horrific ways.

"We will all lose people we love in our lives, but few of us will witness that loss, and very few will witness a loss where it is an extremely graphic, up-close and personal death. What I've realized in my practice is that all the talk therapy and medication in the world do not dissolve the trauma that is stuck in the bodies of these individuals. Clearly, like many of the vets I've worked with, you have experienced a unique amount of violence in a very personal way.

"One of the practices that I have seen the most powerful shift with has been in working on releasing that trauma from the body. There are a lot of somatic-style practices: grounding, breath work, yoga, any type of mindful movement. Channeling that energy rather than suppressing it. Basic things like when an emotion arises running cold water over your hands, jumping up and down, tensing and releasing the muscles.

"I personally am a big fan of screaming, grabbing a pillow, and smashing it into everything you can smash it into, running outside and stomping up and down, much like a child does. What a child is often doing when they are having a tantrum is an instinctual maneuver to release that pent-up energy, this growing rage, anger, frustration—whatever they're experiencing. It's a natural way to release it from the body. Now parenting tells us we have to squash that; we have to discipline and discourage that behavior. We're taught to suppress the emotion.

"One of my goals in therapy is to help people unlearn some of that repression. Mind you I'm not saying if an emotion overwhelms you at the grocery store you should run to the produce aisle and start smashing watermelons, but it wouldn't be the most terrible thing to buy one of those watermelons, drive home and beat it to oblivion with a baseball bat. Or don't buy the watermelon. Just go home and scream at the top of your lungs in the car the whole way, turn on some emotional music and scream and cry and let it out."

Celeste tried to hide her smile as she imagined Eliza coming home to find her beating a watermelon into a pile of pink mush in the front yard.

"A smile," he said. "I think that's the first one I've seen."

Celeste touched her mouth. "Is it?" She thought of the baby book filled with talk about how the mother's emotions directly affect the unborn baby. "*If you're sad, your baby's sad...*" One author had written, the line stamped in her memory like a cautionary tale.

Celeste shifted on the couch and crossed her arms tight against her chest.

Dave leaned over, plucked a heart-shaped plush pillow from a basket by his desk and tossed it to her. "Squeeze this."

Celeste hugged the pillow, resting her chin on one rounded edge of the heart. "This feels like a weird question, but I'm going to ask it anyway," she murmured.

"There are no bad questions."

"Could those kinds of reactions hurt my baby? Screaming? Beating a pillow against a wall? All that rage?"

"Just the opposite. You're releasing it, getting it out of your body. Let me put it this way. Cortisol is like your body's fire alarm. It's useful in emergencies, but imagine living with that alarm constantly blaring. It's exhausting. For a fetus, constant exposure to high cortisol can overstimulate the developing stress systems, potentially increasing risk for anxiety or regulation issues later. Releasing your emotions is like shutting off the false alarms, helping your baby grow in a world that feels safe. You both need that right now."

"OK. Thank you. That's helpful."

"Keep in mind releasing the pent-up emotion will probably not immediately stop your panic attacks. Much like the buildup of stress chemicals in your body, releasing that trauma from the tissue will take some time. If a panic attack begins ..." He stood and walked to his desk and opened a drawer. When he returned, he dropped three brightly wrapped candies in her hand.

Celeste looked at them. "Sour candies?"

"Unconventional, I know. But during a panic attack, your brain is spinning, convinced you're in danger. One of the best ways to interrupt that spiral is by giving your brain something else to focus on, something intense, immediate, and a little unexpected. Cold water on your hands or face, sucking on an ice cube or strong mints are some ways to stop the spiral. Or you can ground through your senses. List five things you can see, four you can touch, three you can hear, two you can smell, one you can taste. Let's try that one now."

"Right now?"

"Yep. Go ahead. Five things you can see."

Celeste gazed around the room. "The two silver picture frames on your desk, your black shirt, the yellow stapler on your shelf, umm ... the tree outside the window, and the pen in your hand."

"And four you can touch."

Celeste rubbed her hand along the couch. "The plaid, it's sort of pilled." She squeezed the pillow. "Soft, squishy." She touched her hair. "My hair." She let her fingers drift to the zipper on a couch cushion. "This zipper, it's gritty and slightly cold."

"And three you can hear."

Celeste closed her eyes. "My breath," she murmured. "The sound machine in your waiting room." She frowned, listened, caught the caw of a bird, a raven she thought. "A bird outside the window."

"Good and two, you can smell."

She inhaled, tried to piece out the smells. "Something musky, maybe your cologne." She unwrapped one of the candies and held it to her nose. "Smells like lime, sweet, but strong."

"And taste."

She popped the candy on her tongue, mouth puckering. "Sour." She resisted the urge to spit the candy right back into her hand.

"Very good. Does that feel like enough? For now, anyway?"

"It does, yes."

"And how about one thing you'll do every day to move the energy? Hmm ...? Yoga? Boxing? Watermelon smashing?"

"Can I do grounding meditations? Lie in the grass and meditate?"

"Absolutely. But when the energy is high, maybe pound your fists against the ground, kick your legs. Visualize it draining into the earth."

"Deal."

**24**

---

Celeste arrived at the Fulton Road house just after four in the afternoon.

"Hey," Andi said, coming from the back of the house. "I thought I heard you pull in."

"I brought the ghost hunting stuff. The EMF detector, voice recorders," Celeste explained.

Andi held open her hands to reveal several flat stones. "I was just collecting some rocks in the backyard to do painted rocks with the kids at school." The knees of Andi's gray sweatpants were dark with dirt and grass stains. Soil was lodged beneath her fingernails.

Celeste took in the shadows beneath Andi's eyes, the way her skin looked sallow, as if she hadn't been sleeping well. There was something in her expression—distracted, off-kilter—that unsettled her.

"Everything been going okay?" Celeste asked.

Andi's gaze had drifted, but she refocused on Celeste. "Sure. Yeah. School's draining some days, but..." She shrugged. "That's to be expected."

Celeste opened the back door of her truck and grabbed the box of ghost hunting equipment Lena had dropped off to her.

When she turned back, Andi had shifted her attention to something across the street. Andi's face was slack, her eyes empty, and yet fixated on the little boy across the road peddling his tricycle around and around in his driveway, a large German shepherd following dutifully behind.

"Andi?" Celeste said, disturbed by Andi's vacant stare.

A UPS truck rumbled by on the street, momentarily blocking Andi's view. She blinked and turned to Celeste, a vague confusion on her face.

"Are you sure you're okay?" Celeste asked.

Andi stared at her. She nodded slowly and then shuddered. "Right as rain."

Celeste glanced again across the road, but the little boy had abandoned his bike and disappeared with his dog into the house.

"Thanks again for doing all this," Andi said, as she led the way up the stairs and through the front door.

"You're welcome. I'm not sure how much faith I put in this stuff, but I figure it's worth a shot." Celeste followed Andi into the house. "I'm going to set a few things up in the parlor if that's OK?"

"Absolutely," Andi said. "I'll wash my hands and meet you in there. I can't stay for long. I have a date unfortunately."

"Unfortunately?"

Andi shrugged. "It's a blind date. I'm doing my best not to dread it." Andi rolled her eyes as she turned into the bathroom.

When Celeste opened the parlor doors, a sudden wailing filled her ears. It was as if she'd opened the door into a movie theater during a peak horror scene, speakers deafeningly loud. Screams of anguish. Children mostly but women too. Celeste dropped the box she'd balanced on her hip and clamped her hands over her ears. She reeled away from the open door and crashed into Andi, who'd just emerged from the bathroom. Andi stumbled back and fell with a whoosh of breath and a yelp onto the hall runner.

The box overturned and scattered its contents into the hall.

"Oh God, I'm so sorry." Celeste's hand shook as she extended it to Andi, who took it and hopped up.

"Not a big deal. Are you OK? You opened those doors and jumped about six inches."

Celeste glanced back at the parlor. "I heard something ... like a scream. You didn't hear it?"

Andi shook her head. "No. Nothing."

"Maybe it was the ..." Celeste gestured at the door. "Squeaking hinges."

It wasn't. And Celeste was surprised to see Andi apparently untroubled by what Celeste had heard.

Andi helped her gather the spilled ghost equipment and together they walked into the parlor. Celeste thought of the article she'd found at the library. The babies who'd been found dead in the house. She thought of Fran's story about the birth that had taken place in this very room and the murders that soon followed.

An urge to leave flowed through her, frantic, urgent. Fight or flight attempting to hijack her prefrontal cortex. She almost listened. The baby inside her mattered more than discovering what occupied this house.

But then Andi lifted something from a little table and extended it to her. "I made you this. It's silly, I know. Too much time with kids, but ... here you go."

Celeste took the bracelet, a colorful trio of turquoise, purple and white beads. Letter beads spelled out her name, Celeste, with turquoise hearts at either end. She was struck again by Andi's youth, not in body, but in spirit.

"I love it. Thank you." A memory surfaced, long and hidden. Celeste doubted she'd ever once landed on it in adulthood, but now it arrived perfectly formed. Elliot, her little friend from Moon Lake, sliding a similar bracelet on her wrist then holding up his own. Each bracelet read "Best Friends." He'd given it to her the summer he died.

———

After Andi left, Celeste took out the ghost hunting equipment. Three digital voice recorders, a handheld EMF detector, a temperature gauge, and a motion-activated camera. Her boots echoed against the hardwood floor as she moved from room to room.

She placed the first recorder upstairs on the antique dresser in the room Andi had been sleeping in, angling the mic toward the bed. She clicked it on and spoke. "Recorder one—upstairs bedroom." The red light blinked steadily.

She walked back downstairs and into the kitchen, hesitating at the basement door. The table no longer blocked it. Why had Andi removed it? After a moment, she twisted the knob.

The air behind the door was thick and oddly warm. She clicked on her phone's flashlight. Its beam pierced the dark stairwell as she descended, one creaking step at a time.

The basement smelled of earth and mildew. The foundation walls were stone and appeared wet. The space was large and packed with stuff. Withered cardboard boxes, furniture warped by the damp. Old rotted-out shelves were stacked against one wall.

Celeste set down a recorder on a workbench covered in rusted tools. "Recorder two—basement," she said, trying to keep her voice steady.

As she turned to leave, her eyes flicked toward the far wall. A dark panel, not unlike the wall in the parlor covered the space.

Nothing moved.

But something was *wrong*. She couldn't name it, but she felt it, like something watching her from just outside the flashlight's reach. Her scalp prickled.

A faint rasping sound drew her gaze back to the paneled wall. She shone her light towards it. At the base a small rat crouched on its haunches, near an ancient looking high-backed chair, its claws working furiously against the wood. Its beady eyes flashed in the light before it bolted into the mess of stuff and vanished.

Celeste climbed the stairs faster than she'd meant to, shutting the door behind her with more force than necessary. The noise echoed through the house like a warning shot.

Back in the parlor, she set up the rest of her equipment. She placed the EMF detector on the mantel, the temperature gauge on the velvet chaise, and the motion sensor aimed toward the hallway. She sat in the stiff armchair with her notebook, eyes flicking from device to device.

She waited.

Minutes passed.

Then an hour.

Nothing.

The EMF meter stayed dead, the temperature gauge steady. No clicks, no drops, no flickers. She stared at the devices until her eyes burned. Still nothing.

That part of her—reshaped by the near-death experience, stretched open in ways she couldn't explain—*felt* it. A presence. Subtle, but unmistakable. Malevolent, hostile, filled with some kind of dark yearning Celeste could almost feel vibrating in the walls, the floor.

Whatever was in the house understood she was searching for it.

And it did *not* want to be known.

As Celeste parked in Eliza's driveway, her cell phone rang. Lena.

"Hello?"

"Hey," Lena said. "How'd the ghost hunt go?"

"A bust. Nothing showed up on the EMF detector, the temperature gauge, the camera. Nada."

"Did you set up the recorders?"

"All three." Celeste's skin crawled when she thought back to her trip into the basement, the terror that had suddenly gripped her when she remembered getting locked in the cellar at the schoolhouse in Graves. She'd become so frightened, she'd almost abandoned the recorder altogether, but managed to will herself across the room to snatch it before tearing back up the stairs.

"Have you listened back to them?"

"No. But I had one set in the parlor where I was at. There were no sounds."

"You can't always hear them in the moment. Listen to the recordings and use headphones. There might be something on there."

"All right."

"Any chance you can work at the store tomorrow morning for a half day? I have three readings scheduled."

"Sure."

"Great. See you then."

Celeste carried the box into her little apartment. Cash and Romeo both stood to greet her then returned to their nap in the corner of the couch.

Celeste sat at the table, rewound the first recorder that she'd placed in the parlor and plugged her headphones into the jack. The recording lasted nearly an hour, and she'd go nuts sitting at the table listening to three hours of static.

She stood and went to the sink, handwashing her dirty dishes.

Few sounds on the recording. Nothing but faint creaks. Her own footsteps in the parlor. The occasional gust of wind outside.

Normal. Or at least explainable.

She cleaned her apartment while listening to the recording she'd placed upstairs in Andi's bedroom. The occasional crackling of old wood settling. Once, something thumped in the distance—but it could've been her making a noise downstairs.

By the time she started the third recording, she was out of tasks in the little apartment. She wandered into the backyard, the cats trailing behind her.

For nearly two minutes, nothing. Just ambient static. A distant drip.

In the back corner of the yard, beneath an enormous maple whose leaves had begun to turn gold, sat a little stone bench. As Celeste paused by the bench, admiring the dozens of Petoskey stones arranged on the surrounding ground, a faint sound arose from the recorder.

A whimper.

Celeste froze. The sound was soft, like it came from far off. Muffled, but unmistakably human.

And then a child's voice. A boy.

*"Help me ..."*

It was barely more than a breath, drawn out and cracking. More silence.

Celeste pulled the recorder from her pocket and rewound it, played it back.

*"Help me ..."*

Goose bumps rose along her arms and neck. She sat on the bench and listened. A minute passed and then two. She suspected there'd be no other sounds and then ... a dragging.

Like something heavy moving across concrete.

Celeste's mind flashed to the cold stone basement, the damp stone walls, the smell of mildew and iron.

Her heart beat faster. She thought of Dr. Dave and worked through his suggestions: "Five things you can see." She looked up into the canopy of golden leaves, then down at the stones, the blades of grass, the fabric of her blue linen pants, the curves of the bench. She didn't feel panicky, but the rapid thud of her heart made her uneasy. Lately it had been the signal moments before her vision narrowed and the world shrank to a pinprick.

The recorder hissed and popped with static ... until something else, something almost too faint to catch, emerged at the very end.

A voice.

Low. Not the child.

"*Mine.*"

**25**

─────────

Andi wished again she had not agreed to the double date. Sober, she'd have refused. The day before, after her nightmarish encounter in the basement, she'd nearly canceled, told Ginnie something had come up. But when she'd encountered Ginnie in the halls, the other teacher had gushed about how excited her husband's friend was to meet her. And in truth, Andi desperately wanted to feel normal again, even if just for a night.

Now she sat at a table in the busy steakhouse, aware of the beads of sweat gathering beneath her arms, staring intently at every person who walked through the door and dreading having to make initial contact. Dating had never been her strong suit. Small talk and uncomfortable eye contact and worst of all the laundry list of accomplishments they were both expected to unravel at the start.

*Hi, my name is Andi. I'm a recently dumped twenty-five-year-old woman with a dead dog on my nightstand chasing a trauma ghost from my teen years. What'd you say your name was?*

"Maverick," he said, offering his hand. "Lovely to meet you."

Andi shook his hand, painfully aware of the marker staining her fingertips, the dirt she'd not managed to dislodge from her cuticles. His hands were large and smooth and unmarred. He wore a crisp button-down pale blue shirt, dark jeans, brown loafers. Andi had worn one of her only dresses, red with white polka dots that she'd originally bought as part of her Minnie Mouse Halloween costume years before.

"Mav for short?" she asked, smiling.

"Just Maverick."

"Oh. Gotcha. Umm ... I already ordered a drink." She gestured at the table where her piña colada sat with its neon pink umbrella poking into a giant slice of pineapple.

Maverick's eyes lingered a second too long on her drink, something akin to displeasure in his face. He sat across from her.

"A glass of red wine, please," Maverick told the waitress when she returned. He straightened his silverware, unfolded his napkin and placed it in his lap, then returned his attention to Andi. "Ginnie says you're also a schoolteacher?"

"Yeah. Boogers and finger paints. That's the life for me."

He offered her a tight-lipped smile. His eyes shifted to their waitress carrying his wine to the table. "Should we order?" he asked.

"Oh, uh, sure. Umm ... I'll have a cheeseburger, no pickles or onions or the special sauce, and french fries."

"The steak salad please," Maverick said. "Dressing on the side."

Their waitress left and Andi plucked her pineapple from her drink and ate the fruit.

"You sell insurance?" Andi asked.

Maverick beamed. "Oh yeah. And business is very good."

He launched into a long-winded story about how he'd gotten hooked up with insurance sales through his mother's best friend who'd opened an office five years before. As he droned on, Andi finished her piña colada and ordered another, doing her best to ignore his eyes narrowing at her second drink.

"Anyway, insurance is where it's at. Everyone has to have it after all. Job security."

Andi didn't think she'd ever met a person less deserving of his namesake than Maverick. She'd lapsed during his insurance sermon and struggled to think of a question to keep the conversation going, anything to avoid an awkward silence.

"I don't have insurance," she admitted. "Not life insurance. I do have car and health, but ..." She shrugged.

He dug out his wallet and handed her a card. "You really should have life insurance. I've gotten my whole family set up. In fact, instead of gifts, I add to their policy each year. It's a gift with longevity. People spend their whole life savings on five-dollar Hallmark cards, seven-dollar lattes." He shook his head. "It blows my mind how little people consider the long term." He held up three fingers. "IRA, life insurance, own your home."

---

"Andi? What are you doing?"

Andi looked up to see Maverick. She stood outside the restaurant, the unseasonably warm night pressing in.

As her gaze drifted down, she realized a little girl stood beside her, hand clasped in her own. Ellie Parker from her kindergarten class.

"Miss Andi's going to show me some kittens."

Maverick's eyes narrowed on hers. "Where in the world are their kittens near here?"

"Oh ..." Andi squeezed the little girl's hand and squatted to face her. "Stuffed animal kittens in my car, honey, but you know what ... umm ..." A bead of sweat rolled down the side of Andi's face and pooled in her collarbone. "I shouldn't have brought you out here. How silly. I'll bring them to school on Monday."

The wind shifted. The air grew heavier. A faint smell—damp leaves and something sweet, like decaying fruit—drifted in with the lake breeze. Andi suddenly felt nauseous. Her skin prickled as if someone were watching her, someone other than Maverick, who stared at her as if he'd just caught her shoplifting.

"But I want to see them now. Please, Miss Andi?"

Just as Andi stood up, a woman, eyes wild, burst from the restaurant. She saw Ellie and strode over, tears spilling down her cheeks.

"Oh my God. You're okay? You're okay." The woman looked up and saw Andi. "Miss Andi. Oh, thank God you were here. Did she wander out?"

Andi nodded, felt Maverick's eyes burning into the back of her head.

"Miss Andi has stuffed kittens in her car!" Ellie exclaimed. "Can we go see them?"

Andi's stomach plunged. The contents of her car consisted of an old fast-food bag, a pair of sandals and a plastic sack with coloring books and crayons she kept forgetting to take into school.

"No, honey, not tonight. Our dinner just came. Your spaghetti looks so good and Daddy is waiting for us." Ellie's mother started to guide Ellie back through the glass door. "Thank you again, Andi."

"Of course," Andi whispered, her voice cracking slightly.

Maverick continued to stare at her, face wary, eye suspicious.

After Ellie and her mom disappeared and the sounds of voices and clinking forks faded behind the door, they stood for several moments in the most excruciating silence Andi had ever experienced. Down the street, a car horn blared.

"I think it's time to call it a night," Maverick said. "I'll go in and pay the tab." He turned and strode back toward the restaurant, walking quickly. He cast a single backward glance over his shoulder and Andi turned away, unable to look him in the eyes.

She tried desperately to remember what had happened at the restaurant and yet it wasn't there. Andi had gone to the bathroom and the next thing she knew she was standing on the sidewalk, Ellie's hand gripped in hers. What if Maverick hadn't seen them? Broken her from whatever trance she'd slipped into.

"He did," she murmured. "He did, and it was fine."

Fine unless she considered that she in fact had turned out to be the nightmare date, the date he'd likely tell people about for years to come, some psycho woman who tried to kidnap a kid. What if he told Ginnie from school?

Andi wiped her clammy hands on her dress and forced herself back into the restaurant to get her purse.

## 26

Celeste looked up when the bell tinkled over the door at The Spirit Lantern. Harris walked in holding a cardboard tray with coffees.

"Are you the coffee delivery guy, then?"

He grinned. "Herbal tea for you. I hope that's okay."

"It's perfect. I already had my one cup of coffee this morning."

"How'd everything go at the house yesterday with Lena's equipment?"

Celeste bent down and grabbed her purse "I didn't think anything at all happened. I had that feeling again, the one I described before, like whatever was in the house didn't want to reveal itself. But then I got home and listened to the recordings." She took out the recorder, plugged in her headphones and handed it to Harris. "You'll hear it within the first few minutes."

Harris put the headphones on and gazed toward the window, head tilted down as he listened. Minutes passed, and Celeste saw the moment he heard the first voice. His eyes went wide, his lips parted, his posture bent forward slightly as if straining to hear more.

When the next voice happened, his face darkened.

Celeste walked from behind the counter, waving to get his attention.

He slipped the headphones off.

"There's no more," she said. "I listened to the entire recording. The only sounds are in the first five minutes."

He wrapped the headphone cord around the recorder and handed it back to her. "You were the only person in the house?"

Celeste nodded. "Andi was on a date. I was alone. The basement, where I put that recorder, was empty."

"The first one sounded like a child."

"Yes," she murmured.

"Any idea who it was? Who he was?"

Celeste shook her head. "I'm not getting any sense of who is in there. But like I told you before, bad things have happened in that house. It's getting difficult to be inside of it, honestly. I keep wondering why I'm continuing to go back. Everything I'm reading in the baby books is how I'm supposed to create some serene environment for the baby. Low stress, lots of rest and instead I'm elbow-deep in this hell house. I don't know how I keep ending up in these awful situations."

Harris raised an eyebrow, but said nothing.

"What? Why'd you give me that look?"

"You said you don't understand how you keep ending up in the middle of these awful situations, but you're obviously choosing it."

"What is that supposed to mean? Of course I'm not."

"You literally are," Harris said. "I've read your columns, Celeste. Why aren't you flying to Pennsylvania to help the lady whose mother-in-law is taking over her wedding? Or driving down to Detroit to work with the guy who's suffering migraines when he pulls into his parking lot at work. It might be unconscious, but you're choosing to get involved with people who have a dark story; something bad has happened, and it's not only that they communicate that in their letters, which I suspect they do; it's also that you can sense the people you're going toward. You're choosing them. There's nothing wrong with that.

"Do you think I became a detective because I detest the ugly part of being human? Well, I do, in a way, but in another way I'm drawn to it. I'm drawn to engaging with this part of society. I don't want to commit violence. I want to stop it, but there's still some resonance in it for me. I thought that would go away after my NDE, that I'd be transmuted to love and light and need to work in a field that showed the best of humanity, not the worst, but on the other side I realized this was part of my soul contract, my work here. I think it's yours too and perhaps your NDE was a bit of path realignment. Maybe this is the work you're actually meant for in this life."

"What work? I'm not helping Andi. I'm digging into all this insane history and for what? What good will it do? At least with Joanna and River there was a focus, a human being who needed to be stopped. Andi is a young woman living in a house that has been plagued by a century of death and darkness. If I really wanted to help her, why haven't I just told her she needs to pack her bags and leave?"

"Would she do that?"

"No. She wouldn't. So, what then? How can I help?"

"By finding out what's causing the bad things to happen at the house."

The bell above the door chimed. Celeste watched, surprised, when Liz strolled through. She smiled at Celeste and waved as if the two were old friends meeting again.

Celeste felt Harris's eyes on her.

"Are you OK?" he murmured under his breath.

She nodded and smiled woodenly at Liz, who marched over and extended her hand.

Liz held out a business card.

Reluctantly, Celeste took it. "What is this?"

"I have a friend who works at this private lab just outside of town. They focus on infectious disease research. He could use someone with your talent, Celeste."

Celeste stared at the card, surprised and a bit wary.

Liz glanced toward Harris, but said nothing. "I'm heading back downstate now, but wanted to drop it by."

Celeste thought she should say something, thank you, goodbye, but her mouth had gone dry and no words emerged.

Liz started for the door, paused and glanced back. "Come on, stop looking at me like that. You're brilliant. Don't let that go to waste."

The door swung closed behind her and Liz disappeared down the street.

"Who was that?" Harris asked.

"I used to work with her at Dynamic Labs."

He took a sip of his coffee. "That exchange felt a little frosty. Not a friendly working relationship?"

"A competitive one. And no, not friendly. I'm surprised by this." She peered at the card. Bio Fusion was printed in dark block letters. At the bottom, the name Torrence Kramer above a phone number and email.

"But you're interested?"

Celeste sighed and stuck the card in the back pocket of her jeans. "I'll have to think about it."

That afternoon, Celeste's cell phone rang just as she sat down to eat her sandwich at her little kitchen table for one. On the screen she read "Kent County Correctional Facility."

Celeste listened to the recorded voice. "You have received a call from: Darlene at the Kent County Correctional Facility. Press one to accept the call."

Celeste pressed one.

Movement on the other end, a kind of shuffling around and then ...

"Celeste?"

Celeste's stomach clenched at the sound of Darlene's voice. It was as it had always been, meek, soft. Not the voice of a killer.

"I'm here," Celeste said.

A pause as if Darlene too was reconciling hearing Celeste's voice for the first time in months.

"I'm sorry," Darlene breathed.

Celeste frowned and stood, abandoning her sandwich.

"I'm sorry for everything, and I'm not just saying that because we got caught. Or I got caught. He's still ... running."

"Whose idea was it?" Celeste asked.

Another pause. "Which part?"

"Killing me." The words sounded far away, as if a stranger had asked the question.

"His."

Celeste stared at the framed photo on the wall, a Petoskey stone partially sunken in the wet sand of a Lake Michigan shoreline, the sun glinting off the smooth water.

"Why?"

"He said you'd kill him if he left you, that you were unstable and had tried before. That you'd never let him go; you'd stalk us."

"What?" Celeste spat the word. "That's a lie—a complete lie."

"He said that ... that you drugged him at least twice and that once he woke up to you standing at his bedside with a knife and he thought you meant to stab him, but then you just turned and walked away and acted like you didn't remember the next day."

Celeste sagged onto the couch, closed her eyes. Cash, as if sensing her distress, hopped into her lap and nudged his face against her free hand.

"He fabricated all of that. All of it. Not a single one of those things ever happened. And you believed it all."

"I know it sounds crazy. It was crazy and looking back now, it seems obvious he lied. I was so caught up ... love-bombed. That's what my counselor in here calls what he did. He just ... started courting me."

"What do you mean? He was pursuing you? Trying to start the affair?" Celeste thought of what Jonathan had told her, that it had just happened. He and Darlene had been working a lot together; Celeste had grown distant. He'd acted like it was as much Celeste's fault as his own, as if she'd practically driven him into the arms of another woman.

"Yes. I was really surprised at first and flattered. I felt weird about it, obviously. But at first, he told me you guys hadn't been happily married in years and then he started adding little comments about how crazy you were, how impossible to live with. He started writing me these little notes on Post-its and sticking them in my locker at the lab, on my windshield, even at my lab station."

Celeste frowned and thought back to her early days with Jonathan. Returning home from class to find yellow Post-its with "You're so beautiful," and "I can't wait to see you Friday."

"Then he started shifting things so we were working in the same lab rooms. He put gifts in my locker, little bags of the tea I like, single flowers, poems he'd printed. I've never experienced anything like that. I've had a couple of boyfriends, but ... no one who ever really seemed all that interested in me. I got so ... wrapped up in it. All the things he said. My counselor here says the behavior is typical of a narcissist. I don't know if that's what he is, but ... she gave me a book and so many of the things make sense. Anytime I'd question what we were doing, he'd love-bomb me again and then as soon as I was wrapped up in him, he'd grow cold, distant. It was a game for him. I realize that now."

A narcissist. Celeste was familiar with the word. The term had become so commonplace, slapped on anyone with remotely undesirable behavior. But then she thought of his girlfriend in high school, Lorna. Had he killed her? And gotten away with it. Clearly, something was wrong with Jonathan.

"And eventually you guys began going out on dates? Sleeping together?" Celeste asked.

"Yes. After ... a month or two. And I felt so guilty at first. I swear to you. I cried myself to sleep. I even told him I wouldn't see him again unless he told you the truth, but then he ... he said you'd kill him, that maybe you'd kill us both. He showed me this nasty gash on his arm. He said you'd broken a glass and cut him with a piece of it during a fight."

Celeste's mouth fell open. "He cut himself at his parents' house moving an old mirror. We weren't even together the weekend that happened." Celeste remembered Jonathan returning from the weekend at his parents with a bandage on his forearm. He'd been helping his dad move an old mirror that had fallen and cracked and sent a splinter of glass into Jonathan's arm. He'd spent the next several days complaining about potential tetanus and other infections.

"I was so naive," Darlene murmured. "Stupid. So stupid."

Celeste sighed and pulled her legs close to her body resting her chin on one knee. Despite what Darlene had done to her, she felt sympathy for the woman on the other end of the phone.

"When did he suggest you guys should kill me?"

"About three months before ... before it happened. We went out for dinner and he said you'd begun to suspect the affair.

You were ransacking his stuff, demanding to search his phone. He'd bought us disposable phones early on and he kept his in his car. He told me he was afraid you were going to do something crazy. That it was us or you."

Celeste squirmed at the lie, rage curdling her blood. During the weeks leading up to her hit-and-run, she'd been obsessed with the latest tests she'd recently run on Sigma-1, which had been showing promising results as an antidepressant. She'd been convinced they were on the verge of a breakthrough. She was the opposite of the woman Darlene described. She'd been absent, distracted, completely mired in her routine as she channeled all of her attention into analyzing the most recent tests for Sigma-1. And all the while he'd been feeding Darlene a pack of lies, convincing her Celeste was a threat. Kill or be killed.

"And the hit-and-run? That was his idea?" Celeste asked.

"Yes. I suggested, well ... drugs. We worked in the lab and there are a lot of options as you know and many of them are painless. It seemed like ... the kindest—that's a terrible word—the least invasive option."

"But he said no to that?"

"He was afraid the coroner would do a full toxicology screening based on your and Jonathan's profession. He didn't want to risk the link."

Celeste heard the words, but they hardly registered. For an instant she saw Jonathan and Darlene tucked in a little booth, heads together, lights low, pasta dishes growing cold on the table between them as they discussed a coroner cutting open Celeste's body, harvesting her organs, taking vials of blood to test for various drugs.

She stood and paced away from the couch, a rumble of nausea in her belly.

"I'm sorry," Darlene whispered. "If I could take it back ... I'd do anything to take it back."

"That morning, how did you know when I'd be on my walk?"

"I had the disposable phone and umm ... Jonathan had his. My brother had rented me the SUV. I'd slept in it the night before in a casino parking lot and then drove to an old video store that had closed near your house. Jonathan had picked that spot because it was close—only five minutes from your neighborhood and no cameras. At least none he'd spotted. He called me and said you'd just left on your walk."

Celeste stared through the window, but her mind had gone back to that morning. Lacing up her tennis shoes, the slap of her feet on the pavement, the early morning birdsong. Her mind had been on the Sigma-1. When she got back home, she intended to tell Jonathan she wanted to run into the lab. The sound of tires on the road behind her had barely registered. She was in the stretch of the neighborhood that was mostly undeveloped, had passed Doris Macintosh's house, the woman who would later say the SUV swerved to hit her. If Celeste felt the impact, she had no memory of it. Only the sensation of rocketing up and away and then seeing her body down there, crumpled, and then Jonathan running down the road wearing only a single slipper.

"Celeste? Are you still there?"

Celeste closed her eyes, took a deep breath. "I'm here. What happened after you hit me?"

Quiet on the line. And then, if Darlene's voice could get even smaller. "I ... drove away. I called Jonathan and I was crying. I don't even remember what I said. He told me to calm down, to drive the speed limit. To get rid of the phone and then the car. He'd pick me up in the middle of the night and bring me back to the campsite so I could call the police and claim the SUV had been stolen."

The details hardly mattered. During those hours when Jonathan and Darlene were desperately covering their tracks,

Celeste had left the earthly plane. And for that she was grateful.

"Darlene, did Jonathan ever mention the name Lorna to you?"

"Lorna? No. Was she ... someone else he was having an affair with?"

"No. She was his high school friend. She died during a hit-and-run his senior year."

Darlene had begun to softly cry. "Did he kill her?"

"Honestly, I don't know."

**27**

———

The following day, Celeste spent the morning on the Internet searching for any other clues about what might be happening in Andi's house. She'd texted her and told her she'd visit again in a couple of days. Celeste had considered mentioning the recordings, but realized it'd be better to simply let Andi hear them.

As she searched for any strange happenings on Fulton Road, her phone rang and River's name appeared on the screen.

"River?" Celeste answered.

"It's so good to hear your voice," River said.

"And yours. Is everything all right?"

"Great actually. I'm calling because we have a gig in Traverse City tonight. In your last email you said you moved there. I thought you might want to come. I know it's last minute so don't feel like you have to."

"I'd love to. Tell me when and where."

After Celeste ended the call with River, she grabbed the business card from Liz and wandered into Eliza's backyard, the cats trailing behind her.

Her thoughts were muddled with the Fulton house and the phone call the previous day with Darlene. She longed for days in the lab, the deep focus of her work. She'd rarely felt scattered. She gazed at the business card, wondering if she could somehow simply step back into that life, shut down the Dear Celeste column, finalize the divorce. Move on.

Eliza appeared, Sassy trotting behind her.

"Simon's bench," Eliza explained, gesturing at the stone carved with initials and a picture of a small boy. Embedded within the stone path leading to the bench were dozens of Petoskey stones. "I put it here for my mom, so she had a place to ... talk to him, feel close to him since we never had a grave."

Celeste patted the bench. "It's really nice."

Eliza sat beside her. "I think so too. A lot of butterflies and dragonflies land here. I've seen bunnies, cardinals, and even a fox. A fox just sitting here on the stones." Eliza smiled sadly. "Simon dressed up as a fox for his last Halloween. My mother had sewn him the costume. Many of these creatures, just like the Petoskey stones, are signs from Simon. Maybe not all of them, but a lot of them. That fox showed up on my birthday and sat here for five minutes staring at the house."

"That's really amazing," Celeste said, thinking of the ravens that had followed her since her near-death.

"What's that you're wearing to bits?" Eliza gestured at the business card in Celeste's hand, the card Liz had given her the day before.

"It's a contact for a lab here in Traverse City. An old colleague stopped into The Spirit Lantern and gave it to me, said I should call the owner for a job."

"Well, that's exciting, or no? I can't quite get a sense of how you're feeling."

"Conflicted. Scientist was the old me, my old job, old life. I've left it behind."

"What's that saying? Don't throw the baby out with the

bathwater? You're obviously good at science-y stuff. And into it. Why not give it a chance?"

"I just started working at the store."

"Oh, come on. Lena could put an ad online and have a hundred applicants next week. You don't need to work at the store if a better option has come along."

Celeste sighed and slid the card back into her pocket. "I'm going to watch River's band here in Traverse City this evening if you feel like going."

"That sounds lovely, but I'm helping my friend Teresa paint her kitchen. She's been putting it off for months and I told her we'd make a party of it."

"That's sweet."

---

Celeste turned into Harris's driveway just after five o'clock. She'd messaged him earlier in the day and he'd agreed to go with her to watch River's band, Grace not Grit, play at a downtown brewery.

She'd never been to his house before. As she eased her truck down the long gravel drive, a sprawling Victorian came into view—white clapboard siding gleaming in the sun, a newer metal roof catching the light. The house was clearly well-kept, its broad wraparound porch framed with neat railings and a lone swing creaking softly in the breeze. Unlike many of the lots lining the street, this one stretched wide and deep, shaded by towering maples and oaks that dappled the yard in shifting patterns of light. To the left, Harris's car sat in the open garage.

When Celeste ascended the porch steps, she found his front door open, the screen door barely latched, swaying in the breeze. She knocked on the aluminum doorframe, but minutes passed with no Harris.

"Harris?" Celeste called.

She peered through the screen door into the interior, but neither saw nor heard the man inside. "I'm coming in to check on you," she shouted.

Celeste opened the door and stepped into the warm interior.

To her left stood a staircase leading to the second floor, work boots on the bottom step. Wood floors ran the length of the hall. An old-fashioned coat rack stood to the right. Celeste's eye caught on a small pink jacket with a rhinestone pony on the back. Near the rack sat a wooden bench and beneath that several pairs of shoes including a pair of women's purple flip-flops and a child's sparkly pink tennis shoes.

Photos lined the walls. A younger Harris pictured with a pretty woman with dark curls and large brown eyes. His wife, Nell. Photos of a young girl, dark curls like her mother, blue eyes like her father. His daughter, Bonnie. Pictures of the little family on the beach, at an amusement park, in a pumpkin patch.

Celeste forced her eyes from the images and called out to Harris again.

No answer.

She peered into a large living room, cozy with fat cream-colored couches. More photos of the family lined the mantel on the large fireplace. There again, Celeste spotted remnants of Bonnie and Nell. A pair of pink reading glasses rested on top of a women's fiction novel. A child's toy piano sat in the corner next to an art table scattered with drawings.

For an instant, Celeste saw the child there, hand scribbling furiously, a fire crackling in the fireplace, her parents snuggled on the couch.

A wave of discomfort swept over her, the sense that she'd crossed an invisible boundary and stepped into a hidden chapter of Harris's life, uninvited.

"Celeste?"

Celeste jumped, startled to see Harris standing in the doorway.

"Hi. I'm sorry I called your name and ..." She felt suddenly foolish for walking into his house. Warmth flushed her face.

"I was out back checking on some saplings I planted last month. Totally lost track of time." His eyes drifted from her to the children's art table she'd been staring at seconds before. He brushed a hand through his hair. "This is embarrassing," he admitted.

"What? No. I shouldn't have just walked in here."

"It's okay. Why shouldn't you, right? It's only a house, only ... stuff."

Celeste nodded. "Are you ready?"

"Yeah. Let me wash up."

***

They drove to the brewery in silence. When Harris parked in the lot, he turned to face her. "I know I should have gotten rid of their stuff."

"I'm not judging you, Harris."

He turned his attention back to the windshield. "Maybe I need someone to judge me." He leaned his head against the seat and clenched his eyes shut. "I've never invited Robin over. We've been dating for five months and I've never let her in my house."

Celeste reached a hand to his, resting on the gear shift. "Perhaps that's a testament to how much Robin supports you. The fact that she hasn't pushed you to change before you're ready."

He looked at her, eyes troubled. "I've tried a couple of times. Collected cardboard boxes, wrote it on my calendar and then ..." He shook his head. "I couldn't do it."

"When it's time, you'll do it."

"There are people who live their whole lives stuck in the past, incapable of moving on."

"You're not one of those people."

"How do you know?"

Celeste gestured through the windshield. "Because you live in the present, Harris. Every day. Here we are. So you've saved their stuff. What's so terrible about that?"

"Eliza thinks it's their energy. I came back sensitive to that and feel it still connected to everything they touched, everything they loved."

"It makes sense." Celeste thought of the Moon Lake house, the sensation of pawing through her mother's forgotten things, each one a silent echo across time. Never had she felt her presence so vividly.

"Does it? Or is that just the story I tell myself to stay rooted in something that no longer exists?"

"It exists," Celeste murmured. "The love exists. Don't be so hard on yourself, OK? I feel honored to have gotten to see a little slice of the life you guys shared. It looks like it was pretty great."

"It really was." His voice had thickened and for several moments neither of them spoke.

In her mind, Celeste traced back to the vision of her Grand Rapids house—bare, sterile, lacking the pulse of life that filled Harris's place. She and Jonathan had both abandoned it, and she suspected no visitor would be stirred by sentiment or nostalgia if they were to step inside.

Harris cleared his throat and turned to face her. "Before we go in, I have something for you." He wrangled several folded sheets of paper from his back pocket and handed them to her.

Celeste smoothed them on her lap and tried to make sense of the words.

"It's the Lorna Hawkins case," he said.

Celeste sighed back in the seat.

"I contemplated even giving it to you. You've got a lot going on, but figured you'd just end up doing the research. Plus, I was curious."

"Can you give me the CliffsNotes? I'm not up for reading this right now."

"Sure. There's not a lot to tell. Lorna was walking home from her job at a nature center and was killed in a hit-and-run. No witnesses. Based on the evidence, police suspected she was dragged beneath the vehicle for several feet. She did not die instantly."

Celeste closed her eyes, imagined the seventeen-year-old girl walking along a dark street at night, remembered her own emotions in the half a second of awareness before impact. And then the beauty that followed, an understanding, suddenly that the body disappearing beneath her was merely a shell. She'd been liberated and was returning home.

"At least she's free now," Celeste murmured.

"Very true. Not that it made it any easier on her family."

"Was Jonathan a suspect?"

"I can't say that without talking to an investigator. They don't have a dedicated cold case unit, but there's a detective assigned to her case. I left him a voicemail. If he's willing to share information with me, I'll tell you what I find out."

"Have you spoken to Bowman about any of this?"

"No. I haven't talked to him. He's got a heavy caseload and so do I. I feel confident if he had anything new, he'd touch base. I'm assuming you haven't heard much either?"

Celeste shook her head. "No, but I did talk to Darlene."

"How'd that go?"

"Frustrating. Jonathan sold her a pack of lies about how I was some unhinged wife who'd tried to kill him. He set the whole thing up."

"That must have been hard to hear."

Celeste rested a hand on her stomach. "I just wish they'd catch him."

---

River saw Celeste and ran across the restaurant, nearly colliding with her. She threw her arms around Celeste and squeezed her tight.

"Celeste! I have so been looking forward to hugging you." She pulled back. "Your hair is different. I love it!"

Celeste touched her brown hair. "Thanks, River. I went back to my natural color."

"It suits you."

"I appreciate that." Emotion rolled through Celeste, and her eyes watered. The warmth of the brewery and the sight of River with her long chocolate hair tied in a braid wearing a colorful skirt and loose white blouse. From the corner where the band was setting up, Celeste saw Owen. He bounced Hope on his hip.

For a moment, she wanted to tell River about her baby. A baby who would one day be like Hope, a bouncing, giggling little girl. She wanted to sit with River in the rocking chairs behind her country house and listen to the birdsong and forget about the eerie voice on the recorder in the Fulton house and Darlene crying over Jonathan and every other terrible thing she'd experienced in the previous months.

Instead, she shifted her attention as Owen and Hope walked over and hugged them together, laughing when Hope planted a kiss on Celeste's forehead.

---

Celeste struggled not to cry during the first set of songs. River's voice, her deep, heartfelt lyrics. A new song about her murdered mother touched Celeste especially and she thought of her own mother submerged in Moon Lake, gone for so long Celeste barely remembered her at all. The emotion she'd managed to restrain for the previous year bubbled up and thinking of Doctor Dave's advice not to suppress, she allowed her tears to flow.

Harris, noticing, pushed from his side of the booth and moved next to her. He wrapped an arm around her waist and leaned his head sideways against hers.

"You OK?" he whispered.

She sniffled and nodded, mopping her face with a napkin.

River started to sing "Old Oak Tree." Owen held Hope and danced.

Next to her, Harris suddenly stiffened.

Celeste followed his gaze to the door where his girlfriend, Robin, stood, eyes scanning the brewery. Harris slid from the booth.

"Robin's here," he said, apparently surprised. "I'll be right back."

They talked for a moment and Celeste tried not to stare, forcing her eyes back to River and the band.

When he returned, Robin was beside him. She sat across from Celeste.

"Celeste, you remember Robin?"

"I do. Good to see you again."

"And you," Robin said, though Celeste detected a coolness in her voice. Robin's eyes drifted from Harris to River swaying, eyes closed, as she sang.

"Can I get you a drink?" Harris asked.

Robin nodded. "A vodka lemonade please."

"I'll be right back." Harris disappeared into the throng of people near the bar.

"Harris says you're friends with the band?" Robin asked,

shifting her gaze to Celeste. Her stare was intense, slightly unnerving.

Celeste nodded, imagined briefly telling Robin how she knew River. *Oh, I helped find her murdered mother and discovered the man she thought was her father had actually abducted her.*

"They're great. Aren't they?"

Robin nodded. "I was surprised when Harris mentioned you guys were coming here. He doesn't go out much."

"He's probably taking pity on me so I don't have to hang out at the bar alone," Celeste joked.

Robin smiled, but the expression was stiff. Celeste realized Harris's girlfriend didn't like her.

Celeste fiddled with her wrapper from her straw. "I hope you know there's nothing between Harris and me. I ... well, I'm married technically and my husband is ... he's gone. The police are looking for him. I moved up here to get away from our home, to hide even. Just in case."

Robin had shifted her attention from River to Celeste. Her face was unreadable.

"You're hiding from your husband?"

Celeste blew out a breath. "In a way, yes. You're aware I had the near-death experience? I was hit and almost killed."

"Harris told me you had an NDE, but he didn't offer details. He's pretty private about all of that."

"The police believe my husband was involved."

Robin's face softened. "I'm so sorry. That must have been terrible."

"It was. It still is."

"Harris has a need to save people. At first that drew me to him. But if you're not in some kind of trouble, it's like he can't figure out what to do with you. It's admirable, yes, but also deeply lonely if you're looking for something more than rescue."

Celeste took a sip of her iced tea, searched the bar, and noticed Harris coming toward them with Robin's drink.

"Are you from Traverse City?" Celeste asked, changing the subject as Harris slid into the booth next to Robin.

Robin shot a sideways glance to Harris, thanked him for the drink and nodded. "Born and raised here."

---

Celeste woke to the boy who'd given her the marble in The Spirit Lantern. As she gazed at him, she knew without question that the boy was dead. His ghost sat in the small wicker chair in the corner of her room, not looking at her, but instead at Romeo, who'd fluffed into a ball of white fur.

From across the room, merely a silhouette in her open doorway, came a hiss. She saw two glowing yellow eyes. Cash.

Her heart thundered in her chest.

"What do you want?" she asked.

He turned slowly, face slack, eyes shining beneath his mop of dark curly hair. He was there and not there.

His lips parted, but no sound emerged. She sensed he wanted to speak, had come for a reason, but could not gather the energy to muster words. She noticed something dark at the corner of his lips. Blood, old dried blood and suddenly she knew who he was.

"Marco." She said his name.

Romeo darted from the bed and raced out of the room. Cash turning and fleeing behind him.

Celeste shivered and studied the boy. A cool mist seemed to rise from the corner of the room, rippling out toward her. It fogged the glass on the dark window. Her hands grew clammy, and she pulled her comforter up and slipped her hands beneath it.

The boy shuddered. For an instant, he was gone and then he reappeared. When he did a flood of images filled her brain.

Marco and Andi rushing into the crashing waves of Lake Michigan, daring each other to swing higher and higher on the elementary school playground, sneaking cookies from a glass case in a bakery, and then a stream of disjointed images, seemingly unrelated to the first.

A young woman wearing a habit, knees pressed to a wood floor, tears pouring down her milky cheeks, eyes big and dark. She held her hands in a prayer pose and whispered urgently. The hooves of horses on a rutted dirt road at night. A candlelit room, fire in the hearth, heavy breathing.

*Push, child!* a woman urged and then a baby's cry followed by screams. The most god-awful, pain-filled wails.

"No!" Celeste's own scream broke the stream of images. She clenched her eyes shut.

When she opened them the wicker chair sat empty.

**28**

─────────

Andi opened the door to find Dante standing on the porch, a picnic basket clutched in one hand.

He grinned. "Don't tell me I just woke you up. It's almost eleven."

Andi stifled a yawn and squinted at the bright day beyond him. "Really? Wow." She held up her arm to look at her watch, but she'd not put it on that morning. "Guess I was tired."

"Time to shake it off. I've packed us a picnic and we're going to the beach."

"Come again?"

He held up the basket. "Italian subs, cannoli, a bottle of white wine. Come on."

"Don't you usually call someone? See if they're available."

He shrugged. "I prefer spontaneity."

"And what if I hadn't been home?"

"Then I'd have been eating for two at the beach. Come on, get changed. Next week is forecasting a drop in temperatures. We're getting a fluke Indian summer and we're going to take advantage of it."

Andi sighed and looked down at her rumpled dog print

flannel pants and T-shirt she'd worn so many times the U of M logo had long since faded.

"All right, give me ten minutes. Come in."

Andi trudged back up the stairs. The hellish date from the previous night playing on a loop in her brain as the memory of it seeped back in. Had Maverick gone straight home and told Ginnie and her husband about his unhinged night with Andi the kidnapper? She'd lain awake half the night wondering, jumping at every sound, her thoughts erratic and unfocused. One moment sure she was losing her mind, the next terrified she was not alone in the house.

"Ugh," she grumbled, stripping off her clothes that smelled tangy, as if she'd been sweating all night. She dropped them in the hamper and paused. Lying on the top was a T-shirt her sister had given her after she graduated from college; Teachers Have More Fun, it read. The pale-yellow fabric was streaked with dark stains. Andi touched it. It was slightly damp, and before she even lifted it to her nose, she smelled blood.

Hands trembling, she dropped it back into the hamper and checked the clothes she'd just shrugged off. Had she gotten a bloody nose and forgotten? Chewing her lip, she shoved the shirt deep in the hamper and tugged on shorts and a clean T-shirt.

She hurried to the bathroom to brush her teeth, grimaced when she caught sight of her reflection in the mirror. Her curls were a tangled bird's nest, her eyes red-rimmed and edged in crusty goop.

Downstairs, she found Dante in the parlor, grinning. "Took ya long enough."

She rolled her eyes. "Come on." She shoved sunglasses on and walked out the door.

Dante spread a flannel blanket on the sand and plopped the picnic basket in the center.

Andi gazed at the lake, the gentle lap of waves against the beach. A couple of kids played frisbee further down the shore, but otherwise the beach was largely empty. The summer people had gone home the previous month and most of the locals were re-immersed in work and school activities.

"These are the best weekends," Dante murmured. "No tourists, hardly anybody at all."

"It is nice," Andi admitted. And it was. She didn't realize how much she needed to get out of the house, breathe in the fresh air. School and the house had been her reality for weeks, speckled with a handful of outings. She thought again of her date the previous night and felt blood rush into her face.

"Sandwich?" he asked.

"Not yet," she said. "I'm still waking up."

"Want me to run to Mister Bagel and grab you a coffee?"

"How about to the vending machine to grab me a Dr. Pepper?"

He wrinkled his nose. "Who drinks pop for breakfast?"

"You're looking at her. Plus, it's lunchtime."

He jumped up. "All right, but your dentist won't thank me."

Andi didn't tell him she didn't have a dentist or a doctor or any type of regular medical professional. She hadn't had a physical since college.

For the next two hours Andi forgot about the sudden strange turn of her life in the previous days. Occasionally she also forgot it was Dante she sat with and accidentally called him Marco. It was the first time in years she could talk about Marco and life growing up in Frankfort with someone who actually got it.

She'd tried once to talk to Luke about him, but he'd been clearly uncomfortable discussing death in general let alone the death of one of her best friends. He'd cut the conversation off and shifted to talking about how crazy the traffic had gotten in downtown Ann Arbor.

Dante lay back on the blanket and stared at the clouds, crossing his legs at the ankles. Andi joined him.

"That one looks like a crayfish," she said, thoughts wandering back to her and Marco and Gwen doing the same thing on the same beach. Gwen had always struggled to conjure images from the clouds. Marco, on the contrary, saw whole scenes playing out in the sky. "Oh look!" He'd once pointed and said, "Do you guys see the elephant balanced on the back of an alligator smoking a cigar?"

Dante cocked his head. "A crayfish? I guess I kind of see it. If he only has one claw and his tail is shaped like a noodle."

For a while they passed into a comfortable silence, then Dante rolled on his side to face her. "Are you going to stay in Frankfort, Andi? Or is this"—he shook his head—"a passing-through kind of thing."

"Passing through to where? The UP? Lake Michigan?"

"You know what I mean."

Andi gazed at a dinosaur-shaped cloud drifting overhead and considered the answer. "I'm not sure."

"Have you thought about it?"

"Well, duh, yeah. But why does it matter? When does the plan ever turn out the way we imagined it?"

"I notice you've gotten really good at not answering questions."

"I answered it. I don't know. That's the answer."

"Where do you want to be in five years?"

Andi groaned and rolled over, pressed her forehead into the sand. "You sound like my sister, or worse, my parents."

He chuckled. "I sound like my own parents, but come on. You must want something, some outcome, some specific reality."

"Do you?" She sat up, sand falling onto her shirt.

"Absolutely. I want to sell the store, help my parents retire, and move somewhere down south—Florida, Arizona, maybe Georgia."

She gaped at him. "Sell the store? How can you sell the store?"

"It's not happening tomorrow, but five years from now, it'd be nice if we were getting ready to make it happen. I came back here to help them. My focus right now is getting systems in place so someone else can take over one day. I'm not my dad. This was his dream, and it's been amazing. I've benefited enormously. Marco and I had idyllic childhoods. I'm grateful, but that won't be the life for me. I hate the winter. Hate it. I didn't when we were kids. Skiing and friends kept me distracted. Now"—he sat up—"now I want to sit on my porch in the winter and drink espresso in sandals."

---

That evening, Dante invited Andi back to his condo for dinner. They sat on the balcony eating leftover lasagna and drinking chilled limoncello.

"Do your parents know you want to move south?" Andi asked.

On the street below a couple holding hands walked a small, eager dalmatian puppy. In the distance, Andi could see Lake Michigan, the orange sun already marbling the surface of the mostly calm lake.

"They do. We talked about it for the first time just before they left for their most recent trip."

"And they're on board?"

Dante took a bite of lasagna and chewed slowly, seemingly lost in the memory. "I think so, yes. I could tell my dad was struggling with it, but my mom seemed almost excited. One of her sisters lives in South Carolina. She'd love to see her more.

Most of my dad's family is in New York. Neither of them is interested in going that way. It'll be a change, sure, but what are we here for after all if not to change, to transform? It would be easy to stay here until the end, but I would be choosing a comfortable, yet unfulfilling life if I did that."

Andi thought of Marco's grave, decorated with blue and yellow flowers in the cemetery. It was hard to imagine his parents leaving it behind. She was suddenly grateful for her little urn with Bo's ashes. The dead could tether you to a place.

"We'll come back, of course," Dante said as if he'd caught the trajectory of Andi's thoughts. "Do summer vacations here maybe. We can visit Marco's grave and friends in the area. Travel is easy now. Fly into Traverse City, an hour's drive and we're here." He snapped his fingers. "Nothing to it."

---

It was midnight when Dante walked Andi back to the front door at the Fulton Road house.

The temperature had begun to drop. Andi shivered and Dante pulled off the sweatshirt he'd slipped on before they left his condo. He draped it around her shoulders.

"I'm three steps from the front door," she said. "I can survive without it."

"I have to take every opportunity to show you how gentlemanly I am."

"And why is that?"

"Because Carla Lombardi raised me right."

She turned to him and he leaned forward, cupped her face, and kissed her.

Some aspect of the kiss felt wrong, as if she were betraying Marco by kissing his older brother. The ultimate sin in childhood was dating a sibling, and yet she did not pull away. She explored the kiss, the softness of his lips, the smell of the bakery, so achingly the way Marco had always smelled and she could almost believe it was Marco who'd kissed her. Marco had not died that night. They'd grown up and, in the way of the very best friends, fell in love. There was a certain symmetry to it.

Dante drew back, his eyes searching hers. "I probably shouldn't have done that." He spoke the words, but there was nothing sorry in his expression.

Andi swallowed, willed the blush out of her cheeks, the breathlessness from her chest.

"Probably not," she murmured.

He kissed her once more, lightly on the lips then turned and trotted down the steps. He glanced back. "Thank you. I really enjoyed spending the day with you."

"Me too."

She watched him climb into his car and disappear down the street.

## 29

Celeste had not allowed herself to search online for Lorna, but the papers Harris had given her had begun to burn a hole through her purse. She dug them out and sat on the couch with her laptop, a cup of decaf coffee on the side table, steam rising from the oily surface.

Using her newspaper subscription, she searched for Lorna Hawkins in Midland, Michigan, Jonathan's hometown. Six articles populated.

*Local Teen Killed in Tragic Hit-and-Run*

A quiet community is in mourning after seventeen-year-old Lorna Hawkins was killed in a hit-and-run late Friday night while walking home from her part-time job at Winterberry Preserve.

According to the Midland Police Department, officers responded to a call around 11:45 p.m. reporting an unresponsive person near Mile Marker 6 on Old Timber Road, a remote, wooded stretch with no streetlights or sidewalks. Paramedics arrived to find Hawkins with multiple traumatic injuries. She was pronounced dead at the scene.

Lorna, a senior at Midland High School, was last seen leaving the preserve's nature center around 10:30 p.m., where she worked as a seasonal assistant. Friends say she often walked the two-mile route home rather than ask for a ride.

"She was one of the kindest souls I've ever met," said Ms. Lillian Brook, a park supervisor who had worked with Lorna the past two summers. "She loved nature and had dreams of becoming a conservationist."

Police have yet to release details about the vehicle involved but believe it was likely traveling at a high speed and fled the scene immediately after the collision. Investigators are urging anyone who may have been in the area that night, or who noticed any recent vehicle damage in the community, to come forward.

Additional articles spoke of the grief of Lorna's family, her brother accepting her diploma at her high school graduation, a funeral that overflowed onto Main Street. In an article titled "Friends Remember Lorna as 'Bright Light' of Senior Class," Celeste found a mention of Jonathan: *Jonathan Cleary, a close friend of Lorna's, said he'd encouraged Lorna to wear reflective gear on the road, but she rarely did.*

Coverage of Lorna's unsolved death tapered off over time. The latest article, printed six years before, quoted Lorna's mother: *"Not a day goes by that I don't think about the sound of her laughter,"* said Sally Hawkins, Lorna's mother, during a small gathering held in her daughter's memory. *"We've lived with a hole in our hearts for ten years. If anyone out there knows who did this. Please, do the right thing. Speak up. My daughter deserves that much."*

Sally's grief moved through time and settled in Celeste's body. Celeste rested a hand on her belly, on the space where her own daughter was only beginning. How would it feel to someday have this child, this child who she'd not even met, but already loved, ripped from her life? Stolen during a moment of insanity on a stretch of dark forest road, left to die on the pavement alone.

The thought was almost unbearable. Tears leaked from her eyes. Had Jonathan done this? Had he intentionally hit and killed his girlfriend? Snuffed out her life because she'd rejected him.

The knowledge of it barely registered. She'd become almost numb to him now. Numb to this stranger she'd shared a bed with, drank her coffee next to, made love to. He was not real.

***

That afternoon, Celeste pulled into Andi's driveway and parked, instantly weighted down by the mere presence of the house. She searched the dark windows and tried to discern some sense of what inhabited it.

After several minutes, she climbed from her truck and trudged up the porch stairs. Celeste knocked three times before Andi pulled open the door. She did not look well. Blue-purple shadows beneath her eyes, her T-shirt wrinkled, hair disheveled.

"Is everything OK?" Celeste asked.

"Mm-hmm yeah, just ..." She yawned. "Must have dozed off. Could be catching a touch of something."

"Would you rather I come back?" Celeste asked. She'd brought the printed newspaper articles about what had happened in Andi's house as well as the recording from the basement and suddenly wondered if it might all be too much for the young woman.

Andi shook her head and offered her a weak wave to come in. "That's okay. I'll snap out of it in a few minutes." Andi led Celeste into the kitchen.

The table was littered with bottles of glue, crumpled newspaper, and scissors. "Papier mâché pumpkin for my class at school," Andi explained. "Gotta get the Halloween decorations started early or I won't have them finished."

"It's not even October."

"Isn't it? No, you're right, it isn't, but it's coming soon. Our weather is turning."

Celeste touched the coat she'd put on that morning. "I noticed it too. Farewell to the extra summer."

"I'm good with it," Andi admitted. "Lately, I've been so hot."

Celeste studied Andi's pale face, the sheen on her forehead. "You do look like you're getting sick, Andi. Maybe we should postpone this and you can rest today."

"One year for Halloween, Marco and I dressed up as Woody and Buzz Lightyear from *Toy Story*," Andi said, ignoring, or perhaps not even hearing, Celeste's comment. "We won the school costume contest. Best costumes ever."

Celeste thought back to Halloween in her own childhood. She'd worn nearly the same costume every year during elementary school. A sheet with two holes cut for eyes. Her father had been too distracted (*too guilt-ridden perhaps*) to be bothered with such things. Celeste usually managed to come up with something new for Adam, a lumberjack one year, a clown another.

"How'd your blind date go?" Celeste asked.

Andi grimaced. "Not great. I doubt we'll be going out again."

"I'm sorry to hear that."

Andi shrugged. "I'd have more fun watching the kids' watercolor paintings dry than yawning through another dinner with that guy."

Celeste laughed. "That bad, huh?"

"Worse."

Andi's cell phone rang. She glanced at it, but didn't answer. Celeste saw "Mom" on the screen.

"You can answer it," Celeste told her. "I can step out."

Andi shook her head. "I'll call her later."

Celeste noted a twinge of something in Andi's voice and suspected she'd been ignoring her mother's calls for some time.

"I meant to show these to you the other day," Celeste said, opening her bag. "I printed them off at the library. They're not about Vivian Walters, but other things have happened in this house. Bad things."

Celeste spread the papers on the table where Andi's menagerie of newspaper and glue sat for her papier mâché pumpkin. Her eye caught on a classified listing with the grainy image of a cottage. She scanned the description: "Quiet lake-front cottage, two beds, one bath, nestled on an acre of wooded shoreline. Needs some TLC. Motivated seller."

She picked the section of newspaper up and squinted closer at the image of the small house. A porch faced the water, framed by tall birch trees, and the lake looked like glass.

She thought of Moon Lake and the story of her mother taking her and Adam in the rowboat drifting around the calm lake in the morning.

"Do you mind if I take this?" Celeste asked.

Andi, who'd begun to scan the articles, shook her head. "Go for it."

Celeste tucked the paper into her purse.

While Andi read, Celeste wandered back down the hall.

Something landed with a hard thud on the wood floor in the parlor.

Celeste peered through the open parlor doors. A wooden ball, a child's toy, rolled across the floor. The image on the ball flashed as it rolled, glimpses of a clown face grinning at her, then disappearing as it spun.

Celeste thought of the photo in Eliza's house, Simon proudly holding up the hand-painted ball his uncle had gifted him for his fifth birthday.

On stilted legs, Celeste moved into the room, followed the ball as it rolled beneath a large antique hutch. She kneeled and peered into the dark crevice. Dust bunnies. No ball. On hands and knees, she crawled first to one end of the hutch then the other searching for the ball. Had it rolled out, disappeared beneath some other piece of furniture. She couldn't find it.

Suddenly a child's hand, fingernails green with mold, snaked from beneath the hutch and grabbed hold of Celeste's wrist. She shrieked and jerked away, fell back on her butt and scrambled, pushing backward on her hands and heels.

For several moments, she stared at the shadow beneath the hutch and waited. A child could not fit beneath it and yet she expected one to emerge, to slither out and unfold itself.

They didn't.

Celeste pushed back to her feet, blood still pulsing in her ears. As she returned to the kitchen, her ears perked at the sound of scratching behind the basement door.

Andi leaned over the printouts, eyes scanning the words, seemingly unaware of the scratching.

"Andi?"

"Hmm?" She didn't glance up.

"Do you hear that?"

Still, Andi didn't look up and when she finally did, her eyes had a glassy sheen. Her skin appeared more translucent, stretched thin over her high cheekbones and jaw. Sweat glistened on her forehead.

"You don't look well, Andi. Why don't you head to bed? I can bring you up a glass of water, even run into the store and get you some cold or flu medicine."

Andi shook her head, gestured limply at the papers. "Very disturbing, isn't it?"

An uneasiness crept slowly through Celeste, a sense that it was not Andi who studied her through Andi's brown eyes.

Someone, something else, had slipped in. The scratching grew louder.

Celeste blinked and shifted her eyes to the basement door, a vision of hundreds of writhing rats briefly filling her head. She refused it, bit her lip, and refocused her attention on Andi.

**30**

———

On her drive back to Traverse City, Celeste tried to call Harris, but got his voicemail.

When she parked in the driveway, she saw lights on in Eliza's kitchen and flashed again to that wooden ball, the grinning clown face, the child's hand.

Celeste hurried into her apartment. She'd barely closed the door when a knock sounded behind her. She opened the door to find Eliza smiling.

"I made a chicken casserole. Want to come over for dinner?"

Celeste brushed a hand across her forehead and wished suddenly she hadn't moved into a house with a psychic, a person who might in an instant know what she'd seen.

"No. I'm ... umm ... feeling a little crummy. I'm going to lie down."

"Oh darn. Nauseous?"

"Just really worn out."

"I can bring you a plate."

"I'm good. Really. Thanks, Eliza. Have a good night."

"Oh real quick," Eliza said. "I'm heading downstate after dinner to spend a couple days with a friend. Will you be okay here on your own? I could see if Lena wants to come over and stay?"

Celeste's shoulders softened, and she tried to keep the relief from her face. "No. I'm fine, really. Have a safe trip."

Eliza started to turn away then shifted back. "I'm taking Sassy with me, but would you mind popping in to check on Pumpkin?"

"I'd be happy to."

"Lovely. Thank you. And your apartment key unlocks the side door."

"Perfect. Goodnight."

Celeste closed herself into the little apartment and sat on the floor, her back against the wall. The wooden ball, the child's hand. The memory of both played on repeat in her head. It didn't seem possible that Andi's house could be connected to Eliza's little brother who'd vanished decades before.

"But it is," she muttered.

---

Despite her exhaustion, Celeste lay awake for a long time thinking about Simon Kent. When she finally slipped away, a nightmare awaited her.

She stood in the parlor at 506 Fulton. She gazed at Andi who lay stretched on the couch, waxen skin too tight on her bony face. Andi's eyes stared at the ceiling. She mumbled something beneath her breath.

"What did you say?" Celeste asked, stepping closer, her legs oddly heavy. Moving across the room felt like wading through water.

"*Dominus infernus ... veni ad me ...*" Andi whispered the words on repeat.

Celeste stared at her cracked lips, blood trickling from her nose. Her heart slammed against her chest; her vision undulated in and out of focus. When she finally reached a hand to Andi's arm the girl's skin was so hot it burned her fingertips. Celeste jerked her hand away, saw steam rising from her singed skin.

Andi turned and fixed her gaze on Celeste. She smiled and her mouth grew wider and then wider still revealing pointed teeth. The skin on Andi's face began to blacken and curl. It fell away and smoked on the parlor floor.

Celeste wanted to scream, to run, but she couldn't move.

The walls of the parlor groaned. Portraits tilted on the nails. A grandfather clock struck midnight, and the deafening chime seemed to split Celeste's head in two.

The double glass parlor doors flew open and wind and rain rushed into the room.

There in the doorway stood a little boy. Eliza's brother Simon, a wooden ball clutched in his pale hands. Suddenly the ball cracked open and a wriggling rat fell to the floor and scurried away.

Andi, now little more than a grinning skeleton, sat up and beckoned the child into the parlor.

Celeste jerked awake, gasping and startling Romeo and Cash from the foot of the bed. In sync they leaped from the mattress and raced from the room.

Celeste fumbled for the lamp and flipped on the switch, chasing out the shadows, sucking in mouthfuls of air as the room focused. No parlor, no Andi with her pointed fangs, no Simon in the doorway.

The nightmare had felt so real, the clamminess of her skin only intensifying the sensations.

She stood and made her way into the bathroom, flipped on the light and started the shower. The pungent animal odor of fear-sweat seeped from her pores. Celeste stepped beneath the cool spray and tried to imagine the horrors of the dream washed away, swirling into the drain below.

It was only a dream. And yet ... Celeste's dreams had stopped being mere dreams after her near-death. They were different now. She'd dreamt of Dee Simmons's house soaked in blood multiple times before the woman was murdered there. Worse, it had been Celeste's warning about those visions that had encouraged Dee to accept a ride from her killer the night she died.

The ghoulish image of Andi, her face peeling away, flashed once more in Celeste's mind.

Celeste turned off the faucet, toweled dry, and slipped on her robe.

When she emerged from the bathroom, the sharp edges of the dream had softened, but the emotion remained. She picked up a pillow and squeezed it tight, channeling Doctor Dave's suggestion to release the energy. As she clutched the pillow, she envisioned her residual anxiety running down her arms, out through her hands and into the pillow.

Body and brain mostly calm, but now wide awake, she walked to the refrigerator and pulled out her bag of spinach. She shook some into a bowl and added honey mustard dressing, then moved to the window and peeled back the curtain, eating her salad standing up.

As her eyes scanned the dark street, she caught sight of a person's silhouette directly across from Eliza's house. She pressed her face closer to the glass and squinted. They stood in the shadow of an oak tree, their form nearly bleeding into the dark trunk behind them.

As Celeste studied the shape of the figure, a pit formed in her stomach. They were real, solid. Maybe a neighbor, a person taking a walk.

She twisted around and stared at the clock on her oven. Two fifteen in the morning.

Eliza's car was not in the driveway. Celeste remembered she'd left town, wouldn't return for a day or two.

Celeste dropped the curtain into place and backed quickly away. She put her bowl in the sink, and slipped back to her bedroom, grabbing her cell phone. She had a missed call from Harris earlier in the evening. He must have returned her call while she slept. After a moment of hesitation, she dialed him back.

He answered immediately, sounding wide awake.

"What's wrong?" he asked.

She didn't probe why he'd answered her call with that question.

Before she spoke, she peeked through the curtain again, confirmed the person still stood there. "There's someone here," she whispered, though the person outside was too far away to hear her. "They're watching Eliza's house or me ... I don't know."

"I'm on my way."

Celeste listened to the sound of him moving, a zipper, the rustling of keys, his car door slamming.

"Can you still see them?" he asked.

Celeste blinked, still unsure if the person was merely a trick of the dark, an ordinary, harmless object made sinister by the night.

"Yes."

---

"They're gone," Celeste blurted when she opened the door to Harris less than ten minutes later.

He turned and gazed across the street.

"Where were they?"

"By that tree over there ..." She pointed at the shadowy pool beneath a large oak. She hadn't seen them walk away, had let the curtain fall back into place, so she could assemble weapons if need be. The only suitable options had been a spray can of bleach cleaner and a dull butcher knife. "But maybe ... it wasn't anything. I mean, it was a person, but ..." She fluttered her hands. "I'd had a nightmare just before and I may have ..."

"Imagined them?"

She nodded.

"No. I don't think so. I had a very uncomfortable feeling right before you phoned. Had you not called, I was calling you."

"You had an uncomfortable feeling?"

"Yeah." He followed her into the apartment. Brushed both hands through his hair and gazed around. He moved into her bedroom, opened the closet door, then into the bathroom and pulled back the shower curtain.

"What is it?" she asked, trailing behind him.

He extinguished the lamps she'd turned on and walked to the window. He pulled back the curtains and stared into the night. "I was going over a case and had this sudden"—he tapped two fingers on his temple—"feeling that I needed to call you, that something was wrong."

Celeste shuddered and pulled the belt on her robe tighter.

"I'm going to do a quick perimeter check," he said. "Lock the door behind me. I'll knock four times to come back in."

Celeste followed him to the door and locked it. She watched through the window as he crossed the street and scanned the dark yards, moving quickly along the sidewalk.

He returned several minutes later and rapped on the door four times.

When he walked in, he shook his head. "No sign of anyone. Any sense at all of who it might have been? Has anyone been following you?"

"No. Not that I've noticed."

"What did you do today exactly?"

Celeste sat on the couch, body both tired and buzzing with adrenaline. "Not a whole lot. I spent the morning here looking up stuff about Lorna Hawkins. In the afternoon I went to Andi's and the experience was pretty strange. She seemed kind of out of it. When I first visited her, she told me about the odd sounds and things happening in the house. Today she acted like she didn't hear it," Celeste explained.

Harris scratched his jaw. "That is weird."

"It is. And it's more than that. She's changing. Sometimes she has this distant look on her face or worse, a totally blank look, like no one's in there. I almost felt like ... like it wasn't her I was talking to today. It was ... and yet it wasn't."

Harris was quiet for a long moment, fingers laced in his lap, expression troubled. "You think what then? That she's losing it or something in the house is ..."

"Possessing her."

He flinched at the word.

"There's something else," Celeste murmured. She saw again the wooden ball rolling beneath the hutch, the grinning clown face, the child's hand. "I think what happened to Eliza's little brother is connected to the house on Fulton Road."

Harris leaned back, steepled his fingers at his lips. "Why?"

She told him about the nightmares, the toy wooden ball, the child's hand that grabbed hold of her.

He shifted in his seat. "I don't even know what to say right now."

"Yeah."

They talked for nearly two hours. Celeste showed Harris the printouts from the library and eventually, eyelids heavy, she dozed off on the couch as he sat at the table using her laptop to see if he could find any other clues that might connect Simon to the house on Fulton Road.

**31**

---

Andi sat up, startled to see Gwen outlined in the parlor doors.

"I knocked," Gwen said. "But no one answered. The door was unlocked."

"Oh ... hi. How are you?" Andi had been drifting, lost in thoughts of ... What? She suddenly couldn't remember what she'd been daydreaming about. Radiohead played low from her cell phone. The song "Street Spirit." Andi hadn't heard a knock, and yet it wouldn't have surprised her if Gwen had banged for five minutes and somehow, she'd not registered it.

"I'm just fine. Right as rain." Gwen crossed the room. As she had before, she appeared perfectly put together. Crisp white pants and a sky blue shirt with a plunging neckline. So pretty.

Andi brushed both hands through her hair, felt clumps of curls sticking at odd angles. She glanced down at her T-shirt, stained with marker, and paired with purple sweatpants, a hole in the right knee.

"I was at the pier today and thought of you," Gwen said. "Do you remember when I almost drowned there? That big wave came up and pushed me right off. You and Marco saved me, didn't even hesitate, just jumped in and rescued me."

Andi nodded, the memory causing a visceral sensation in her body, the icy cold lake, the burning when she'd sucked in a mouthful of water. But they'd gotten her. She and Marco had each grabbed hold of one of Gwen's arms and, struggling, they'd made it to the shore, and lay heaving on the prickly beach sand. Afterward they'd laughed, laughed so hard they cried. It had been October, cold and gray, and they'd cheated death.

Andi's eyes drifted to Gwen's shoes. Lake grass had gotten tangled in her blue strappy sandal. "You've got some seaweed stuck in your shoe."

Gwen stared down for a moment and then looked back at Andi and shrugged. "How funny."

Andi could smell it, the seagrass, musty, faintly fishy.

"So tell me about your love life?" Gwen urged. "Single, dating?"

"Single."

"And happy to be?"

Andi pictured Luke, and a little knot tightened in her belly. She nodded, but didn't look Gwen in the eye. "How about you?"

"Engaged, actually." Gwen extended an arm. On the ring finger of her slender left hand clung a beautiful and weirdly familiar diamond ring.

Andi leaned closer. "This is strange to say, but I feel like I've seen that ring before."

"You have. It belonged to Carla Lombardi."

Andi's mouth fell open. "Marco's mom?" And now she recognized the ring from the dozens of times she'd sat on a stool in Marco's kitchen watching his mother deftly form arancini or meticulously roll out bread dough.

"Dante's mom," Gwen corrected.

"You're engaged to Dante?" She couldn't hide the shock in

her voice. Andi's face burned. The sensation of the kiss they'd shared warm and recent on her lips.

"Yeah. We've been dating for years, pretty much since he came back from college."

Andi squirmed in her seat. "I had no idea. I've ... talked to him a couple of times. He didn't mention ..." She trailed off, unsure of what to say. No one wanted to hear their fiancée hadn't talked about them, and why hadn't he? She and Gwen had been close. How could he hide that from her? How long had he expected her not to find out?

"Dante is a private person. I haven't told him, but I want to have three babies, and we'll name one Marco," Gwen said wistfully. "And who knows if we have a girl, maybe we'll name her Andi after you."

Gwen continued talking, waxing poetic about her idyllic future with Dante, but Andi struggled to concentrate, too fixated on the kiss she'd shared with Dante and the terrible betrayal they'd both committed against Gwen.

By the time Andi reached Dante's family store, she was seething. She'd replayed it a hundred different ways in her head, but none of them made sense. How could he possibly justify keeping his engagement from her? There was no reason good enough.

She found him in the back, sitting on a stool behind the deli counter, restocking cold cuts.

Andi stared at him, hurt. She'd never had a poker face, and all her big plans to confront him got washed away by the family photos on the wall, the smell of the store, the memories of Marco so heavy and poignant. She'd not even spoken, and her eyes welled.

He stood up, started to smile, but the expression quickly dissolved. "What is it? Why are you upset?" he asked.

It took her a moment to get the words out, to choke down the tears gathering in her throat. "You didn't tell me about Gwen."

His face paled, and he shook his head slowly.

"Why?" she demanded.

Dante ran a hand through his dark hair, a signature Marco move. A single tear slipped from her right eye and carved its way down her cheek.

"I don't know. It never came up."

"Because you didn't bring it up."

He shoved his hands into his jeans pockets. "Andi, I figured you already knew. You guys were always close. I just assumed—"

The bell over the door chimed, and an elderly couple walked in.

Dante plastered on a customer service smile. "George, Rita. How's the day treating you?"

The couple bustled to the counter both talking at once: the man about how his lawnmower had decided to malfunction on the very weekend of his daughter's wedding in the backyard and the woman about how she told the man to hire a lawn company but did he listen?

Andi backed away. She wanted to wait, to demand more answers, but the tears would not stay down, and standing in the corner of the store bawling was not an option.

Her cell phone rang three times on her drive back to the Fulton Road house. Her mother, her sister, and finally Dante. She ignored all three calls and shoved through the front door, her grief giving way to rage.

Dante had kissed her. He'd already ruined any chance she and Gwen would have of reconciling. He'd tainted it before it could begin again.

In the kitchen, she picked up her half-finished papier mâché pumpkin and smashed it on the ground. She stormed through the house, weeping, the weight of the previous weeks and months wringing her out.

Why had she returned to Frankfort? What sick, confused instinct sent her back to the town where she'd experienced the worst pain of her life?

---

It was after ten and pouring rain when Dante arrived at her front door. She saw his car through the window and almost ignored his thunderous bangs. Finally, she pulled the door open, still angry, but exhausted now, more tired than she could ever remember being.

"What?" she snapped.

He stared down at her, confusion and frustration in his features. "What do you mean, what? You came into the store and yelled at me and then took off. I, for one, prefer to deal with my problems instead of running away."

"What's that supposed to mean? You think I ran away? You of all people are judging me? When two days ago you kissed me and you're engaged to Gwen." Spit flew from her mouth as she spoke. Some landed on his dark jacket, but he seemed oblivious to it. His eyes had gone wide, his mouth had fallen open.

"What?" she demanded. "No snappy comeback now?"

"What are you saying, Andi? Gwen is dead."

Andi gaped at him, her mind flooded instantly with fear. Why was he lying to her?

"How can you say that? How dare you say that? She's been here in this house with me. I saw your mother's ring on her finger. Do you think that's funny? To talk about your fiancée that way?"

"Fiancée?" Dante stared at her, incredulous, wary. He took a step back.

"You admitted it. I asked you at the bakery, and you told me it was true."

He gaped at her, shaking his head slowly. "No ... you ... you asked why I didn't tell you about Gwen. I thought you meant her death. Andi... Gwen is dead. She's been dead for three years."

## 32

Harris was gone when Celeste woke in the morning. Her neck ached from her awkward sleeping position on the couch, and Romeo and Cash both lay curled on her legs, which were numb and tingly. She winced as she stood and limped across the room.

A note from Harris hung by a magnet on the little refrigerator: "Early day for me, so I had to go. Call me if you see anyone suspicious around the house."

Celeste showered, ate two pieces of toast and made a cup of half-decaf coffee. She made a quick stop at Eliza's to feed Pumpkin. As she started for the door, she paused at the wall of photos of Simon. She plucked the framed picture of Simon holding the wooden clown ball and slid it into her bag.

On her drive to Frankfort, Celeste thought of the person she'd seen lurking outside the night before. Had they been watching her? Or were they merely a passerby, and she'd projected her fears onto them?

She drove to the Golden Oaks Assisted Living house, parking as she'd done before on the street.

The extended summer was gone, and fall had fully replaced

it. The sky was a mass of gray, swift-moving clouds. An icy wind blew in from Lake Michigan. The trees that hadn't already turned to reds and golds had begun to change rapidly, many of their leaves falling in the gusting wind.

No one sat on the porch.

Celeste pushed open the front door, which led to a large foyer, an antique-looking chandelier hanging overhead. A wooden desk with a landline phone and a day planner sat just inside the door, but the seat behind it was empty. Off to her right stood a large living room, an electric fireplace in the corner.

Six or seven people sat in the room in wheelchairs or on couches. She saw Porch Prophet Gus at a table across from a heavyset man playing a game of Battleship. Both men's hands shook furiously as they attempted to fit the tiny pegs into the holes as they sunk each other's ships.

"Goddamn it," the bigger man barked. "Just goddamn it to hell. I can't get this peg in to save my life. Where's Tracy?"

"Tracy is emptying the bedpans," a woman snapped from the couch. "She doesn't have time to play the game for you. Why don't you play checkers or chess? A million games in the damn closet and you two have to pick the only one that needs the fingers of a child to work it properly."

"Pipe down, Janine," the man said. "No one asked you."

"Shhh...," another woman, closer to the TV, said. "We're missing *The Bachelor*."

This comment elicited another wave of grumbling from the group.

Gus looked up and spotted Celeste in the doorway.

"Hiya!" he called, waving. "I forgot your name."

"Celeste," she told him, walking over. "I'm sorry to interrupt your game."

"Not a problem at all. Here." He dropped four little red pegs in her hand. "If you could plug those into D1, 2, 3, and 4."

The man across from him waved angrily. "I sank your submarine first. Here, look." He gestured at Celeste. "I need you to get these into A6, B6, and C6."

"Gus, I wanted to find out more about the Fulton Road house. Is Fran around today?" Celeste asked as she pushed the pegs into the plastic board.

He chuckled. "Is she around? Where do you think she'd be? In Aruba?"

Celeste gazed toward the hall. "Where can I find her?"

"Behind the door marked Fran, I reckon."

The woman on the couch leaned over. "Up the stairs, third room on the left. Gotta ask a woman if you wanna clear answer. If your legs aren't up for those stairs, the elevators are in the back of the house next to the washroom."

"Thanks," Celeste told her.

Each room had a hand-painted wooden sign with the occupant's name. Fran was painted in purple and yellow with green ivy along the border. For a moment, Celeste saw her own name hand-painted on a sign on her bedroom at the Moon Lake house, a little sign her mother must have painted in the scant years she had with her children before her life was stolen.

Celeste knocked, but the door, already cracked, slid open. Fran sat in a reclining chair near the window, a large-print romance book propped on a swivel stand before her.

She turned as Celeste peeked in.

"Hi, Fran. I don't know if you remember me. I stopped by the other day."

"Oh sure, asking around about the Fulton house. Had this place buzzing like a bees' nest that night. I heard nothin' but Fulton this and Fulton that over the supper table."

"Really? Are there other people here who are familiar with what's happened in the house?"

"Familiar? If by that you're askin' if they've believed every scuttlebutt for the last fifty-odd years, then sure."

"Did you hear any stories from people who actually seemed to have knowledge of what happened in the house?"

Fran started to speak, and then a coughing fit took her. She hunched over in her chair, hand flailing to a little nearby table until she secured a wad of tissue to cough into. "Chester Sutton," she finally choked out. "He's the only one who had somethin' worth listenin' to. He lived across the street from 506 Fulton back in ..." Another cough silenced her. She pounded on her chest and cleared her throat. "Allergies in the spring, allergies in the summer, allergies in the fall. My granddaughter says, 'Move to Florida where it's warm.' Ha. Winter is my only reprieve. Things finally die and give an old lady some peace."

Celeste's eyes drifted to the blood-streaked tissue Fran had returned to the table. The cough had a deep, chest-rattling sound to it. It wasn't allergies. "Can I get you a drink or—"

Fran waved the question off. "Chester lived across the street from the Fulton place back in the forties. Long time ago now, and he wasn't real chatty about what went on. But he said that house is no good. He said if you"—she pointed at Celeste—"came back askin', we should tell you to steer clear of it."

"Chester is living here at Golden Oaks?"

"Sure is. First floor. Can't hardly use his legs no more, so the second floor's out for him."

"I think I'll go talk to him. Thanks, Fran."

"Before you go, toss that quilt on my legs? Hmm... Starting to feel a chill in the air."

Celeste took the throw from the foot of Fran's bed and tucked it around her legs. Fran leaned her head back and closed her eyes, saying nothing more.

Celeste made her way back to the first floor, careful to avoid the sitting room full of residents. Like Fran, Chester had a hand-painted wooden placard on his door. Someone had painted little classic cars on a border around his name.

She knocked on the door. Inside, she heard the low

murmur of the television. After the second knock elicited no response, she twisted the door handle and peeked in.

A man slept in a wheelchair angled toward the window.

Celeste chewed her lip, reluctant to wake him and yet desperate to hear what he had to say. She cleared her throat. He didn't stir.

"Chester?" she called.

Still no response. As she looked at him, she searched for the telltale rise and fall of his chest. His body appeared still, too still.

From the sitting room, she heard the raised voices of Gus and his counterpart arguing over Battleship. She searched the hall behind her for a nurse or caretaker but saw no one.

On wobbly legs, she crossed the room and reached a trembling hand to Chester's shoulder. She feared it would be stiff, cold to the touch. Instead, the moment her fingers touched the fabric of his flannel shirt, he jolted awake, eyes flinging open, hands spasming in his lap.

"Oh!" Celeste jumped and knocked her hand against a large Styrofoam cup on his rolling table. She managed to right it before it toppled to the ground.

He blinked at her, chest heaving, and seemed unsure if he could trust his eyes.

"Chester. Hi. Gosh, I'm sorry I startled you. Startled us both, really." She released a shaky laugh and took several steps away from him.

He continued staring at her, mouth agape, eyes opening and closing in rapid succession.

"Are you OK? Can I get you something?"

"My... my heart. I think it's on the ceiling."

Celeste looked up, slow to catch the joke.

Chester released a slow chuckle that ended with a cough. "Don't think I've been awoken to a pretty stranger in my room since California, 1973. And turned out she was lost. Lookin' for my best friend, Zander's, room." He laughed again and leaned his head back, squeezing his eyes shut. "What I wouldn't give to go back to that little shack on the beach for just one day."

"I'm really sorry I scared you."

He opened his eyes and gazed at her. "Scared is walking point in the jungles of Vietnam and praying you'll see the booby trap before it sees you. Scared is getting jackknifed by a semi on an icy highway outside of Detroit. This was more like a strong cup of coffee and a slap to the face. So thank you. I probably needed it."

Celeste smiled, though her own body hadn't quite come down from her scare. "Do you mind if I sit?" She pointed at one of the two chairs upholstered in antique cars, not dissimilar from those painted on his nameplate.

"Not at all. Take a load off. Are you working here now? Gina said something about applying for a fancy new job downstate."

Celeste shook her head. "You might have heard about me. I stopped in the other day asking about 506 Fulton."

His eyes narrowed slightly. "Ahh ... you're the one. And now you caught wind I might have a story to tell?"

"Fran said I should talk to you."

"Fran is right."

"You're familiar with 506 Fulton Road?"

"Very. My father called the woman in that house the bride of Satan."

## 33

Celeste made a face and echoed Chester's words back to him. "The bride of Satan?"

"I know." Chester rubbed his hands up and down his arms. "Creepy. And maybe a little over the top. I remember my mom swatting him and saying not to talk like that, but when she left the room, he leaned in real close to me and said, 'You take heed, son. Don't ever, ever, under any condition go near that house. I don't care if you saw Jocko'—that was my dog back then—'run right up the porch and through the front door because I'm telling it to you straight, it wasn't Jocko, it was some abomination, some imposter meant to lure you in and once she's got you inside, you ain't ever coming back out.'

"Let's just say I took that advice to heart. My father did not delight in scaring little boys. I saw the fear in his eyes myself. Years later, after my father had passed, and we'd moved far away from Fulton Road, I asked my mom about it, why my father was so convinced the woman who lived in the house was bad. She got real quiet for a bit and then admitted that my father had seen something about a year before my birth. This little girl from the neighborhood disappeared without a trace. Leslie was her name. Leslie Twitchell.

"The day she disappeared, she was going to houses selling calendars for the Girl Scouts. It was wartime then, and rationing had caused a shortage of butter, sugar, and flour, so the girls sold calendars instead of cookies. She came to our door, and my dad ordered a calendar. Leslie hopped off the stoop and headed across the street to 506 Fulton, where the woman lived; Nadine was her name. My dad lit up a joint and sat on the porch and watched her. He got awful tension headaches, and he'd found marijuana dulled that pain a bit. This would come back to bite him later on. Nadine opened her door and invited Leslie inside. She never came back out. Around five when Leslie hadn't returned home for supper, her mom, who was raising four children mostly on her own as her husband had gone off to the war, started walking the neighborhood looking for her. My dad said, yeah, he'd seen her, and she'd gone into 506 Fulton and never came out.

"Well, Nadine denied it. She told Leslie's mom she'd not seen the girl all day. Now, if she'd have said Leslie stopped by, came in for a few minutes and left, my dad would never have given it a second thought, but when the woman denied the girl ever entering the house, that's when he lost it. The police came. They're crawling all over the neighborhood, questioning everyone, and my dad's ranting about the woman across the street lying. The police questioned him about what he'd been doing, and he admitted to smoking a joint because he was an honest man, honest to a fault, obviously because that put him right in the crosshairs then.

"You gotta remember the 1940s was the age of Reefer Madness. People thought pot smokers should be tossed in prison. He regretted telling the police about that joint until the day he died. An admitted drug user, high, lures this little girl into his house. That's how the law pegged him. They searched our house, found a baggie of weed, and arrested him. Interrogated him for years. I kid you not, years. Every time a new cold case investigator would get ahold of the file, they'd go after him again.

"About six months after Leslie disappeared, he confronted Nadine on the sidewalk outside the house. My mom witnessed the whole thing, and Nadine didn't say a word, but she looked very ... strange, like she stared right through my father, right into his soul. That's how my mom described her. That night he developed a bad fever, so bad my mom had to drive him all the way to the hospital in Traverse City. We didn't have a local hospital in those days. No cause the doctors could find, but he spent two weeks in the hospital. He said he dreamt again and again of Leslie Twitchell trapped in 506 Fulton Road."

Gooseflesh crept up Celeste's arms as Chester spoke. The fever story marked the first she'd heard that mirrored Andi's account of Marco—and, far worse, the thought of a little girl stepping through that door and never emerging again lodged cold in her chest.

"What happened to Nadine?"

"She died when I was eight—a gruesome death too. Freddie Lincoln lived in the house next to mine. He saw the paramedics taking her out. And he snuck up to the house and peeked in, said there was blood on the walls, the floor. Like a slaughterhouse."

"Somone murdered her?"

Chester shook her head. "Coroner called it suicide. I only know because when I was about middle-aged I did a bit of looking into things. I found Nadine's brother. Barry. He told me Nadine had been possessed. Honestly, at the time, I didn't believe it. Bullshit. I figured. Barry trying to distance himself from whatever horrors that woman inflicted.

"Still, I was curious and asked him what he meant. He told me Nadine insisted a demon lived in the house and at night she gave herself to it. Barry said that on the last day he saw her, which was a few days before her death, Nadine leaned in close and whispered, '*I suspect it is nearly finished with me now.*'"

Celeste folded her arms across her chest. "Finished with her."

Chester nodded. "And the next Barry heard, Nadine had died. Police found a gory, pretty horrific scene, but they ruled it a suicide. Though unlike anything they'd ever seen. Slit her wrists in the upstairs bathtub and ran through the house rubbing her arms along the walls, flinging blood as high as the ceiling and I'm not sure if you've been in that house, but there are some high ceilings."

"Barry's family didn't push the police to investigate, see if she'd been murdered?"

"I asked that same question. But no, he said. There'd already been suspicion surrounding Nadine, so many whispers. They wanted only for her to fade away, I guess. And that's what she did."

"Was Barry reluctant to share the story? Had he told other people or—"

"These aren't the types of stories people share—that families pass down. This is the kind of story a family hides, that a town wipes from its history, like genocide and slavery. Nobody wants to claim a story like this, not even the part before the real spooky, horror movie-type stuff went on. So, answering your question, no. I went into my conversation with Barry with a plan. I found him at Smokey's Bar and I started chattin' to him about the football game. I could see he was real into it. I started buyin' rounds and slowly, once I'd gotten him loosened up, then I started pushing.

"He still didn't want to tell me, but finally I dropped Leslie's name and started talking about how devastating it would be to lose a daughter and never know what became of her. That softened him up, that and the booze. He cried a lot, said a few sorrys, insisted he didn't know what happened to Leslie, but he clearly suspected Nadine had done something to her."

"Did Nadine live alone in the house?"

"When Leslie went missing, she did live alone, but my dad told me she'd had a husband, a real nice guy named Wally who was always asking other guys in the neighborhood if they wanted to go fishing with him or grab a drink at the bar. He and Nadine were perfectly normal for a couple of years. And they did have children. Four. Three of them died. A pair of twins, cradle death, my dad said, but later he was convinced Leslie probably smothered them in her sleep. They found three of them in the house dead."

"I read about that," Celeste whispered.

"Yep. And even with that kind of history, they put the spotlight on my dad for little Leslie's disappearance. The cops just could not believe a woman living alone would have done it. And I get it. I watch the detective shows. The perps are usually men. Still, you'd think they'd take a closer look at her."

"What happened to the fourth child? You said three died."

"The dad took her when he left Nadine."

Another story that echoed Vivian Walters. "Any idea why Wally left?"

"Because his wife was batshit crazy." Chester shrugged. "I'm not sure. I might have asked my dad, and maybe he even gave me an answer, but I can't recall it. Now my turn for a question. How come you're asking about 506 Fulton? Don't tell me you're living there?"

Celeste shook her head. "No, but I'm helping the young woman who is."

"Tell her to get out. Pack her bags and get the hell out of there."

Celeste thought of Andi. It was such a simple suggestion. But she suspected the young woman wouldn't take it. Whatever lived in the house had gotten ahold of her already.

"She won't leave, right?"

"Why do you say that?"

"Because Barry said something like that with Nadine. He tried to carry her out. When she told him about the thing nearly being done with her. He picked her up and tried to carry her out of the house. She bit him and clawed his face. When he put her down, she ran into the basement and locked herself down there. He'd already tried to get her to move, offered her a room at his place, then even said he'd rent her a house somewhere else. Nope. She wouldn't hear of it."

"That's very disturbing."

"It is. You need to speak to Alvin Kready."

"Who is he?"

"He used to be an exorcist here in Frankfort. I heard he went into that house more than once. He can tell you more."

"Where can I find him?"

"Now that I can't say. He's lived a colorful life. Try the Holy Trinity Church. They try to distance themselves from the guy, but someone around there usually keeps tabs on him."

## 34

———

"You know what I found this morning?" Andi asked Colton as he bit back tears, trying to cram his stuff into his backpack. The zipper was broken, and twice his *Minions* lunch box, water bottle and library book had fallen onto the floor.

He looked at her, eyes watery.

"Kittens," she told him.

His eyes went big and round. For a moment, he forgot his scattered stuff on the floor. "Really? My cousin Mandy's cat had kittens in her barn. Six of 'em. This big." He held his thumb and index fingers inches apart.

"These are about that size," Andi said. "Two orange, one black and white, and one all black."

"All black?" he asked.

She nodded. "Maybe you can come by and see them sometime? Would you like that?"

He nodded. "Yeah."

A voice yelled from the end of the hall. "Colton Ramsey, you are about to miss your bus. Come on, buddy. They're waiting for you."

Andi turned to see Mrs. Keller, one of the office staff, standing in the middle of the hall, hands on her thick hips. She had a sour look on her face.

Andi quickly helped Colton cram his fallen items back into his bag and pinch the top closed so they wouldn't spill out again. He stood and ran down the hall. Mrs. Keller waved him hurriedly toward the front of the school.

Andi stood, legs stiff, and swallowed the thick saliva running down the back of her throat. Her head felt fuzzy. She made her way back into the classroom, gaze bouncing off the children's drawings and the maniacal smiles of the colorful alphabet people on the wall. The room was too bright. It burned Andi's eyes.

She steadied her hands on the desk, bent over and pulled a shaky breath into her lungs.

Why had she said those things, lied to Colton about kittens, invited him back to her house? It was the same lie she'd told Ellie the night she'd walked her out of the restaurant.

She sat heavily in the chair, nauseous, face slick with sweat. Andi touched her forehead. It was hot.

On her desk lay a single printout. Gwen Richard's obituary. She'd found it online that morning and printed it in the staff room. Gwen stared out of the photo. Her eyes looked sharp, almost accusatory.

"Andi?"

The voice startled her. Carrie Davies stood in the doorway.

"Are you OK?" she asked.

Andi blinked at her and tried to shake off the fog, the sudden urge to wade into the cool waters of Lake Michigan and disappear into the dark depths.

"Yeah. I think so." She pulled a Kleenex from the little box decorated to look like a frog and mopped her forehead. "Maybe I've caught a little bug."

Carrie smiled, her face soft. "Life of an elementary school

teacher. Last year I was sick eight times. Eight." She shook her head. "Amazing that any of us come back."

Andi nodded. She steadied her hands on the desk and stood up, eyes drifting to the wastebasket decorated in pink and yellow polka dots. She wasn't sure if she shouldn't drop to her knees in front of it, might not spew her turkey and cheese sandwich. Her stomach rumbled, but her lunch stayed put for now.

"Yeah. I better get home and lie down."

Carrie nodded. "Good plan. A hot bath, and some honey lemon water. Works every time."

"Thank you."

Despite Carrie's kindness, Andi noticed the other teachers as she walked from the building. Teachers who'd previously called out hello or stopped to chat quickly looked away as she passed them. In the parking lot, she briefly encountered Ginnie getting into her car. The woman rushed to climb in, the locks engaging with an audible click. She started the car and drove away, but Andi could see her eyes locked on her in her rearview mirror.

---

As Andi drove home, her old Civic rattled with every pothole. Each vibration jarred her already aching head. She blinked hard, trying to clear the gauzy fog that pressed against her temples. Maybe it was the start of the flu. Or maybe it was just the long day of wrangling eighteen five-year-olds with sticky fingers and relentless questions. That day had been worse than usual. Twice she'd had lapses, realizing fifteen or twenty minutes had passed in what felt like seconds. Add in Hunter breaking Ella's show-and-tell toy pony and Delia wetting her pants and the end of the day hadn't come soon enough.

*And let's not forget about Gwen.*

The thought was a hot knife to the brain, instant and searing.

Her eyes watered as the fiery sun glared through her windshield. She was so hot, burning up, but the air conditioner had broken months before. She cracked the window, the cool air blowing in from Lake Michigan offering instant relief. But with the open window came the sounds. A car honked, a woman yelled across a parking lot, and the lake ground against the shore. The world seemed too bright, too loud.

She barely registered the soft voice behind her.

"Does it hurt to die?"

She nodded absently, her mind too sluggish to catch the wrongness of it. "Sometimes," she murmured, her voice distant, automatic, like she was answering another question about snack time or glue sticks.

Andi glanced in the rearview mirror, caught sight of the little boy, face pale, big eyes staring back at her. She slammed on the brakes. The car behind her swerved viciously to the left and careened back in time to miss an oncoming pickup. She glimpsed the driver's red screaming face, listened to the fading blare of his horn and the swear words, *Fucking idiot bitch*," muffled, as he sped away.

She coaxed her car onto the shoulder and, with shaky hands, tilted the mirror to see the child. He wasn't there. The back seat sat empty.

---

When Andi got home, her entire body felt as if she'd doused it in gasoline and lit it on fire. Her face was burning up. Sweat beaded on her temples and rolled down her neck.

A sane person would have gone to the urgent care, but the thought of sitting in the too-bright reception area, antiseptic smells and fluorescent lights beating down, made her want to climb right out of her skin.

No, she needed to be in her own bed, curtains drawn. The call of the cool, dark house was the only thing keeping her going.

As Andi parked in her driveway, she saw the neighbor children across the street. A little boy, around three, and a girl a year or two older. The little girl carried an armful of dolls toward the plastic blue playhouse in the side yard. The toddler boy ran after her, and a dog followed them both, tail wagging.

Andi smiled faintly. Something in her chest ached. A longing, maybe. Or a memory. The kind that felt like it didn't belong to her at all. The fever seemed to be rising, her eyes floating in boiling soup.

Her gaze lingered on the little boy, and the longing grew, an anguish beneath it. The way she'd felt when the vet told her Bo had to be put down, or worse, when her mother woke her in her childhood bedroom, tears leaking from her eyes and barely choked out the words: "*Marco died last night.*"

Suddenly the dog, a large German shepherd, stopped and turned to look at Andi, ears perked.

"Hi, buddy," she rasped.

The dog snarled. He took a couple of steps toward her and then lunged and broke into a run.

Andi flinched, confused.

As the dog closed the distance, her fuzzy brain struggled to make sense of what was happening.

The shepherd's eyes were locked on her, teeth bared. Not wild. Not feral. Focused. Controlled. Protective.

Andi turned to run, but her feet didn't move.

As the dog reached the edge of its yard, it let out a sudden, sharp yelp and skidded to a halt.

Andi stood frozen, her whole body trembling. Her clothes stuck to her sweaty body like a second skin.

The German shepherd whined and backed up.

The dog had an invisible fence.

"Chewy, come here!" the little girl called, face scrunched. Her brother stood beside her, gazing toward Andi.

Slowly, the dog trotted back to the children, circling them, tail rigid and eyes still watching her.

Andi swallowed and turned, trying to calm her quaking legs as she lumbered up to her house and through the front door.

Andi leaned heavily against the wall. Relief flooded through her. Her vision swam as she stared down the hall, struggling to make sense of the figure there—a woman, blood pooling on the floor between her legs.

Andi blinked, and the woman was gone. The hall stood empty.

"Hallucinating," she murmured. Because of the fever. The fever that was climbing—that would soon prevent her from walking upstairs.

Somehow, she got to her bedroom, stripped off her clothes and climbed beneath the covers. She was burning up and simultaneously chilled, needed the shroud surrounding her, the weight of the blankets to hold her in place.

## 35

After her talk with Chester, Celeste drove to the library in Frankfort. Bjork was not behind the desk. Instead, a middle-aged man stood at the post typing on the computer.

Celeste smiled at him and made her way to the computer with the newspaper archives. She searched for Leslie Twitchell.

Her case had been covered extensively. More than twenty articles with headlines like "Missing Girl Scout," and "What Happened to Leslie?"

Chester's dad was not named as the last known person to see her. Only that a man living in her neighborhood allegedly purchased a calendar around two o'clock on Friday. The article mentioned that the man and others had not been ruled out as suspects. There was no mention at all of 506 Fulton Road or of Nadine.

Later articles printed on the anniversaries of Leslie's disappearance were less neutral. One stated that police looked heavily at Granger Sutton, the neighbor who claimed to have bought a calendar from the girl and even arrested him on an unrelated drug charge. Again, no reference anywhere to Nadine.

The same two photos of the little girl accompanied nearly every article. One appeared to be a school picture. Dark hair on her narrow shoulders, big brown eyes and a little gap between her two front teeth. The other was a picture of the little girl standing next to a lopsided sandcastle on the Lake Michigan shoreline.

Celeste next searched for Nadine and found only one article. An obituary: *Nadine Miller died unexpectedly Tuesday at her home in Frankfort. She is survived by her brother, Barry; her father, Lawrence; her estranged husband, Edward; and her daughter, Louanne.*

Nothing else.

Celeste returned to the search bar and typed in "Alvin Kready." To her relief, several articles popped up, the most recent of which was dated two years prior. The first article mentioned Alvin's involvement with a large fundraiser for the Holy Trinity Church. The second two were quotes from Kready regarding his affiliation with the Frankfort Elks Lodge.

---

When Celeste arrived at the Elks Lodge, the parking lot was full. A sign near the door read "Spaghetti Dinner and Silent Auction to Support Eugene Ritch in His Fight Against Cancer."

She pushed open the heavy glass door. Rows of long folding tables, covered in red-checked vinyl tablecloths, filled the room. Most of the tables were packed with people eating and talking. Along one wall, crock-pots of spaghetti and baskets of garlic bread covered two more folding tables.

A woman seated at a card table just inside the door beamed up at her. "Here for the benefit dinner?"

"Actually, I'm looking for Alvin Kready. Any chance he's here tonight?"

Celeste did not know if Alvin was still a member of the Elks Lodge, if he even still lived in Frankfort for that matter, but the woman shook her head right away.

"No Alvin tonight. He wanted to be here. I can tell you that much. He and Eugene have been friends for ages, but Alvin busted up his back helping take a dock out last week, and he'll likely be laid up for another few weeks at least."

"OK. Do you happen to have his phone number or an email?"

"Email?" She raised an eyebrow and laughed. "I think Alvin would send a carrier pigeon before he sent an email. Hold on, hon. Let me get ya his number." The woman bent down and hoisted a large leather purse onto the table, rifling through for a phone. She quickly swiped the screen, clicked twice and turned the cell to face Celeste. "There ya go. He doesn't always answer. Half the time forgets to put his hearing aids in, but he'll call you back."

Celeste added the contact information to her own phone, thanked the woman, and left.

As Celeste drove away from the lodge, the lighthouse caught her eye, and she turned toward the beach.

The evening breeze off Lake Michigan had teeth now, sharp with the first hints of October. Celeste thought of Andi's papier mâché pumpkin, half formed on her kitchen table. Soon skeletons and pumpkins would appear on porches. People would plop inflatable monsters in their yards and string purple and orange lights in their trees.

Shoes off, she made her way to the water's edge. Cold sand pressed beneath Celeste's feet, and she watched people walking the long pier that stretched to the lighthouse. Further down the beach, closer to the sprawling mansions, a bonfire flickered, surrounded by people wrapped in blankets.

Celeste sat and stared out at the choppy water and considered everything she'd discovered at 506 Fulton.

What did it all mean? The little girl, Leslie, who'd gone to the house to sell cookies and vanished without a trace? Eliza's long-ago abducted brother? Babies dying in the house, the women going insane?

Andi seemed more and more distant each time Celeste visited. Celeste wasn't sure what she'd expected when she agreed to help Andi, but the whole situation seemed to be getting more convoluted and uglier. Andi's experience as a girl was not the only bad thing connected to 506 Fulton. In fact, it was the least of the bad things. And now Celeste was involved. As if she didn't have enough on her plate. A pregnancy, a homicidal husband, panic attacks.

Celeste thought of her mother and wished as she had a thousand times in the past that she could call her, call her in the way other daughters called their mothers and asked for advice or simply went to visit them, lay on the couch while their mom listened and offered a hug.

"What do I do, Mom?" she whispered to the sky. "Walk away? Tell Andi to call a priest?"

She imagined Nettie on the porch at Moon Lake grappling with her own questions, her own struggles as she watched her husband grow more distant and a teenager move into her place. Nettie too had lost her mother. What would Celeste's life have been if her father had never started an affair with a schoolgirl? If he'd never decided her mother was an inconvenience.

Adam had told her he'd cried, was remorseful, ready to take his punishment. But what difference did it make? The damage was done. None of it could bring back her mother or the years of Celeste and Adam against the world because their father was too eaten by guilt to show them any real affection.

"I chose this life," she murmured. "I chose it." And she had. It had become clear to Celeste when she'd died. She'd come into this life seeking growth, and growth had come through pain, loss, betrayal.

Night had fallen when the rain began. It started slowly, with a few drops, and by the time Celeste reached her truck it had become a steady drizzle. Frankfort lay largely deserted as she drove through town.

Celeste intended to drive straight back to Eliza's house, but instead found herself turning down the familiar streets that would take her to 506 Fulton Road.

The house sat dark. Still, Celeste eased to the side of the road and parked. The rain had lessened slightly, and Celeste stepped from her truck and walked toward the house, bypassing the front porch and moving toward the side yard.

She imagined Andi more than a decade before making the same journey, giddy with excitement and fear, her two best friends nearby, the last few precious seconds before her life was forever altered.

Light flickered in the parlor, and Celeste stopped, the sudden urge to leave nearly overpowering her. She thought of how Andi's whole life had seemingly been cursed by gazing through this very window, as if it weren't the woman inside who'd cast the dark spell, but the mere act of witnessing her feverish secret writings.

Forcing her feet to move, Celeste stepped closer and closer to the house. She stood on tiptoe and peered inside.

Andi sat hunched on the floor, her long hair damp and tangled around her face. A dozen half-melted candles twitched from surfaces throughout the room. The walls were scrawled in jagged, messy words that glistened wetly in the flickering light.

For a second, no less, Celeste's brain tried to rationalize what she was seeing as if Andi might have decided to perform the act of writing on the walls to make sense of the night Marco died.

But no, as she stared at the words, her gut told her they were written in blood.

Andi lurched unsteadily to her feet, dipped her finger into a dark jar, and continued her feverish writing, her mouth moving in a whisper Celeste couldn't hear. Her eyes were glassy, her skin pallid and slick with sweat.

The wood panel that covered the wall stood angled against the parlor doors as if it were merely a prop designed to hide the writing beneath.

*It was.*

Celeste blinked, heart hammering, and for a moment the candlelight warped, flickered, *changed.*

The room shimmered before her.

Suddenly, it wasn't Andi in the parlor—but a young woman screaming, soaked in sweat. Her hugely pregnant body heaved on a pile of blankets in the center of the room. The walls were clean, the furniture elegant and crisp. A phonograph played music in the corner, but it did little to muffle the cries. Four other women occupied the room. Three wore white linen aprons and hunched close to the young woman on the makeshift bed. The fourth woman stood in the corner, hand clasping a golden cross attached to a delicate gold chain around her slender throat. She appeared to be praying.

The girl screamed again, her voice echoing through Celeste's bones. The infant crowned, and suddenly through the glass parlor doors, shapes loomed. Men, rain-soaked, red-faced, burst into the room. They carried knives.

A sudden splash of blood.

The world pulsed white.

Then—

Darkness.

The vision snapped back like a rubber band. Celeste gasped and staggered away from the window.

Her breath had grown short, shallow, raspy. Celeste pressed

a hand to her chest and stumbled through the dark yard toward her truck. The rain had picked up. Her vision narrowed, and instead of slowing, she moved faster. Her foot caught a divot in the yard, and she sprawled forward in the wet grass.

The darkness edged in. She couldn't see, couldn't breathe.

A warm hand pressed against her back, not pushing, but soothing, reassuring. She looked up, but no one stood nearby. Celeste was alone in the dark yard, the rain beating down.

"Mom," she whispered, sensing her presence even as the touch on her back faded.

Celeste forced herself to focus on the sensation of the grass, cold and wet beneath her palms. Slowly, she pressed her knees into the muddy ground, pulled her breath deeper still, focusing on the sensation of the grass and now also the mushy earth and the smell of wet leaves and cool rain pummeling her back, soaking her coat and pants.

On her feet, trudging now, that old ache crying out in her hip, she limped to her truck and collapsed inside.

## 36

Andi woke to something sharp poking into her back. For a moment, she thought she was dreaming, but the cold was too real, as were the smells. Wet morning grass and the pungent decay of leaves.

She blinked and stared at the unfamiliar space. Pale blue walls pressed close around her, decorated with decals of cartoon rabbits and puppies. A pink plastic children's table was wedged in the corner, its contents a set of purple teacups, two dolls and a small blue truck. A single pink rain boot lay discarded beneath the table. Light leaked through the plastic window, silver and washed-out, the thin dawn.

Confused, mouth and eyes sticky, she sat up and tried to make sense of the space.

Slowly, horrifyingly, it dawned on her. She was in the playhouse of the children who lived across the street. The house with the German shepherd.

"What's happening?" She murmured the words calmly, but her brain was an inferno of fear and panic. She had to get out of there now before someone found her. They'd think she was insane, maybe call the police. Or worse, they'd let the dog out for his morning pee and he'd discover Andi. No invisible fence would protect her this time.

Her hands and feet prickling from her awkward sleep, she crawled to the little plastic doorway and peered toward the house. It was early morning. Dew sparkled in the grass. A cool mist hovered over the lawn.

Praying that no one stared out their windows at that exact moment, Andi leaped to her feet and sprinted across the lawn, her body tensed for the growl of the German shepherd, the sudden pain as he sprang onto her back. He didn't come. Andi made it across the street, not slowing until she reached the door of her house. She twisted the knob and practically fell across the threshold.

---

Everything in Andi wanted to crawl back into bed and forget she'd woken up in the kids' playhouse. She had no memory of leaving the night before, had fallen into bed feverish, cell phone close in case she needed to call an ambulance in the night. That's how sick she'd felt, but this morning the fever had gone.

Fatigue pulled at her like an undertow, dragging her deeper with each passing hour. In the bathroom mirror, she hardly recognized herself—eyes rimmed red and a crust of dried blood beneath her nose. Another nosebleed.

She looked at her shirt. Clean. Not the shirt she'd gone to bed in. She must have changed it in the night, but had no recollection of doing so.

"Probably right before you wandered off for a tea party across the street," she mumbled, her voice raspy.

The nosebleeds had started after Marco's death. She'd wake with blood pouring from her nose, pooling in her hands, soaking her pillow and bedding. When she'd confided to Gwen that she was afraid she too had been cursed by the woman who killed Marco, Gwen had grown hysterical, crying and shaking her head and telling Andi to stop trying to scare her.

*Gwen is dead.*

It couldn't be true. She'd spoken to her, touched her. But it was true. She'd read her obituary. Gwen, like Marco, was dead.

She brushed her fuzzy teeth and eyeballed her hair. It needed to be washed. Instead, she shoved it into a sloppy bun. As she started from the bathroom, her eye caught on a little glass bowl on the chest that held towels. It was filled with a dark liquid, smudged with red fingerprints. She stared at it, stomach sinking. When she picked it up, her fears were confirmed. Blood. The bowl contained blood. Hers, likely, from the nosebleed. Had she held the bowl beneath her nose? And if so, why had she dipped her fingers in it?

Andi dumped the blood into the toilet, trying not to watch the swirls of red as she flushed it down. She cleaned the bowl in the sink, squirting it with hand soap and scrubbing until no remnant of red remained.

In a pair of baggy jeans and a hooded black sweatshirt, Andi grabbed her backpack and hurried out to her car, groaning when she realized her tank was on empty.

---

Andi had called in sick to school and she felt criminal as she hurried into the middle school where Marcy Kilwin taught music on Thursdays.

Marcy had been one of Gwen's closest friends at the end of their senior year.

Andi found Marcy alone in the music room tuning a violin. "Marcy?"

Marcy looked up and smiled, though her smile faltered as she took in Andi's appearance.

Haggard, unkempt, sloppy. The list clicked through Andi's mind. *Oh, and don't forget unhinged.* This morning, she'd woken up in a child's playhouse.

"Hi, Marcy. Sorry to bug you at school. Do you have a minute?"

Marcy stood and propped the violin back in its case. "Sure, yes. Let's see." She looked at the clock over her desk. "The next group of kids won't be in for twenty minutes. How can I help?"

Andi pulled her hood down. "I wanted to ask you about Gwen."

"Gwen?" Marcy frowned.

"Yes. Umm ... someone told me, well Dante Lombardi told me she died."

Marcy nodded slowly. "She drowned in Lake Michigan."

Andi breathed, her body feeling weirdly light, ungrounded. She walked to a chair, kid-sized, and sank into it.

"Do you have any idea what happened?"

Marcy's mouth turned down. "I can't say for certain, but ... I believe she took her own life."

Andi looked up sharply. "She killed herself."

"That's what people said."

"But why? What was happening in her life before it happened?"

Marcy returned to her seat, crossed her legs and squeezed her hands together. "She'd been dating Dante for a while. I was surprised when that started. But"—she shrugged—"I knew she still had issues from what had happened with Marco, but she never talked about it. And for a while she seemed really happy with Dante. But then they broke up, and she started to get ... weird."

"Weird?"

"Yeah. Like ... out of it. I thought maybe she had started using drugs. She'd forget stuff, where she'd been, that kind of thing. I would see her car parked on Fulton Road by that big old farmhouse. It was vacant then. I heard you're living there now?"

"I am," Andi murmured, Gwen in her mind's eye walking up to her on the back patio. A new and improved Gwen. A Gwen that didn't exist.

Marcy's eyebrows drew together, but she didn't comment on Andi's choice to live in the house. "She was going into the house. I'm sure of it, but when I'd ask her, she'd look at me like I'd lost it. She insisted she hadn't been there. I told her, Gwen, I saw your car with my own two eyes. It had your Radiohead sticker on the bumper. Anyway, she denied it, and I started to distance myself from her because, like I said, I thought she might be doing drugs." Marcy's eyes teared up. "And then she was dead, just ... dead. My mom called and told me. They'd found her on the beach in Frankfort. They thought she fell off the pier at night, but then ... I guess there was a note in her car."

"Do you know what it said?"

Marcy shook her head. "I didn't read it, but do you remember Zach Vickery?"

Andi nodded. "Yeah. He used to ride my bus."

"He's a cop now. He's the one who found her and he saw the note. He said it was strange, but honestly, I can't remember the specifics now—maybe I never even knew them. It confirmed my fear she'd been taking drugs, but later I heard that her autopsy didn't show any drugs or alcohol in her system. About a year after she died, her parents moved away. I don't know where."

---

Andi parked at the Frankfort Police Department and walked inside. She asked the desk sergeant for Zach.

He appeared several minutes later. In school, Zach had

worn his hair bleached blond. He'd been into skateboards and chain wallets, baggy jeans. Now his hair was dark, cropped close to his head, and he wore a police uniform.

"Zach, hi," Andi said, bouncing on the balls of her toes, half expecting Zach not to remember her.

"Oh shoot, Dandy Andi. How are ya? I heard you were back in town."

"You did?"

"Yep. My sister's got a kid in your class, Hunter Williams."

Andi pictured Hunter from the previous day standing on his chair, hands over his ears, yelling he wanted the blue dinosaur that Elijah was playing with.

"Hunter, really. Okay. He's a … good kid," she lied.

Zach raised an eyebrow. "You must have been working in the Detroit schools if you think Hunter's a good kid." He guffawed. "Cute though and got his mom wrapped around his little finger."

"I bet," Andi murmured, though in truth she knew. She'd seen Hunter shout demands at his mother during morning drop-off, and the woman always complied. "I'm sorry to bug you at work, but I wanted to ask about …" She glanced quickly in either direction to make sure no one was listening. "Gwen. I spoke with Marcy Kilwin, and she mentioned you were there the day she died."

Zach nodded slowly. "That's right. You and she were real close back in the day. I remember now before …"

"Marco died. Yeah."

He gestured at the plastic lobby seats. "Have a seat. I'll tell you what I can."

Andi sat, noticing something slightly sticky on the edge of her chair. She wiped it on her pants.

"We got a call into the station about a car parked overnight at the pier. The parking lady had ticketed it and was going to walk away, but then she noticed a couple of things that bugged her. A purse in the passenger seat and a pair of shoes sitting on the ground outside the driver's door."

"Shoes?"

"Yeah. A pair of light blue sandals with beaded straps. Kind of looked like somebody slid them off to walk on the beach or in the water and planned to come back. She took a closer look and saw a little smear of blood near the car door. It spooked her a bit. She called it in. We went out there, and by the time we arrived, a jogger had found her body washed up on the beach."

"She drowned?"

He nodded. "We didn't know that straight away; had to wait for the coroner to confirm, but in the meantime, we searched the car and found the note."

"What did the note say?"

Zach scratched his jaw. Andi could see little nicks where he'd cut himself shaving. "Oh boy, umm ..., let me remember. It wasn't addressed to anyone in particular. I think 'to whom it may concern' or something odd like that. There was this sort of rambling story about seeing a little girl in the mall and walking up to her and holding her hand and that's how easy it was to take a little kid and parents needed to be more aware because at any moment their kid could vanish. It was strange for sure. And then near the end she wrote, *'I'm not myself anymore, and so I'm leaving. I'm afraid if I don't, something bad will happen.'* I can't remember her exact wording, but that was the gist."

A cold sweat had broken out on Andi's body. She saw herself outside the steakhouse, Maverick interrupting her as she attempted to walk Ellie to her car on the promise of kittens.

"So, she's definitely dead. You saw her body?"

He looked at her funny and then nodded. "Yes. She's dead. I went to her funeral. Most everyone who graduated with us did. It was the right thing to do for her family."

Andi drove to the Frankfort Pier and parked. She stepped from her car and stared at the cracked pavement parking lot, imagining Gwen's blue sandals, the strappy ones she'd seen her wearing in the Fulton Road house days before.

What had been going through Gwen's mind when she'd parked in this lot? Had she already written her suicide note? Had she known what she intended to do?

A chill fall wind breezed from the lake. The water was choppy, waves crashing against the rocky pier. For a moment, Andi saw her there, Gwen, walking alone at dusk, singularly focused on ... what? Her own death.

Despite her tiredness, Andi felt clearer than she had in days.

*Because she'd slept in the playhouse.*

The thought popped into her head, and she considered it. Why would sleeping in the playhouse make her less foggy? If anything, the lack of sleep, the strangeness of it all should have left her more disoriented.

And yet it didn't, because 506 Fulton was the reason her mind had started to slip. It was as if something in the house were poison, and the longer she breathed it, the sicker she became.

---

When Andi returned to the house, she resisted the urge to visit the parlor. The previous night's antics had caught up with her, and exhaustion tugged at her eyelids. But no, she was going to pack, finally take everyone's advice and get out of the house on Fulton Road.

In her bedroom, she peeled off the lid of an empty tote and started to fill it with clothes, yanking shirts from hangers and dropping them in barely folded. As she moved, an urgency vibrated through her arms and legs. From the first floor, she heard the tick of the grandfather clock.

"Andi, you've got to see this!"

She jerked her head up at the sound of the voice.

Marco.

It wasn't him. Marco was dead, and yet ...

Andi heard the pound of tennis shoes on the stairs as if someone, a kid, were running down them. She stood and bolted into the hall.

What if, like Gwen, Marco could somehow visit the house from the afterlife?

"Andi! Come on."

She caught a glimpse of him, the back of his Michigan Wolverines sweatshirt, tousled dark hair flying as he rounded the bottom of the stairs and ran down the hall.

Common sense was overridden by desperation. To see him, just once.

She ran down the stairs and saw tennis-shoed footprints, muddy and wet-looking. Down the hall and into the kitchen. The basement door stood ajar.

She plunged down after him.

## 37

Celeste curled up on her small sofa, her body heavy with exhaustion. She'd barely slept. The night before had been a blur—returning from Andi's house shaken, on the verge of calling Harris, her finger hovering over his name in her phone. But she hadn't. She couldn't bring herself to summon him again in the middle of the night, not for the second time in as many days.

Still, there'd been one small victory. Outside Andi's house, she hadn't spiraled into a full-blown panic attack. That, in itself, felt like progress. She'd used Doctor Dave's techniques, grounding herself just enough to shift from the edge of collapse to something resembling control.

Driving home, she'd cranked the radio, letting the music carry her. One song after another from her college days poured through the speakers—unexpected and familiar. She sang loud, defiantly, as if shouting the lyrics could keep the fear at bay. As if reclaiming those old anthems could tether her to a version of herself that hadn't yet been cracked open.

As she cooked eggs and spinach and sipped her coffee, her cell phone rang. She didn't recognize the number.

"Hello," she answered.

"This is Alvin," a gruff voice said.

It took her a moment to remember. Alvin Kready.

"Alvin, hi. My name is Celeste Cleary. Chester Sutton told me to give you a call."

"Chester Sutton? He still alive?"

"Yes. He's living at Golden Oaks in Frankfort."

"Huh. All right. Maybe I did hear that a while back. What can I do ya for?"

"I'd like to talk about 506 Fulton Road."

Alvin released a long whistle. "Ain't even finished my first cup of joe, girlie. If I knew that's why you were callin' I'd have started with a glass of whiskey. I'll make ya a deal. You run into Mr. Bagel and get me one of them onion donuts with the herb cream cheese and I'll tell you everything I know."

Celeste nodded, quickly scooping her eggs and spinach into a plastic Tupperware. "I can do that. I'll need about an hour. I live in Traverse City."

"Golly gosh. That's a drive, huh? You sure it's worth it to ya?"

"It is. Just tell me your address."

---

Celeste stepped onto the creaky wooden porch of the old Victorian-turned-triplex, the bagel bag crinkling in her hand. The morning hung overcast, cool enough to make her grateful she'd grabbed her jacket. A wind chime tinkled above her, clanging softly against the chipped white paint of the eaves.

She knocked on the door marked 1A.

A muffled voice called out, "It's open!"

Celeste pushed it inward and was met with the smell of coffee and dust. The living room was dim, despite the tall windows. Heavy curtains hung halfway shut, filtering the morning light.

An elderly man sat in a battered recliner near a dark fireplace, a heating pad looped behind his lower back and a paperback resting on his chest.

"Alvin?" she asked.

"You're lookin' at him."

Celeste handed him the bag with the bagel and sat on a small green sofa.

"You get one for yourself?" he asked, pulling out his bagel and arranging it on a napkin on his armchair. "These babies are better than drugs."

"I bought one for later," Celeste told him.

"Good girl." He slathered his bagel with cream cheese and took an enormous bite, closing his eyes. "Oh boy, that is good," he mumbled as he chewed.

After he finished, he stared at her across the room, expression curious. "Why are you asking about 506 Fulton. Don't tell me we've got another demon on the loose over there."

"A demon?"

He took another bite, chewed and swallowed. "Don't know what else you'd call it."

"I'm helping the girl who lives in the house. She's ... experiencing things."

"I bet she is," he muttered. "I told Robert he needed to burn that house to the ground. Think he listened? Course not."

"Who's Robert?"

"He's the one who needed that place exorcised back in the sixties."

"Can you tell me what happened?"

"Sure, I can, but let's begin with a bit of backstory. For starters, I'm not your usual exorcist. I was not a God-fearing man in my youth. If anything, I constantly looked for him and came up empty. But then beggars can't be choosers, as they say. I found God in the fifties when I nearly died and got really close to the devil and lived to tell. That's when I changed my life around, went into the church and eventually started helping people get the evil out of their houses. It's not the usual path to performing exorcisms, and there are plenty of priests who'd say I'm not the real deal, but I've performed more than a hundred exorcisms."

"And you did one at 506 Fulton?"

He held up four fingers.

"Four?"

"Who originally asked you to perform an exorcism there?"

"Believe it or not, Father Dixon originally contacted me."

"Father Dixon?"

"If you've been lookin' into 506 Fulton, you've likely heard of him. Way back in the early 1900s he was here in Frankfort and invited Georgina Atwater back to his rectory to become a sister, a nun."

"The priest who got her pregnant?"

"No. But that's what the Frankfort rumor mill would have you believe. He told it to me straight. Georgina had come to him desperate for help. She'd invited a demon into the house."

Celeste tried to keep the skepticism from her face.

He closed his paperback and returned it to the table. "By the time Father Dixon reached out to me he was conflicted, tortured even over what had gone down in the Fulton house. And the whole sordid tale had occurred more than fifty years before. So, I sat back and listened. I'm good at that." Alvin leaned back and folded his arms across his stomach as if to show what he'd done all those years ago. "The priest said back in 1910, he visited Frankfort and filled in for a Catholic priest on sabbatical for a month. Not a bad gig considering it was summer and his usual parish was further inland. One morning, this teenage girl hung around after the service. Her family had already left for the Communion breakfast. She told the priest she needed help, and it took him the better part of an hour to drag it out of her. Finally, she confessed that she'd brought a demon into their house."

Celeste's brow furrowed. She felt the reflexive rise of her old life—the rational, clinical mind, her years in a lab coat. A quantifiable, measurable, predictable world.

"A fiend, a devil, a Beelzebub, an evil entity," he went on. "Take your pick. The priest internally dismissed her claims. He felt sure the girl was afflicted by not enough God, so he told her to start coming to mass every day, and she did. He kept an eye on her and noticed in late summer she started to decline. She put on weight, developed dark circles beneath her eyes, and looked a bit run-down. He decided to pay a visit to the Atwater family.

"He went over to 506 Fulton Road, and from the outside everything appeared peachy. Late summer flowers blooming in the window boxes, Mary and Fred Atwater sitting out front drinking lemonade. Two other daughters reading their Bibles on the porch swing. Picture perfect. And he said he got a little"—Alvin brushed his fingers along his collarbone—"tickle along here. Not scared, just a tad uneasy. But he's the arm of God and he's not afraid of a tickle. He greeted the family and asked about the girl, Georgina. She's inside, the mother said and offered to go get her, but Father Dixon asked if he could go into the house to speak with her. The mother agreed, and the whole family traipsed into the parlor, where Georgina sat alone at her father's desk.

"She wrote letters for her father with this ink and quill. She had the best handwriting in the family, so she wrote her father's correspondence, and he'd sign the letters. Anyway, Father Dixon spoke with her, but she appeared to be quite distant.

"By this point, Father Dixon started getting an uncomfortable feeling in the house. He couldn't put his finger on it. He used the bathroom and thought he saw something dart behind him. Nothing there. When he returned to the parlor, the doors closed on their own. Just the wind, Georgina's father insisted, which made no sense at all because according to Father Dixon, it was a still summer day and not a breath of wind in the place. Still, Father Dixon wrote off the peculiar events.

"He talked the parents into letting Georgina return to his parish with him to begin potentially training as a nun. She didn't resist. She had a sort of flat affect. He didn't describe her that way, but it's what I gathered. I think he said emotionless, numb. In late August, Georgina joined the group of sisters in his parish and began her religious life, the postulancy it's called.

"For the first weeks at the monastery, Georgina showed signs of improvement. She rose early, learned the morning prayers, and took her meals in the company of Sister Agnes. Yet there remained an unquietness in her. When she gazed at the crucifix above the rectory hearth, her mouth would tremble and she'd often cry.

"By the third week, her pallor grew worse. Father Dixon observed her retching behind the stables, her shoulders convulsing. Soon everyone could see she was with child and she'd have to leave the monastery for a home for unwed mothers. The priest tried to ask her about the father, and she became violent, hysterical. She insisted the demon in the Fulton Road house impregnated her. The night before her scheduled transport to a maternity home, Georgina fled.

"That's when rumors flew that Georgina had fallen pregnant by the priest. It was all a lie, but it caught on as any good scandal does. Father Dixon was not at the Catholic church in Frankfort when Georgina got pregnant. He hadn't even met her yet. Sister Agnes told Father Dixon that Georgina had confided to her that her own father, Fred Atwater, had made her pregnant. He'd been coming into her room for years."

"Her father?" Celeste murmured, stomach churning.

"Unfortunately, yes. Father Dixon went to the Atwater residence, but the parents claimed Georgina was not there. He was unaware that her mother had hidden her in the basement of the house. He attempted to counsel the father about the sexual abuse, and the man became very quiet, and then he marched Father Dixon from the house and threatened him. Father Dixon didn't tell me what he said, but I suspect it was pretty nasty. Father Dixon returned to the rectory and prayed. He heard nothing from the Atwaters and thought perhaps Georgina had made her way to a safe place, had given birth and found the help she needed.

"He learned soon enough that was not the case. Georgina's mother, Mary, appeared at the rectory one early morning. She looked haggard, had set out by horse and carriage in the middle of the night. The Atwaters were one of the few Frankfort families in that day who owned an automobile, but Mary Atwater was not permitted to drive it.

"She told him Georgina's baby had died and Georgina had gone mad and been sent away. He'd later learn in a confession, from one of Fred Atwater's hunting party, no less, that Georgina, the baby and a midwife had been violently slain. But at the time, Mary Atwater withheld this information. She told Father Dixon that something terrible was happening in the house—blood dripping from the walls and the most awful screams that sounded like Georgina, but of course Georgina had been shipped off to a sanatorium, again a lie, but one he wasn't aware of.

"Mary also said her husband had begun to ... act strangely. And children were going missing in Frankfort, babies. And one man said Fred Atwater had taken a child right out of a pram and spirited it away. The police, reluctant due to the family's strong standing in the town, searched the house but found no trace of the baby. But Mary Atwater confided to Father Dixon she'd heard a baby crying. Mary Atwater begged for help, and Father Dixon returned to the house and began an exploration to see if an exorcism would be appropriate. Eventually he determined it was.

The exorcism took place, but Father Dixon called it a strange incident. As he'd noted before, the house stood weirdly quiet and utterly still. At one point, the wind began to blow outside, yet the structure never creaked. Father Dixon glanced toward a window where a rose bush scratched the glass, but no sound reached the parlor. He doubted he had driven the demon out—and his doubt proved correct. Six months later he returned. Two more children had vanished from town, older ones this time, and Mary Atwater admitted she feared her husband had taken them and killed them. Fred Atwater believed a midwife had slipped away with Georgina's baby, that the child was evil and he needed to destroy it."

**38**

———————

"Father Dixon thought back to what Georgina had told him about drawing a demon into the house," Alvin continued. "He started to suspect she'd actually done it and after several more conversations with Sister Agnes, the young nun admitted Georgina had confided that she'd called for a dark lord to protect her from her father. She told Sister Agnes that God had not stopped him, so perhaps the devil would.

"He was quite guilt-ridden for not having listened to her in the beginning. Not only had he ignored the demonic aspect of her story despite many of the Catholic teachings speaking of such evil, he'd not helped her with the incest and he'd allowed her to leave the rectory, which ultimately ended in the brutal slaying of both Georgina and her infant child.

"By the time I met Father Dixon, he'd done seven exorcisms at 506 Fulton."

"Seven?"

Alvin nodded. "Yes. Three during the Atwaters' time, two more in the forties, and the two most recent in the early sixties. And that's when he found me. He was in his eighties, and he needed to pass the torch, so to speak. No other priests wanted anything to do with the Fulton house. In fact, he implied his preoccupation with the house had stunted his upward mobility in the Church."

"What happened to the Atwaters?"

"I asked that same question. Townsfolk ran 'em out. After the third baby went missing, they attacked Fred in the street. He survived and managed to escape. His wife and daughters fled in the night. No one knows where they went."

"Can you tell me what happened during the exorcisms?"

Alvin nodded. "I tried hard to rule out something fact-based. Lead poisoning, black mold, arsenic left out for rats a hundred years ago that had gotten into the water supply. As I said, I'm not your usual exorcist. I'd heard Father Dixon's story, and I gave it some weight. I did, but I still like to go in and rule out the poison behind the poltergeist, so to speak. It's all muddled up, God and science. The supernatural is just another form of energy we haven't figured out how to measure. So initially I took in test kits for mold, lead, water and soil. By that time, I'd done a few exorcisms and had a few situations where something in nature was to blame.

"I'd helped a family with an alleged possession down in Muskegon. This child was experiencing hallucinations, seizures, and had even attacked his mother quite violently. I found a tin tucked away in the back corner of the basement of this house full of lead paint chips. The child was eating them. I know how this sounds. Why would a kid do such a thing? They do it because there are components in lead paint, specifically lead acetate, that taste sweet. Anyway, the culprit in that case was simple. Not so with the Fulton Road house. I realized pretty quickly that something supernatural had actually taken up residence in the house.

"Father Dixon and I went back with all the usual culprits: holy water, incense, his Bible. He went through the opening prayer, and I moved through the house sprinkling holy water. We did a lot of that in the big room with the double glass doors, a lot of heaviness floating around in there, and also in the basement. Those were the hot spots. Then he called upon God to assist us, and he read passages, and finally he commanded the demon to leave the house."

"And the exorcism didn't work?"

"Apparently not, because Father Dixon called me again a few months later, and things had gotten worse. He said that for maybe a month after, everything calmed down. The sounds at night, the blood on the walls and floor had stopped, and then they started up again. So he and I went on back, and I brought a few other charms with me. Figured we needed the big guns for this house. I'd learned a few new things in my travels. I hung raven's feathers, dipped in honey and grave dirt, in the corners of that big room. Met an exorcist in the Caribbean who turned me onto that one. I also rearranged all the furniture and tried to confuse the evil spirit. Opened the windows and ran through the house screaming the psalms and chasing the energy out with incense. Father Dixon couldn't do it on account of being so frail and getting more exhausted by the day."

"Was the family there for this?"

"Oh yeah, Robert and his wife, Mo. She was the one truly afflicted. She was ... spooky. Don't know how else to say it. She watched every move I made, eyes glued right to me and not nice-lookin' eyes either. She was pregnant then. Had her hands curled right up in her lap. Robert walked with us as we blessed the rooms, but Mo stayed in that room with the double doors.

"The next time I went back, I was uneasy right away because I knew the instant I laid eyes on her that demon was getting to her."

"How did you know?"

"Because she looked like little more than a shell, like that demon had used her up. Eyes as hollow as ash pits where fires used to burn and a body little more than a scarecrow draped in skin. A crying shame too because that woman had been beautiful just months earlier when I visited; of course, even then it had gotten its grip on her."

Celeste saw Andi—face pale, eyes distant. "You said the demon had used her up?"

"Oh yeah. That's what a demon does. It's a parasite, moves in and feeds on the host until there ain't nothing left. Vile as the night is dark. I seen some bad things in prison. Some of them real baddies have got a demon, somethin' that slithers in at night and moves right into their body. Prolly they're prayin' to it for all I know." He rubbed his aged hands on his jeans as if they'd grown sweaty. "Praying to the devil to help them escape or some nonsense. You ever been in Jackson Prison? Razor wire to the clouds, men perched on a tower with a trigger finger so happy a guy dies every other week because one of the snipers has a cold. There ain't no escaping. Do your time. Do your time and don't re-offend. It ain't easy, but it's helluva lot better than goin' back in."

"You were in prison?"

"Four years for B&E. I was young and dumb, full of my own hot air. Probably needed it. Let me tell you, prison either straightens you out or spits you out. I got straight. And found God. That near-death I told you about? Shanked by a guy who thought I stole his sneakers, which I didn't." He shook his head. "God works in mysterious ways, don't he?"

"You had a near-death experience?"

"Yep. Greatest forty minutes of my whole life, or death." He chuckled.

"Did you ... see things? Like an afterlife?"

Alvin grinned. "I saw my mother. And not the one who died either, eaten up by cancer. Nope, this was my mother in her prime. Sheila Kready wearing her favorite yellow sundress and sitting in a field of wildflowers as far as the eye could see. I sat down there beside her and she said, in the way she had of putting it to you, but gentle too, she said, Alvin, 'You're messing it all up. You've strayed from the path, and this is your one chance to get back on it.'

"I woke up in the prison hospital a changed man." He snapped his fingers. "Just like that. I feel bad for the poor souls who live their whole lives never getting to peek at the other side. If we could all go there, for a minute, shit, for a second, we'd have a different world."

Celeste nodded, her own near-death floating at the periphery of her mind. She understood exactly what he meant. If all the beings on the planet could get only a glimpse of what existed beyond the human construct of reality, everything would change in an instant. But the material world had its own kind of power, and the veil that dropped over everyone's eyes when they entered, it was not easy to displace. In the years before her near-death, in many ways, ignorance truly had been bliss.

"I did my first exorcism in prison. Self-taught in the library and listenin' to the old-timers. There was a young guy who'd come in, younger than me, believe it or not, only nineteen and serving life for killing this woman. He told me, and by God, I believed him, that he left his body. That something had gotten inside of him and he was hovering over, watchin' it all happen, horrified, but helpless."

"Don't most murderers say that?"

"Some of 'em do, to be sure, but this guy, Jamie, he was different. Had a real softness in his person. Anyhow, I did the best I could tryin' to exercise that demon out of him."

"Did it work?"

Alvin shrugged. "That's the trouble with this kind of work. It's pretty hard to tell. And a demon is sly; it knows how to hide, to play dead, so to speak. After I got out of prison, I walked the straight and narrow. Met my Wendy, who's gone now. Died in

'87 from heart failure. We had two boys, Grady and Callum. Grady's out in Texas now. Callum's over in Traverse City. Owns a coffee shop. I've got grandkids and the Elks and my books and shows. I'm one of the lucky ones, and I know it."

"Did you ever do any exorcisms in the house after the sixties?"

"Nope."

"Did you know a couple named Conrad and Vivian moved into the house in the nineties?"

"Oh yeah, I was aware of them. And I drove right over there when they bought that house and tried to warn 'em off. I told Vivian, this house ain't right. There're ten other houses in town, and they should sell the one on Fulton and buy a different one. She looked at me like I had a screw loose. So I tried again, spoke to Conrad. My first thought when I met him was this is a guy who probably irons his underwear. Still, I told him that we'd done exorcisms in the house, multiple, and that some very dark, nasty things had gone on there. You know what he said? He said, 'Sir, if you don't leave my property immediately, I'm calling the authorities.'" Alvin shrugged. "And so I did."

"Are you aware that Vivian went missing?"

Alvin took a bite of his bagel. He nodded. "Oh yeah. And I heard there'd been some kind of violent altercation with her too. I tried to track her down with no luck. That house got real dark. Never saw any lights on. I asked around, and nobody knew. She'd just up and vanished. I went over there once and kind of picked around, and while I was out back behind the house peeking in the kitchen, I got this"— he shuddered—"this feeling like something wanted me to come inside. I ran back to my truck. I'm dead serious. I ran like somebody had set my pants on fire. I never did another exorcism again.

"Being in that house, seeing how things can slither in and get ahold of you, that changed me, too. Made me real careful about the purity of my soul. Not in the religious sense, the virgin bride and that nonsense, but in my thoughts and feelings. You know that saying 'the crack is where the light gets in?' Well, it's where the darkness gets in too. Thinkin' ill of others, worse yet, thinkin' ill of your own self. Black moods, depression they call it now, fear, grief, greed, desperation. It's all an invitation of sorts, an open door for something to walk on through."

Celeste considered Andi, who'd moved into the house during a time when her life was falling apart, when everything had cracked and broken open.

"Where do you think it came from? The demon?"

"Where do such things come from? If someone could give us an answer, could we even grasp it? Do we understand where we ourselves come from? No matter how much we learn, it's like pulling on a thread that never ends. You can trace a flower back to its seed, to the cells, to the atoms—and there's always another layer underneath.

"Still, I'll share my theory with you. It came from a twisted heart so desperate, so unmoored that the person's soul called out to some ancient black place that we forgot eons ago; perhaps we forgot it long before we even existed on two legs, walking upright, fumbling to make tools and wheels. There are other worlds parallel to our own, layers perhaps and in some of those layers dwell beings who are so dark and evil and low they cannot be called upon, unless someone descends into the horror, unless their soul becomes so despondent they develop the grumble of that place and then they can reach there and draw something back. The girl, Georgina, I think she touched that place.

"There's an interesting conundrum with children in the case of evil supernatural entities. The demon is drawn to a child far more than to an adult. In some ways it is easier for the child to call out to them. They are closer to the other realms, the worlds we slipped through when we came to this one. Now if you can get the right kind of child, the child who's been molded by the parent into compliance, into politeness, the good girl is the perfect target because they struggle to say no; they override their internal warning system in lieu of behaving in the manner that's expected of them. According to what the priest found out about Georgina's childhood, she was that compliant child, the good girl. A good girl being horrifically abused. She was desperate for help and too young and naive to imagine what she might unleash if she invited it in."

Celeste's eyes drifted down to the friendship bracelet Andi had given her. Andi, like Georgina, possessed a naivete, an openness. Had it been that part of her that something lured to the house all those years ago on Devil's Night? Andi believed it had been mere chance that she, Marco and Gwen had targeted 506 Fulton, but perhaps it was by design.

"Evil is insidious, you know?" Alvin continued. "Uncontainable. It's not housed in a single person, even a single house, for that matter. Energy doesn't work that way. It needs to move. And it does. Don't go telling yourself that the woman living in that house is the only one affected by it. There are others. Spend enough time there and you'll count yourself among them."

Celeste rubbed her eyes. Tiredness had begun its work. "There's a young woman living there now who seems to be ... losing her mind."

"It's gotten to her then?"

"I don't know. I keep searching for, well, to use your example, the fact-based answer."

Alvin shrugged. "There isn't one. Not in that house."

"So how do I help her?"

"Find what the priest couldn't. The way Georgina called the demon in and bound it to the house."

Celeste thought of Simon Kent. He had disappeared in 1965. During the time Alvin and Father Dixon had been working with the family in the house.

"Robert and Mo? What happened to them?"

"Robert died. Fell down the stairs in the house. Mo had some serious problems too. I believe she lost a baby, maybe more than one."

"Robert and Mo what? Do you remember their last names?"

"Sinclair."

Celeste frowned. "Wait, was Mo a nickname?"

"Yep. Legal name was Maureen. Robert and Maureen Sinclair."

## 39

Andi stared at her in the darkness, Gwen at the foot of her bed. Moonlight caused her skin to glow, her eyes to look as bright and shiny as the stones they'd plucked from the water on the Lake Michigan shoreline, brilliant beneath the surface, dull and dead once they'd dried.

"Gwen...," she breathed.

Gwen walked to the opposite side of the bed and slid beneath the covers. She smiled, and her teeth glowed too, appeared strange, perfect. Gwen had had a slight gap between her front teeth. This Gwen did not, and her teeth also seemed... pointed.

*The better to eat you with.* Andi thought of how she'd read "Little Red Riding Hood" to her class of first graders in Ann Arbor the year before.

"Remember how we used to have sleepovers?" Gwen murmured, lying on her side, face inches from Andi's, her long dark hair cascading over the pillow.

Andi, too scared to speak, nodded.

"We'd watch *Beauty and the Beast* and eat popcorn, and your sister would usually come in and make fun of the movie, and you and she would fight." Gwen's smile grew bigger. "I always wanted a sister, always. And then you became like my sister, didn't you? We were that close?"

The question hung between them. Andi parted her lips, croaked something like "yes."

A shadow moved across Gwen's face—anger and then sadness. "And then we weren't. We came here and everything changed."

"Gwen," Andi whispered. "Everyone is saying you're dead."

Gwen smiled, those pointed teeth again, her lips red, bright, blood red. "People lie, you know."

"They do," Andi agreed. Like Luke. He'd lied about his relationship with Lisa, the girl from work. He'd lied even after Andi saw the text messages between them.

Andi's eyes moved to her half-packed tote, a T-shirt draped over the edge. She'd been packing earlier and then ...

"You have a choice now, Andi."

Andi blinked, shifting her attention back to Gwen. She'd begun to drift.

"You can resist what's happening, or you can seize the power in this house. It's here for you."

Andi, dozing now, wondering why Gwen hadn't left, nodded, but let her eyes slip closed.

"If you resist, you'll die. And that's okay. We all die, don't we? But if you take it, if you open yourself, you can have whatever you want."

***

Andi sat at the kitchen table, hands sunk into a bowl of gluey newspaper as she attempted to form the head. The previous night's dream tugged on her brain, stretching and warping, causing the latest headache to pulse near her temples and behind her eyes.

She'd woken to a pillow soaked in blood—another nose-bleed—and she meant to finish packing, to rent a hotel room, to drive far away. Instead, she'd sat at the kitchen table and returned to her papier mâché to form not a pumpkin, but a baby.

Andi tilted the head and pressed both her thumbs into the soft shape to form eyes.

Her cell phone rang—Torrie. She ignored it. Not two minutes later, her mom called and then texted. Andi glanced at the words as they appeared.

Mom: *Please call me back, Andi. We're all worried.*

Andi's mouth grew dry, and she wanted a drink, but didn't want to wash her hands until she'd completed the baby's face. Her tongue stuck to the roof of her mouth and finally she gave up, standing and turning on the faucet with her elbow, feeling the cool water run over her hands. She leaned down and drank directly from the faucet. The water was slightly metallic, but satisfying. She gulped until she'd soaked the front of her Michigan Theater T-shirt.

Scratching behind the basement door. He looked up, stared at it. The knob twisted, and the door cracked. Two eyes peered out at her, Gwen's eyes, sharp teeth as she smiled.

"Knock knock," she whispered.

A sudden sharp knock came from the front of the house. Andi twisted around, peered down the hall.

The knock came a second time, louder.

The basement door was closed once more.

Andi opened the front door to find Dante, mouth grim, forehead creased.

"Look, I'm not going to presume what's going on. I'm here to say I'm sorry for the way I reacted the other day when you asked about Gwen. I don't know what's happening and frankly, it scared me, what you said."

Andi nodded. "It scared me too."

"You meant it? That you've been talking to Gwen in this house?"

Andi wanted to lie, to say of course not. Gwen was dead. How preposterous. Instead, she mumbled, "Yes."

"Do you think you might be ... imagining it?"

"Aka going insane?"

"No." He shook his head. "I was lying in bed thinking about it last night. Maybe there's like ... something toxic in this house, you know? A carbon monoxide leak or something really crazy like arsenic-infused wallpaper. That was a thing back in the day. I saw it on the History Channel."

Andi wrinkled her forehead. "Arsenic-infused wallpaper?"

"Gwen was visiting this house a lot before she ... took her life," he said. "We were seeing each other. It was a weird time in both our lives, I guess. I'd come back from school feeling like I'd failed at life. Gwen was struggling too." He smoothed his palms on his pants as if his hands had begun to sweat. "She was in a dark place. That's how we reconnected, really. She came into the bakery one night. There'd been a terrible storm, and she'd gotten caught in it, was soaking wet and a little delirious. She kept talking about Marco and that night on Fulton Road and how she drove by the house all the time and sometimes she saw faces in the windows. I ended up closing early. We talked for hours. I don't think I'd ever understood how Marco's death affected her, affected you both, really.

"I have this idea that something about what happened that night, the age the three of you were, I mean, maybe I'm grasping at straws here. I'm not a head doctor, but I think it was some kind of perfect storm and it messed you all up. Marco died of a burst appendix, but it felt bigger than that and like imprinted itself on your and Gwen's psyches. Both of you became obsessed with this house and what happened to Marco."

"I'm obsessed?" Andi stared at him, incredulous. "You dated

Gwen, Dante. You kissed me the other night. Claim you're not stuck on what happened with Marco, but why the interest in Gwen then? And me? Huh. You showed up here with that fucking picnic basket. You came here today for Christ's sake. You know it wasn't a burst appendix. Some part of you knows!"

Dante's face paled. "You need to move out of this house, Andi. Do you not see that? Find an apartment, rent a hotel room, shoot, come stay with me until you figure it out."

From the kitchen, Andi heard the basement door creak open once more. She imagined her half-packed tote, her decision the day before to leave. It was a logical choice. How many times had she heard it from Torrie?

But now, deep in her gut, the thought made her furious. She wanted to scream, wanted to attack Dante and claw his pretty blue eyes out, wanted to grab a knife from the kitchen and stab him in the neck and watch his blood spurt onto the wood floor.

"Andi?"

She jumped. For an instant the gruesome vision had been so real, as real as him in the room now, as real as Gwen.

"I'll think about it," she lied. It was the only answer, the right answer to get Dante to leave.

"Promise?"

She nodded. "I have to get changed now. I have a school thing tonight."

Andi didn't have a school thing. The principal had called her that morning. She was no longer needed in the kindergarten class. No explanation, but Andi knew Maverick had told Ginnie and Ginnie had told the principal that Andi had walked out of a restaurant with a little girl, was trying to lure that child to her car.

Andi closed the door behind Dante, walked down the hall and slipped into the basement.

## 40

Celeste knocked on Andi's door. She intended to ask Maureen about Simon, but first wanted to check on Andi. Seconds passed, a minute. She peered through the glass near the door, but saw no movement inside.

The memory of Andi hunched at the wall in the parlor writing in blood caused her heart to beat faster. What if Celeste had left and Andi had hurt herself? What if she'd hurt someone else?

When she tried the knob, Celeste found the door unlocked and pushed it open.

"Andi?" she called.

Quiet in the house except for the steady tick of the grandfather clock.

As she reached for the glass-inlaid parlor door, Celeste froze. A woman stared back at her. A woman with shiny yellow skin and frantic eyes and a gash across her throat that had gone purple and black.

Celeste took a startled step back, but already the woman had faded to nothing. Hand shaking Celeste reached again for the door handle. It released a groan, almost human-sounding, as she twisted it and swung it open.

The parlor was dim, the curtains pulled mostly shut, stripes of pale daylight cutting the wood floor.

Andi lay stretched out on the velvet sofa. Hair unwashed, eyes glassy as she chewed the cuticle on her thumb.

Celeste pulled a chair close to her, pushed an oily lock of hair off her forehead and forced a smile. She didn't want Andi to recognize the alarm in her face, but her whole body vibrated with it.

"Andi?"

Andi's eyes didn't shift to hers.

"Are you feeling sick?"

A tiny bead of blood bloomed on Andi's thumb where she chewed it.

"Andi, if you don't talk to me, I'm going to call an ambulance."

Across the room, the parlor doors slowly creaked closed. Celeste glanced back at them, wondered briefly if they'd also locked.

Celeste touched Andi's forehead. The young woman's skin was warm to the touch, but not alarming. Andi's eyes drifted shut, and her breath deepened.

Doing her best not to make it obvious, Celeste stood and walked to the paneled wall. She ran her fingers along the edge and felt it give. When she knelt and examined a bottom corner, she spotted a strip of Velcro. The panel was being held to the wall with Velcro. The faint scent of copper clung to the air. Celeste's stomach rolled, and she breathed through her mouth.

A prickling sensation crawled up her spine, and she turned to see Andi watching her.

Celeste's heart kicked. Without moving her head, she let her gaze slide sideways, just enough to catch Andi in her periphery.

Andi stared at her.

Not drowsy, not unfocused, but with intent.

Celeste's pulse hammered in her throat. She was certain this wasn't Andi looking at her. Not really. The story of Leslie Twitchell walking into the house and never reemerging, of Nadine committing a violent suicide, of Georgina and her infant stabbed to death in the very room Celeste now occupied exploded in Celeste's brain.

For a long moment she stayed frozen, staring at the seam in the wood, refusing to turn. It felt like if she acknowledged Andi, no not Andi, but whatever occupied her, something terrible might happen.

Finally, she swallowed and made herself look directly at Andi.

The instant their eyes met, Andi's gaze dropped. Her eyelids drooped, and her body slackened back into the couch.

Celeste stood and backed away from the wall, fear ratcheting up her heart rate.

"Andi," Celeste said, returning again to the chair, "I think you need to see a doctor." Celeste spoke the words, but knew they weren't true. A medical doctor could not fix what ailed Andi.

Andi nodded. "Maybe. I just need to sleep for a little while."

"OK. I'm going to walk down the road and have a talk with someone I met the other day. I'll stop back in to check on you."

Celeste cast Andi a final glance, then hurried from the house.

Maureen did not sit on her porch. The cooler temperatures had likely driven her inside.

Celeste knocked on her door. The windows on either side of the door were clouded with grime and impossible to peer through.

When she pulled open the door, a draft of sour-smelling air hit Celeste in the face. She struggled to conceal her repulsion.

"Yes?" The woman stood in the dark hall. Her sightless eyes aimed toward the space to the left of Celeste.

"Hi, Maureen. It's Celeste. We spoke the other day."

Maureen leaned forward, head slightly tilted. Her nostrils flared as if she were sniffing Celeste.

Gooseflesh prickled down Celeste's spine, and she took a step away.

The woman was blind. Perhaps it wasn't all that unusual, and yet it gave Celeste a sick feeling.

Maureen nodded slowly. "Oh yes. Come in. I'd like some tea, but my girl didn't show up today. Maybe you can fix me a cup?"

Celeste did not want to step foot inside Maureen's house. Her stomach clenched, and her mouth began to water. Excuses piled up in her brain, but she needed to talk to this woman, and how could she deny making her a cup of tea? "OK, sure."

Celeste stepped inside. The foul smell of mildew and something rotten coiled in the house. With Maureen facing away, heading down the dark hall, Celeste pulled her shirt over her nose.

As Celeste moved into the kitchen, she recoiled. Dishes piled a foot high in the sink, crusted with layers of blackened food. A colony of flies buzzed near a bloated garbage bin.

Maureen's breath sounded wet, phlegmy as she lumbered to the kitchen table and felt along the back of a chair. She sat down heavily, and the spindly legs of the chair groaned beneath her.

Maureen's face was turned toward Celeste. Her white hair hung in stringy clumps, and her nightgown was stained brown in places that once might've been blue. A fly landed on Maureen's cheek and crawled toward one puckered, sightless eye.

Celeste swallowed back the bile rising in her throat. She forced her eyes away from the woman and searched for the teapot. It sat on the stove next to a frying pan coated with a congealed substance alive with bugs.

She was going to be sick.

No, she could do this.

She stared only at the kettle, grabbed it and stuffed it beneath the faucet, filling it halfway with water.

"Maureen, where do you keep your tea?" Celeste asked after she turned the burner to high.

"In the cookie jar. The one shaped like a rooster." Maureen gestured at the counter.

Celeste spotted the rooster, kept her eyes carefully averted from the spilled food, the bowl of peaches green with mold and buzzing with fruit flies. She plucked off the rooster's head. "Umm ..." Celeste forced her eyes to see the contents, to refuse her stomach's desire to eject her breakfast. She picked through the tea bags. "Let's see chamomile, peppermint or green."

"Peppermint."

"Cups?" Celeste asked, plucking a peppermint tea and tearing open the package. She could have opened the cupboards herself and found the mugs, but didn't want to risk opening a food cupboard.

"Above the sink."

Celeste took down a pink and white polka-dot mug. It was chipped, and when she tried to choose a different one, she saw that every cup in the cupboard had cracks or bits of ceramic broken off the rims or handles. She stuck with the pink one.

"Maureen, I wanted to ask you about 506 Fulton again. I heard you used to live there."

"I was twelve," Maureen said, one hand trailing along the table. Her fingers landed in a puddle of something dark and sticky-looking. She didn't seem to notice. "And I wanted to see the baby."

41
---

Celeste's skin prickled. "I don't understand. You were twelve when you moved into the house?"

Maureen looked annoyed at the question. "I was twelve, and a woman named Nadine lived in the house. And she'd had a baby. My family lived on Monroe Street. I walked over one Saturday and knocked on the door and asked Nadine if I could see her baby. I loved babies. Nadine took me to the parlor. The baby slept in her pram in the parlor after their morning walk. The most beautiful pram, but years later I saw one just like it in that movie *Rosemary's Baby*. Did you watch that movie?"

Celeste had seen it. She'd watched it in college with two of her girlfriends on Halloween. The memory of the baby's two glowing yellow reptilian eyes played across her mind.

"That poor lady died, you know. And so did that beautiful little baby." Maureen's cracked lips thinned into a frown.

On the stove, the kettle began to screech, causing Celeste to jump. She spun and clicked the burner off, wincing at the hot handle as she lifted the kettle and filled Maureen's cup. The smell of the peppermint offered relief from the intruding funk. Celeste grabbed another mug and made tea for herself as well.

"Here you go, Maureen." She slid the woman's cup in front of her. Then she held her own tea, the mug hot, in her palms and kept it close to her face, inhaling the peppermint steam.

"When did you decide to move into the house?"

Maureen picked up her tea and sipped it delicately. "My grandpa used to carry peppermints in his pocket, you know. But then he got hit by a train, and my mother and brother were with him. My brother said peppermint candies were flung all over the gravel, splattered with blood. My brother never ate them again. But not me. I wasn't there. Peppermint is still my favorite. Peppermint tea, ice cream, candies."

"It is good," Celeste agreed, disturbed by the story and having no intention of drinking out of anything in Maureen's house. "When did you say you moved into the house?" Celeste tried again.

"When it called me."

An involuntary shudder rippled through Celeste, and she spilled a drop of burning tea on her hand.

"It called you? What does that mean?"

"I was special. I knew that when I started dreaming of that house. The rooms filled with the sounds of babies. Laughing and crying and gurgling little babies." She laughed. "Babies are a gift. The most precious, the most valuable of all gifts. But most women, and the men especially, take that for granted. As if anyone at all should be allowed to have babies." Maureen shook her head. "People think so, but it isn't true. There are forces at work. Deciders of such things. She giveth, and she taketh.

"I told Robert I wanted that house, and so he bought it. A nightmare of a man, more interested in nights out with the boys than his own wife, than in keeping up his yard, tending to my chickens. My rooster, Zany, hated him. He'd run right across the yard and sink his talons into Robert's leg." She chuckled. "Zany knew, and the house knew too. We all knew."

Celeste inhaled another breath of tea. "Knew what?"

"That he had to go away."

"And so he did. Fell right down the stairs in that house."

"He fell down the stairs and died?"

"Oh yes. And you know, my sister had told me he would die. The house shows you things," Maureen murmured. "My sister used to visit me there, she and her three sweet little babies, all blue-eyed and blond curls. The most beautiful little babies you've ever seen. And they behaved like perfect angels, never made a peep. My sister would talk about her perfect life and her perfect husband."

Maureen adjusted in her chair, releasing a little moan. "The strange thing is my sister was dead. She died at sixteen. She and a group of friends driving too fast out in Mesick, wrapped their little car around a tree. Michelle got ejected, wasn't wearing her seat belt. None of 'em were apparently. She and her best friend both died. The driver lived, but he had stuff wrong in his head after. But what I'm telling you is she'd come and sit with me, and she was as real as this table." Maureen rapped her knuckles against the table, sending the dishes clinking together.

The sound grated on Celeste, but she forced herself to stay put, to focus on the woman's story even if every fiber of her being wanted to leave.

"I could touch her. Sometimes I believed the house showed me another dimension, another reality. Other times I believed it tried to trick me, though I can't say why. What was the point of showin' me my sister and this life she never lived, at least one I got to see?"

Celeste's hands shook as she pulled the framed photograph

of Simon from her purse. She couldn't show Maureen the photo, wasn't sure why she'd brought it at all.

"Maureen, do you remember a little boy who went missing from a house just outside of Frankfort in Honor many years ago? He vanished in 1965."

Maureen's white eyes fixed on her. "Simple Simon met a pieman, going to the fair." She sang the nursery rhyme in a high voice.

*Simon*. Maureen had said his name.

"Yes," Celeste breathed. A fruit fly buzzed near her ear, and she brushed it away. "Simon Kent. Do you remember him? He was five years old."

"He was not mine to remember."

"What does that mean?"

"He belonged to her."

Celeste's legs weakened with Maureen's words, and she felt one knee jitter. She edged back away from the woman.

"Her?"

"Oh, I called it *her*. Mostly she felt like a woman, but not always. She came to me as a man too, as a handsome suitor. From the corners of my eyes, I could glimpse his true form, a massive, black shadow, oily and changing. I saw her as a serpent, as a child with black eyes, as a man with heavy boots who stank of tobacco and whiskey. She had many forms."

"And this was someone in the house?"

"Something in the house and the house itself and maybe even the land beneath the house. Massive, endless. I grew up in the church, but I learned early that either the church doesn't know or the church doesn't want us to know what can only be seen from the corner of the eye."

"And this thing took Simon?"

"I had a dream one night ..." Maureen moved her hands to a crucifix she wore around her neck.

The cross looked wrong, and Celeste realized it hung upside down.

"I was a hunter," Maureen continued. "A predator, a wolf staring into a field of sheep, scanning, searching for the vulnerable target, the one slightly different, alone, left behind. I drove for days, burning through fuel, passing neighborhoods, schoolyards, parks. And then there he stood. I knew instantly by the shabby curtains and the discarded toys in the yard that no one watched most of the time and for every hour he played outside a caregiver, most likely a disinterested older sibling or a babysitter, would set eyes on him for five seconds and then they'd go back to what they were doing. He had this little wooden ball painted with the face of a clown, and he tossed it up again and again."

Her description of Simon as neglected, forgotten infuriated Celeste. She imagined the wall of Eliza's photos. The little brother she had loved snatched away in the middle of an ordinary day.

"He had the skinny look of a child who rarely got treats, who probably ate a lot of noodles and cans of soup. Cheap bread, no butter, nothing substantial to put meat on his bones, but I didn't mind. It wasn't meat I was after. I pulled to the curb and rolled down my window. I held up a tube of SweeTarts. I had a whole basket of candy, but somehow I knew he'd want the SweeTarts. I told him if he'd hop in and show me the way to the post office, I'd drive him right back home and he could have the candy."

"What happened after that?" Celeste tied to keep her voice measured. Maureen had called it a dream, but in her gut, Celeste felt certain the woman described how she'd abducted Simon Kent.

"After that nothing. And everything. I woke up, and she gave me what I had been yearning for."

"What did she give you?"

"Babies. Four." She held up four gnarled fingers. "But I kept only two. Keep one, kill one."

"You killed your babies?"

"Of course not."

"But you just said—"

"They weren't mine. They belonged to... her."

## 42

Maureen had all but admitted it. She'd abducted Simon. The revelation made Celeste sick to her stomach, furious. Some part of her wanted to fling her cup of hot tea into the woman's face.

"Maureen, do you have any idea what happened to Simon? Did you have any dreams about ... him dying?" Because he had died. Celeste was sure of it. And he'd died at 506 Fulton Road.

"Death is merely a bridge from this world to the next. We're all going to walk it."

"Did you kill Simon, Maureen?"

Maureen took another sip of tea. Some of it dripped down her puckered chin. She leaned forward again, nostrils flaring as if she again were smelling Celeste. Then she tilted her head as if listening. Celeste strained to hear whatever sound Maureen might have heard, but she caught only the steady hum of flies, an occasional drip from the faucet.

"You're having a baby," Maureen murmured. "How lovely."

Celeste jerked back, spilling tea down the front of her white shirt. "How do you know that?"

Maureen reached a single curled hand to her ear. "She told me."

Celeste blinked at her, disgusted, scared. As she turned to leave the kitchen, something caught her eye: a check pinned to Maureen's refrigerator with a magnet. It was made out to Sinclair Properties, LLC. In the top left corner: Andi's name. Her signature scrawled along the bottom. On the memo line, one word: *Rent.*

Celeste looked back at Maureen, who'd angled herself toward Celeste.

"Do you still own 506 Fulton?" Celeste asked.

Maureen smiled. "Oh yes. Vivian gave me a very good deal."

---

Celeste wanted to go back to her little apartment at Eliza's. She wanted to curl up on the couch, with the cats nestled against her, a blanket to her neck, and go to sleep. She never wanted to step foot on Fulton Road again.

But Andi's house was in view, and Celeste couldn't drive away without checking on her. As she walked along the sidewalk, she noticed a dark SUV parked at the curb. A man sat in the driver's seat, and until Celeste had turned her gaze toward him, he'd been staring at her. She'd felt it, caught the jerk of his head as he quickly looked away and tried to conceal that he watched her.

He wore a baseball cap and dark sunglasses. She could make out no other distinguishing features.

Celeste knocked. She expected Andi not to answer, to again have to open the door and walk in on her own. But she heard footsteps in the hall and suddenly the door swung open.

Andi stood inside, smiling, hair wet on her shoulders. She wore a clean T-shirt with stonewashed jeans.

"Hey there. I was just thinking about you," Andi said. "I

meant to ask you about the ghost hunt. If anything had shown up on all your gadgets."

Celeste blinked at her. She looked nothing like the Andi an hour before.

"Are you feeling better?"

"What do you mean?" Andi appeared confused.

"Well ... I was just here and ... you were ... you looked sick. I sat with you for a bit in the parlor, even suggested we go to the emergency room, but you refused. That's why I'm here now. To check on you."

Andi wrinkled her forehead. "What? No, you were here ... the day before yesterday. I mean, right?" A flicker of fear skittered across Andi's face.

Celeste shook her head. "No, I stopped here and then walked down the road to talk to Maureen Sinclair."

Andi smiled, but the expression appeared forced. "Huh. That's weird. I did have a fever at school a couple of days ago and ... yeah. A fever can do that—make you forget some things. But no big deal."

"Andi, I think you need to move out of this house. Tonight. Right now. I'll help you. I'll rent you a hotel room. Whatever you need."

Andi's smile fell away, and she grew very still. Her head drooped and cocked slightly as if she listened to something, just as Maureen had done minutes before.

"Andi?" Celeste asked, stomach plunging. From somewhere behind Andi, the kitchen Celeste thought, she heard the creak of a door groaning open.

Andi did not turn to look at her. Celeste saw the shift, the subtle ripple along the smooth lines of her face, the sudden sheen over her eyes.

"Andi?"

Andi turned her head and nodded. "Yes. That's a good idea,

Celeste, but not tonight. First thing in the morning. I'm exhausted. I need to sleep."

Andi did not look exhausted; the opposite, in fact. High, buzzed, feverish. Her eyes had taken on that weird glint in only a split second's time.

Celeste stared at her, trying to think about how to break through, how to bypass whatever had taken hold of her. Instead, the words that floated through her mind were Alvin's: *"Evil is insidious, you know? Uncontainable. It's not housed in a single person, or even a single house for that matter. Energy doesn't work that way. It needs to move. And it does. Don't go telling yourself that the woman living in that house is the only one affected by it. There are others. Spend enough time there and you'll count yourself among them."*

Celeste was in over her head, and the tenacious part of her wanted to dig in, shake some sense into Andi, force her to pack a bag and drive away with her. But the baby growing inside of Celeste caused another desire, a more powerful one, to get the hell out of there, to put distance between herself and whatever had taken hold of Andi.

Celeste swallowed and forced a brittle smile. "OK. I'm going to come back tomorrow, and I think ... Would it be okay if I bring some friends?" She needed help, and the Memento Mori group was the only option. Police would scoff at her claims, and if one of them listened, what could they possibly do?

Andi stared at her. Her gaze was patient, unnatural. Beneath the veneer, something cold glimmered.

"OK then," Celeste breathed, pulse quickening as she backed toward the steps. The normal thing would have been to turn around, walk down the steps and head for her truck, but Celeste could not bring herself to turn her back on the young woman.

Only when Andi slipped into the dark hallway and closed

the door did Celeste turn away. She walked fast, practically ran, to her truck.

---

Celeste's hands shook on the wheel. Her mouth was dry, her legs like Jell-O.

A convenience store loomed on her right, and she turned in, parked near the road, and forced her breath to steady. She'd run out of sour candies and desperately wanted a bottle of water. More than either, she craved proximity to something normal—a cashier who wasn't possessed, a place so ordinary it might scrub away the lingering horror of the past few hours.

The bright fluorescent lights, the smell of recently cleaned linoleum, and the colorful packages of potato chips and bottles of soda soothed her. She took her time walking through the shelves. She considered a bag of salted almonds, but knew she couldn't stomach anything just then. She grabbed the sour candies and a bottle of water. As she started toward the cashier, her eye caught on a tube of SweeTarts, the candy Maureen had used to lure Simon into her car. The momentary good feelings drained away.

As she crossed the parking lot to her truck, the man she'd seen parked near Andi's house stepped from his dark SUV.

Her pulse surged.

She didn't recognize him, but he was focused on her. Her thoughts went to Jonathan, still on the run. Had he hired someone to attack her? Finish her once and for all.

She fumbled in her purse, hands trembling as she yanked her keys free and clicked to unlock her truck. The headlights blinked in response. Twenty feet. Fifteen. She broke into a fast walk, trying not to sprint.

"Stop," he yelled as he bolted forward.

As Celeste yanked open her driver's side door, the man shoved his hand against it, forcing it closed.

**43**

___

Celeste ducked away before he grabbed her.

"Please stop. Wait. I'm here about Andi. She's my wife."

Every instinct screamed for her to run back inside the convenience store, but her pace faltered—sprint melting into a jog, jog into a walk—until she finally turned to face him.

He'd taken off the hat and sunglasses, had shaggy dark hair and brown eyes. He was tall, handsome, though his face looked drawn, his body slightly hunched in something akin to defeat.

"What do you mean she's your wife?"

He held up his left hand, twiddled his fingers. A gold ring encircled his ring finger.

"That doesn't prove anything," she said, not moving any closer.

"Andi Marie Cooper. Daughter of Tim and Lynn Cooper. One sister named Torrie. She's an elementary school teacher. Graduated from the U of M. I'm Luke Elmore. We met at the University of Michigan during our junior year. We have a condo in Ann Arbor. We had a dog together, her dog technically, but he felt like mine. Bo, a sheepdog. He died a year ago."

Celeste frowned. "Andi said Bo died a few weeks before she moved here and that you broke up with her."

"Bo didn't die right before she moved. He died a year ago. I proposed to her right after. The timing was... shit, obviously, but I'd already bought the ring, and she was so depressed I thought it might cheer her up. She didn't want a big wedding. We got married in New Orleans. We both love it there."

"How long ago was that?"

"About six months ago."

"How do I know you're telling me the truth?" Celeste demanded.

"Why would I lie?" he asked.

"Why would Andi?"

"Fine, here." He took a cell phone from his back pocket, scrolled, then turned it to face her.

Slowly, reluctantly, Celeste crossed the parking lot toward him. She peered at his phone. Andi in a white dress with a lace bodice, hair pinned up with little white flowers poking from her dark curls. She held a bouquet of white lilies. Luke was leaning in, kissing her cheek. He wore a navy blue tux, his dark hair, longer then, brushing the collar.

He handed her the phone. "Swipe. You'll see more."

Celeste took the phone and flicked through the photos. Andi and Luke appeared again, framed by a flower-covered gazebo with an officiant before them. Only one person stood beside each of them, the moment pared down and personal.

"That's Torrie, Andi's sister. And next to me is Joey, my best friend and best man."

Celeste scrolled to an image of a long table, Andi and Luke still in their wedding garb, everyone else at the table similarly dressed in formal attire. A wedding cake decorated with Mardi Gras flowers in the center.

"Andi's parents"—he pointed to faces in the image—"then Torrie, her husband, Calvin, and their two kids. My parents, my best man and his girlfriend. That was our wedding reception. We had a big dinner catered at our Airbnb."

The photos seemed pretty impossible to refute.

He took the phone back, scrolled again and showed her the screen.

"This is Bo on his last day. She wanted me to take one final picture of them together at the vet."

Celeste studied the image. The large sheepdog lay on the linoleum floor. The steel table in the background. Andi stretched on the floor beside him, her face tear-streaked, her head angled against his fluffy back. The dog looked tired, eyes rheumy, snout resting on its paws.

The timestamp proved the photo had been taken just under one year before.

"Please, I'm telling you the truth. I only want to help her."

Celeste nodded, conflicted by her loyalty to Andi and her reluctance to believe the young woman had lied to her. Yet, she could not deny there was something wrong with Andi. "There's a late-night diner up the road a couple of miles. Let's go there and talk."

Luke followed Celeste in his SUV. She parked near the door at the diner she'd passed on each of her trips to Frankfort. The large neon sign read The Late Shift.

As had become her new norm, each time Celeste walked into a diner, she was blasted back to the Sidewinder in Graves. When a server stepped from the kitchen holding a tray of pancakes, for a moment she had Joanna's face, and then Celeste saw that no, this woman was much older than Joanna. Her name tag read Barbie.

They sat in a booth next to a line of plate-glass windows that reflected their own faces back to them. When the waitress appeared, Celeste ordered a ginger ale, Luke a cup of coffee. He looked worn out, like he hadn't slept well in days.

"Why did you follow me? Why not just walk up to the door at Andi's house and knock?"

Luke brushed a hand through his hair. "I've tried. She won't answer the door, won't take my calls."

"Why?"

"I don't know why. In August, she just … freaked. Uprooted our life. I came home from work and found a note on the dining room table. She'd left and didn't want to hear from me."

"Out of the blue? Nothing else happened?"

"I cheated on her."

"Wow. Well, I think it's clear why she wants nothing to do with you."

"It was one time, an accident, so stupid. Things had been strained and…"

Celeste held up a hand, annoyed. She knew too well the betrayal Andi had faced. No wonder she'd left. "I'm not interested in your excuses."

"Okay. I get it. I do. I'd do anything to take it back, but there was something else that happened before the infidelity." Luke rubbed his jaw. "Three months ago, about a month before the infidelity, she had a miscarriage."

A quiet stirring deep in Celeste's womb. She almost placed her hand on her low belly, but resisted the urge. "She lost a baby?"

He nodded. "She was four months along. We thought we were out of the dangerous phase, so we told people. Her parents and mine, her sister. And then one night… I woke up and found her in the would-be nursery sitting in the glider chair. We'd bought it the day before. She was rocking and… mumbling some pretty creepy stuff." He stared at the table, seemed unable to meet her eyes. "There was blood. I guess when the baby… the fetus left her body. She dipped her finger in the blood and wrote stuff on the walls. It was scary, honestly. I… didn't handle it well. I called the police and had her committed. I was afraid she'd hurt herself. Maybe I shouldn't have done that."

It physically hurt Celeste to imagine Andi in that chair, alone in the dark, blood seeping from between her legs. She must have been in shock, heartbroken. All things Celeste herself would feel if she were to lose the child growing inside her.

"What was she saying?" Celeste asked.

Luke blew out a breath. "I couldn't make out all of it, but she definitely said two or three times, '*Keep one, kill one.*'"

It was after midnight when Celeste returned to her apartment at Eliza's. She fell into bed, exhausted.

The nightmare took her immediately.

Celeste sat slumped in the parlor chair, her hands curled in her lap. The weight of her own body pressed her down, rooted her to the brocade cushion. She could not rise. Could not run.

Around her, five women sat in a loose circle, occupying high-backed chairs as if this were an ordinary afternoon visit.

The woman nearest the hearth, Georgina, had a long slit across her pale throat, a dark seam that opened when she spoke. Her voice poured out in a soft, gurgling hush. "Your daughter will have your eyes." She smiled, and fresh blood soaked the collar of her white linen nightgown, blooming down the front until it reached the red-wet fabric between her legs.

Celeste tried again to stand, but her legs refused the frantic command from her brain. The second woman, Maureen Sinclair—her eyes two cavernous sockets—stared at her. Tears of blood traced thin rivulets down her hollow cheeks. She rolled a wooden ball in her hands, the painted clown face leering with each rotation. "The red bedroom," she whispered. "That's where you should place the crib."

The third woman, Nadine, sitting primly with her wrists laid across her skirt, had gashes that leaked dark streams onto the faded upholstery. Her mouth curved in a pleasant, almost motherly smile. "Oh yes," she said in a voice that was too calm. "The red bedroom is lovely."

Celeste tried to force her hands onto the arms of the chair to push herself up. Her fingers would not move. She felt tears hot on her face, though she could not feel herself crying.

In the corner by the paneled wall, the fourth woman lifted her chin. Somehow Celeste knew this was Vivian Walters. Her skin was the color of ash, her eyes hollow black pits that swallowed the lamplight. A heavy looking silver and turquoise necklace hung around her slender throat. She parted cracked lips, and a trickle of dirt spilled out, pattering onto her blouse, into her lap. A rat scurried from beneath her chair and disappeared beneath the velvet fainting couch. When she spoke, her voice was dry, like wind through brittle grass. "It will be a beautiful nursery. You'll see."

Andi was the fifth woman, and she didn't speak. She watched Celeste with a fixed, hungry gaze, her hands folded neatly over her belly. Blood seeped from one nostril, and the side of her face appeared battered and bloody. Her arm hung limp at her side.

Celeste's heart banged harder; her breath grew shallow. Black spots swam behind her eyes.

No, she could not have a panic attack now. Could not lose consciousness in this room. She had to get out.

Slowly, all the women stood and moved toward her. The room seemed to tilt. Celeste's body sank deeper into the chair, as if she were already being swallowed.

Around her, the women began to hum a lullaby.

## 44

———

Celeste woke drenched in her own sweat, clawing at the covers. She'd bitten her lip and winced at the sharp pain when her dry tongue brushed across it. The metallic taste of blood lingered in her mouth.

She rolled to her side, broke free of the blankets and sat up. She discovered a raven sitting on the small bird feeder outside her window. It stared in at her, its black eyes shining.

Romeo suddenly jumped from the chair beside the bed at the window. The raven squawked and flew away.

The nightmare had not faded. She could smell the parlor, the women, the decay; could feel her paralyzed limbs, her fluttering heart.

She wasn't working at The Spirit Lantern that morning, but after confirming Lena was at the store, she texted Harris and asked if he could stop in.

———

"I need help," Celeste told them, glancing anxiously toward the door and hoping no customers chose that moment to visit The

Spirit Lantern. "You were right, Lena. I think Andi is possessed by whatever is in the house."

"What happened?" Harris asked.

Celeste laid out the previous day starting with her visit to Alvin and then her stop at Andi's. She held back her discovery that Maureen had abducted and likely murdered Eliza's little brother, but ended with her conversation with Luke.

"And she didn't tell you she was married?" Harris asked.

"No. She said her boyfriend broke up with her, that her life had fallen apart, her dog died, but the implication was that it all happened weeks before she moved back to Frankfort."

"She's totally in the grip of whatever is in that house," Lena said, picking up a stack of tarot cards and shuffling them quickly.

Celeste shook her head. "What I don't understand is the part with her husband. She left him before she moved into the house. She married him six months ago. How does that line up with her being possessed?"

"Can't both be true? She had a menty B, and the house is crawling with evil?" Lena asked.

"A menty B?"

"Mental breakdown, psychotic split, mind meld, whatever you want to call it. You're a scientist, right? Isn't that what all this quantum stuff is about? You can be insane, but that house can too?"

"I'm not that kind of scientist, and honestly ... I have no clue."

"But what you have had is a vacation to the other side, a front-row seat for the delusion that is our reality," Lena continued, flipping three cards face down.

Celeste nodded. And she'd also experienced the house first-hand. It was haunted, and not in a friendly way. In her near-death experience, there'd been no evil, no demons, no hell and damnation.

"Did you tell her about Simon?" Harris looked at Celeste.

"Simon?" Lena glanced back and forth between them. "Eliza's little brother, Simon?"

Celeste shifted her attention to Lena. "A woman who lived in that house, Maureen Sinclair, kidnapped Simon. I think she murdered him."

"No fricken way."

"It's true," Celeste murmured. "I saw his little wooden ball." She took the framed picture from her purse and handed it to Lena. "And I confronted Maureen. She basically admitted it though she framed the whole thing as a dream."

"She did?" Harris looked surprised. "She's still alive then?"

"Yes. She lives a few houses down from 506 Fulton. She still owns the house. Technically, she's Andi's landlord."

Lena studied the picture.

"Why did you decide to help Andi?" Lena asked. "Of all the letters, why her letter?"

Celeste thought back to the email that had come in to the Dear Celeste column. She'd opened it at three in the morning, during one of the many sleepless nights contemplating where Jonathan had gone after he'd fled West Virginia.

"Something in it ... struck me, I guess. I'm not sure why to be honest."

"How did Andi find you online?" Harris asked.

"She said she was looking for an exorcist."

"And your advice column came up?" Lena handed the photo back to Celeste.

Celeste nodded. It was hard to connect the two. She tried to recall if she'd ever responded to a letter writer who asked about exorcisms. It was possible. Since her near-death, the frequency of letters involving hauntings, unsolved disappearances and uncanny experiences had grown tenfold. Before her accident —*attempted murder*—she'd rarely received such questions.

After, it was as if the algorithm itself had been rerouted by some invisible hand.

"No accidents," Lena said. "Everything's connected. What more proof do you need than Eliza's baby brother, who disappeared fifty years ago, showing up in that house?"

Celeste closed her eyes. She was hungry, craving a spinach salad, and simultaneously nauseous and exhausted. She wanted to rewind the clock and have written a quick response to Andi's letter, except she never would have done it. So, what had motivated Andi to write her? Was it Andi or something in the house?

Lena flipped the first tarot card. A pale, watchful moon gazed down on a twisted landscape of wolves and shadows. "I pulled these for insight into Andi. The Moon. Deception. Things not being what they seem. Secrets. Maybe even self-deception. Someone's walking around in a fog—either by choice or because someone or something put them there."

She turned the middle card. "The Nine of Swords. Not a happy card. Nightmares. Anxiety. Breakdown stuff. Someone's unraveling. Losing their grip."

The door opened, the bell above chimed, and two women walked in. Lena greeted them and pointed them to the books on astrology before flipping the third and final card.

The Devil. The artwork was stark. A horned beast towered over a cowering figure.

Lena looked up at them, expression serious. "I'd say this one speaks for itself."

"I thought the tarot was meant to be symbolic, not literal," Harris murmured.

"It's both. Like everything in this world."

"I need you guys to help me," Celeste said. "To come back to the house with me."

Lena clapped her hands together. "Yes!"

"Of course," Harris agreed. "And... well, does it make sense to call the entire group together? In some ways, this is why we formed the Memento Mori group. There is power in the collective energy, and we all have different ... insights into things."

Celeste nodded. "Yes. And I need to tell Eliza. I saw her car parked at the house this morning, and I slipped out without even saying hi, which I feel terrible about, but I knew the moment I saw her, I'd blurt the whole horrible story out."

"Let's tell her together," Lena suggested.

---

They'd started the group text at noon, and by five the entire Memento Mori group was on their way to Traverse City.

Celeste had stayed away from the house most of the day. She'd eaten lunch alone at a little restaurant overlooking Traverse City's West Bay and then taken a walk downtown, impulsively purchasing a plush black raven and two sets of pink baby pajamas.

Afterward, she dug the classified ad about the cottage for sale from her purse and left a message with the realtor.

By seven, she'd returned to the apartment, pacing around as she waited for everyone to arrive.

At a quarter to eight, she looked out and saw Harris park in Eliza's driveway.

"Hey," she said, stepping into the cool evening.

He held up a small stuffed cat. Pink with white button eyes.

"For the baby," he said. "It was Bonnie's."

Tears bubbled up. She took the cat, buried her face in it for a moment and waited for the emotion to settle.

When she opened her eyes, Harris too looked on the verge of tears.

"Thank you," she murmured.

He held her gaze, and a quiet magnetism passed between them. For a moment, Celeste forgot about Andi's house, about telling Eliza that Simon had likely died there. She forgot what they had planned for the following day.

Harris stepped closer, started to lean in, and then headlights washed over them. A car pulled into the driveway. Lena, Taylor in the passenger seat. The two women climbed out.

Lena grinned. Taylor looked back and forth between them.

"I'm just going to put this in the apartment," Celeste breathed. "I'll meet you guys at Eliza's."

Celeste rested the little cat on her pillows next to the raven she'd bought that day. Her body was light, buoyant, the tiredness that had plagued her that evening washed away in an instant.

When she walked into the kitchen, Jack, too, had arrived. The group stood talking. Eliza had made a pot of coffee and glanced nervously between them, clearly sensing that whatever was coming involved her.

"All right, guys, let's sit." Harris gestured at the kitchen table. "Celeste, the floor is yours."

Celeste gazed toward the wall of photos. Simon's smiling face, one nail hanging empty, the picture she'd taken of Simon holding the little clown ball. Eliza's eyes followed Celeste's stare, a crease forming between her brows.

"You guys know I started helping a young woman in Frankfort, Andi," Celeste said. "She'd moved into a house at 506 Fulton, and she had a history with the house. As soon as I went there, I felt … something. That something wasn't quite right."

Taylor's gaze too had shifted to the missing photo on Eliza's wall. When she looked back at Celeste, her eyes had gotten large.

"I believe a woman who used to live in that house abducted Simon, Eliza." She'd meant to offer more backstory, but she'd seen the dawning in Eliza's eyes.

Eliza stared at her, face pale. She put a hand to her necklace, a Petoskey stone with a piece of leather looped through it.

"Why?" Eliza whispered.

"Because I've ... seen him. I've seen his ghost and I've seen" —she produced the picture she'd taken from the wall—"this ball."

"His ball is in the house?"

"Well... I saw it, but then it wasn't there. But I'm sure, Eliza. I'm as sure as I've ever been about this gift ... this sight. He was taken by a woman named Maureen."

Eliza frowned. "Maureen Sinclair?"

Celeste gaped at her. "You know her?"

"I met her on the five-year anniversary of Simon's disappearance. She joined a search in Honor and stayed in contact for years, first with my mom and then later with me when I took over as the family spokesperson."

"That's sick," Lena muttered.

"Seriously?" Jack asked. "Wow. I mean... this is... what are the chances you'd end up at that house?"

"It wasn't by chance," Taylor murmured.

"No. I don't think so either," Celeste agreed.

**45**

———————

Andi stared at the dizzying wallpaper inches from her nose. Her arm lifted, her fingers curled around the quill. She wrote the words, listened to the scrape of the pen, inhaled the earthy metallic scent of blood. She stood in the parlor, and he was coming, thunderous footfalls on the wooden staircase. Sweat dripped into her eyes. She wrote faster. Somewhere a baby cried, but the sound was muffled, distant.

Later—though she couldn't say how much later—Andi stood in the bathroom. In the mirror, a stranger blinked back. Hollowed eyes, sunken cheeks, a bloodstain beneath one nostril. She touched the glass, the stranger's movements mimicking her own.

In the shower, the water ran pink, swirling in spirals down the drain. She stood beneath the icy spray, her body too hot, and waited until it turned clear.

The weak light of dawn filtered through the windows when she walked into the kitchen. Clothed in fresh jeans and a T-shirt, feet bare and sticking slightly to the wood floor. The grandfather clock ticked down. Something scratched behind the walls.

She filled a glass of water and drank it, then another.

The basement door creaked open.

Gwen peeked through, eyes glittering, sharp teeth glowing. She pushed the door all the way open and walked into the kitchen, her shoes squelching as if waterlogged.

She cupped Andi's cheek, tilted her head. "Don't forget the candy." Her voice sounded bloated, wet and gurgling.

Andi nodded, absent. She picked up the candy from the counter and left the house.

Outside, the world was barely awake. Light touched the tops of the trees. Across the street, the blue playhouse stood empty. The boy's red tricycle lay on its side next to the driveway.

Andi stared at it for a moment.

She got in her car and started to drive.

**46**

———

As they drove toward Frankfort, Harris behind the wheel, Celeste in the passenger seat, she tried to calm her quaking nerves. She'd dreamt again of Andi's house the night before, and though the details were fuzzy, she could still smell the blood and something else, a burning. As they drove, Celeste had tried repeatedly to call Andi, but her cell phone clicked straight to voicemail. Celeste's texts went unanswered.

"Are you afraid?" Celeste asked.

He glanced at her. "Not to die. But"—he touched her hand—"it would be hard to leave you ... all of you. The group I mean." He swallowed, eyes trained on the road.

Harris's phone beeped. He picked it up and frowned.

"What is it?" she asked.

"An Amber alert. A child disappeared today from the elementary school in Frankfort. Paisley Kincaid." He showed her the phone with the image of the little girl, smiling gap-toothed, her light hair held in place by a rainbow headband.

Celeste's heart skipped. "That's where Andi works."

Harris said nothing. He gripped the wheel tighter and

accelerated. Celeste glanced in the side-view mirror. Lena, Taylor, Eliza and Jack followed in Jack's Suburban.

They parked, and Celeste and Harris jumped out. Celeste didn't wait for the others. She hurried to the door and knocked. Andi didn't answer. She tried the knob. Locked.

Behind her, she heard Harris. "Did you guys get the Amber alert?"

"Yes," Eliza said. "You don't think ..."

"We don't know, but... it's possible."

Days before Andi had left Celeste a key beneath a flowerpot on the porch steps. She tilted it and saw the key still in place. She took it out, inserted it into the lock and twisted the knob.

"Andi?" Celeste called.

No response.

She turned to the group. They crowded onto the porch behind her. Taylor held Eliza's hand. Eliza blinked through teary eyes at the dark interior. Jack hung back, scanning the house, frowning.

Lena held a lighter to a bundle of sage. "Might as well get started straight away," she said.

"I'm going to go in quick and find her. I don't want to startle her with all of us rushing in together."

"What if she has the kid?" Lena asked, waving the sage toward the open door.

Celeste listened, but the house was quiet. She desperately wanted to believe the Amber alert was unrelated. Andi would never have taken someone's child.

"Celeste." Harris put his hand on her forearm. "If she has her, you may not want to be the one to find them."

She nodded. "No. You're right. Let me just... call out to her a few times. Maybe everything is fine and she's having a nap or ... something totally benign. I don't want her to feel like we just barged in."

He stepped closer. "I'll wait in the doorway."

The hush in the house had deepened. Celeste's footfalls sounded muted.

"Andi?" she called at the base of the stairs.

No response.

She moved to the parlor, peeked in. Empty. Into the kitchen, also empty. The basement door was closed. Fear coiled like a snake around her feet when she twisted the knob and opened the door. Darkness and silence.

"Andi?" she shouted.

Her voice echoed back to her. The basement was utterly still and soundless.

She returned to the group. "I don't see her, but... her car's here."

"Is she hiding?" Taylor asked.

Something about the question caused the fine hairs on Celeste's neck to rise. She imagined Andi, hunched, glassy-eyed, waiting.

"She might be."

"Safety in numbers," Jack said. "We all go in together."

Harris unclipped the gun holstered on his hip. Celeste eyed it warily. Harris would never shoot unprovoked, but she was afraid of a confrontation, with Andi suddenly hurling herself at them from a closet, the gun going off.

She shook the thought away.

"Let's split up in pairs and do a quick sweep of the house," Harris said. "Jack, you and I will go up. The four of you just cover the ground floor here."

"There's also a basement," Celeste said.

"We'll do the basement after we check upstairs," Harris told her.

Jack and Harris disappeared up the stairs.

Celeste led the others first through the living room—empty. They separated and opened doors into the bathroom, the laundry and utility room and walked through the kitchen. Then they backtracked to the parlor.

The paneling had been removed from the wall. It lay on its side in the back of the room. Fresh words had been written in blood, but the dark wallpaper made it difficult to decipher them.

"Where might she be if her car is here?" Taylor murmured, looking at the ceiling where Harris and Jack moved from room to room.

"I don't know," Celeste said. "It's possible a friend picked her up, I guess."

It didn't ring true, though.

"I think we should get started," Taylor said. "Let's rip down this wallpaper."

Celeste nodded. The evening before the group had agreed that Georgina Atwater had likely been writing on the walls in blood as a way to summon the dark entity into the house. By removing and destroying the writings, perhaps they could also loosen the demonic hold on Andi.

Celeste tugged at the corner, and it peeled back like old skin. More words beneath.

Taylor joined her, helping rip the paper away. Lena twirled the sage through the air, murmuring under her breath.

A faint scratching noise came from behind the walls.

Taylor froze. "Did you hear that?"

Celeste nodded. "I've heard it before."

Eliza stood before the large painting above the fireplace, her small frame trembling. Her eyes were locked on a single figure in the painting.

"This is Simon," she whispered.

Celeste, Taylor, and Lena crossed to the painting.

Eliza pointed at a little boy depicted in profile. His hair was dark, with a cowlick curling at the back. He wore a yellow shirt with black stripes.

"That's what he had on the day vanished," Eliza said. "My mom always said he looked like a little bumblebee."

Lena's face twisted in unease. "This place is so wrong," she murmured, just as the ceiling above them creaked again.

Taylor stepped back to the wall. Another flap of wallpaper hung loose. She ripped it free.

Celeste joined her. As more wallpaper came down, the temperature in the room seemed to climb. Sweat beaded at Celeste's hairline.

"It's fucking blazing in here," Lena complained, setting the still-burning sage on a little glass dish and trying to force a window open. "It won't budge," she muttered.

The plaster beside the window suddenly cracked, a spiderweb of lines scurrying toward the floor.

Celeste stared at another layer of writing, brownish red, long dried and partially cracked away. *Keep one, kill one. Help me.* A line of Latin she couldn't make out.

Glass rattled in the windowpanes. Lights flickered. The ceiling above them groaned as if something large crawled across it.

"Only beings of light are welcome here," Taylor murmured as she yanked off another strip of wallpaper.

Celeste paused, closed her eyes, and imagined her mother. Not the mother she barely remembered from life, but her mother she'd met during her near-death. A presence so loving, so all-encompassing. She imagined that presence now, surrounding her, filling the room, the whole house.

Taylor suddenly stopped and gazed intently at the corner. "Do you see her?"

Celeste followed her gaze, almost thought she'd see a vision of her mother there. But the corner stood empty.

"Her name is Leslie," Taylor murmured.

"Leslie was a Girl Scout last seen coming into this house in the 1940s," Celeste said.

"The lady told her she had kittens. They were in the basement," Taylor said. She tilted her head, seeing and hearing something the others could not. She shuddered and gave Celeste a horrified look. "When Leslie looked in the box, she didn't find kittens, but rats."

A loud crack sounded as a raven crashed into the window. Celeste flinched.

A voice spoke inches from Celeste's ear: *He's coming.*

She spun, heart hammering. No one was there.

Celeste knew the voice that spoke was Georgina's. She could feel the young woman's spirit hovering close, invisible yet unmistakable.

Celeste did not need to ask who *he* was. Georgina was speaking about her father.

Something thumped overhead. One of the parlor doors creaked open and banged closed so hard several panes of glass in the door shattered.

Eliza, who hadn't left the painting of Simon, gasped.

Jack strode in, face pale. He glanced at the glass on the floor. The doors upstairs opened and slammed shut. "I got locked in the bathroom. Holy shit... this is..."

"Batshit crazy," Lena finished.

"Where's Harris?" Celeste asked.

"He crawled into the attic to make sure Andi isn't hiding there."

"I'm going to check on him," Celeste said.

"No," Taylor said sharply. "Don't go up there."

Celeste's eyes rose to the ceiling, alarmed as she heard something thud followed a dragging sound.

"He's OK," Taylor said.

Seconds later, Harris appeared in the hall, hair full of dust and cobwebs.

"What was that sound?" Celeste asked.

"It was... nothing. I mean nothing I could see, but obviously… not nothing."

"We need to go in the basement," Celeste murmured.

Taylor nodded.

"I'll go," Harris said.

"And me," Jack added.

*And you.* The words were not whispered. They appeared in Celeste's mind. "I have to go too," Celeste said.

"I don't think that's a good idea."

"She does," Taylor agreed. "Celeste, I think Andi's in the basement, and she's not alone."

"I'll join you," Lena said. "Probably could use some of this down there." She picked up the bundle of sage.

"I'd like to stay here," Eliza told them. She'd returned again to the painting as if Simon's spirit was captured inside the small figure on the canvas.

"I'll wait with Eliza," Taylor offered, "and keep working on this wallpaper."

Harris led the way down the dark, creaking staircase, Celeste second, Jack and Lena behind her.

Harris pulled the string that dangled from the basement light. The bulb sputtered weakly before flickering out with a soft *pop*, plunging them into near darkness.

Jack turned on the flashlight on his phone. Then Harris did as well.

"Jesus. It's a hoarder's dream," Lena muttered as the beams lit the stacks of junk.

A sour, mineral stench hung in the air.

"It reeks down here," Jack complained.

"Inhale this." Lena thrust the sage toward him.

"Shh…," Harris whispered, holding his fingers to his lips.

The voice came from the far end of the basement, near the area Celeste had placed the recorder days before.

Andi's voice drifted out, shrill and angry.

They moved slowly, Harris's light cutting through the

gloom and piles of clutter. As he moved the beam, it illuminated the piece of wood paneling that blocked one wall.

"They're back there," Celeste whispered.

Jack crouched to move a battered trunk, grunting as dust puffed around them. Harris tugged aside the high-backed chair. One of its legs snapped and it clattered to the floor.

They all froze, listening. No sounds from behind the panel.

Celeste's heart hammered. She wiped her palms on her pants and blinked away the sweat dripping into her eyes. The stink of the basement and the headiness of Lena's sage made her feel dizzy.

"Are you okay?" Harris touched her arm.

She drew in a breath, forced it deep, focused on objects in the room. Five things she could see.

"I'm okay," she whispered,

Jack grabbed the edge of the panel and lifted it aside.

Cold air spilled out. The scent here was different—rancid.

Celeste's stomach rolled. She clenched her teeth and breathed through her mouth.

"It's a tunnel," Jack whispered.

Celeste stepped inside, her footsteps muffled by the damp dirt floor. The narrow tunnel sloped down slightly, the walls rough-hewn and glistening.

The tunnel curved, and ended at a sagging, mildew-streaked sheet tacked up like a curtain.

Celeste reached out, hand trembling, and pulled the sheet down.

The room beyond was larger than she expected—stone walls, arched low, slick with moisture. The stink was sharper, metallic and foul. Dirty white sheets hung on several of the walls.

Candles flickered along the edges of the floor. In one corner stood a rocking chair. A skeleton sat in it. Bone-white and still, wearing the remnants of a once-lavender dress. Thin bangles circled a wrist that ended in curled, skeletal fingers. A silver and turquoise necklace sagged between brittle clavicles. Celeste remembered the necklace from her dream. They'd discovered the final resting place of Vivian Walters.

Andi stood crouched in the opposite corner, her nails crusted with dried blood, her hair tangled and matted across her face. In front of her, a little girl lay on a dirty cot. It was the same girl from the Amber alert. Paisley Kindcaid.

"Holy fuck," Lena breathed.

"Andi... We're here to help you," Celeste said, stepping deeper into the room.

**47**

---

A ndi's vision swam in and out of focus. She heard Celeste's words, but they hardly registered. Others crowded in behind Celeste.

Gwen lay on the bed, her giant wicked grin stretched wide. Pointed teeth gleaming. Andi had restrained her and needed everyone to see.

"Look! It's Gwen," Andi shouted. "She's not dead. She has everyone fooled."

But Celeste stepped closer, her brow furrowed in concern. "Andi," she said gently, "that's not Gwen. That's Paisley Kincaid. She's a missing child from the elementary school. People are out searching for her right now."

"No," Andi whispered, blinking. Her eyes flicked to the cot again.

In that instant, the grin was gone.

The face beneath her gaze was no longer Gwen's, but a little girl's—pale lips, eyes closed, skin ashen. Her small arms were folded neatly across her chest, as if someone had lovingly arranged her that way.

Like she was *dead*.

"Dead!" Andi shrieked the word and jumped away. She'd killed her. Andi had killed Paisley.

A scream gurgled from her throat. The wail seemed to split her in two. It grew louder, deafening. It was not her own anymore, but something deeper, a cry that spanned decades, centuries even.

Andi bolted past Celeste and the others. A man tried to grab hold of her shoulder, and she raked her stubby fingernails across his forearm. He jerked his hand away.

She fled through the narrow stone hallway. Breath wheezing, sweat dripped into her eyes. Andi crashed into a stack of boxes and nearly fell, but managed to keep her feet beneath her. Barely illuminated by light trickling down the steps, she glimpsed Vivian Walters. The woman's face was gaunt, her eyes sunken. She reached a gnarled hand toward Andi, but Andi scrambled past her, up the basement stairs, and into the house.

Through the kitchen, down the hall. Two women she didn't recognize sat on the parlor floor. Beyond her in the back corner, a woman in a blood-soaked nightgown rocked an infant. The baby's skin was gray. The woman's was too, a gash in her throat.

A baby cried—then another—followed by a woman's anguished wail. Thunderous footsteps pounded the floor, shrieks tore through the air, the savage slash of blades, fists pounding flesh, something heavy and wet thudding to the ground. Screams piled upon screams, overlapping, spiraling into a maddening chorus. Beneath it all, like the house's own dark heartbeat, rumbled a growling, guttural sound—hungry. Ancient. And inside her. The noise wasn't just around her. It came from within.

For a sickening second, she saw Gwen at the foot of the stairs, hair dripping, face bloated and flesh-eaten.

And she suddenly understood why Gwen had done it. It had gotten inside of her too.

Andi shoved past her, inhaled the rank stench of her rotted

body, and ran up the stairs. Her mind was a confusion of urges. To live and to die. To feed the monster inside her and to starve it.

Another woman, dead, the flesh of her wrists peeled back, blood pooling beneath her, stood at the end of the hall.

At the threshold of her bedroom, the red walls seemed to ripple and bleed with a strange life, and she faltered.

*Run.*

She could gather a few things, run to her car and escape. She could get away.

The urgency to flee, to hide, sizzled in her blood.

But in her mind's eye she saw Marco, Marco who'd died because of the thing that lived in the house, the thing that now lived in Andi.

"No," she muttered. "I won't. I won't kill for you." Because that's what it wanted, what it demanded.

She spun in a circle, breath ragged, eyes scanning the room. Panic blurred the edges of everything. Her gaze landed on the window.

Time stopped.

A whisper curled in her ear, soft and urgent. *Save yourself.*

She shook her head. No.

Her feet moved before the voice could come again, lure her away from her decision. One step. Then another. Then faster. She was running.

She lowered her head.

The glass rushed toward her.

And then—impact.

A deafening crack. A burst of cold air. The window shattered around her like ice.

"I have to go after her." Celeste turned, but Harris followed her into the tunnel.

He grabbed her hand and pulled her toward him, kissing her hard and fast. Before she could speak, he broke away and strode back down the tunnel.

Celeste stood, stunned, watching him fade into the darkness. Her body buzzed, blood thumping.

"She's alive!" Lena's voice drifted out.

The sound snapped Celeste out of her daze, and she fled the basement. In the parlor, Eliza and Taylor stood hand in hand, encircling a ring of salt drawn carefully on the floor. For a brief moment, Celeste's eyes caught flickers of other presences in the room—Simon in his bumblebee T-shirt, Leslie dressed in her Girl Scout uniform, clusters of babies and toddlers, and other children. Marco, wearing his worn Converse, stood nearby, silently pointing toward the hallway and the stairs.

Celeste spun and ran toward them, taking the stairs two at a time, her breath puffing, a cramp gripping her hip.

She reached Andi's bedroom in time to see her hit the window headfirst.

Celeste screamed and reached for her, but it was too late.

---

For one weightless moment, Andi was flying ...

And then she plummeted toward the stone pathway below.

**48**

---

ndi lay crumpled on the cracked flagstones, the sky a shade of blue she'd never seen, pale and swirling. Her heart stuttered in her chest, and somewhere she heard crying. Paisley. She had taken Paisley, but it was okay. It would all be okay.

The voices melted into stillness; the world dimmed. She was elsewhere now—in a memory not hers, yet somehow deeply hers.

A candle burned low in a chipped porcelain holder, wax dripping onto the floorboards. Georgina would need to clean it before morning. But not now; now she needed the candlelight as she kneeled and dipped her fingers into her blood. Blood she'd waited weeks for. Menstrual blood.

Her hand trembled as she lifted it to the wall behind her small, iron-framed bed. The floral wallpaper was dizzying with her face so close. Shaking, she wrote the words...

*Dominus infernus... veni ad me...*

She mouthed the words soundlessly. The words had been scrawled months before on a boulder near the rectory. The parishioners called it blasphemy. Georgina had heard two choirboys whispering about how a devil worshipper had written the phrases, a person summoning a dark angel for help. She hadn't believed them—*not really*—until her father had started coming into her room again at night. She'd lain beneath him, her cries muffled by his large hand stinking of tobacco and ink, and vowed to call upon her own dark angel.

Georgina traced each letter carefully, her breath hitching in her throat.

*Help me. I beg you. I will give you anything.*

Each word in blood made her head swim with fear. Her gaze darted to the door. The hallway was silent except for the grandfather clock's deep ticking. She finished and picked up the painting of Saint Agatha and returned it to the nail that jutted above her plea.

Her chest was compressed with guilt. If her mother found the words, she'd scream and faint. But her mother, she thought bitterly, had done nothing, and neither, for that matter, had God. For more than a year she'd prayed every night, begging for salvation from her father. Her knees were bruised and bloody from kneeling beside her bed. He'd come even in the midst of those prayers, his heavy feet creaking down the hall.

Georgina wrote her pleas in blood night after night for months. When her menstrual blood faded, she made use of the rats in the cellar. She slipped quietly from room to room as her parents and sisters slept. She tugged paintings from the walls. Images of pastoral farms, landscapes, saints. And behind them, she called upon the dark angel and she pleaded for it to come, to help her.

Still, her father came as well. He came sometimes stinking of tobacco and ink and sometimes of soap and grass. And on those nights after he'd gone back to his own bed to sleep soundly beside her mother, Georgina crept through the house begging the dark angel to save her, to strike her father dead, to set her free.

And then one night after she'd written her call on the parlor wall and then slipped quickly to bed, blowing out her guttering candle, the grandfather clock struck three.

And in the silence between the chimes, she heard a voice—soft and rasping—answer her prayer.

"Now you are mine …"

The farmhouse faded, Georgina's memories falling back like a curtain. Gone.

Andi drifted for a while in darkness and then...

She stood on the beach in Frankfort, the summer sun baking down, a warm breeze lifting her hair.

"You're here!" the voices called from the pier, and she turned to see Gwen and Marco running toward her, laughing. They collided with her on the beach. The three of them fell in a giggling heap of limbs.

Marco leaned close and whispered. "We knew you'd come."

---

Celeste rushed down the stairs and out the front door.

She froze when she saw Andi on the stone path, her body twisted, a trickle of blood at the corner of her mouth.

"No!" She dropped to her side, searching for a pulse.

Jack emerged from the house, with Eliza and Taylor on his heels. He held Paisley, who'd woken, her face pale, fearful.

Celeste's fingers searched Andi's neck, her wrist. She couldn't find a heartbeat.

In the distance, the sirens split the quiet.

Behind her, the soft crunch of dry grass under slow-moving feet caused Celeste to twist around. Maureen approached with eerie precision, tapping her cane once, then stopping at Andi's side. Maureen crouched and reached a pale, gnarled hand toward Andi's chest. Her fingers hovered... then made contact.

Andi's body gave a sudden, slight jolt. A ripple moved through it—no breath, no gasp, just a tremor.

Maureen exhaled sharply and rose, unseeing eyes fluttering. A faint smile curved her lips. Celeste stared, a chill prickling across her neck.

Maureen turned and walked straight toward the old farmhouse, slippered feet shuffling along the walkway, her cane twitching over the porch steps as she ascended them and disappeared inside.

Celeste turned back to Andi. Blood had begun to trickle from one of her nostrils, and more spread in a pool beneath her head.

The smell of Maureen lingered. And for a moment Celeste couldn't make sense of the scent.

And then it came to her.

Gasoline.

Celeste forced herself to her feet and ran toward the house.

She searched for Maureen, didn't see her, but the smell of gasoline was stronger now, pungent and dizzying.

The fire took hold so fast Celeste fell back when the blaze suddenly exploded through the parlor doors and raced across the hall ceiling.

"Fire," she screamed. "The house is on fire."

She sprinted to the kitchen to the open basement door, where neither Lena nor Harris had emerged. "Get out!" she shrieked. "The house is on fire."

Behind her, the blaze overtook the hallway and obscured the front door. Celeste stared into the dark basement, but heard nothing.

Suddenly, Taylor was beside her, grabbed her around the waist and dragged her out of the house through the back door.

"Harris and Lena!" she shrieked. "They're still inside."

Taylor shoved Celeste. "Get away from the house now. I'll go back in."

As Celeste stumbled around the side of the house, coughing, eyes watering from the growing smoke and flames, she saw the front yard filling with people. Paramedics and firefighters rushed from their vehicles. Two men lifted Andi onto a stretcher and hurried her to a waiting ambulance. Firefighters shouted orders as they uncoiled their hose and dragged it across the lawn.

More paramedics had Paisley. An oxygen mask over her face as they took her to an adjacent ambulance.

The fire howled as if the house itself were protesting its own death. The downstairs windows exploded out, carrying bursts of bright hot orange. Somewhere deep inside, a moan rose up —not quite human, not quite structure—like a thing alive and in agony, being dragged to hell.

Taylor ran from the back the house, coughing, eyes red. No one else was with her.

Celeste hurried to a firefighter and clutched his jacket. "There are people in there, two in the basement. Harris and Lena. Please. And"—she thought of Maureen. Too late to save her, but—"there's an older woman. She went into the parlor."

"Got it. Get back. Go." He gently pushed her toward the road. Eliza and Taylor grabbed her arms.

Voices rode the crackling heat. The cries of an infant, the pleading of children, the wails of the women who'd lost themselves to the house. For a moment in the flames she saw faces. Beside her, Taylor and Eliza stared at the house, their mouths open, their wide eyes reflecting the firelight. They could hear them too.

"Simon," Eliza whispered, her voice cracking. She lifted a trembling hand as if to touch him, but he was not there, had not been there for a very long time.

They waited. Minutes passed, but no one appeared from the house. The fire had overtaken it now.

Celeste began to cry. She touched her lips, the still warm place where Harris had kissed her minutes before. Her knees shook and she slowly sank to the ground. Taylor gripped one of her elbows and dropped with her. She cried too, face streaked and blotchy as they watched the house with their friends inside it burn.

**49**

———————

Time passed and yet it seemed time had stopped.

The roof was gone, swallowed by fire. More people filled the street, drawn to the heat, the chaos. The wind off Lake Michigan fed the flames. The fire surged higher.

Suddenly, through the mirage of smoke, Celeste saw two figures hobbling down the road toward them.

Harris and Lena.

Celeste stared at them, believed she glimpsed their spirits, but no. They were solid. Their faces streaked with soot and dirt and damp.

She tried to stand, but couldn't get her legs to obey. Taylor made it to her feet first and helped her up. They rushed toward them. Celeste collided with Harris, nearly brought him down, but he caught her, buried his face in her hair.

"It's okay. We're okay."

"I thought … we thought …" She couldn't get the words out.

"We found another tunnel!" Lena exclaimed. "It was partially blocked with stones, but we saw rats running through an opening at the bottom. We managed to heave the rocks aside and get through. Talk about claustrophobia. And filled with spiders. We crawled through it and came out in the woods in this little stone hovel full of firewood. It was nuts. We tried to get out through the basement, but smoke was pouring down the stairs." She paused and turned to stare at the house. "Holy shit."

Jack and Eliza joined them, and they all watched 506 Fulton burn.

---

Andi opened her eyes and blinked at the panel of fluorescent lights above her. A needle pricked the inside of her elbow, held in place with white tape. An IV bag hung from a stand beside the bed, its tube snaking down to her left arm.

She turned her head—too fast—and winced. A foam sling cradled her right arm which was also encased in plaster and gauze. It didn't hurt, not exactly, but she could feel something wrong beneath the numbness.

Dante dozed in a chair next to her bed.

As if sensing she'd woken, he opened his eyes, sitting up quickly.

"I saw Marco," she exclaimed. "Just now at the Frankfort Pier. Marco and Gwen and they're good. They're so happy."

He stared at her, slowly reached a hand for her fingers jutting from her cast.

"It was real, Dante. They were there."

He smiled sadly. "I believe you," he murmured. "But stop trying to sit up, OK? You're hurt pretty bad."

She reached her hand with the IV to the gauze encasing her head. "Am I?"

He nodded. "Your parents and Torrie are all in Frankfort. And... umm... your husband is here, Luke. He's been here on and off for the last few days. They all drove to their hotel to shower and grab some lunch like an hour ago."

"My husband," she murmured. And yes, the memories all came rushing back, the blur of the previous year no longer hidden in some vault she'd locked and thrown away the key. The death of Bo, her marriage to Luke, the baby, Luke's affair—stark and ugly and painful.

"I've been in the hospital for days?"

"Three."

A wave of nausea rolled through her as another memory clicked into place, the image of Paisley on the basement cot. "Paisley Kincaid."

Dante held her hand tighter. "She's fine. She's perfectly fine."

"I took her...," Andi whispered. The memory flickered—there, then gone—like a film reel skipping frames. She saw herself, or someone wearing her face, pulling an enormous lollipop from her bag on the school playground, offering it to Paisley, then guiding the girl to her car and driving away. No one stopped them. Maybe no one even noticed. Or maybe they had, seen the teacher with her student, and thought nothing of it.

She eased back against the pillows, noticing for the first time the other aches running through her body.

Dante's expression appeared troubled. "Gwen told me something... a few months before she took her life. She'd stayed overnight at my condo, and I woke up to find her on my balcony. She was upset and said she'd had a dream that she'd tried to take a little girl from the shopping mall in Traverse City. I told her it had only been a nightmare, that nothing had actually happened. She pulled this hair scrunchie out of her pocket. It was pink and had Barbies on it. In her dream, the little girl had been wearing it."

He withdrew his hand from hers and rubbed the hollows of

his eyes. "I dismissed her worries. I figured... she'd picked the scrunchie up somewhere and forgotten. She'd been going to that house, and three days ago when that fire raged through it, I went to 506 Fulton. The fire department had pretty much given up on putting it out. They were just trying to contain it. People were standing all over watching. And"—he couldn't seem to look at Andi—"I saw Gwen... I saw her clear as day just for a moment in the crowd. She watched that fire burn, and there was something in her eyes, this relief. I've never believed in ghosts. I still don't know what I believe, but... I think it's real. What happened to you and Marco and Gwen."

"It's real," Andi said.

The door opened, and Luke stepped into the room. His eyes searched Andi's.

"I'll give you guys some time," Dante said. He stood and slipped into the hall.

Worry lines creased Luke's face. He walked over, leaned down and kissed her on the forehead. "Thank God you're all right." He sat in the chair Dante had vacated and hesitantly took her hand.

"I am," she said.

"The doctors... they weren't sure. When you first got here..." His voice cracked. "They weren't sure if you'd make it. You fractured your skull, and your brain was ... inflamed, and..." Tears leaked from his eyes, and he took in a big shuddering breath.

"I'm sorry," Andi told him. "For leaving the way I did."

The weeks she'd spent in the house drifted through her mind like smoke—unreal, distorted. It felt less like a life she had lived and more like a story someone had whispered into her head. She saw herself again, running toward the window, gripped by a desperate need to escape whatever darkness had taken root inside her.

"It's okay. We can forget all of it. All right? It's over and done with and—"

Andi shook her head. "No. We can't do that. I am so sorry I left the way I did, but Luke ... I want a divorce."

His mouth fell open. "But... Andi, I know this year was bad and the thing with Lisa, that was so fucking stupid. I have no idea what came over me. You'd lost the baby and become so... distant and I just..."

"It's not your fault." She squeezed his hand, thinking again of Marco. "Fourteen years ago, I lost my best friend, Marco. That was his brother here a few minutes ago."

"Dante," Luke murmured, frowning.

"Yes. And when Marco died, I... I never healed from that. But when I fell from that window, when I jumped because that's what I did, I jumped."

"You jumped?" He stared at her, horrified.

"Yes. It was the only way to get rid of the evil. But..." She smiled, though it hurt her face. "That doesn't matter now. I'm going back to Tennessee with my parents to heal, and then I'm going to France or Amsterdam to see Radiohead play live."

He stared at her. "What? Why? You can probably watch Radiohead right here in Michigan. And Tennessee? Are you moving to Tennessee?"

"I don't know. Maybe. But Luke, you're going to be fine. We both are. We weren't the right fit. I can see that now. I appreciate you coming here and I don't regret a second we had together. But... I'd like a divorce."

---

"Well look at you," Celeste murmured from the doorway.

Andi sat up in bed eating a bowl of soup.

"I hope that's not the hot foot soup," she said, walking into the room.

Andi studied the soup and then looked back at her. "I hope it's not too. They told me it was chicken noodle."

"How are you feeling?"

"Physically? Like I jumped through a second-story window and landed on a bunch of rocks. Mentally and emotionally, better than I have since... well, since Marco died."

"That's so good, Andi." Celeste sat in a chair near the bed. "You gave me quite a scare."

"Yeah, I'm sorry. I had no idea when I asked you for help... how real it all was. You know? I spent all these years half believing I'd made it up."

"You didn't," Celeste told her. "It's hard to believe. I'm still struggling with it myself, but ... it happened. It all happened."

Andi chewed her lip, swirling her soup for a long moment. "Umm ... I have this memory and I'm not sure if it was a dream, but I was lying on the ground after I jumped and someone touched me. They... they took it. The thing that had moved into my body."

"It wasn't a dream. Her name was Maureen Sinclair, and she lived in that house in the sixties, and she did some terrible things while she was there. Except I suspect *she* didn't really do those terrible things."

"Is she still alive?"

"No. She started the fire."

Andi's face fell. "Do you think it's dead then? That it can die?"

Celeste frowned. She didn't honestly know, wasn't sure anyone could know. "I believe it is yes. I went there yesterday. The house is a pile of ash." Celeste imagined standing in the road, feeling into what remained of the house. There'd been no sense of foreboding, of something crouched and watching. Had it truly died or merely gone dormant? Who could say? "I think it's gone."

"I hope so," Andi whispered.

"Here." Celeste dug into her purse and found the marble

Marco had given her in The Spirit Lantern. She handed it to Andi.

Andi leaned closer, winced as if the movement hurt. "Where did you get this?"

"Marco gave it to me. I'm sure he meant it for you."

"Marco…," Andi breathed. She shifted her eyes from the marble to Celeste's face. "I saw him," she murmured. "After I jumped from the window. I saw him and Gwen."

Celeste nodded. "They're always with you, Andi. Even when you can't see them. All this time, Marco has been with you."

Tears leaked from Andi's eyes. She picked up the marble and kissed it. "He collected these. This one, the yellow and blue, was his favorite."

"What's next for you?" Celeste asked.

"The doctor said they'll likely discharge me early next week, and I'm going back to Tennessee with my parents and sister. My mom is already making grocery lists, and Torrie's been on the phone to Calvin insisting he get the spare room at my parents' house ready. After that, I'm going to find a Radiohead concert somewhere cool, Paris or Amsterdam or maybe Italy. Marco, Gwen and I always said we'd do that after we graduated from high school. That was our big dream. I might even ask Dante to meet me there."

"Dante brought you a box of cookies from his family's bakery a couple days ago, but you were still unconscious. He seems like a pretty nice guy."

"He is," Andi agreed.

Celeste stood and squeezed her hand a final time. "You know how to reach me."

# EPILOGUE

Celeste took the elevator to the top floor of the Park Place Hotel, where she'd agreed to meet Harris for dinner. The doors opened to the soft clink of glassware and low conversation. He was already there, sitting at a small table by the windows. Behind him, the view stretched wide—downtown Traverse City fading into the shimmer of Lake Michigan, the sunset casting a warm glow over everything.

"What a view," she said when he stood and pulled out her chair.

He returned to his seat, and their eyes locked. Warmth flooded Celeste's face. She swallowed and broke the gaze, shifting her attention back to the downtown skyline.

"Did you hear any more about the bodies they recovered from the Fulton Road house?"

"Yeah. They found Maureen in the parlor. It was pretty clear she'd started the fire. They discovered evidence of the accelerant all around her. At her house, investigators found a can of gasoline in the middle of her living room. She'd spilled a lot of it.

"As for the bodies in the basement, they've found six. They suspect Vivian Walters was the skeleton in the rocking chair. On the floor were several empty bottles of pills. They'll likely never know her cause of death, but the implication of suicide is pretty clear. The other bodies, the children and babies, were all in another tunnel that dead-ended five or six feet beyond the secret room. Eliza identified Simon's shirt among the remains. It'll take a while for the DNA results, but we all know he's among the recovered. Another skeleton had on a tattered Girl Scout uniform."

"Leslie Twitchell."

He nodded. "I'd say yes. Her parents are both dead, but she has a brother still living, so there will be some closure for her family. At least three of the skeletons had cracked skulls. Bludgeoning was the likely cause of death. How long they were there, what was done to them." He shook his head. "Best not to even imagine."

Celeste saw Simon in her mind's eye, a flash of a memory, his not hers, eating a tube of SweeTarts and then suddenly the whoosh of something arcing down toward the top of his head. Followed by only darkness.

"It's sad," Celeste murmured. "So very sad."

"Yeah. How's Eliza holding up?"

"Pretty good, I think. We had coffee this morning, and she said she's relieved to finally have answers. They're hard answers, but ... now she can plan a burial for Simon. His parents bought him a plot years ago next to theirs, so ... she's keeping busy with that."

"That's good. And how are you doing?"

"Excited actually." She took out her cell phone, clicked a link and handed him the phone. "I put an offer on this cottage this morning."

"You did?"

She nodded. "And the seller accepted. Financing and

closing will take a month, but yeah. That's what's next. I'm moving into this house."

"Emberleaf Lake, huh? That's a nice spot and not too far from me. A fifteen, twenty-minute drive." He swiped through images, then turned the phone to face her. "Check out that willow. That's a beauty."

The large weeping willow rose near the lake, its long branches brushing the top of the water.

"You kissed me," she said, finally speaking the words that had been on her mind for days.

He stared at her, face serious. "I did."

"Why?"

He studied her. "Because I've wanted to for ... a long time. Probably since the very first day I saw you at the Unitarian Universalist Church Near Death Meeting. I had this." He rested a hand on his heart. "Jolt. I couldn't stop thinking about you after I left."

"You're dating Robin."

"No." He shook his head. "I ended it last weekend. We had an argument. She was angry about my relationship with you, and at first, I got defensive, denied it, and then I realized I was lying to her, lying to myself. I do have feelings for you. I've had them since the beginning, but ever since Nell and Bonnie died, I've not allowed myself to feel anything, really. I climbed onto this pedestal of indifference. I'd been to the other side. This physical world is a game, a play, a performance. I refused to ever be taken in by it again. But then I met you and started to realize we don't come here to cut ourselves off from emotion, from physicality. We come here to sink into it, get lost in it. Fall in love, wail in our despair and all the moments in between. I'm done being detached. I want you. I've wanted you since the beginning."

Celeste reeled with his words, tried to grasp them, to register what he was saying. She put a hand, unconsciously and then with awareness, to her belly, to the place where she carried the child of another man. No relationship in her future could be separate from that.

"I want her too. I want you both."

---

After dinner, they lingered in the parking lot, the night quiet around them. Harris opened her truck door, but before she climbed in, he stepped close and kissed her—longer this time, deeper. His hand slipped gently into her hair. She let herself lean into him, surprised by how much she'd missed the sensation of being close to someone, of being wanted. As the kiss deepened, a flicker of fear stirred beneath the warmth. To feel this again—this pull toward love, toward trust—was its own kind of risk. Jonathan's face flashed through her mind, but she refused to let his betrayal ruin the moment in front of her.

When the kiss ended, they stood in silence staring at each other. Harris smiled, then tucked a piece of her hair behind her ear like he'd done it a hundred times before.

"I've been waiting for that," he said quietly. "For this. And to be honest, some part of me knew the second I met you, we'd end up here."

Celeste thought back to the moment she'd first seen him stride into the near-death meeting. Maybe even then—long before she'd uncovered Jonathan's lies, before the harrowing year that followed—some part of her had known something deeper would unfold between them.

Even at the best of times with Jonathan, there had always been a sliver of distance, a part of herself she'd kept guarded. With Harris, that barrier felt thinner. They shared a secret, a profound understanding of what lay beyond life itself. It forged a connection between them that she could never have experienced with Jonathan.

"I haven't felt... excited for the future in a long time," she told him. "But right now I do."

"Me too." He kissed her again, softly on the lips.

When she climbed into her truck, she watched him walk across the lot. He turned back and grinned. "I'll bring coffee into The Spirit Lantern in the morning. Half decaf?"

"Perfect. I look forward to it."

As she started her truck, a text pinged on her cell phone. Celeste saw the message from an unknown number and read:

*Hi, Celeste. Sorry to text you out of the blue. I'm a friend of Liz Ratcliffe's. I believe the two of you worked together at Dynamic Laboratories in Grand Rapids. She mentioned you moved to the area and might be looking for work. I have a position I desperately need filled.*

*Any interest in stopping by the lab tonight? We can meet, you can take a look around and I'll explain what the position entails. No pressure if you're not interested, but you'd be saving me even if you only filled in for a few months. I'm at the lab right now if you're up for it. Or if now isn't good, you tell me the date and time and we'll schedule it.*

Buoyed by the conversation with Harris, by the parting kiss and the promise of so much more, she texted the number her response.

*I can stop by tonight. Text me the address.*

When the message came through, she plugged the address into her GPS and drove south out of Traverse City. She turned onto Rudolph Road, oddly rural, but it made sense. A lot of private labs were located in rural areas. The land was cheaper, the permits easier to come by, the taxes lower.

The driveway had a chain-link fence that blocked the entrance, but the gate stood propped open. Celeste slowed and turned in.

As she made her way down the dark gravel road, a sudden unease crept through her. The building slid into view. She was surprised at how dark it appeared, how empty. The man who'd texted her had implied the lab was open, and that he was working. And she knew plenty of labs kept overnight hours; some of the most significant breakthroughs came in the dead of night, when the world was quiet. She frowned, scanning the shadowy outline of the structure. It didn't seem abandoned, just ... off.

Still, a private lab would mean health insurance, a decent salary, and an opportunity to use her education and skills. And it was possible the research rooms in use at night were deeper in the building, making the light impossible to discern from outside.

She parked and climbed out and started toward the front door. A dark van occupied a space near the entrance. The driver's door swung open.

She faltered as she got closer, realizing the person who'd stepped out was not a man, but a woman.

Liz Ratcliffe.

Suddenly a sound behind her, shoes on the gravel.

Celeste whirled around, saw a man in a ski mask running at her. She threw her arms up to protect herself.

But the flash came first. A blue-white bolt of lightning leaped toward her.

A Taser.

Celeste's body seized, legs buckling. In the half-second before she collapsed, she glimpsed eyes behind the ski mask. Familiar eyes.

Jonathan.

# AUTHOR'S NOTE

**Hey There, Reader,**

Thank you for picking up the latest novel in the *Dear Celeste* series. I hope you enjoyed Celeste's chilling journey into the dark history of 506 Fulton Road.

While many of my novels draw partial inspiration from true events, *She Writes in Red* didn't come from any single real-life story. However, a small seed for it was planted years ago—back when I was a teenager, filling notebooks with unfinished tales. One of them told of a woman who kept a diary on the walls of her apartment. Across the way, a child watched from his window at night, catching glimpses of her as she wrote, and wondering what secrets her walls held. Like so many early stories, it trailed off into nothing... but the image never left me. Years later, it resurfaced, twisted into something darker, until it became *She Writes in Red*.

Most of my books keep one foot in the tangible world, brushing the edges of the supernatural. But every so often, I let the shadows pull me further in. Possession has always been a fascination of mine—its mysteries, its terrors, its question of what can slip inside when the door is left open.

Across the world, countless cultures believe the boundary between the living and the spirit realm is thin, and that unseen forces can shape our health, our fortunes, even our thoughts. In some traditions, spirit possession is sacred—a deity or ancestor entering the body during ritual. In others, it is feared—a demonic force bringing sickness or madness. My curiosity about these beliefs helped guide me as I shaped this story.

I hope you found *She Writes in Red* as unsettling to read as it was for me to write.

Until next time—

Stay spooky,

**Jacki**

# ALSO BY J.R. ERICKSON

**Dear Celeste Novels**

Come Home, Katie

The Worst Kind

Dread the Night

She Writes in Red

Veil of Pines

**Troubled Spirits:**

Where paranormal fiction and true crime meet.

**The Northern Michigan Asylum Series:**

Ghost stories inspired by a real former asylum.

*You can find all my novels and join my reader team to find out about new releases, book giveaways, and more at www.jrericksonauthor.com*

# ACKNOWLEDGMENTS

Many thanks to the people who made this book possible. Thank you to Team Miblart for the beautiful cover. Thank you to Emma Moylan for copy editing *She Writes in Red*. Many thanks to Emily H.,Saundra W., Melissa E., and Robin W. for finding those final pesky typos that slip in. Thank you to Leslie Twitchell for offering up her name as a character in this novel. Thank you to my amazing Advanced Reader Team. Lastly, and most of all, thank you to my family and friends for always supporting and encouraging me on this journey.

# ABOUT THE AUTHOR

J.R. Erickson, also known as Jacki Riegle, is an indie author who writes ghost stories. She is the author of the Troubled Spirits Series, which blends true crime with paranormal murder mysteries. Her Northern Michigan Asylum Series are stand-alone paranormal novels inspired by a real former asylum in Traverse City.

These days, Jacki passes the time in the Traverse City area with her excavator husband, her wild little boy, and her three kitties.

To find out more about J.R. Erickson, visit her website at www.jrericksonauthor.com.